Advance Praise for *Fawkes*

"*Fawkes* is the perfect mix of history and magic. I was up late in the night reading, waiting to get to the fifth of November to see how the plot would actually unfold, and it did not disappoint. An imaginative, colorful tale about choosing for yourself between what's right and what others insist is the truth."

—Cynthia Hand, *New York Times* bestselling author of *My Lady Jane*

"Hold on to your heart as this slow-burning adventure quickly escalates into an explosion of magic, love, and the truth about loyalty."

—Mary Weber, bestselling author of the Storm Siren Trilogy

"A magical retelling of the seventeenth century's famous Gunpowder Plot that will sweep you back in time—to a divided England where plagues can turn you to stone and magic has a voice. Deft and clever, *Fawkes* is a vibrant story about the search for truth and issues relevant to us, still, today."

—Tosca Lee, *New York Times* bestselling author

"*Fawkes* is a tale full of spiritual depth, tragedy, and hope. A beautifully written allegory for the magic of faith, with an achingly relatable hero who pulls you into his world heart and soul. A must-read for all fantasy fans!"

—Lorie Langdon, author of *Olivia Twist*

"A brilliant book that fulfills every expectation. Brandes turns seventeenth century London into a magical place. I was captivated by the allegory of her magic system and how she blended that fantasy with history. I highly recommend this gripping and beautifully crafted book to all. It will leave you both entertained and pondering matters raised in the storyline long after you've finished reading."

—JILL WILLIAMSON, CHRISTY AWARD-WINNING AUTHOR OF *BY DARKNESS HID* AND *CAPTIVES*

Fawkes

NADINE BRANDES

THOMAS NELSON
Since 1798

Fawkes

© 2018 by Nadine Brandes

Published in Nashville, Tennessee, by Thomas Nelson. Thomas Nelson is a registered trademark of HarperCollins Christian Publishing, Inc.

Thomas Nelson titles may be purchased in bulk for educational, business, fund-raising, or sales promotional use. For information, please e-mail SpecialMarkets@ThomasNelson.com.

Publisher's Note: This novel is a work of fiction. Names, characters, places, and incidents are either products of the author's imagination or used fictitiously. All characters are fictional, and any similarity to people living or dead is purely coincidental.

Library of Congress Cataloging-in-Publication Data
Names: Brandes, Nadine, 1986- author.
Title: Fawkes : a novel / Nadine Brandes.
Description: Nashville, Tennessee : Thomas Nelson, [2018] | Summary: "Thomas Fawkes is turning to stone, and the only cure to the Stone Plague is to join his father's plot to assassinate the king of England."-- Provided by publisher.
Identifiers: LCCN 2017059943 | ISBN 9780785217145 (hardback)
Subjects: LCSH: Fawkes, Guy, 1570-1606--Juvenile fiction. | CYAC: Fawkes, Guy, 1570-1606--Fiction. | Gunpowder Plot, 1605--Fiction. | Plague--Fiction. | Christian life--Fiction. | Fantasy. | Historical fiction. lcgft
Classification: LCC PZ7.1.B75146 Faw 2018 | DDC [Fic]--dc23 LC record available at https://lccn.loc.gov/2017059943

Printed in the United States of America
18 19 20 21 22 LSC 5 4 3 2 1

For Daddy,
who has been everything God designed a father to be—
and who bought me the fountain pen
with which I wrote this book.

Remember, remember, the fifth of November,
The Gunpowder treason and plot;
I know of no reason why the Gunpowder treason
Should ever be forgot!
Guy Fawkes, Guy Fawkes, 'twas his intent
To blow up the king and Parliament;
Threescore barrels of powder below,
Poor old England to overthrow.
By God's providence he was catch'd,
With a dark lantern and burning match.

Grey

One

York, England
Late spring, 1604

I wasn't ready to turn to stone.

I leaned so close to the small wall mirror that my nose left a grease spot on the glass, but I held still. Or tried to. I couldn't control the trembling. The grease spot smeared.

My right eye reflected a bright-blue iris, but it was the left side of my face that held me a whisper away from the mirror. Cracked stone blossomed from the chiseled marble that *should* have been an eye. The ball didn't move; the lid didn't blink. I lifted shaking fingers to my face. Petrification tickled the hairline of my eyebrow. A single infected hair protruded like a stone needle.

The plague was spreading.

I broke off the hair, as though that would help, but I knew better.

"Come sit, Thomas."

I stumbled backward before facing the apothecary, Benedict Norwood. Norwood stood at his dented and stained herb table, the backdrop of his curio cabinet displaying rows of green-hued bottles and jars, most of which held some sort of powder, paste, or plant.

He bent over my leather eye patch, picking at the seam threads with a small knife. Norwood wore his color mask—deep Green with gold laurels on the crown. Though no expression painted its face beyond two eye holes and a carved nose, it emitted a sense of calm. I imagined Norwood's hidden expression as one of care and kindness, like his voice—a balm I'd come to rely on.

I felt naked without the patch covering my plagued eye. If any of the other students at St. Peter's Color School saw me . . .

"Norwood, it's spreading." My voice was weak and childish— the opposite of what I needed on the day I was to be declared a man.

"Barely." Norwood poked a series of eyelet holes in the new edge.

My breath quickened. "It's stayed contained within my eye socket the entire past year since I caught the plague. Why would it spread? And now?" Why on the day of my Color Test?

"Thomas Fawkes, come sit." With a single whisper, he sent a thick olive-green thread through the eyelets and tied it off in a perfect knot. Norwood muttered another color command and mixed a green paste in a wood bowl beside him. Then he removed his mask and leveled me with a stare so commanding, it left no room for panic.

When he took off the mask, we switched from student and professor to friends. I wiped my sweating palms on my doublet, straightened my cuffs, and sat on the three-legged stool before the counter. He lowered himself onto his own stool, across from me.

I glanced over my shoulder at the closed door. Then to the window leading out to the garden. "Shall we put the eye patch back on?"

"In a moment. The paste needs to set a little longer." He placed a black cowhide bag on the table and withdrew seven wooden spheres, each painted a different color and none larger than a chess pawn. "Focus on the colors, not the plague. Your Color Test is *tonight*."

"Norwood, if I don't bond with Grey, then the plague will spread to my brain. If I'm blind, I can't bond with *any* color—"

"You worry like a woman!" He tossed me the Brown sphere. I caught it with one hand by reflex. "Help me polish these."

I halfheartedly snagged a spare rag and rubbed the cloth over the wood. It looked plenty polished to me. Besides, I didn't want to become a Brown. My gaze strayed to the Grey sphere. It sat there. Still. Dull. Mocking me. What if, when I put on my new color mask, Grey didn't bond with me?

"I was nervous for my Color Test too." Norwood spit on the Green sphere and rubbed it in practiced circles. "When my father handed me my mask for the first time and I put it on, all fear fled. I looked through the mask at the spheres and, clear as the sun in the sky, Green glowed like a beacon. The moment I spoke its language, it bonded to my mask." His smile grew and I found myself smiling with him. "It was magnificent. You'll understand after tonight."

My hands stilled. Would that be my story? I pictured myself wearing my new mask in a few hours . . . and none of the colors glowing. Everyone watching. *Father* watching. What would I become without a mask? Without color power?

The plague would spread and I would be consumed by the stone.

"Even if Grey does glow brightest when you call, you need to be ready to speak the other languages." Norwood rolled the Blue sphere to me. "Go on."

I gave a final polish to Brown. "Brown obeys warmth and smooth authority." My voice sounded bored. I set aside the Brown sphere and picked up the Blue. "Blue speech is like poetry—rhythmic and flowing."

"And Green?" Norwood rested a hand on his mask at his belt.

"Requires a calm and pleasant voice. It can sense your emotions." Reciting the color languages was like reciting a nursery rhyme. "Is this really—"

"What about Red?"

I reached for the Red sphere, but then my hand bypassed it, almost of its own accord. I picked up the Grey sphere, my fingers sliding across its textured surface. "Grey."

Grey obeyed a firm voice. A command, not a request. Confidence. Authority.

I clenched my fist around it so tightly a knuckle popped. "It has to be Grey. That is all I want." Once I had my mask, I would spend the rest of my life commanding the Stone Plague to recede from my body.

"There is no cure, Thomas, even if you bond with Grey." He sounded resigned.

"There has to be."

"Others have tried Grey speech—"

"I am not others!" I slammed the Grey sphere onto the table. "I am the son of Guy Fawkes. The blood in my veins is the blood of color warriors." I wanted to say more, but the walls of St. Peter's Color School were thin. And even in the heat of the moment, I dared not say what *type* of warriors my family was.

I barely dared to think the word.

Keepers.

Even though Norwood was a Keeper, too, an agreed silence always hung between us. The war between Keepers and Igniters was too real—even at St. Peter's, an Igniter school. That was why I needed to live. To find a cure for my plague—so I could join the fight.

"No matter whose son you are, this is *your* Color Test. You must be adequately prepared. All masks take on the color with which the bound person is strongest." He picked up his mask and tied the cords to hold it in place. Then, with barely a whisper, he spoke to the green paste in the bowl and a thick stream of it spread itself on the inner edges of my eye patch.

I never tired of watching color power.

A knock on the door. "Benedict?"

I startled, knocking the Brown sphere off the table with my elbow. It rolled into the folds of a cream-and-green gown. Emma Areben stood in the doorway—her oak-Brown mask firmly attached to her face with a white rose covering one eye.

I clapped a hand over my plagued eye, but the stiff silence was confession enough of my secret.

She'd seen.

The girl who hung on the arm of my greatest enemy knew about my plague.

"I'll be finished in a moment, Emma." Norwood's usually collected voice was stripped of all warmth.

Emma stared a moment longer, then whispered something. The Brown sphere soared through the air and back onto the table. Then Emma backed out of the room, closing the door behind her.

Norwood and I sat in silence. Doom had come in the form of an elegant masked lady, all of sixteen.

My hand drifted down from my eye. "She saw—"

"I know."

"It's over." I would be expelled on the day of my Color Test. In front of Father and my peers.

Norwood picked up my eye patch. "She won't tell."

"She's an Igniter. She's with Henry Parker. One slip—"

"She won't tell."

I leaned forward and he affixed it to my face. The green sealant paste hardened and I adjusted to the stickiness. I tapped the eye patch. Nothing in my sight changed—I was half-blind already—but I breathed in the safety that came from a hidden secret.

"As you say." I didn't see how Norwood could know what Emma would do, but I trusted Norwood. And worrying would do nothing to help me survive this terrible day. Too much was happening—the spread of my plague, the Color Test, the arrival of Father, who would present me with my mask.

Only with my mask could I bond with a color.

It had been a year since his last letter . . . and thirteen years since he last saw me. A mere babe then, I didn't know his face—or his mask. He had spent most of my life away, fighting in battles, saving lives, upholding a cause. He stopped writing when I told him I was plagued. But until today it hadn't spread. It hadn't infected others. I wasn't endangering anyone.

Perhaps Father was ashamed. After tonight, I hoped he would be proud.

Norwood scooped the spheres into their pouch. I rose from the table, but hovered—not quite ready to reenter the drama of St. Peter's Color School, where I would dress for the supper and endure Henry Parker's insults and possibly be expelled for my plague.

"I expect Father will be ashamed to see my infection."

Norwood's eyes crinkled in the shadows of his mask eye holes. "The great Guy Fawkes is traveling across all of England to bring you the mask he carved." He placed a hand on my shoulder. "He ought to be nothing but *proud* of you."

The great Guy Fawkes. The mighty solider. How could I live up to such a legacy?

"Thank you." I strode to the door, then looked over my shoulder. Norwood still watched me. I grinned and raised my good eyebrow. "Get a firm look at my face, sir. For after tonight you shall not see it again."

I tied the final ribbon from my doublet to my breeches—both of which were newly fitted for my coming-of-age day by York's not-quite-finest tailor. I combed my brown hair away from my face as best I could.

In a few minutes I would descend the steps of St. Peter's Color School for the last time as a maskless. Father would be waiting. If Norwood was right and Emma kept her mouth shut, I would start my final year of training, complete with color power and mask.

I forced a deep breath. Confident. Commanding.

"Mr. Fawkes." Headmaster Canon entered my room. He wore a Blue mask with two painted keys of sky blue crisscrossed in the center. I tried not to let my nerves show. I couldn't read his face behind his mask.

Was he here to confront me about my plague?

"You should be downstairs already, boy. Guests are arriving." His voice was as smooth and singsong as the Blue language he commanded. My fear fled, replaced by relief and then irritation.

Boy. Even today, on my coming-of-age day, the headmaster called me *boy?* I would not stoop to remind him that I was the son of Europe's mightiest color solider—or that I would receive my mask today and then be his equal.

I perfected my posture and strode past the headmaster to the stairs with a curt, "Sir." Halfway down, my steps slowed. I was about to see Father. My knuckles whitened against the banister. What would he say about my eye?

I recalled Norwood's words. I must go into this ceremony confident. Commanding. I didn't need Father's—or anyone else's—approval.

9

I entered the sitting room. Dark carved oak paneling covered all four walls, interrupted by a white stone hearth. A fire blazed inside it, draping a blanket of warmth over me as I entered. My throat tightened, urged to whisper a command to the flame and see if it obeyed.

Of course it wouldn't. Yellow speech was extremely complex and required the crown's permission.

Other hues hummed around me, as though begging me to speak to them. Brown wood beneath my feet. Grey from the candle brackets lining the wall. Woad Blue from a fellow's doublet.

Oh, to control them all! But I would command only one—that was the Keeper way. My family's way. To lust after multiple colors was shameless. Greedy. The way of Igniters.

After tonight, one color—I prayed it was Grey—would obey my voice.

I am the one you want.

I stumbled and glanced around.

Which one are you? A color had never spoken to me before. That made it the most alluring of all. Could it be Grey?

"Ah, the Cyclops has emerged from its den."

I ripped myself from the search for the mystery color. Three older students hovered by the fire, pewter goblets of wine cradled in their hands. Their masked faces turned toward me.

Henry Parker—the spokesman of the three and as pleasant to look at as a muddied swine—lifted his goblet. His Grey mask bore a set of painted black lips resting in a side-smirk. That simpering smirk would keep him from ever being taken seriously. Father would know better than to include something so immature as a *smirk* on my mask, wouldn't he?

Father.

I scanned the room.

Headmaster Canon chatted with some strangers near the entrance. My grandparents—Denis and Edith Bainbridge of Timble Hall—stepped into the room, leaving their cloaks with the entry servant. A few professors examined one of the school bookshelves holding tomes about color languages.

Then I caught the curled dark hair. The oak-Brown mask. The painted silver eyelashes and a white rose over one eye. Emma Areben joined Henry's crew. I once thought her beautiful despite having never seen her true face.

She'd arrived at St. Peter's a year ago, already masked.

I envied her for never having to take St. Peter's test. The Color Test was one "student honor" I wouldn't have minded forgoing. She and Henry would graduate tonight after my maskless peers and I took the Color Test.

She turned her head my way and I darted my gaze to the rest of the room.

I'd expected Father to arrive with Grandmother and Grandfather. I glanced out the window. Rain. That explained his delay.

"Have you decided which colors you'll start with, Cyclops? I suppose you don't care, as long as you have a mask to hide that fencing wound." After years of Henry's barbs, I should have been able to handle them better. At least his insult proved he knew nothing of my plague.

Teeth gritted, I walked away, mainly so I wouldn't hear Emma's laugh.

I heard it anyway.

I crossed the room to greet my grandparents—the two who had raised me long enough to send me to St. Peter's. Grandmother, her broad-brimmed hat like a crown atop her feathered hair, wore a dark petticoat with a modest neck ruff. Both she and Grandfather wore their masks on their belts, Grandfather's a river Blue carved with the swirls and flow of rushing water. Grandmother's a dull Brown.

I embraced Grandmother, but when I shook Grandfather's hand, I scanned the entryway again. It was empty save for the maskless servant, his eyes downcast. No father to carve his mask.

Where *was* Father?

"Thomas, let's step outside." Grandfather took my arm. "I would have a word."

My knees locked. Outside? For a word? *Now?* It had to be bad news. Now was *not* the time.

Grandfather steered me toward the door, but Headmaster Canon called out, "Thomas, come here, boy."

Boy again. Fueled by nerves, my feet obeyed his singsong voice and I left—no, *fled*—Grandfather's news.

I passed the testing room. The door hung open, the interior lit by a lone candle. The six color spheres rested in a line on the surface of the table. Awaiting me.

I walked on.

Headmaster Canon led me to the strangers. One man wore a slate-Grey mask at his belt and the other a Brown one textured like tree bark. "This is Master Connor,"—the Grey inclined his head—"and this is Master Haberdasher." The Brown held my one-eyed gaze, then the Headmaster went on. "They each seek an apprentice and will join us for supper and for your Color Testing."

The two masters bowed, but neither seemed impressed. Instead, their attention drifted to Henry—St. Peter's most skilled.

Within the hour, I'd have my mask and they'd give me the time of day. I would be like Emma—never taking my mask off. They'd see the power that flowed in my Fawkes blood. I shook off my nerves. Confident. Commanding. I must be a Grey. I gave a small bow. "You are both most welcome."

"Perhaps Fawkes's mask will have only one eye," Henry commented to his peers.

Do. Not. Turn. Red. The possibility of a cyclops mask *had* crossed my mind. Father might fill in an eye hole when he saw my patch. I wouldn't mind—

Father.

Why wasn't he here yet? I avoided Grandfather's scrutiny, though his posture leaned my way. If my suspicions about his bad news were right . . .

No.

Grandfather gestured to Headmaster Canon. My stomach lurched. They both spoke in low tones, then Grandfather withdrew an envelope, his gaze drifting to meet mine.

I strode over.

"Thomas." Grandfather faced me.

I shook my head. *Please, no.*

"He's not coming."

The room muted as though a giant pillow pressed upon it. Cloying. Suffocating. "Of course he is—"

"We've only just had word from London." Grandfather kept his voice low, but it still rang like a cathedral bell in the silent room.

This discussion couldn't be happening. Not in front of everyone. "He promised. In his last letter. I will not doubt him." I didn't mention that the letter came before Father knew I was plagued.

Headmaster Canon handed me the new letter. It contained one sentence.

There will be no mask for Thomas from me.

Below that, Father's signature.

No explanation.

I faced Grandfather, more to hide my shame from others than to meet his gaze. "But . . . everyone's here." My voice rose. "He *has* to come." Everything rode on Father's presence . . . on the mask he was to give me.

I needed him on this day only. I would never ask for another favor.

Norwood slid into the room from the hall. His appearance caused my good eye to burn.

Henry's whisper cut the silence from my blind spot on my left. "He really thinks the great Guy Fawkes will show up with a mask. Does he actually believe the man is his father?"

No one responded. Emma didn't laugh.

"I'm sorry, son." Grandfather sounded remorseful, but he had no idea what he'd done. He'd announced this shame publicly. Before my peers, my professors, the masters. Master Connor and Master Haberdasher inched toward the other students—the masked students.

Giving up on me.

Headmaster Canon cleared his throat. "I need to have a private word with Mr. Fawkes." He took my arm and led me from the room. "Come along, boy."

I craned a look over my shoulder until I located the Green mask and gold laurels. The man I *wished* was my father. "Norwood?"

He could fix this—*explain* this. He was our herbalist. Healer. My friend.

Norwood strode after me. "I'm here." His quiet words were for my ears alone. In one swift moment, the buildup of emotions that had filled me deflated, leaving me empty. But I did not stay hollow long. Anger trickled into the space.

Drip.

Drip.

Drip.

Headmaster Canon opened the door to his private study, allowing me to enter first. Muted moonlight filtered through the rain-speckled windows across the room.

"Give us a moment." He closed the door on Norwood, then lit a candle. "Without a mask, there's no reason for you to continue at St. Peter's." Canon's usually singsong voice came out monotone. "We cannot apply color training when you have no color power."

"You want me to *leave*?" I croaked. I couldn't leave with one year left—the final and most important year that resulted in an actual profession. The year I would hone my skill with the color of my choice—Grey—and maybe heal my eye. Despite the school and its dog-eat-dog students, I *couldn't* be cast out now. I had a mere sixpence and shilling to live on.

Headmaster Canon hung his head and I caught a muffled sigh. "Only your father can carve your mask and pass on the color powers. Unless you can track down Guy Fawkes for a mask, you cannot be bound with a color."

"Why cannot my grandfather pass on his color power? Or even Norwood?" My voice sounded shrill.

"It comes through blood, from father to son and mother to daughter. Denis Bainbridge is not your grandfather by blood." He folded his arms as though steeling himself. "You no longer have a place in our society."

I could not harden my heart fast enough to block the sting. Not just in the school, but in *society*.

I no longer had a purpose.

The servant in the entrance hall came to mind. Me—the son of Guy Fawkes and the grandson of the master and mistress of Timble Hall—*maskless*? Viewed as an orphan? *Treated* as an orphan? Not just that, but . . .

A *plagued* orphan.

They were casting me upon the street. No Fawkes had ever been maskless before.

I wouldn't allow it. I would *not* be the first.

"You are welcome to remain for the graduations—"

"I will find him." My voice emerged strong. Commanding. Like a Grey.

"I wish you all the bes—"

"Good eve, Headmaster." I forced winter into my voice. I wasn't in the mood to hear his well wishes when he was the one sending me from St. Peter's.

I strode from the room and nearly plowed into Norwood. He gripped my hand in a firm shake.

A farewell.

I nodded, clenching my jaw, and then continued through the halls of St. Peter's Color School. I would find Father. I would get my mask from him . . .

And then I would make him regret ever having a son.

Two

A mud clod struck my cheekbone, sending a spray of grit and slime into my open mouth and good eye. "Get out of our town, plague!"

On my first day of travel, the rain had slipped into the cracks of Norwood's paste and loosed the eye patch. On the second day, it fell off. It now rode in my pocket. Had I been wearing a mask, no one would see my eye. No one would see my plague. No one would *dare* throw mud.

But my departure from St. Peter's had not gone as imagined. I left that very night. Grandfather and Grandmother tried to convince me to come home, but that would be defeat. I wanted nothing to do with them—I had to be my own man now, mask or not.

So I'd set out for London.

Four days later I entered the city of Tuxford as a plagued—via the main road, as a gentleman would do. But I should have taken the alleys, where other maskless and plagued might have provided food or shelter. Or at the least withheld their mud clods.

A second scoop of mud formed into a ball a few feet away from me, commanded by a Brown too cowardly to get his hands dirty.

Stop, I sent to the mud, though my color speech had no power without a mask. I turned my face in time to avoid another mouthful of horse waste and sludge.

I wanted to be a Yellow and burn these cowards.

I wanted to be a Grey and send my plague into their skin.

I wanted to be a Blue and drown them in the spring snowmelt.

"Do ye not hear us, plagued scum?" Two burly men rolled up their sleeves as they came toward me.

I forced my weak limbs to propel me in the opposite direction. Out of Tuxford and back to the postal road, without a warm meal or shelter for the fourth night in a row. Had it not been the end of May, I'd have perished from chill alone in my attempt to walk to London. I still might perish. Seventy-five miles got me to Tuxford with a torn cloak and a sixpence remaining in my pocket. Still one hundred thirty miles to go.

My navel gnawed on my spine with each disheartened step.

The clouds glared down on me, preparing to open their fists of rain as a welcome back into misery. With the post road as muddy as the streets of Tuxford, my thin boots were already soaked through. It was a day's journey to Newark—my next hope of food and lodging.

I stumbled on my fourth step down the road. I couldn't do it.

But I must. Father was in London—the man who caused this suffering and cared nothing for his son. The only person who could give me a mask. Bile rose in my throat at the thought of accepting help from such a man. But I couldn't make my own mask. No color would respect it enough to bond.

I urged my feet into action. As long as I moved, I could cling to hope. If I allowed myself to collapse in the poplars off the road— even for a moment—that would be the end. One step over the other. One more step.

London.

London.

London.

The clouds released their gale. I pulled my cloak around me, but the mud soaking it made me colder. With no one else to beseech—not that they'd answer my pleas—I reached out to the colors. *Help me,* I cried to the green broadleaves on the roadside. *Send me a Green with a good heart.*

Was it even possible to send messages through colors? Without a mask?

Help me. I sent the same to the brown of the dirt.

I will help you.

The mystery voice that had reached out to me four nights ago! The one I couldn't place and had never mentioned to Norwood.

I focused. *Where are you?*

A clap of thunder drowned out any answer. I ducked my head and quickened my pace, the shivers keeping my muscles working. The rain persisted for hours. A neigh lifted my head and a rider passed by, hunched over the neck of his trotting horse.

"Sir!" I jogged after him. "May I ride with you?"

He reined his steed and waited for me. Water dribbled from the wide brim of his hat over his Red mask. As I drew near, a relieved smile broke my face. I could already picture the sigh my body would release upon taking weight off my feet.

I caught the man's eyes and tried to convey my gratitude through a grin. His gaze settled on my stone eye and he recoiled. I slowed, my face burning—the only heat in my body.

Without a word, he turned his gelding.

"No, wait!" I reached out. "Please!" He threw up a hand, palm-out, as if to ward me off. I flew backward as though yanked from behind.

Color power.

He kicked his gelding into motion. Mud flew up from the horse's hooves and I shielded my face. Gone. Curse this plague!

I reached Newark in Nottinghamshire at dusk the next day. By that point, my face held so much mud I prayed it would conceal my infection. I felt for the sixpence in my sodden pocket and crossed Trent Bridge. Then I turned down an alley lit by two flickering candles blurred behind oiled linen windows. The yellow glow kept the shadows from suffocating me.

The dirt underfoot did not squelch so much beneath the overhangs of two wood-framed wattle-and-daub homes. The stench hit me in waves—horse manure and human waste tossed from windows.

I exited the alley and caught a swinging sign out of the corner of my good eye: The Castle and Crown, Pub and Lodging. The roof was peaked and light shone from an upper lattice window. A cheer went up from the inside. Such a warm sound that I stepped up to the threshold, prepared to drop to my knees in want of a bed.

The door flew open before I could reach for the latch and two men strode out, waving to some comrades inside. "Another Keeper hung in London. Good riddance."

I let them pass, then entered as the door closed. Warmth struck me and I gripped the frame to keep my knees from buckling. The brick walls bore dents and splashes from the rowdier tenants. Tables filled every nook and a group of men had drawn chairs to the hearth of the open fire—cards in one hand and tankards in the other. Aside from them, the pub seemed mostly empty. 'Twas not yet suppertime for the masses.

A masked man in a white shirt with a russet doublet and jerkin refilled the men's ale and stoked the fire . . . all with color speech. His mask was composed of plaited Brown cords, but I knew he was an Igniter because he controlled two colors at once. The ale pitcher hovered in the air, pouring its contents into the empty tankards, while his hands served chunks of bread. He turned toward me. I resisted the temptation to shrink against the wall, Norwood's reprimand sounding in my mind. *"Be commanding."*

Right.

I stepped toward the innkeeper. "I am in need of lodging and supper." Only then did I realize I hadn't spoken more than a few sentences in the past five days. My voice came out hoarse and tired. Not at all commanding.

The innkeeper came closer. "What was that, boy?"

I cleared my throat, not having enough energy to be offended at the *boy*. "Have you a room?"

"Have you coin?" He said nothing of my eye. The mud was doing its job.

I pulled the sixpence from my muddied pocket.

"It be another three farthing for board and ale, unless ye want fruit and cheese. That'll be a farthing."

I pulled out another pence. I was so close. "Board, ale, and a bath, please, good sir."

"Ye might need two baths to rid ye of the grime." He laughed and gave me a groat in change. I forced a laugh, too, and followed him up the creaking back stairs to a room half the size of my bedroom at St. Peter's. A straw bed lay on the floor. "Will you be supping up here or below?"

"Up here." Despite my deep desire to sit near the fire, once I was bathed my infection would be evident. And that would forfeit my lodging.

My muscles trembled, awaiting my food and bath. Four pence

left in my pocket. When I finally sank into the steaming water, it was with a tankard of ale in one fist and a loaf of bread in the other.

As my bones thawed, I felt less and less like a street beast and more like a human.

After bathing, I washed my clothes as best I could in the bathwater. It muddied within seconds. Had I been a Brown, I could have commanded the mud out of the fabric.

But I wasn't a Brown.

I wasn't anything.

At a knock, I jumped up, frantic for something to cover my nakedness. Snatching the blanket from the bed, I wrapped it around my body and cracked the door. A maid peered through and her eyes widened behind her sky-Blue mask.

Then I recalled . . . I was clean. The mud was gone.

My plague was exposed.

She stumbled backward. Then she coughed out a timid sentence. "I'm here ta fetch yar dishes, sir."

I grabbed the empty board and tankard from the floor and shoved them at her. She backed away but managed to grip the items using the cloth of her apron as protection. With a bob, she avoided my gaze and disappeared down the stairs.

What a fool! Would I and my wet clothes be thrown back into the stormy night? Back into the cold with no help and no fire?

I glanced around the room. There was nothing with which to block the door. The best I could do was use my own bare skin as a weapon. They wouldn't force a naked boy onto the street.

Anticipating an invasion any moment, I did the only thing I could: I climbed into bed. Perhaps I'd gain a wink of slumber beneath a soft feather blanket before being wrenched from my reprieve.

And perhaps they'd leave me be. I paid good coin after all.

The slam of the door against the inner wall startled me from my dream of London, Father, and my mask.

"There he is, Sheriff Nix. The plagued." I blinked away my confusion, only to recognize the innkeeper's shout. "Contaminating my room!"

Someone yanked the blanket off me. I instinctively curled my limbs against the rush of chill air, not just to shield myself from the cold, but also from blows. My good eye finally focused and took in the scene.

Still dark. The innkeeper stood in the door, while the maid gathered my feather blanket into her arms. I should have paid her off.

"Burn it outside." At the innkeeper's command, she disappeared.

A third person filled my vision. His tall frame caused his head to skim the ceiling. He wore a shining Grey mask and a saber at his side. He threw my clothes at me. Still wet, they slapped me in the face and drew a gasp. "Dress, boy. It's to the prison with you."

"But what—"

The sheriff raised a fist. "I give you ten seconds. Then I'm dragging you out whether you're clothed or not."

I struggled to pull on my wet clothing—every muscle tense against the ice. "Please, sir. I've been traveling long. It's no crime to be infected!"

"Have you a pass to travel?" Sheriff Nix rounded on me as I tied my leggings. "Urchins like you are spreading the plague by wandering from town to town!" He yanked the doublet over my head and then pulled me after him. I barely managed to snag my dripping cloak.

"No one's caught the plague from me since I contracted it a year ago." I stumbled from the room. "It's dormant!"

But that was now a lie. Five days ago it had spread. Overnight.

The inn had filled with the late-night revelers, all of whom stopped their drinking to watch the sheriff drag a half-clothed, maskless, one-eyed boy down the stairs and out the front door. I ducked my head to block their stares.

Father would be ashamed.

But who cared about him? He was the true swine behind my predicament. At least I had food in my belly, though my body ached and my good eye stung from the need for rest.

———※※———

The prison was an enormous stone gate that arched over the road. Barred windows flanked the street. I'd seen plenty of prisoners through the windows in York's prison, begging for alms so as to pay their debts.

The wooden door creaked as Sheriff Nix threw me to the ground, then rifled through my clothes. His fist emerged with my remaining groat. I scrabbled for footing. "That coin is mine!"

"This is payment to the innkeeper for a new mattress and blanket." Sheriff Nix tucked it in his own pocket.

My eyes narrowed. "You're keeping it for yourself, aren't you?"

He smacked my head, then shoved me into a cell with a barred window and a huddle of sleeping inmates. He slammed the door and with a harsh whisper, the lock clicked.

I gripped the bars. "How long do I have to stay in here?"

Sheriff Nix turned, but I caught his low mutter. "Depends on if the inmates leave ye alive." He left.

I heaved my weight against the door, but it didn't budge. "Come back!" A prisoner shushed me and then rolled onto his other side. I pressed my face against the bars to stop my shivering.

"If the inmates leave you alive."

I looked over my shoulder. Five lumps of cloth and stench. Five men, from what I could tell. Those men would wake in a few hours, and when they saw they were imprisoned with a plagued . . .

They would surely kill me.

Three

"What's wrong with your face, boy?" A maskless prisoner with wild hair and even wilder eyes peered at me through the morning light.

I pulled my makeshift bandage lower over my stone eye. "Sheriff struck me." While the prisoners slept, I'd ripped a sleeve from my shirt and tied it around my head.

The man's spidery eyebrows popped upward. He scooted closer. "Let me see."

I jerked away. "Thank you, no. It is tender."

"A cloth won't help the tenderness. Give your bruise some air."

"Leave me be!" My heart thudded.

He shrugged and made his way back to the window. Early risers were out on the streets, passing by our cell. "Marie!" the old man cried. "Marie, do ye not love me anymore?"

A young lady with a Green mask and a basket of flowers over her arm wended her way to the window. "My farthings sure don't." With a gentle whisper, she sent a sunshine-yellow flower through the air and into his outstretched palm. "That's worth a ha' penny.

Perchance ye can sell it to a passerby, yes?" She blew a kiss and disappeared through the gate.

"Until tomorrow, sweet Marie!" The old man brought the flower to his nose and remained that way until another passerby returned him to begging.

The other prisoners, once woken, peppered me with questions.

How old was I?

"Sixteen."

What got me thrown in prison?

"Traveling without a permit."

What had I heard during said travels?

I recalled the passing chatter of the men at the Castle and Crown. "Another Keeper was executed in London."

They all went silent. Then . . . "Poor soul."

One man in the back corner snorted. "Those Keepers are causing this plague. The faster we rid our country of them, the sooner the plague leaves. King James is too soft on 'em."

"Too soft?" The window man sneered. "Keepers are being executed every month!"

"Should be every *week*," the corner man said.

None responded and that's when I knew. The rest of them were Keepers. Like me. Imprisoned for believing that color power should be limited to one color.

The window man turned his face toward me. "Be ye from a Keeper family, boy? Or were you raised Igniter?"

As if any man would answer such a question.

The creak of a door preceded a beam of light as Sheriff Nix entered, wearing his Grey mask. It reflected the sun and blinded me for a moment. "Keepers, out."

The cell lock clicked without a key.

All prisoners but myself and the corner man exited, dragging their chained feet. I didn't want to incriminate myself. They'd hang me—mask or no, I was sixteen. And once you hit sixteen, you could swing for your beliefs.

Nix moved to close the door but paused when his gaze landed on me. "Boy, you're to be sent back home. Keep the plague to your own people."

"Plague?" one of the Keepers squawked.

Now Nix had done it. He hauled me out and then locked the door again. "Where did you come from?"

I opened my mouth to say York, but with a single hiccup of thought, I switched. "London."

"I thought so." Before I knew it, I was on my back in a cage wagon with the four Keeper prisoners, trundling toward London. Had my heart not been thumping so frantically, I might have cheered.

The Keepers huddled in the opposite corner. Even they were wary of my plague, despite the fate of execution awaiting them in London. I stared at them with my good eye.

These men were going to die.

Suddenly obtaining my mask and getting revenge on Father seemed inconsequential. They were being taken to London to be hanged. What was going to happen to me? I needed to escape. *They* needed to escape. I had roughly one hundred ten miles in which to figure out a plan.

The May sun was finally shining, warming my core and drying my clothes through the window and door bars. I settled myself on the wooden bench next to the door. Thick wood blocked the metal lock from view, but I tried Grey speech anyway.

Unlock. Let me out. Not even a tickle of Grey obedience touched my mind.

I tried again and even touched on Brown to talk to the wood surrounding the lock, to no avail. I needed a mask. Curse Father!

But what about that color that spoke to me on the road to Nottinghamshire? It had to have been Grey. What had it said on the evening of my testing? *I am the one you want.* And then on the road, it said it would help me.

Hello? Grey? I thought, though I didn't know where to place my focus.

No response. I would keep trying.

The bumps on the road jarred my body and interrupted my focus every few seconds. I slumped over my knees and set to scraping mud off my shoes with my fingernail while I thought. Since I had just one good eye, perhaps the colors didn't feel like they had my full attention.

At noon, I was let out to relieve myself. I took my time soaking in the warmth of the sun. The cart drivers kept a sharp watch on us, masks on and matchlock pistols in hand. No opening for a bolt.

Once we returned to the cart, I tried Grey speech again. And again.

Open. The lock didn't even wiggle. *Open!* I glared at the lock, trying to show authority. This was simply a lock. It would obey me. It was my slave. I was master of the lock. I was a Fawkes.

"No matter 'ow 'ard you stare at that lock, it won't obey you 'less you 'ave a mask." One of the Keepers sat nearer me than before. Perhaps he figured that catching the plague didn't matter if he was about to hang.

"You could help," I said. "I'm doing this for all our sakes."

"I can do nothing without my mask. It was taken. Broken."

My throat tightened. They *broke* his mask? Would they allow no honor to ascend the gallows? "I have to try."

"Best accept your fate."

Accept my fate? That wasn't the way of a Fawkes. "Has a color ever spoken to you without a mask?"

The response was instant. His eyes narrowed and the heads of the other Keepers snapped up. "Only one color ever speaks *to* a person," said the Keeper with spiked eyebrows who flirted with Marie.

I waited.

He looked around and the others avoided his gaze. My intrigue increased. He finally looked back to me, grim. "White Light. It is the color through which all other colors come." The carriage struck a rut in the road and we knocked into each other. He rested his elbows on his knees to steady himself. "White Light is the cause of war between Keepers and Igniters."

Huh. That didn't align with my understanding of the war. In my mind, it wasn't that complicated: Keepers were loyal to *one* color, and had been for thousands of years. Whereas Igniters wanted to control *all* colors. Igniters broke the laws of color magic to bind with multiple colors.

Apparently monarchs loved power, because both Queen Elizabeth and King James were Igniters. Consequently all Keepers were exiled, hunted, and executed for "resisting progress."

And that was the war in a nutshell. Simple as skipping. The only time I'd heard of White Light was when Norwood said to ignore it—it would turn me into an Igniter. "So is it good or bad?"

"Depends which side you're on."

"I'm on the side of whoever and whatever will get me out of this cage." They went silent at that. So much for answers.

I leaned against the wall of the cart and closed my eye as though trying to nap. I doubted I fooled them—no one could nap in this bumpy hand basket.

Leicester came and went, adding three more infected prisoners and four Keepers to the cage—all of whom were older than me. We passed through Northampton, then Bedford, and finally Henford.

With each passing day, I grew more and more desperate to escape the cage of eleven prisoners and get some real food in my body.

I'd spent the previous three days of the jostling ride thinking about Father. London was ten times the size of York. He would take some time to find, but I'd track him down. Father kept to the Keeper way. If I found London's Keepers, I would find him.

"Home sweet hell." One of the prisoners used the window bars to hoist himself to a crouched position. I popped up from my bench and joined him at the window.

We trundled through a junction marked not by signs but by gallows. The worn structure bore the carved street names and also three swinging naked bodies—a couple days old by the looks of their swollen corpses and the flies that swarmed around them.

Distant bells rang. "They ring for the dead," one Keeper said. "The plague is heavy in London."

The horizon gave way to the rise of steeples and an expanse of houses with thatched roofs. The sun sank, taking the light with it and leaving behind a damp fog settling over the city. I wanted to stare longer—but a bump sent us sprawling.

"Get a good look, Keepers," one of the plagued men said. "London be your graveyard."

I didn't want to think about these Keepers or their looming executions. I didn't want to think about these men I'd spent three days in a cage with . . . dead. Perhaps it was cowardly of me, but I pushed them out of my mind and shored up any soft emotions.

I climbed back onto my bench spot. I needed to escape before the light completely left so I'd be able to navigate the city. *White? Are you there?*

Blast it all. What was its color speech? Did I need to command it? Coax it? Bow to it?

Free me. If you can.

How could White do anything? Nothing in my view was White, except the clouds above. It would do no good to move clouds—they could not help me escape from the prison wagon.

The cart trundled along, jostling my already exhausted and bruised body. I clutched my hands tight in my lap. The city grew nearer. I looked to the clouds, zeroing in on the White. *Please. Please. I care not whether you're for the Igniters or Keepers . . . Get me out of this place.*

The other prisoners drooped like water-starved shrubs. None paid attention to me, each caught in his own dread. Buildings passed by the cart window, blocking my view. Blast it all! Blast the White color!

Just be quiet already! It's your turn to listen.

There it was. I gripped the bench edge to keep from falling over. *Please. Free me—*

LIST-EN.

I stilled, willing myself to listen to the color that spoke in the deep recesses of my mind. What was I going to hear? Instruction? A command? Perhaps it was going to bargain with me—and I was willing to give it what it wanted.

Click.

The door creaked as we went over a bump. Then . . . it opened with a swing and a *clang*. I stared. The other prisoners jumped at the sound and the crack of dusk light that entered the paneled cage.

One breath.

Two.

Three.

On the fourth breath I overcame my shock and leapt out of the cart. My knees buckled when I landed and I collapsed to all fours. Mud slid between my fingers. I scrambled back up, joints protesting.

Shouts arose. Some of the other plagued prisoners ran free too. But the Keeper with spiked eyebrows stood in the doorway as the cart trundled on. I gestured with a caked hand for him to jump out.

He was old. Did he need help?

I didn't have time for this! The drivers would notice the commotion any moment. I ran after the cart. I'd catch him if needed. "Come on!"

"How?" he called as I caught up. The other Keepers hovered behind him.

"Just jump!" I reached out with a hand, my limp legs quaking from lack of sustenance and exercise. "I'll assist you."

"How?" the Keeper bellowed. Only then did I realize he wasn't asking how to get out of the cart.

"The White color did it!" I was losing momentum. "Now jump, old man!"

He shook his head and backed into the cart. "I cannot. A Keeper does not use White Light for his will. You have dabbled in it like the Igniters."

I stumbled to a halt. Was he jesting? He was going to stay in that blasted wagon because of . . . because of some twisted *conviction?*

"Have it your way." I ran off as I caught the shouts of the drivers and the whinny of a reined horse.

I darted into an alley. I shouldn't have left those Keepers there. I should have forced them out of the cart. Or perhaps followed and freed them a different way.

But what were they to me? They chose death. I chose to hide. I forced away the guilt. They made their choice. I could do nothing about that.

Still, a single word chanted in my brain as I turned my back on the road and the Keepers.

Coward.

Coward.

Coward.

My chest pounded and I couldn't swallow. I crossed the street and entered the opposite alley. Then I ran, though my weak limbs swung to and fro and my mind didn't process the streets of London beyond the fact they were a maze. A coward I might be, but at least I was a free one.

Four

The apple crates behind which I huddled smelled of rot. I crouched low, my stomach grumbling . . . craving even the rotten apples. But I knew better. For the moment, starving would fare me better than an ill stomach.

No shouts. No pursuit. I allowed a solid quarter hour to pass before moving again, wandering through the narrow alleys lit by single lanterns, dodging the evening shoppers and slosh of urine tossed from upper windows.

As I navigated the streets, my mind traversed the map in Norwood's apothecary. Norwood was from London. It seemed unfair to be here without him.

At last I found a name mounted to the herringbone brick of a corner home: Tooley Street. It didn't ring a bell, but as I continued down it, I stopped at the base of a cathedral. Its tower stretched so high, I expected it to puncture the moon.

The giant wooden door groaned as I entered on muddy tiptoes. Ahead were lines of pews beneath an impossibly high ceiling with equally tall stained glass windows. Spiral stone stairs waited in an alcove to my left.

I climbed them two at a time, until my chest heaved. They deposited me near the top of the steeple, where the bells hung. The walls were open, arched windows, and wind tried to push me to my death, all the while whistling threats in my ears. I stepped upon the ledge, one hand on the beam support.

The city lay below, roofs and smoking chimneys of varied heights creating a sea of angles. I could see down into the narrow pathways strewn with lodgers' laundry. The sunset glinted off the water-filled footsteps imprinted upon the mud.

From up here, I was king of London.

I finally knew where I was. To my right, the River Thames separated me from north London, flowing like a grey slug that had fed on human waste for the past century. Fog flirted with the water's surface, sending tendrils of mist into the streets and over the last few boaters coming in to dock.

Ship masts swayed back and forth and lined the opposite shore, their flags drooping like disheartened soldiers. Pointed steeples interrupted the sunset, declaring their majesty. And I saw London laid out like the map in Norwood's apothecary—perfectly to scale. St. Helen, St. Andrew, St. Dunston . . . I was in the tower of St. Olaf church.

And I needed to cross the Thames.

Straight ahead, London Bridge rested on stone arches spaced across the river, with three-man wherry boats rowing upstream through them. Atop the bridge rose apartments with rounded corners and pointed roofs. Billowing chimney smoke and warm candlelight. An exotic place to live, despite the view of severed heads on spikes rising every which way from the top of the Bridge Gate. Convicts, criminals . . . Keepers.

I once heard Emma Areben whispering about how William Shakespeare crossed London Bridge every day. Perhaps I'd run into the famous playwright.

For now, though, I pocketed my awe. I must find Father.

I descended the tower and reentered the now-darkened streets. No lights lit my way, the alleys blocking any moonlight. The blackness so deep and thick I felt as though I walked through a tunnel. Groans, evil laughs, and sinister whispers floated on the current of darkness. No man was safe on these streets once night fell.

I made my way to the end of Tooley Street and ended up in an open square facing the Bridge Gate. The displayed heads of convicts stared down at me from the gate like menacing demons, their broken masks covered in bird excrement.

I hurried through the entrance, passing homes, shops, and openings to view the Thames in darkness.

Once on the opposite side, I turned left on Thames Street. A few of society's neglected lay tucked in shadowed corners, snoring or nibbling bits of old bread. I might join them after a few hours of the bell, but not yet. My mission fueled me.

I made my way to Fleet Street and quickened my steps under a clothesline that displayed dripping breeches and peasant shirts. Were they hung a little lower, a thief could snatch himself a new outfit.

Did I want to be a thief tonight?

My honor slipped a notch at the thought. I passed the butcher's, where whole pigs hung gutted, their legs stretched on wood ribbing. They stank and flies buzzed where their innards should have been. My empty stomach turned over.

Fleet Street bridged the river and wound through a giant gate with towers on each side and an arch in the middle for passing. The air cleared a bit. With the recent spring storms, the Thames had likely flooded and washed away some of the street filth. I observed the barred windows from afar. Unlike the Keeper prisoner in Newark, no one begged for alms from these windows.

I glanced around. The bridge and streets were empty. I approached the windows. "Keeper," I hissed. "Is there a Keeper in here?" I wasn't exactly subtle.

"What's it to ye?" someone grumbled.

"I need to speak to him." I pressed my face against the bars. The interior was too murky for me to see anything. Then a pale ghost of a face—deprived of a lifetime of sunlight—loomed from the darkness and stopped inches from my own.

I reeled backward.

"You're plagued." The man hissed through broken and blackened teeth.

I stood agape. "Y-Yes."

The Keeper leaned closer until the tip of his nose squeezed between the bars—an inch of freedom. "Listen close. Stay faithful to the Keeper way. Never speak to the White Light, and never turn your ear from a Keeper's request." At this, he slid a trembling hand through the bars, palm up.

"I haven't any coin."

"Let the boy alone," someone grouched from deeper inside, with a tired edge to his voice.

"Why do Igniters hate us? Why does King James exile and execute you?" I asked.

"King James is jealous. Afraid. Everyone else wants White for themselves. Igniters think they are strong enough to speak to it."

"What *is* White?" I didn't dare tell him it spoke to me. That it had freed me. "Why is it so powerful?"

The Keeper shook his head. "It is not for the common man to explore. It is too powerful for us and it breeds greed."

But White spoke to me.

And I spoke back.

I had betrayed the Keeper way without knowing.

"He's lyin', boy." If that shadowed prisoner called me *boy* one more time . . .

I shifted my weight and lowered my voice. "Do you know Fawkes? Guy Fawkes?"

The Keeper leaned back. I couldn't see his expression, but the whitening of his knuckles on the window bars told me enough. "The great soldier?"

I swooped closer. "I need to find him."

"Who are you?"

"A tavern would be the most likely place to find any soldier," hollered the annoyed voice.

"Please, tell me how I can find him," I whispered to the Keeper.

"I can't."

"Please." I reached toward him.

A long pause. "An acquaintance of his resides at the Duck—"

"Hey!" A shout from behind sent me careening away from Fleet Prison. I caught movement in the shadows. On instinct, I sprinted away. Had the person seen my face? Was it a guard from the prison cart? Did they hear the name Fawkes?

I ran until I hit a street called the Strand, where I took refuge behind some ale casks by a tavern. I breathed in the oak, aching to wet my throat. I didn't dare drink Thames water. I'd heard the stories. I pressed my forehead against the rough wood.

That imprisoned Keeper knew Father. I was sure of it.

I raised my head above the edge of the barrel. A doorway lantern illuminated the tavern's sign: The Duck and Drake. Four men exited, bringing the wafting aroma of bread and fire behind them.

My thoughts slipped to dishonorable considerations . . . like the coin purse swinging from the belt of one of the four men exiting the inn. I frowned.

The men spoke in low tones on the doorstep. The nearest man tucked the coin purse in his belt but didn't tie it. Ah, the blessing of oversight brought on by ale.

The men headed away from the Duck and Drake, and I made my decision. A homeless plagued man could retain only so much honor. I had to let go of some.

I followed at a distance, keeping my eye on the purse. One man walked faster than the others, as though trying to distance himself from his companions. At the next alley, he turned right while the other three continued straight. Soon a second man left the pack.

We entered a long alley and I took a chance, dipping out of sight and running ahead of them, praying they kept a straight path. I reentered the main alley just off the deserted market square and sank myself down into a shadow, slouching like a sleeping street man. I made sure to keep them on my good side.

I squinted my eye. They continued down the alley toward me—their gait unchanged. My heart galloped. I shouldn't steal. But what was more shameful, stealing or begging? I couldn't bring myself to beg. These men had swords. If I could acquire one of *those*, the streets of London would be mine.

Closer they came, not speaking. It was too quiet. They would know.

I'd have to be fast. Like when I jabbed my rapier. I willed up the reflexes. Just as they passed, I darted out my hand and gripped the money pouch. It slid from his belt like melting butter. I didn't move my fingers for fear of clinking the coins together. Slower than a prowling street cat, I brought my hand back down to my side and waited until they entered the empty market.

Then I slunk away, keeping an eye on them. Going . . .

Going . . .

Gon—

"Wait." The one in the lead—the one whose purse I'd snatched—held up a hand. He wore a Black mask, so dark the shadows seemed washed out against it. I'd never seen a Black before.

They doubled back.

I ducked behind an empty market cart. Black continued my way, though nothing in his stance said he'd noticed me. Instead, he seemed to be . . . searching. Glancing this way and that, stepping carefully. As though trying to *sense* me.

He drew his sword and scanned the area. I crouched deeper into the mud, but the cart had a wood frame. If he came much closer . . .

His companion pointed my direction. How could he possibly see me? Their footsteps squelched my way. Deliberate. Confident. Fast.

"Here." The Black's voice sounded far more menacing—and far less intoxicated—than when he'd been on the steps of the Duck and Drake.

I shut my eye. Blast it all. I should have begged.

A hand came over the stall counter and grasped the back of my jerkin. It hauled me onto the street and threw me in the mud. Two sword points pressed against my chest. I tried not to breathe and instead blinked the mud out of my good eye so I could see my assailants.

The companion was short, wearing a Brown mask. "Who are you?" Black asked.

I shook my head, trying to untie my tongue. Speak, foul muscle! "N-No one!" It came out like the response of a frightened boy.

"He lies." This from a third voice in the blind spot to my left. "Questioned the Keeper at Fleet Prison, he did. Asking for Guy

Fawkes." The speaker came into view, wearing a Red mask, and placed a third sword point against my chest. This one pricked through the fabric and into my skin.

"N-No . . ." I let the coin pouch drop into the mud. They could have their blasted money.

Red pressed the sword point harder. "And his lies continue."

"I-I mean yes, I was looking for Guy Fawkes."

"Wintour, we need to get out of the street." Black snatched up his coin purse and looked around.

Red jabbed me with the saber and I yelped. "You'll have to kill this one. He's small. You can dump him in the Thames."

Wintour—the Brown—released a sigh. "We know nothing about the boy."

"Deal with it." Red sheathed his saber and then trotted off, not even sparing a backward glance for the sake of my life.

"Please." I focused on my two assailants. "I am a friend of Guy Fawkes." If I could get one of their swords in hand . . .

Black laughed and his sword slid away from my chest. "Your lies are more putrid than the waste in which you lay. I am sorry your life must end, but it has come to this from your own slinking."

There was nothing else I could say. My life would end without food in my belly or a mask on my face. "Am I destined to die honorless?" I muttered, more to myself than as an actual question.

"Honor comes from the interior of a man, not from his situation. A lesson you would have been wise to learn before this moment."

I liked this man less and less, not that my opinion mattered. "Why won't you believe me?"

The man's grip tightened around the hilt. "Because *I* am Guy Fawkes. And I've never seen your foul face."

He plunged his sword.

Five

"I'm your son!"

The sword tip twitched and crashed against my stone eye. I jolted from the impact and the weapon deflected into the dirt, nicking my cheek. I tensed for the second blow.

"That . . . is not possible." Black—the man who *claimed* to be my sire—sounded stunned. "My son is in Yorkshire."

My fear evaporated and I lunged to my feet. "You speak as though you would know!"

Wintour's sword tip held me at bay, but my words surged forward as my weapon. "You *abandoned* me. I was to have my mask a week ago for my Color Test. You vowed you would come. And instead I find you reveling with fellows at a tavern. I may be plagued and maskless, but *you*, sir, discarded your honor when your absence caused me to be thrown from St. Peter's mere hours before my Color Test."

His sword arm drooped and his comrade, Wintour, stood as though carved of the Stone Plague. My chest heaved. Blood slid down my cheek from the sword nick.

As we stood there, I finally took in the man who sired me. I couldn't stop the sneer as I surveyed him. He was everything the rumors said he was. Tall and valiant, with the bearing of a great soldier.

A great soldier who had speared a lost street boy on a whim.

His mask was Black with painted eyebrows, a mustache, and a goatee. Blacks were so rare that the sphere wasn't even included in Color Testing. Blacks were strongest at night, when shadows darkened the colors. Some called them Judases.

An apt name for my father.

"We'd best get below." Wintour returned his rapier to its scabbard. "Bring the boy if you must."

My father did not touch me. He headed toward a set of stairs that led to what seemed to be a cellar. I didn't wait for an invitation. I followed and caught the muddy squelch of Wintour's footsteps after me. Only then did I realize my every limb trembled and I could barely keep my feet.

Once inside, Wintour lit a candle. The cellar wasn't much—a dark room filled with some old crates. It smelled like earth and mold and too much passed time. Wintour stepped into the center of the room and spread his hands. He stood for several minutes. I remained silent, prickling from Father's unbroken stare.

I didn't want to join these men, but I wanted a mask. That was enough reason to keep Father in my sight. All he'd need to do was give me my mask and then let me go on my way.

The earth beneath Wintour's feet rumbled. I stepped back when the dirt began to churn as though being stirred, then spin, then twist like a whirlpool until a hole appeared in the floor. I tried not to gape, but the man's Brown powers were worthy of a slack jaw.

"Into the hole." Father's first words since learning I was his son were spoken as though commanding a disobedient color.

I peered into the cyclone. Was he trying to kill me again? "Why—"

"I'm right behind you."

Those words brought me an unwelcome comfort. I didn't want his assurance. I didn't *need* his assurance, but I silently hoped that—despite his attempt to stab me—he might feel some amount of remorse.

I stepped to the edge of the hole. The skin around my stone eye throbbed.

"There's a ladder. Go!"

I lowered my limbs in, closing my eye against the floating dust. My feet found rungs; my hands located wood. Down I went, hand over hand, blindly trusting the man who hadn't even recognized me as his son.

The ladder went deep into the black earth. I smelled water and my shoes squished on soggy ground as I stepped away from the ladder. The shadowed walls pressed against me. My lungs grew tight.

Father descended next and then Wintour with the candle. At his command, the dirt settled into an obedient mass over the opening. It felt like he'd sealed a tomb.

Wintour lit a lantern that illuminated a long tunnel with a river in the center of it. The water carried lumps and blobs of stench. Thames water. Little better than poison.

Father nudged me. "Follow him."

We traveled along the underground river, through several stone arches and past stained walls holding unlit torches in brackets. The smell grew stronger until we turned down a separate tunnel.

We wound our way through several more, and I committed them to memory as best I could should I need to escape.

Eventually we made it to a wood door. After all the skulking, I expected a secret password or a knock pattern. Instead, Wintour lifted the latch and waltzed through. I followed and he lit three torches along a room of curved walls. A cobblestone floor supported a rough wooden table in the center, covered with papers and half-melted candles. A door on the opposite side was open and a breeze blew in while our door was open. Once closed, the breeze ceased.

Wintour plopped on a bench and scraped mud from the sole of his boot. "What now? We've a boy to deal with."

"Thomas . . . how did you come to London?" Father asked.

I told him how I left St. Peter's after being denied my Color Test. I told him about prison and about my escape—saying a prisoner used color speech and controlled the lock. Not a lie. Not the truth.

"I arrived only today and now I've found you." I did not include that it was accidental that I happened to pickpocket my own father in the largest city of England. What chance brought me to him?

"So the boy has a story. What are we going to do? Catesby will arrive any minute and he'll want to know why a plagued boy is here."

Father surveyed me. "He could be of use."

"All I want is my mask." I straightened my shoulders. "You owe me that much."

"We have need of a maskless to gather information on the streets for us." Father rested his elbows on his knees. "Wait a few months. Then I will have a mask for you."

A small part of me latched onto the invitation, pushing aside the fact that he wanted me only to be his errand boy. "What sort of information? What exactly are you *doing* hiding in tunnels and stabbing people who follow you?"

Wintour stood by the opposite door. He glanced our way. "Catesby's coming."

"Good. He'll decide."

Decide what? Whether I lived or died? "Would you really let

him kill me, *Father*?" I used the title as a jab—as a challenge for Father to be a man and, in the process, teach me how to be one too.

Wintour looked between the two of us, shifting his feet. Father hovered like a balanced statue. Light flickered in the tunnel beyond Wintour. Likely a lantern held by the man called Catesby.

I looked hard into Father's mask.

He broke his stance and reached me in three firm strides. "Keep silent, Wintour. We'll not be long." My father yanked me from the room, striding back the way we'd come. The door clicked behind us, but he didn't stop. As we traveled down the tunnel, my thoughts took a new turn—I was an inconvenience. He clearly had no qualms about eliminating inconveniences . . .

We entered an offshoot we'd passed on the way there.

No light. How could he see—

I rammed into his back. He'd stopped. A *crack* and then a spark flew past my face. I jerked away as a flame blossomed on a torch head. Light.

Father leaned against the tunnel wall and dragged a hand down his mask. Had he brought me here to kill me quietly?

He leveled a gaze at me. "Thomas . . . forgive me."

I backed away. "Let me go." I took another step back. "I won't bother you again."

He pushed off the wall and I stumbled. Suddenly I didn't want a mask. I just wanted my life, or a sword with which to defend myself. "Please, Father!" I held out a hand, all pride gone.

He grabbed it. "Stop."

"Let me go and I'll never tell a soul. I'll return to Yorkshire." My voice caught and I tried to tug my hand away.

I awaited the ring of steel, but instead Father grabbed both my shoulders and shook me hard. "Stop this! I am not going to harm you. Thomas, look at me."

I obeyed, staring into the impersonal eye holes of his mask. What did his true face look like beneath?

"I am *not* going to harm you." This time *his* voice caught. "Take a breath and then open your ears. We have little time and I have much to tell you, though it goes against my better judgment. Can I trust you?"

I nodded, feeling more like a boy than ever before.

Father released me and I straightened as his words finally penetrated my mind. He wasn't going to kill me. He was going to give me information. "Yes. You can trust me."

"Do you consider yourself a Keeper?"

Swallow. "Yes. Though I have much to learn." Like how to avoid communicating with White Light.

"Good. That will make this easier. Igniters have been using White Light to control multiple colors for the past eighty years, feeding off the lust for color power. Keepers protected the language of the White Light for twelve centuries. Once the Igniters rebelled and stole the language of the White Light, our beloved Europe was cursed with the Stone Plague."

He kept his voice low. "Wintour and I have made a pact with three other men to free England of the plague . . . and Igniters."

Too much too fast. "How can you possibly do this if the plague is a curse?"

"It's a curse linked to Igniters. Igniters are hunting us down and having us hung or beheaded. King James is allowing Keeper executions. He's annihilating us."

He took a deep breath, as though gathering the strength to continue speaking. "To free the Keepers, to stop this plague"—he stretched out his fingers inches from my stone eye, but not close enough to touch—"we must put a Keeper on the throne."

His voice turned to steel. "We have vowed to kill King James."

Before I could respond or even move, he rested one hand on his sword hilt and gripped my shoulder with the other. "You must decide. Now. Are you in or out?"

In or out? Was he serious?

"Do you understand what I'm asking, Thomas?" His fingers bore into the muscles of my shoulders.

"I understand." And at last, I did. My father was asking if I wanted to stop the plague. He was asking me to join the cause.

To these I could answer yes! But there was another side. He was also asking me to be part of a plot to kill the king. I'd most certainly be hung for treason if I were caught.

It was a lot to think about.

Still . . . doing this might stop the plague. I'd be cured—or at least not dead. Then I'd have my mask.

I looked at Father's mask. Did he want me to join?

"The decision is yours alone to make, Thomas." He released my shoulder.

Mine alone . . . a man's decision.

I wanted to be healed. I wanted England to be healed. I wanted to be part of something great.

I breathed deep through my nose. No matter my answer, there was no going back. I was committing to either treason or coward-ice. I'd been a coward once already that day.

No longer.

I clasped Father's shoulder with the firmest grip I could mus-ter. "I'm in."

Six

Father knocked the mud from his boots on the threshold of the Bear at Bridgefoot. I hung back, the sting of stone tugging at the skin around my eye. I couldn't enter—the innkeeper would expel me.

"Come, Thomas. It's only an inn." Father opened the door and raucous reveling billowed out, thickening the air with noise as efficiently as a well-used pipe did with tobacco smoke.

"I'm plagued," I snapped.

Father tensed. We stood in stalemate. "The Bear has seen worse than your face, son." He transferred his hat to my head and walked inside. "Just keep your head low."

I tugged the hat down and followed. The few intoxicated patrons who looked up focused mainly on Father and his Black mask, then averted their gazes. Father strode past the blazing hearth and rough tables sticky with mead. I followed him up a set of stairs and into a room, trying to ignore the scent of roast lamb filling the inn.

A bedstead rested against a wall with a straw mat beneath a mattress. A folded blanket and quilt sat at the foot. Opposite it, a table, washbasin, and chamber pot. A carry pack lay near the washbasin.

"Bed here. I will take the truckle bed." He retrieved an extra quilt from a chest near the table and then pulled the straw mattress from beneath the bedstead. Straw stuck out from the seams and indentations from too many bodies. "I'll bring food in a moment. Then I must go out and speak with Catesby."

Without another word, Father left. No information about the plot I'd joined. No direction for the future. If not for his pack being left behind, I would have questioned his return. The moment the door closed behind me, exhaustion and hunger resurfaced with a slap. My knees buckled and I caught myself against the wainscoted wall.

After a second thought, I allowed myself to slide down onto the prickly truckle bed. I'd not have Father take the servant's mattress for my sake. It received me like an embrace—though I'd received so few of those that I wasn't sure I'd recognize one.

My eye drifted closed. I managed to kick off my boots so as not to muddy the quilt more than my grungy clothes already did. Despite Father's assurances, I still expected a sheriff and the innkeeper to burst in any moment.

As my muscles slowed, my mind quickened. I'd done it. I'd found Father, though our reunion had been less than satisfying. I had joined his plot to kill King James.

To kill. The. King.

That would earn me my mask. But a final question swirled in my foggy consciousness before I drifted off . . .

Was my mask worth a murder?

The bedroom door burst open and I sprang to my feet. "Let me get my boots on," I blurted before my vision cleared.

Father stood in the doorway carrying a lit candle in one hand and balancing a tray in the other. No sheriff. No innkeeper. No tattletale maid. I swayed as the sleep-dizziness passed, then hurried to aid him.

I reached for the candle, but he shoved a platter of roasted lamb and potatoes forward. "Take this instead." I snatched the tray and cleared space on the small table. It took every ounce of restraint to keep myself from ripping a chop from the platter with my teeth.

Father gestured to the food. "Eat."

I needed no further encouragement. I tore a chunk of meat from the bone, trying to restrain myself from stuffing it all in with one go. He pulled up a stool. "I've ordered a bath for you. And tomorrow we will get you a set of day clothes, boots, and your own hat."

I swallowed my lamb. "I've no coin."

"You can go to the market—it is the beginning of summer season and hawkers will be looking for errand boys."

My eye narrowed. "I am not a boy."

Father chuckled. "There is nothing shameful about being an errand boy if it will provide food for yourself and loved ones."

Who were Father's loved ones? Apparently not his son. "I don't need your advice." I wasn't here for a relationship. I was here for my mask and to fight for the Keepers.

Father sighed, then lowered his lamb chop. "Thomas, I'm sorry I wasn't . . . there."

"Are you?" I snatched a potato as though it were a weapon. "Then tell me *why*. Why didn't you come?" That was all I really wanted to know.

"This silent war between Keepers and Igniters . . . is still fresh. New."

"I know—"

"When I was a student at St. Peter's, the headmaster was a Keeper. I married his daughter, in fact. Your Headmaster Canon is the first Igniter. You were under the influence of an Igniter. How could I give you a mask when I knew they'd train you up in White Light? How could I watch you take a Color Test against my very morals?"

"I've never been an Igniter! If you hadn't cut me off, you'd know that! Norwood kept me safe. Grandmother and Grandfather Bainbridge remain loyal Keepers. I never desired anything more than to bond with Grey."

"I know that now. I saw you bleed—there was no White in your blood. You're no Igniter."

"Then give me my blasted mask!"

"I haven't even *made* it, Thomas. My focus is the plot. When time allows—and Catesby permits—I will make your mask when you are ready."

I glared. Might as well get my glares in while I was still maskless. "So tell me about this plot."

"It's fragile—we've constructed only the base plan."

"And that is . . . ?"

"Before King James took the throne, he made a promise to protect Keepers. To lift the oppressive laws. To be an ally. But once he took the throne, he exiled us. He commanded practicing Keepers to leave this country. He broke his word."

"But . . . where would we go?"

Father shrugged. "That's not his problem. So we are going to eliminate him, create a new Parliament, and raise up one of his heirs in the Keeper way. By freeing England of an Igniter king, we will also free England of the plague. It is perpetuated by the one who sits on the throne."

I wasn't sure I believed that aspect, but at least I understood the deeper reason behind the plot. And I was proud to defend my people. I was proud to stand for something.

⸻ ⚞⚟ ⸻

The next couple of days taught me a lot about Father's patterns. He slept during the day, went into town in the evenings, and left at night. His comings and goings reeked of mystery, but whenever I asked, he said, "In time."

I used a string to bind my patch to my face so I could go out but had to be cautious about it slipping. I took brief walks and jousted with branches to regain what muscle was consumed by my travels. The market provided no employment, but I sought it every day. Coin in my pocket would permit me to purchase a new sword. And once I had a sword in my hand, I could show Father some of my skills. I didn't need a mask to be a warrior.

When Father returned to the inn one night with a package of new clothes, I barely managed a thank-you. "Why didn't you let me join you?"

"I had other errands to run. I found myself at the shop and took care of your needs since it was on my route."

I stared out our room window that hung over the Thames. Ship masts bobbed back and forth, stretching higher even than our window. "So I am to be left in this room like baggage?"

"It is your own choice to act like baggage. You're not helpless and you weren't raised helpless. You had St. Peter's, as I did. Our paths are not so dissimilar, Thomas. Only I left school with a *vision* for my future."

I spun from the window. "Our paths are not so dissimilar?" I sneered. "I am *plagued* and *maskless*. Tell me, can you relate to those?" I gestured to his stoic Black mask. "Try taking that off for a day. See how it changes you."

Father straightened. "A man's mask is his honor. His identity."

"Your mask is your *pride*." To my knowledge, no one but Father and Emma Areben left their mask on day and night.

"You can't understand—"

"So *teach* me!" I gripped the windowsill, feeling a satisfying crunch of wood beneath my fingers. "I am at your mercy. Teach me. Train me."

Father barely seemed to breathe. Then he clasped his cloak and swung open the door, like he had every previous night. Mask tight, boots clean.

"May I come with you?" I asked this time.

He paused in the doorway. "Can you handle a sword?"

"Well enough." I'd let my sparring speak for itself.

"'Well enough' loses duels and costs hasty men their lives."

I raised my eyebrow. "You are dueling, then?" At his silence, my patience flickered. "I'm getting the impression you're trying to tell me no."

"I'm trying to inform you of how prepared you will need to be to join me."

"Why not inform me of your outings? That seems the best way to prepare me rather than these vague tidbits."

"The night breeds terrors that prey on the helpless. Those oft cannot be fought."

What sort of terrors? Did he mean people? Or something else? "What makes *you* able to fight them?"

He looked over his shoulder. "I am a Judas." With that, he left.

And I understood. Only Judases could speak the language of Black. It was tricky—trickier than Yellow or Red. At night, all things were Black. That gave other ill-intending Judases a hefty power.

I had no color power.

I had no sword.

But neither piece of knowledge stopped me from following Father.

Seven

I threw my cloak over my shoulders, pulled on my stiff new leather boots, and slipped down the stairs. Father bid the alewife good eve and then exited, heading left through London Bridge. Night had fallen. People milled about London Bridge, clinking ale cups and sharing secrets under the noise of the rotating waterwheels in the bridge arches.

Father was swift. His black clothing mixed with shadows as naturally as though he were one. As he passed a glowing brazier, I caught the sword strapped to his side.

My heart thundered and I quickened my pace. The new boots squeaked as though I trod on a mouse with each step. I stopped to rub a little mud on the exterior, keeping my eye on my father. I didn't want to get involved in whatever he planned to do. Not yet. I wanted to observe. To know.

We exited London Bridge and the moonlight eased the strain of locating him amidst the shadows. He headed up Grace Church Street, then turned left toward Cheapside. Just as quickly, he turned right around the corner. I slowed and peeked into the alley. Nothing. Had he entered one of the houses?

Wait. There. A swish of cloak. I hurried so as not to lose him—my boots sounding louder and louder the farther we got from the revelers. But when I turned the corner again, there was nothing. I glanced behind me. The moon no longer seemed so bright.

I stepped back into the shadows, only then realizing how quick my inhales came. I slowed my breathing. If I'd lost him, I'd lost him. I slunk out of the alley back onto Grace Church Street, allowing the moonlight to reach my path once more.

Steps clicked on the cobblestones behind me. I spun as a firm hand clamped my shoulder. "You think I didn't know you were following me?"

"Yes, actually." I tried to sound as nonchalant as he did. I pushed his hand away. "And why shouldn't I? I have a right to come and go as I wish."

He steered me toward London Bridge. "But a gentleman with integrity will respect the wishes of another." He stopped and faced me. "Your curiosity not only endangers you, but it endangers me and my mission."

"You're on a mission?" For the plot?

"I have my own purposes and I *will* share them with you. But not tonight." He turned on his heel and disappeared in the alley shadows branching off Grace Church Street.

This time I didn't follow. But I didn't return to the Bear either.

I stood in the street, grimly aware of my failure at stealth. Blasted boots. I took in the night of London, feeling both dangerous and foolish for lingering in the abandoned dark. Better that than feeling worthless and bored in the Bear.

Tell me about it. Let's do something fun.

I whipped my head toward London Bridge.

Yes, I'm talking to you, Thomas.

Someone—no, some*thing*—knew my name. The mystery color voice. White. I backed away from the bridge. What did it want with me? Payment for freeing me from the prison cart?

How about a game of hide-and-seek? The hollow echo of the bodiless voice in my mind made the child's game sound sinister.

I turned opposite its voice and barely kept from running, as though I could outpace a voice in my head. White breeds greed. That was what the Keeper from Fleet Prison said and I could see what he meant. An itch inside my chest wanted to answer. To speak to White . . . to ask how it freed me from the prison cart.

And to ask what else it could do for me.

I settled for a brisk walk, the air suddenly chill in my lungs. The Thames flowed on my right, reflecting the moonlight as I passed alleys that led to the bank. Multistory houses tilted toward me from my left. Reaching for me.

I glanced over my shoulder, as though the color could follow me. How could White Light exist in the darkness? I saw no White anywhere.

Thooooomas. From my right.

No more fun and games. From my left.

I need you tonight. By the water.

I lurched left and sprinted up an alley, almost shouting, "Leave me be!" but that would mean acknowledging it. And that was the first step to becoming an Igniter.

I paid no mind to the street names I passed, but every time the voice said, *This way!* I went the opposite. I should have returned to the Bear like Father said.

As I turned up another, wider alleyway, the church bells rang, signaling night curfew and that the gates were to be locked in a quarter hour. Their clang added to my nerves.

Amidst the cacophony, I caught a human cry from the direction of the White voice. Or was it a cat?

I skidded to a halt.

Was the cry a farce? Something caused by the White Light to lure me in?

The cry came again, heavy with distress. And definitely human. Female.

Reality hit.

How dare I hesitate?

Thomas. Hurry!

I had no weapon and no color magic. I barely had any courage, but I raced toward the scream . . . and the mystery voice. If it was a trick and I was to die, at least my heart had honor.

I burst out of an alley, crossed Wood Street, and strained to hear anything. The bells made it impossible. I kept running. If only I had a sword.

A flash of light. Another scream—male this time.

I lunged through a dark passage, splashed through a sewer drain, and exited into a tight street in time to see a cloaked girl kick a downed man in the face.

I halted.

She smashed the heel of her boot against his nose and he sprawled backward.

The lady seemed to be doing fine on her own. That was . . . until the flicker from a nearby brazier glinted off a mask clamped in the downed man's hand. The girl scrabbled for it—dark curls sticking to her sweating and muddied face.

Hot fire built in my chest. No one had the right to take someone's mask—to deny them their color power.

I glanced around for a weapon. Where were the watchmen?

A second man lunged from the shadows and grabbed the girl

before she reached her mask. He wore a mask of Brown. He pinned her arms.

She growled. Feral. "I'm not . . . a Keeper!"

Brown Beast slapped a hand over her mouth. "They all say that." His hiss slithered through the abrupt silence into my own ears, carrying a slime that would gag a slug. "But now the gates are closing and you've no horse. Keeper or not, I'm sure we can find *something* to do with you."

Then he cried out, yanking his hand away from her mouth. I caught a splash of blood from his palm. The girl spit out a chunk of his flesh. He raised his first to strike her, but she elbowed him in the midsection.

The hood of her cloak tangled in her wild hair. She fled a few steps, but he caught her arms and dragged her back along the street. Something glinted in his hand—a dagger.

I lurched from my hideout, weaponless.

Now it was my turn.

I planted my feet. "Leave her be!" Not the most threatening line, but it was the only weapon at my disposal . . . unless I could somehow get that dagger.

The man stopped—more stalled than threatened. The girl moved quicker than a blink. She lunged out of his grasp and snatched her mask from the downed man—adding another kick to his ribs.

She slapped the mask to her face . . .

. . . and fire exploded from the brazier, sending coal chunks flying. Flame latched onto the cloak of the Brown. Then mud slammed into the downed man's face, slithering beneath the edge of his Grey mask. He tore it off, but the grime clawed its way into his mouth and down his throat.

A mud bubble popped from his mouth, but no sounds of air.

Brown Beast—the one on fire—shouted something at the

mud. It stopped long enough for Grey to free his lungs with a harsh vomit.

I scanned the shadows. No sign of anyone aiding her. Could she truly be *that* powerful with both Brown and Yellow? She must be an Igniter through and through.

The girl stumbled back, panting. One hand still held her mask to her face. The fire abated. The mud calmed.

The men fled.

The girl plopped in the mud and I hurried to her, reaching out a shaking hand. She tied her mask and finally looked up.

I lurched back. An oak-Brown mask with silver lashes and a white rose over one eye.

Emma Areben.

The girl I spent endless nights of adolescence dreaming of impressing. The girl against whom I'd hardened my heart as firmly as the Stone Plague had hardened my eye. The girl who rode in Henry Parker's twisted pocket.

The one person whom I both loathed and longed for.

Here.

At my feet.

She accepted my hand with her gloved fingers, but mine now hung limp. I shook myself free of my shock and pulled her up. Hadn't I always dreamed of being her knight? Saving the day? Only I'd saved nothing. She'd been her own knight and I'd stood by like a gaping spectator.

The moonlight cast enough reflection for me to catch the flick of her eyes behind the deep eye holes of her mask. "Thomas."

So, she remembered my name. Not just that, but she spoke it with a tone of gratitude—so different from the stiff, impersonal tones at St. Peter's.

"So you *are* plagued."

My patch had slipped off and hung around my neck. I looked away. If she had been unsure before, there was no doubt now with the moonlight illuminating my stone eye. "Why didn't you tell anyone?"

She steadied herself, pulled her gloves tight, smoothed out the neck ruff of her dress, and then stepped back. "Everyone has a right to their own secrets."

"You're not . . . afraid of catching it?"

She shook her head. "Sometimes it spreads, and sometimes it goes dormant in a person. You've had your eye patch for over a year. If I didn't catch it at St. Peter's, there's no reason I'd catch it from you now."

If only others shared this perspective. I stared at her mask, unable to say anything more.

"I need to get to the gates before they close."

"I'll take you." At least I could start acting the part of a gentleman. I pulled her after me, half expecting the thugs to leap out from an alley. Then I saw the Brown Beast's dagger sticking up from the mud, hilt-first. The handle was white like bone, with threads of red, but the blade itself was made of stone, not steel.

I reached for it, but Emma kicked it away. It tumbled into the gutter of refuse.

I wasn't about to put my hand down there. "Why would you do that?"

"You have no idea what color Compulsion they've put on it."

"Color Compulsion?" I would know about those had Father given me my mask and I stayed at St. Peter's.

"Strong color users can permanently bind a Compulsion to items. That dagger was unusual. It held signs of color power."

"How do you get rid of a color Compulsion?"

She stared at the spot where the dagger had disappeared. "The person who set it has to die."

Oh. "Do these happen often?"

"They're extremely hard to create—and even the simplest Compulsion can render a person unconscious for days." She would know better than I.

We headed toward the gate. As we walked, she sent mud off her dress using color speech. "They waited until the curfew bells so that no one would hear me scream." Her voice quivered, though it held no fear. Only anger. "Cowards."

"What are you doing out so late?" Alone? Unescorted? The dark streets of London were no place for a lady—masked or not. They were no place for anyone these days, with Igniters on the hunt for Keepers.

She lifted her chin. "Tending to my own business as is an educated and masked woman's right." She snapped her face toward me. "Are you offering to escort me home?"

Not exactly what I meant, but . . . "I'd be happy to." As if my meager companionship would be any use against ruffians.

"I reside in Hoxton as ward to the Baron Monteagle." Hoxton? That was a good walk beyond the city gates. "I had a horse, but she likely bolted home. Poor thing."

We reached the gates just as the gatekeeper tied on his Brown mask and commanded them closed.

"Wait!" He spun and I led Emma through the opening without another word. As pleasant as it might've been to have my former dream lady on my arm, I did not want to be responsible for her an entire night trapped inside the wall. Best to get her home. Swiftly.

The dark night spread before us as we continued along Curtain Road, flanked by homes, inns, and the alleys between.

"How did you come to London?" Emma kept her arm in mine, but I knew better than to imagine it was for any reason other than support in the dark. She was no damsel. She strode with steps swift enough to match a man's, her chin held high.

I chose my words carefully. "I came how anyone might—by foot a turn and then by cart." Never mind that it was a prison cart.

I expected her to ask why I came, but then she glanced at me for a spell. What would I see on her maskless face? Disgust? Amusement? "I am sorry for how your Color Test turned out. It wasn't right of St. Peter's to dismiss you as they did."

What did she care? She'd graduated. She was starting her new life. She'd accomplished what I couldn't.

We passed Old Street Road and I breathed a sigh of relief as we passed a patch of moonlight. Then back into the dark, narrower Hoxton Street. The houses grew in stature. Emma turned us down a lane. Soon she would be home and the excitement of this night would be over. Did I truly want it to end with my unforgiving silence? She did *seem* to be trying to show kindness. I didn't expect kindness came easily for her, what with residing with Henry Parker.

"How were you able to control two colors so adeptly like that?"

Her arm stiffened in mine. "Practice."

So she didn't want to say. "But your mask is Brown." I wanted to hear her say, "I'm an Igniter," so I could quash my growing respect.

"Masks take on the color with which you are strongest." She pointed. "Here is the home of my guardian, the Baron Monteagle, William Parker."

The house rose from the night shadows, marked by a line of lit lanterns. Moonlight illuminated a manicured garden to the right of the house complete with gilded bench and an orchard. I tried not to think of Grandmother and Grandfather in Timble Hall. Did they think of me at all?

Emma withdrew her arm. "Thank you for coming to my aid, Thomas. Truly. You are a good man."

She was being gracious. I'd taken two steps and spoken three words in that alley. Hardly worth a nod.

Beneath the wavering lantern light, she looked into my face. I resisted the urge to step out of the light and hide my infection, even though she'd seen it in Norwood's apothecary before. Emma stared. She barely blinked. What did she think of me? I swallowed. Hard. Waiting for it—for the moment that always dehumanized me . . .

But it didn't come.

She didn't. Look. Away.

Eight

"Where have you been?" Father looked as tired as I felt when I stumbled into our room above the Bear at dawn. His posture resembled a sapling birch tree weighed down by wet snow.

I wasn't about to tell him I'd spent the night in the gutters waiting for the gates to reopen. And I certainly wasn't about to tell him about Emma.

She hadn't recoiled from my plague. I never imagined a single moment of acceptance could reverse a year of bitterness and prejudice.

One moment. So powerful.

Powerful enough to sustain me through a sleepless night at the gates.

I rubbed my stone eye, as though that would ease the gritty feel. "I will divulge my activities if you agree to do the same."

Even from the doorway I could see the narrowing of Father's eyes behind his Black mask. He rose from his cot and pulled on his boots. "No matter, and no time to rest. Your night business is your own—as is mine—but today you meet Catesby."

I'd have liked nothing more than to collapse on my cot, but

Father's jab at my exhaustion stoked my stubbornness. I gave a firm nod. "It's about time."

"There's sealing paste for your eye patch there." He pointed to a clay jar with a cork in the top, sitting on the windowsill.

"Thank you." I applied it and pressed the patch against my face. We let it dry during a quick breakfast of bread with butter and sage.

Then we headed to the tunnels. I did not look forward to returning to their damp and lightless bellies, but it would be a relief to finally meet the mastermind behind the plot. The man so passionate about returning Keepers to their rightful state that he managed to sway my father to his cause.

"Two Fawkeses. Our blessings are great indeed." Robert Catesby strode forward and held out his hand. He was tall and almost regal—everything one would expect in the leader of a rebellion. A bit older than Father with a mottled Grey mask swinging from his belt.

I shook his hand, willing my grip to be firm and confident. "I'm honored to join." His pinkie bore a brass ring dial by which to tell time.

"Welcome, Thomas. I wish I could say that a man trusted by Guy Fawkes is a man trusted by us all . . . but that wouldn't make me a wise leader now, would it?" His smile was neither warm nor cold.

"I don't expect you to trust me upon first meeting me," I replied.

"Well answered. Let's you and I have a chat then, shall we?" He swept his hand toward the door in the wall opposite the one we entered. The other side looked dark. Sinister.

A chat?

I looked at Catesby. He raised an eyebrow, so I sucked in a silent breath and strode across the room.

The darkness twisted invisible chains around my chest. But Catesby followed with a lit torch. The light revealed a few chairs and some rough barrels with random paper slips and candle stubs. An old rapier leaned in one corner of the room, point down. Not even a scabbard. What fool left it like that? Whoever it was would have a blunt tip in their next duel.

The clank of a bolt echoed in the small room. I turned. Catesby stood in front of the now-bolted door. Sword drawn. Mask on.

"What are you—"

He lunged. I dove out of the way, knocking the table aside with my hip. The torch flickered from the pass of my body. I didn't stop there. A roll deposited me by the blunted rapier and I came up on my feet, armed, facing Catesby.

I glanced toward the door, but escape wasn't my goal. Would Father hear a shout? Then again, Father had brought me down here. For all I knew, they were all against me. Catesby was my first fight. I needed to dispatch him quickly to retain energy if I were to fight Father and Wintour next.

Catesby waited. Confident. His stance spoke of experience.

Nerves settled into place.

I slid my right foot forward, my free hand back, and curled my forefinger about the quillons, aligning my knuckles with the true edge. Then adopted medium guard.

No words needed to be spoken. Only breath passed my lips. I rested my weight on my back foot, so as to keep my head and torso as far away from his blade as possible. The memories and training and practice flowed into me like a warm draught.

Jeopardous blades met.

And thus, the dance began.

We tapped edges, a battle of inches for the high blade. He got his blade on top, but I slid forward so my forte could deflect the weak part of his blade.

Back. Forth. Back. Forth. Testing reflexes, awareness, strike strength.

I needed to strike true.

Catesby feinted a thrust, but no feint could substitute good technique. A trained opponent won't fall for a feint and an untrained opponent won't recognize it. So I held my ground.

He went for another thrust, a slight inhale giving him away. I deflected with my guard. I looped my blade to the top of his, gaining the advantage, and thrust. He retaliated expertly, deflecting the blow with his guard and bringing a bit more fun to the duel. But I was in my element—the one area in which I excelled.

I attacked. He deflected. Attack. Deflect. He stepped back. I pushed forward until he fought from the corner, his elbows knocking against the stone. His arcs grew sloppier and sloppier. I could taste the victory.

But would I kill him?

Sweat trickled from his forehead. I had barely warmed up, but I didn't want to wait until my own brow perspired. A skilled fencer will use only the number of strikes required to vanquish an opponent. Nothing wasted.

When Catesby went for a strike, I gained with a swift *contra tempo*—seizing control and stepping forward with a quick jab. But before the tip connected, my rapier jerked out of my hand and flipped around in the air, and I had two metal blades at my throat—Catesby's and my own.

Only mine hung in the air.

Catesby's mask had done that. Blast!

We stood. I didn't back away. The room was too small—without a weapon, I was already dead. Perhaps I could lunge for his knees and knock him down.

But Catesby lowered the swords. He released his own and sent it back into his scabbard with a color command. My sword returned to its corner—tip down. I cringed, both for the treatment of the sword and for the revelation that hit me.

"This was a test."

Catesby pulled off his mask and tied it to his belt. "A swordsman like your father. I warrant you'd give Jack Wright a run for his honor."

I didn't know who Jack Wright was, but at least Catesby seemed impressed. Still, I was irritated. "You might have asked if I could handle a sword."

"It's not just handling a sword. It's handling yourself and your emotions. In a tight location, at that." Ironic how I loathed tight spaces . . . unless I held a sword in my hand.

So I passed the test.

"Why didn't you call for aid?"

I crossed the room and adjusted the dull sword so it wasn't resting on its tip. "For all I knew, Father and Wintour were my enemies too."

"Shrewd. I daresay, you would have beaten me without my mask."

That brought no comfort. Catesby's use of his mask felt dishonorable . . . like a pistol at a sword duel.

Catesby wiped a sleeve across his brow, then waved a hand toward the two chairs. "Take a seat, Thomas." He uprighted one of the fallen chairs. "By my honor, you're not even out of breath!"

I grinned. "I am quite a bit younger than you."

"That you are."

I sat across from him at the table. I had an idea what this was about. Father and the others had made a pact in the Duck and Drake. They wouldn't include me in the plot at Father's word—no matter how honorable he was.

This was my interrogation.

"Thomas, your father says you are plagued, maskless, and uncertain about being a Keeper?"

He wasn't one to mince words. Neither, apparently, was Father. He had no right to reveal my secrets like that—particularly the one about the plague. "That's an outsider's perspective. I do have the plague, but it's remained in my left eye for just over a year. I continued at St. Peter's all that time. No one got infected."

"And how did you contract the plague?"

I leaned back, trying to convey a posture of ease, though the chains about my chest pinched and my breath quickened. "Does anyone know the answer to that?"

Catesby leveled me with a stare. "Perhaps not. But you know."

Sure I did. I'd analyzed that day repeatedly, but I wasn't about to tell this stranger.

We sat at a stalemate, though not quite king-against-king on a chessboard. More like king-against-pawn . . . and I was about to be taken.

"When you join this plot, you hold the life of every plotter in your hands. Are you willing to sacrifice your own?"

It was a valid question. While I'd shaken Father's hand and said, "I'm in," and daydreamed about danger and duels and treason and fighting for a cause, was I truly willing to commit?

I met Catesby's stare. "I don't think it wise to reveal all my secrets. I don't yet know—nor trust—all the men in this plot."

"What you share with me will not be shared with them. I don't ask you to trust the other plotters—I ask only that all the plotters trust *me*. That is a leader's role."

I still wasn't fully convinced. But as I hesitated, Catesby added, "I've had this conversation with everyone—even your father. And I will have it with every person we add after this. I understand if you need time to consider."

If I took time to consider, it would show a fickleness—a nervousness—that no amount of courage or commitment would erase from the plotters' memories. So I steeled myself and sat taller. "I stole a mask. I had been visiting my mother's grave in the York cemetery. Some headstones bore the masks of the deceased. I'm not proud of what I did. And I certainly wasn't thinking logically."

I didn't say what prompted me to steal it. I didn't mention the plagued woman weeping over her husband's grave, waiting to die from her own plague and join him under the earth. "I shouldn't have even been in the cemetery. The signs warning of plague corpses acted as a fence around the cemetery. But it was Mother's birthday. And I imagined she felt alone with nothing but the pigeons pecking at the seeds on her grave."

I had paid dearly for my visit. And for my theft.

"So you stole the mask and tried to use it?"

I tried to save that woman. I was so sure the mask would let me cure her. My passion had been so strong. "It didn't work, of course. I'd bonded with no color and it wasn't carved by my father, so the power hadn't fused with it. It was too small—too tight for my face. My skin itched for hours afterward. And in the morning when I woke, I was half-blind by the plague." And then I stomped the mask to dust in my fear and anger.

"The school didn't expel you?"

"They didn't know. The apothecary, Benedict Norwood, covered for me." An ache throbbed in my chest—Norwood was the one person who knew all my secrets. Who knew my full story. Soon Catesby would be added to that list, but my relationship with him didn't carry the same connection of friendship.

Sharing my story with Catesby ran more along the lines of giving him a handful of blackmail material. "He told the headmaster I'd had a dueling accident. He kept me in his cottage until he was sure the plague wouldn't spread. Fiddled with concoctions and mixtures to keep me healthy. Risked his own life, he did. And then he sewed me an eye patch to cover the plague." I gestured to the patch.

"But *why* would Norwood do that?"

Why indeed? "He's a good man. That is the only reason I can think of. I've asked myself the same question." My personal opinion was that Norwood viewed me as much a son as I viewed him a father.

That was enough for Catesby. He moved on. I spoke of my studies. He asked about romance.

"Nothing to report there," I said.

"Good. The fewer ties you have, the better."

I told of traveling to London, lying to Sheriff Nix, and hunting down Father.

"How do you feel about being denied your mask?"

My voice emerged darker than the corner shadows. "Betrayed."

"But he's explained it will come."

"He hasn't explained *why*." I lifted my gaze. "Do you know?"

Catesby's nod sent the betrayal deeper. Father would tell Catesby about his choice to deny me my mask, but not tell me? "I understand your frustration, Thomas. But it must be Guido's choice."

I frowned. "Guido?"

His mouth quirked. "You have a lot to learn about your father."

I knew that, but I also knew—at least—my own father's *name*. Guy Fawkes.

"Last question and then we can return to the main room."

I felt like we'd been talking for hours. While it was no easy task to share my secrets, the experience acted as a purge. It cleared my core of the bottled secrets, leaving room for new ones. "I'm ready."

And I was. I was prepared to tell Catesby whatever else he needed. He knew plenty to condemn me. What more was there?

"Has White Light ever spoken to you?"

Chills ran from skull to soles. I couldn't answer this question. To say yes would be to betray Keepers. To say no would be a lie, and if he found out I'd lied . . . "What do you mean?"

"You come from an Igniter school. And while I know you didn't enter the final year of color training, I'm sure White Light was welcomed and encouraged."

But I'd avoided it. I'd avoided the lessons, I'd spent most of my time with Norwood, and it wasn't really discussed with the maskless students other than, "White Light is what allows you to control multiple colors."

The first time it spoke to me was on the day of my Color Test—and I hadn't known it was White Light.

Tell him.

Oh blast. Not now. Not here.

Tell him I'm here. I'm powerful. You could tell him I'm in your head, but he might think you're crazy.

Hush! I *was* going crazy. Could Catesby hear?

Teeeeell hiiiiim.

Was this a game to White Light? It wanted me to tell Catesby. It wanted me to be expelled from the plot.

Now you're just being paranoid.

"Thomas?"

"Yes," I gasped. "Yes, it has spoken to me. It's still speaking to me." The words kept coming, and I could sense White Light chuckling in the back of my mind. "How do I make it stop?"

He leaned back. "You ignore it."

My panic subsided. "You're not . . . concerned?"

"White Light speaks to everyone at some point in their youth. If you'd have said no, I'd have known you were lying. This is why Keepers are so important. We used to help protect people from its voice—train them not to respond. Because once you respond, you can't stop. It gets ahold of you—of your mind. Of your very blood."

Doesn't that make me sound awesome?

The torchlight reflected off his grim face. "Will you resist its voice?"

My hands shook and I clasped them in front of me.

Don't do it, Thomas.

If I said no, Catesby would expel me from the plot and I'd receive no mask.

Not to toot my own horn, but remember how I freed you from that prison cart?

It had saved me. It had offered freedom to everyone—even Keepers. Didn't that mean it was good?

I also led you to Emma. Don't forget that one.

But what did that do? Emma hadn't even needed me.

Catesby waited. Watched. I needed to be strong.

Thomas. No. White Light's playful tone was gone.

And now I could see why it was so dangerous.

Because I almost heeded it.

I stood. "Yes. With every breath and muscle and thought . . . I will resist it."

Nine

"He's in." Catesby's announcement resulted in a hearty cheer from my father and Wintour.

I swelled. Strong. Proud. One of them.

"Thomas's plague is known only by us. We will not share this information. I do not believe he's contagious. Now . . . let's plan." Catesby led the way to the main table. It took all my effort not to glance at Father—to assess his reaction or scan for approval.

I was my own man. Catesby made that clear. He didn't call me *boy*. And he spoke as though respecting my story. "Thomas, we need a maskless who can gather information that we cannot. Without a mask on your belt, Igniters won't hunt you."

Father stepped into my line of sight. "Igniters get paid for turning in men with masks. And when we've succeeded in this plot, you will receive color power and get your mask. No one will know you and you'll be free to come and go as you please. How does that sound?"

How did he think it sounded? "Swell, Guido." My voice came out flat.

Catesby chuckled.

"Guido is my Spanish name," Father explained. "From fighting in the Spanish army for many years."

Catesby clapped a hand on my shoulder and faced Father. "The success of this plot will rid England of the plague. It will free the Keepers and put White Light back where it belongs—out of reach of those greedy Igniters and back under the guardianship of the Keepers."

Catesby seemed to speak from passion, not just ambition. His earnestness compelled me to follow him even more.

"Most of all, it will rid us of that wretch, King James." A tall man slipped from the shadows as smoothly as his voice slithered into our conversation. A mask of Red hung on his belt and stark white hair capped his brow—though it didn't seem to match his age. He looked to be in his forties. Harsh angles defining his face marked him as a dangerous man.

The man who'd encouraged Father to kill me and dump me in the Thames that first night in London.

"Ah, Percy." Catesby grinned at the fiery man. "At last you're here."

"By your approval, I would happily kill King James with my own hands," Percy said.

Catesby shook his hand. "We shall do something even better. We shall kill him with our *intellect*." Catesby faced me and I stood a bit taller. "This is Thomas Percy—the funds behind most of our actions and the fire in our bosoms."

I nodded to Percy, not particularly inclined to shake his hand.

"And Tom Wintour"—Catesby stretched a hand toward the short man, Wintour, who had held me at sword point upon first meeting—"is my cousin, a skilled Brown, a linguist, and an intelligent lawyer."

Linguist? Lawyer? Was everyone in the plot named Thomas?

"We've met." I shook Wintour's hand anyway and a warm smile stretched his round face. I surpassed him in height, but his stature didn't minimize the aura of intelligence that surrounded him.

"Jack and Kit Wright—our other conspirators—are at their home in Lapworth, so you'll meet them upon their return in a fortnight."

I gave a firm nod. Catesby, Percy, Wintour, Jack, and Kit. Add Father and me to the mix and we had seven whole conspirators.

That wasn't enough to dethrone a popular Igniter king.

Catesby turned to a pile of parchment on one of the tables. "I've thought over all the suggestions from our meeting at the Duck and Drake." He lifted his eyes to my father. "Guido, you say Spain will not invade."

Again with the odd name. Was that Catesby's way of showing Father honor?

Father shook his head. "They do not trust that there are enough Keepers here to join in the fight."

"A single assassination attempt is not enough," Catesby said. Percy opened his mouth, but Catesby cut him off. "We need something bigger. Something more permanent."

Wintour cocked his head with a thoughtful frown. "We have limited manpower. What are you envisioning?"

Catesby struck a finger against the table, tip down on a map location. "Parliament. We must strike at Parliament."

All eyes snapped to the map.

"Are you mad, Catesby?" Wintour breathed. "You want to strike him when he's surrounded by hundreds of his Igniter followers? When the royal bodyguards are at their most alert?"

"It is those very followers and supporters who have been passing legislation to *hunt* Keepers. To hunt us down and murder us. Wintour, you are always urging us to 'seek the source.'"

"I meant that when seeking information and knowledge—you

cannot base judgments or decisions off the opinions of others. This"—he gestured to the papers on the table—"is different."

"Only because it is bigger and our actions will send a greater message. Parliament *is* the source. This is the Igniter hive." Catesby straightened and clasped his hands behind his back. His expression held confidence and authority.

It made me want to listen. It made me feel *heard*, though I'd yet to speak.

"We cannot rush into this plot." Catesby took a calming breath. "King James is alert and paranoid. Since his birth, the Scots have made attempts on his life. He thinks England is a tamer stallion than his home country, so while he feels safe we must plot to such thoroughness that we *cannot* fail."

"But Parliament?" Wintour asked with calm curiosity. I could see the lawyer side of him. "Does that not put us at the most risk? What about during one of his hunting expeditions?"

Catesby's voice lowered to a level of such intensity it struck my core. "If we eliminate Parliament, we eliminate its anti-Keeper laws. Don't you understand, men? This is our last attempt. If this fails, we are finished. There is no more we can do."

The most I knew about Parliament was that it took place between the king and all members of Parliament across England. They talked about the country, the uprisings, and then the king made decisions.

I really needed to brush up on my politics. "When is the next Parliament meeting?"

"I've yet to unearth the date," Catesby admitted. "We need someone who can better access such information. *That* is when we'll strike."

Percy sat at the table. "The longer we wait, the higher the chance of us encountering mishaps. Or being caught." He eyed me. Did he think I'd betray them?

"Ah, but the more time we have, the better we can perfect our plans." Wintour stepped up to the table. Though he remained standing and Percy remained sitting, their heads were at the same level.

"How will we strike?" We had too few men to launch a physical assault with swords. Perhaps they'd send in a single assassin. Father maybe?

"With gunpowder." Catesby unrolled a furled piece of parchment. I glimpsed a string of numbers and scrawled notes.

Gunpowder. An explosion. Not an assassin.

Percy studied the new parchment and then his thin lips spread to a grin.

Catesby's shoulders tensed and when he spoke, the mixture of mettle and sorrow in his voice struck my heart. "We must cripple our beloved England in order to heal it."

This was real, this plot. And I was part of it. My pulse burst into a canter as I envisioned a ball of flame consuming the king from his seat in Parliament. That would send a message to the Igniters. With this plan, we could also take down other Igniter leaders.

Even as a plagued man without color power, I was part of something that could very well change the world.

I was in the thick of the fight.

What would Emma think if she saw me here instead of half cowering in a darkened alley as she saw yesterday?

"How can we possibly acquire enough gunpowder for such a task?" Wintour asked. "We've neither the funds nor the supplier and to purchase it would arouse great suspicion. Where would we store it? How would we get it into Parliament?"

My confidence in Catesby's plan wavered. Wintour asked good questions and I realized how intricate this mission would be. One slip, one mistake, and the king would have our heads on spikes over London Bridge.

"That is what we must figure out—our next step, gentlemen. And we need to confirm the dates for the Parliament meetings." Catesby removed his hands from the scroll and it bounced back into two rounds. "Put your ear to the ground, collect what contacts you have. If you aren't sure how we'll accomplish something, find a solution."

Wintour nodded and pushed himself off the table as though scooping his questions and doubts back into his pocket.

And then we went our separate ways—no plans about our next meeting time, but a mutual understanding that we'd taken a permanent step of treason.

We could hang for our words.

But only through taking such a risk could we free England and cure the plague.

Ten

"Grab us some dinner from Pudding Lane." Father handed me a few pence. "I'll meet you back at the Bear."

I headed toward the London Bridge market, not fully certain where Pudding Lane was. The sun hung above, warming both my skin and the putrid streets. One woman, masked, stood at her third-story window, wringing the washing water from a sheet with color power. I crossed to the other side of the street to avoid the stream. As she shook out the sheet, a child climbed the sill and yanked off her mask. The sheet slipped from her fingers and fluttered into the mud at my feet.

"Blast!" She ducked back inside. I lifted the sheet from the ground and tried to shake off the muck. The door opened and her tirade jerked to a halt as her gaze met my face.

I held out the sheet, but she backed away, hands upraised.

Oh. My eye patch. While she couldn't see the plague, plenty of people were suspicious. "Forgive me . . ." I let the sheet fall back into the mud, half tempted to drop it in the waste gutter.

But it wasn't her fault I was plagued. And it wasn't my fault she was paranoid. Hundreds of plagued could be walking around London, hiding behind their masks or clothes, spreading the infection as efficiently as the rats, without anyone's knowledge.

Was that why Father never removed his mask? Or Emma? Were they both plagued?

I continued toward the market. The timber jetties of the narrow house roofs projected outward like a salute of swords, shutting out the light despite the beat of the sun. As I strode past the parlors and workshops, I felt as if I were in the tunnels again.

Then I was deposited onto the street and heard the market before I saw it. Voices battling each other for hawking dominance until they enticed a customer. The smell of too many bodies hit me next. The lane opened up into a wide space where wooden booths and carts created pathways. Wooden signs hung by metal hooks above each market stall, depicting lions, barrels, cauldrons, hammers . . . Nearest the Thames, wool and sheep were being traded. A bit farther down the bank, swine were handed from farmer to butcher.

Other stalls housed glovers, tailors, needle-makers, and hosiers. The odor of fish mixed with the scent of roses, berries, fresh bread. Blood from the slaughter stall constricted my throat.

Ahead, four young cobs with Blue masks apportioned water to buyers from five water jugs by the Great Conduit. Few people could afford clean water. I surveyed the rest of the market, glancing at street signs for Pudding Lane.

Scan.

North Street.

Scan.

Market Street.

Scan.

A Brown mask with a white rose.

I stopped. Emma browsed a flower booth as though undisturbed by her recent attack. The flower man wore a Green mask and a bundle of daffodils hung suspended in the air between them. The man gestured to the bundle and it rotated gently.

Catesby said to put our ears to the ground and to examine our contacts. Could Emma provide any information?

She handed over a coin. Before she could reach out to take the bundle of daffodils and dampen her nice white gloves, I was at her side. "Allow me." I snagged the flowers from the air.

"Thomas!" Did I catch a smile in her voice? I couldn't be sure since I'd never seen her smile. But I let the illusion lie.

The flowers lurched out of my arms at a whispered command from the flower man. "Lady, do you know this boy?" He eyed my patch.

My arms dropped. The plague paranoia in London surpassed any I'd seen before. Even with my patch against my eye, they seemed only to see plague.

Emma's smile no longer marked her tone. "Mister Fawkes is my escort."

The florist stilled. Then the flowers smacked me in the face. "Thank you for your business."

"It's certainly the last you'll see of it," Emma replied.

Harsh. I grinned.

We left and I brushed the fallen daffodil petals off my sleeves. "I apologize for the state of your flowers."

"His buds are too weak if they are already shedding petals. Had he grown them in a windy location, they would be much more robust."

We meandered past other stalls and my tongue remained leaden. The pence from Father burned in my pocket, but I focused on Emma instead. "How do you fare after the other night?"

"I am excellent, thank you." Her gloved hand drifted up to her mask. It patted the edges, as though making sure it was secure. "My guardian, the Baron Monteagle, would like you to call."

"Me? Why?" Did she tell the Baron about my plague?

"To thank you, of course."

That was the last thing I wanted from her guardian. I deserved nothing—Emma had defended herself. Besides, I'd rather not risk running into Henry.

We passed the candlemaker's stall. Perhaps I ought to hand her back her flowers and continue with my dinner duties.

She folded her hands behind her back. "The other night in the alley. Did you . . . did you see them take my mask?"

"Yes. Blasted cowards. Rotten of them to manhandle you so."

"I see." She kept her gaze fixed ahead as we walked without a destination. "Did you see anything else?"

Perhaps she wasn't asking about my cowardice. This could be my chance to ask her again about her color power. "I saw you command two colors at once—Brown and Yellow."

She said nothing else.

"How many colors have you mastered?" I wished she'd take off her mask.

She lifted her masked face toward me and stopped. "It's not about mastering individual colors. It's about studying White Light."

White Light. She spoke to it. She knew how to *control* it.

"I know you come from a Keeper family, Thomas."

A chill cloaked me. How did she know that?

"But someday the White Light will reach out to you—it happens to everyone—and, well, you should answer it."

I couldn't tell her it already had. I couldn't tell her it frightened me almost as much as the plague. I couldn't tell her it freed me and then led me to her. And I certainly couldn't tell her I vowed not to respond to it for a plot of treason. "So you're really an Igniter."

She laughed lightly. "Of course! The decrees against Keepers and their followers are for a reason. We're in a new era—where we don't have to confine ourselves to one color—"

"Igniters caused the plague," I cut in with a low voice. "It all started when your kind broke the laws of color speech."

"That's not true. *Keepers* caused the plague by hiding White Light from the public for centuries."

I thrust the flowers into her hands. "Good day, Mistress Areben." I left the market breathing hard. She was one of *them*. She was perpetuating the plague through her ideals.

We needed to get a Keeper on the throne as soon as possible.

I pulled Father's pence from my pocket. And then I ran.

Eleven

By the time I returned to the Bear, I had two lukewarm pasties in my hands and a sour attitude. At St. Peter's, Norwood and I had hidden our Keeper beliefs. I'd hoped Emma was hiding them too. I'd hoped she was secretly a Keeper. Like me.

I entered our room. Father lay awake on his mattress. I tossed the pasties onto the table. "Why do the Keepers avoid White Light?"

Father held out his hand for a pasty. "You mean, why do *we* avoid White Light?"

"If the differentiation is that important to you, then yes." I handed him one, then sat back. I wanted to see him eat it without taking off his mask.

"It is."

I waited. Yes, I identified as a Keeper, but I still had questions. And now that I was around people who could talk about the Keeper way, I intended to educate myself.

"White Light is powerful. Unpredictable." I wished I could see an expression besides the painted mysterious half smile on his mask. "Dangerous. Only the oldest and most advanced Keepers understand it. Only they are knowledgeable enough to contain it." Father tore off a piece of the pasty crust with his fingers and slipped it under his mask.

"What do Igniters have to gain by attacking us? They already have a king on the throne and they use the White Light to control as many colors as they like. What are we to them?"

He chewed for a moment, his mask bobbing left and right with the motion of his jaw. Swallow. "Roaches."

The Igniters were stamping us out simply because they didn't like us. "It doesn't make sense. It's inhumane!"

"Most revolutions are." He pinched off another bit of pasty. Meat and corn filling oozed out. "Keepers protected every masked for hundreds of years, and now the people—and our very *king*—are turning against us. Exiling us. Beheading us." His fist tightened, sending a dribble of pasty filling down his knuckles.

I thought of Emma. "Why is it so wrong to control multiple colors?"

"It changes everything, Thomas." Father's tone drove apprehension into my joints. "They are willing to kill people for the power. Is that not reason enough for you?"

"So are we," I said softly, thinking of the plot.

"That's different."

"How?" Igniters killed our people. And we were planning to blow up their king. "Help me understand." I wanted to know the things he knew and to share his passion against White Light.

"That is all you need to understand. Stop meddling with it."

"I *haven't* meddled with—"

"Stop asking about it!"

"Then give me my color power!" My voice rang in echo before settling. Likely everyone in the Bear had heard.

"You're not ready."

Anger closed my throat. He didn't even know me—nor was he bothering to try. He asked me not to meddle with White Light, yet he wouldn't give me my color power or a mask. Did he not realize he was the only one who *could*? If the Gunpowder Plot was exposed, Father could be captured and killed. I'd never have a chance to try to heal my plague, nor have any profession higher than a caddy.

I would die.

My chest heaved. The anger reached a peak where it transformed into a silent iron, encasing my heart and chilling my tone. "What must I do to be ready?"

"You need to commit, Thomas." Father tossed his half-eaten pasty back onto the table and lay down again. "You can't ride both sides."

"I am part of the plot," I said. What more did he want?

"But it is not yet *your* plot." He crossed his hands over his chest. "You are too curious about the Igniters."

"I just want to know the truth."

"I've given it to you."

I shook my head, though I suspected his eyes were closed. "You've given me *your* truth. I have to find it for myself for it to become mine. And curiosity is the first step."

―――✠――――

7 June 1604

Greetings, Norwood,

London is different from what I imagined. Louder, dirtier, busier. A wild, untamed place. I can see why you love it, and also why you left it.

I found my father. He nearly stabbed me before I revealed my relation. You and he are quite the opposite. Father refuses to give me my mask. He doesn't think I'm loyal to the Keeper way.

I'm part of something that I think you would be interested in joining. The details are not fit for a letter, but I can tell you that—should this pursuit succeed—we will be cured of both war and plague.

Thomas

The Bear at Bridgefoot

"I have been promoted." I couldn't tell if Percy's face bore a grin or a grimace. Possibly a combination of both. Beneath his shock of white hair, he looked ghoulish in the dim light of the tunnel room.

Father, Catesby, Percy, and I stood beneath the streets of London for what I hoped would be the last time. The drip of water fueled my discomfort with each splash. I rubbed my thumbnail along the tips of my other fingers. The darkness made the space feel even smaller. Tighter. Closing in.

"Northumberland appointed me a gentleman pensioner to the king." Percy slapped a hand onto the hilt of his sword with a definite grin now, but something about it still seemed sinister. "I am one of the king's fifty mounted bodyguards." He burst out laughing. Catesby, too, released an exclamation and shook Percy's hand.

The irony wasn't lost on me. King James had promoted a man who was set on murdering him as one of his personal protectors. This made the plot so much simpler. So relieved and encouraged was I that I stepped forward and shook Percy's hand myself.

"Will that allow you to kill him?" I asked.

"Nay." Percy's mirth faded. "Catesby is right in that destroying all of Parliament will best cleanse our country. But"—he held up a finger—"this does provide many solutions to our current problems."

Catesby crossed his arms and leaned back against the wall. Father patted Percy on the back. "Enlighten us!"

"I am required permanent residence in London, and Northumberland assigned me to Whynniard's old apartment. It is in the precincts of Westminster!"

Father straightened.

"At the very *foot* of Parliament! There could be no better location."

Father whistled. "Your friendship with the Earl of Northumberland has served us well." But Catesby was frowning. Percy's glee snapped to a narrowed alertness. "What is it?"

"Are you not required to swear the Oath of Igniter Supremacy if you are to hold this position?" A drip of water fell from the damp tunnel ceiling and splattered his forehead.

Percy nodded. "Aye. But Northumberland did not impose it upon me."

"Then he must suspect you are a Keeper." The room stilled at Father's statement.

"He has promoted me and not questioned me nor turned me in. We must trust in this good fortune."

Father shook his head. "I don't like it."

Catesby pushed himself off the wall. "It is an opening. We must take it and we must trust that it is White Light inviting us in to return it to its rightful place."

For the first time, I wondered if White Light had ever spoken to Catesby, Father, or Percy, because it didn't strike me as a good listener. It didn't seem to be pining for man's intervention.

I kept these thoughts to myself.

"The Scottish commissioners will be staying in Parliament for a time, connected to the Whynniard apartment. I expect they'll be returning to their land soon."

"I should hope so," Father said. "The reek of those Scots will fill the apartment every time they pass by." I sniggered. The Scots did carry a certain unwashed odor about them.

The excitement in the room latched onto me, sending even my doubting thoughts swirling. This was happening. This was *working*.

"Whynniard's apartment is not far from mine, separated by the Thames." Catesby wiped away another water drop. "On the bank, even. This could not be more perfect. When the time of Parliament draws near, we can row our supplies over under cover of the river fog. How large is the apartment?"

"Barely enough room for living. I will mainly lodge at Gray's Inn just down the way. I shall need to set up a servant at the Whynniard house." Percy's gaze shot to me.

Father stepped forward. "I can fill that role. I have served as a footman and am familiar with the duties."

When had Father been a *footman*? Before becoming one of the most skilled masked soldiers of England?

His head inclined toward me. "Thomas can come as a caddy."

"You cannot use your real name." Catesby scooped up the remaining parchments and bits of quills from the table.

"Johnson," Father said. "I shall be John Johnson."

Johnson? There was no imagination in that. But perhaps that was the point.

Catesby paced, and with each footfall his smile grew. "Things are moving forward nicely. Now, if we had eyes upon a Parliament member . . ."

I wanted to ask if we were finished. I wanted out of these tunnels, dripping their Thames saliva down my neck and closing their claws around me. "That may come yet." Percy laughed. "One victory at a time."

Catesby clasped Percy on the shoulder. "Well done, Percy. We shall depart these wretched tunnels immediately."

I let out a relieved breath.

Catesby tipped over the table and slid it against the wall. Now the tunnel room looked less like a meeting place. "Our next step is to observe King James at his first Parliament meeting—see if you can discover the date, Percy. Then . . . we'll seek out the gunpowder."

I followed Catesby out of the tunnel, not waiting for Father. I would show him my commitment to the Keeper plot. I wanted this plot to succeed. The planning, the risks, the passion arose from a true desire to free Keepers from the oppression of King James and the plague.

No one should be imprisoned or beheaded when they desired only to protect people.

I would help free them.

The market wasn't as busy as the last time I went. The rakers were out—scooping up the waste from the street gutters and depositing it into wagons so as to cart the filth to a laystall or the countryside. It was worst near the market and shops. Animal entrails, feces, old floor rushes, and rotten food overflowed the gutters. I pulled out a handkerchief and held it to my nose. Even after the rakers cleared the gutters, the market square still stank.

I diverted to the food stalls and bought a pasty for myself with some leftover coin, but slowed as I walked past the smith. A man dunked a short blade in a barrel of water and an explosion of steam responded. Sweat poured down his leather vest.

I needed a sword. The smithy looked up. I could tell the moment he caught sight of my patch. First came the surprise, then curiosity, then suspicion. His body tensed and he returned to his work with renewed vigor, angling away from me. Would he respond the same way if I had coin?

I loathed the idea of asking Father for any money—especially for something as pricey as a blade.

So I did the only thing I could.

I headed out of the market, across London Bridge, and toward Hoxton.

Toward Emma.

Twelve

I stood frozen in the lane before the Monteagle house. Should I go to the back? I wasn't a servant, but how did one go about asking for reward money?

I lifted my chin, straightened my spine, and checked the seal on my eye patch. The door bore a round brass knocker. Each slam of the knocker against the metal plating struck my nerves.

The seconds passed. Then a minute. My hand hovered over the knocker. Perhaps it was bad form to knock twice. But I needed coin. I needed a sword. So I reached for the knocker again just as the door swung open.

A servant answered and his narrowed gaze settled on my eye patch. "Messages are to be delivered in back."

"I'm here to speak to the Baron Monteagle."

He raised an eyebrow. "He's occupied at the moment. You may leave your message with me."

"He requested my presence." The man's eyebrow rose even higher. "Alongside his charge, Mistress Areben," I added.

"Ward, who is at the door?" A familiar voice—swollen with

hot air and self-adoration—preceded the appearance of a face I loathed even more than my own.

Henry Parker.

His blond hair rested in a sweep away from his forehead in utmost obedience—not a strand out of place. His smirking Grey mask hung on his belt. Henry recoiled upon first seeing me, but then a smile spread. Not a friendly smile. "Cyclops, my old friend?"

The footman—Ward—stepped aside. "He is asking for Mistress Areben."

Henry's smug look disintegrated into one of narrowed suspicion. "What do you want with Emma? And how are you in London?"

I removed my hat. I'd enjoyed having forgotten about this toad-stool. "I was requested by your father, the Baron Monteagle." I shot a one-eyed glare at the footman for failing to mention that part.

"Now why would my father—a Parliament member and friend to the crown—wish to speak with a one-eyed, maskless street rat?"

I never knew Henry's father belonged to Parliament. Then again, prior to the plot, I hadn't paid much attention to Parliament in any capacity.

Henry waved Ward away and then leaned against the door-frame. "He *has* been inquiring after Emma's rescuer and she refused to tell him." He gave my face a once-over. "I see now why she was embarrassed."

I wasn't her rescuer. I'd stood there like a slack-jawed toddler as she defended herself. Why didn't she tell them?

I gave a small bow that exhausted the last of my patience. "Good day." I turned to leave, but Henry blocked my exit with a rush.

"You cannot leave without allowing Father to shower you with his thanks." He swept me inside. The shutting of the door struck my eardrums like the fall of the Edinburgh Maiden.

It was a mistake coming here. The Baron would ask about

me—about my father. About my mask. My irritation with Henry fled as I focused on taming my tongue. I must not allow any slipups regarding the plot.

We wove through an elaborate hallway and entered a sitting room. The Baron Monteagle reclined on a daybed, his neck ruff crooked beneath his round chin. He sat up—with much effort, given his rotund stature—when we entered.

"Father, this is Emma's rescuer. Thomas Fawkes." Henry stepped away as though presenting me as a gift to the Baron.

I stood tall, like a gentleman. "It was my honor to escort your ward home after she was set upon by thugs."

"*You* were her savior?" The Baron's pink face slackened. He scanned my belt. "Are you not even masked?"

"Not yet, sir."

His fingers twisted the hem of his handkerchief. "Tell me how you came upon Emma. What did you see?"

Desiring nothing more than to depart from the Monteagle place, I didn't mince words. I told of how I heard her cry over the church bells, so I pursued. I came upon her fighting the men. I stepped forward and threatened them and they fled.

"I heard Emma's mask was taken."

I recalled, with amusement, the vision of Emma kicking her attacker in the nose. "She retrieved it quite expertly."

"And . . . did she seem in pain? Could you see it . . . on her face?"

Something about how the Baron choked out the question seemed odd—too concerned. "She was shaken, but well. The shadows did not permit me to see if she'd been struck on the face, but she did not speak of any such wound."

The Baron sank back onto the couch and Henry sat down in a chair near the empty hearth. "Thank you, Mister Fawkes. How can I ever repay you?"

That was the question I had come for, but now that it was spoken, I dreaded answering. How badly did I want the sword?

A new thought struck me. Catesby said we needed the inside information of a Parliament member. Could I secure that? It would send a rather loud sign of commitment to both Catesby and Father.

Henry wore a smirk that matched the painted mask at his belt. He wanted to see me ask for something.

I wanted to humble him. To erase that cockiness from his face. And I could . . . with the plot. He was an Igniter, and the Gunpowder Plot would strip him and his people of their pride.

So I swallowed my own. "If my lord is willing, I would be ever so honored to serve the Monteagle household . . . as an employee."

They both went silent, but Henry's smile spread. I angled my head so that he rested in my blind spot. Ah, much better.

"We have no use for another servant," the Baron said, as I'd expected. "But Henry will give you some coin as thanks when you exit."

At the very least, I'd tried. As I turned to leave, Henry spoke. "Tell me, Thomas, did you ever locate your father?"

My throat dried like a strip of leather in the summer sun. Did Henry suspect something about the plot? Why would he care if I had found Father? "Aye."

He folded his arms. "And what of a mask, then?"

I didn't want him knowing anything of my mask situation, but there was no tactful way to remain silent. "I will receive it in time."

A moment of silence. Then, "Father, I think Thomas is just what we need."

I barely held my suspicion in. Why would Henry speak up for me? Something had changed between my dismissal and his questions about Father. Had I given something away?

The Baron laughed through his nose and turned his chubby face to his son. "How so?"

"He could be Emma's new escort."

"She has escorts."

"Yes, and they crawl back to us like whipped pups every time she gives them the slip. Thomas here"—Henry wagged a finger in my direction—"Thomas is trusted by Emma and he's proven his mettle against a couple fraters. He's also an excellent swordsman."

I felt dirty having Henry stand up for me.

The Baron raised an eyebrow. "You have a sharp mind, son. Conclude the agreement."

Henry faced me at his full height and authority. "You'll be paid ten shillings per month. Your role will be escorting Emma to market once a week and, on occasion, caddying for the Baron and myself. What say you?"

Ten shillings? That was half what a caddy would be paid. The Baron leaned forward at this. Apparently saving a few coins and taking advantage of a one-eyed maskless caddy was his idea of a reward.

But I needed a sword. The plot needed a spy. And I was tired of living on the graces of Father's purse. A man provided for himself and a snobbish ten shillings was far more pay than no coin at all. "I am . . . appreciative." I was going to say honored, but best not start off my employment with a lie.

"The Baron and I will work out the details. Come by Wednesday to start and we'll talk it over." I managed a single nod and Henry saw me to the door. His smile chilled my spine. "It's like old times, eh, Cyclops? You are in your rightful place and I am in mine."

I ought to have thanked him for the employment. Instead, I walked away.

"Come back here, *boy*."

I stopped but didn't turn. So this was how it would be. Were ten shillings per month worth it?

"A servant bows to his master."

I thought of my own home, my own land, curing the plague. Saving the lives of other men and plagued whom Henry spat on. So I turned and bowed. "Good day, Parker."

"The proper term is *my lord*."

I held my tongue. No final retort. No backward glance. My silence would burn a blister of fury more effectively than any final words could. I learned that long ago.

The door closed, separating me from one of the most unusual interactions I'd ever had. Henry Parker offered me employment.

Why would he want me to work for him? I'd take his coin if it meant bringing me one step closer to my goal—crippling the Igniters, freeing the poor, persecuted, and plagued . . .

. . . and humbling Henry in the process.

Thirteen

"*You* are my new escort?" The way Emma asked it made me feel like I was a slug she'd trodden on.

Not exactly the reaction I was hoping for.

She stomped out the door and toward town. I could do nothing but follow. Did she think I'd asked to be an escort? When I asked the Baron for employment, I'd hoped for something subtler. A stable hand or some sort.

But I didn't expect Emma to understand having to do whatever it took to secure employment. She needed only ask for a purse of coins or baubles and the Baron would indulge her.

I jogged to catch up. "Um . . . Mistress Areben—"

"Ugh. Emma is fine."

I strode alongside her. "Your guardian offered me employment and I accepted." Not to mention that Catesby had clapped me on the back and called me a "proactive young soldier" when I shared my success. "If it is upsetting to you, then I will desist."

"I can *make* you desist, thank you very much." Her pace increased. How did one so much shorter than myself carry on such a long stride? I hurried to catch her, but my boots stuck in the mud, releasing a louder and louder squelch each time I ripped them free. "I"—pant—"must do"—squelch—"what I can." I looked behind me and almost tripped.

Little rolls of mud were *chasing* me. Like a miniature ocean, the goop pulsed after me, snagging at my boots. "Will you stop?"

Emma snorted and the mud returned to its regular, immobile state. She waited for me to catch up, a tilt to her head. I tried to imagine what expression I'd see behind her mask. Amusement? Anger? Curiosity?

"You used your color power on me." I shook the remaining bits of mud from the leather, but a whisper from her sent all the dirt and mud into the street so that my boots looked nearly new.

"Yes." Then, when I did nothing but stare, she added, "My apologies." She didn't sound apologetic.

I needed to earn her approval so I could spy on the Baron. *"He has a loose tongue,"* Catesby had said. *"Make sure you are there when it wags."*

I calmed my tone. "I need the coin." I didn't intend to sound so blunt, but I felt no shame in saying that. "I don't want to follow you around. I don't want to be your lapdog carrying your dress packages or shopping in market all day. But I *do* want to be able to eat and sleep somewhere other than the streets. There aren't many options for a . . . plagued."

Emma crossed her arms, looking much more like a petulant child than a lady of stature. But I'd seen her smash a man's face in with her boot, and explode an alley. I envied this girl's brawn, and I cringed at the fact I'd made her sound like a lady of shallow pursuits.

"I will not reveal your secret, Thomas. But if we are to spend my outings together and you don't want me to abandon you to crawl back to the Baron or his controlling son, then I have rules."

That was the first time I'd heard her speak ill of Henry. If anything, it made her more attractive. "Very well."

"You will *never* lie to me."

My muscles snapped to attention. I was part of a plot to dethrone her king. Never lie to her?

That was a request I couldn't keep.

We stood there for a breath—she waiting for my response and me not giving one. It was too late to save the moment. She knew I'd lie.

"Look, I'm not asking you to lay out your life story. I just want to know that when you *do* speak, truth is coming out of your mouth. I will not question your silence. I'd also like to not have to question your words."

I let out a breath. Perhaps I'd regret this, but I held out a hand. "Very well." I realized a shake was an action men would make to seal the bond, but before I could withdraw my hand, she met it with her own gloved one.

"Any other rules?"

"Of course." She resumed walking. "We will shop every day."

Groan.

"I will purchase something every day."

I stifled a real groan.

"You shall carry whatever that item is for me."

That time I didn't stifle. "What an honor," I muttered.

She rounded on me. "And that is *all* you will report to Henry or the Baron."

I ground to a halt so as not to run into her. Then my gaze narrowed. "Meaning?"

"Meaning that whatever *else* I do during my day, you are to share nothing with them."

I wanted to ask what else she might plan to do—but as her

escort, I'd get to see it firsthand. The realization compelled me to follow close on her heels. "You wish me never to lie to you, but you ask me to lie to your guardian and his son?"

Her chin lifted so high in affront that I almost apologized. "You will not be lying. You will be reporting truth to them. But to tell them everything would be . . . unnecessary." She planted a hand on her hip. "If you do not agree to all my terms, Thomas Fawkes, then I shall tell my guardian that you forced yourself upon me and—after he castrates you—he will string you up on the gallows without a tongue!"

The words out of this woman's mouth would make a bawdy soldier balk. For some reason, I couldn't imagine the Baron Monteagle, in all his elaborate clothes and powder and pudginess, even thinking of such a retribution. But Emma's ferocity was enough to make me say, "You have my word, then."

A sharp nod and then our walk continued.

I had a feeling I would enjoy this job.

— ✶✷ —

We reached the market and Emma purchased a set of summer gloves. I couldn't imagine wearing gloves in this June heat, but every inch of Emma's fashion gave the impression she was chilled. Where other ladies displayed cleavage on all ranges of the scale, Emma's lace neck ruff went right up to her masked chin and high up the back of her neck.

It made her look elegant and a natural step above the other ladies.

The glover wore a Green mask, and after placing Emma's new light pink gloves on thick parchment paper, he whispered color commands and the paper folded and bound itself into a perfect square. She thanked him and handed me the square.

I tucked it dutifully under my arm. "Now where to?"

"This way." She withdrew a sealed letter from inside her sleeve. I couldn't catch the name or address on the cover, but she held it firmly in one hand. Confident, like her stride.

Wherever we were going, it wasn't near the square. I dodged a small girl leading two pigs on a rope. "If it is a letter, why not hire a caddy? Or give it to me to deliver?"

"It is one I must deliver myself."

We walked in silence through several alleys. Emma's pace quickened. My good eye darted to the shadows. We left the market and food streets, entering more of the art district. I hadn't spent much time in this area. Carts and horses kicked up dust from the dried ground. People crowded the streets, holding handkerchiefs to their mouths to breathe more easily.

"You do realize the Baron and Henry are both Igniters, too, don't you?" Emma sounded agitated, as though we'd been carrying on an argument instead of walking in silence for several minutes.

This was about my response the other day. I had better put an end to this conversation before it started. "I can't discuss White Light."

And especially not with her. I was part of a plot that rebelled against the Igniter movement. We were opposites, in more ways than just our stances on White Light.

"I only wanted . . . to talk."

"I can't."

"You're afraid." She didn't say this as an insult—more as an observation that I wanted to refute. Was I afraid? "The very topic of White Light has caused Igniters to hunt down and murder Keepers. Wouldn't *you* be wary if you weren't an Igniter?" So much for not discussing White Light. And murder was a dangerous topic during the calmest of times, let alone during a silent war. "Think on that."

"I will." She lifted her head and I caught a glimpse of her shadowed gaze.

We headed along the outer rim of the square toward the Thames. It was a breezy day after a fresh rain, so the stench of the river and streets had departed for a time.

"Why do you always wear your mask?"

"It's what I prefer." The tension in her voice hinted at more.

"I ask because my father does the same thing and I wondered if there was a reason that a maskless like myself couldn't understand." I added a laugh to try to hide the ache. Those with color powers all shared an understanding and a unity that I would not be part of until Father deemed me worthy.

Perhaps he never would.

"I know of no special reason someone else might wear a mask day and night, unless he desired anonymity."

"Is that what you desire?"

She just hummed. Now I wanted to know even more. "Does wearing your mask day and night make you stronger with your color power?"

Emma shook her head. "The only advantage it gives is to make my color power constantly accessible. I suppose you weren't taught this since you didn't receive your mask."

"I appreciate the reminder." It was meant to come out as humor, but even I detected the bitterness in my words.

Graciously, Emma didn't remark on that. "Your mask stores color power. The more time you spend speaking with the colors, the more power the mask stores. And then once you send a command, your mask releases that power."

I maintained my pace and interested expression, but inside I craved more information. I wanted to know everything about the colors and mask that were denied me. "And then what?"

"Then you need to rest. Using color power is exhausting." She let out a deep breath.

"So how are some masked people better at color power than others? Do their masks store more of the power?"

"Color power is like any other skill—you grow in capability. The more you speak to colors, the more you learn how they respond to you. Each color responds differently. Sometimes you need to coax, command, or compliment a color to convince it to obey you. Eventually you build trust and relationship with the colors. For Igniters, that means trust and relationship with White Light, because all the other colors obey it. If you can speak to White Light, you can eventually command all colors. Though your mask will only ever reflect your strongest color."

I went silent. White Light again.

"Here we are." She jerked me to a halt at the corner of Cornhill and Broad Streets. Cobblestones lay beneath my boots and not the dry dirt. No dust hung in the air here.

We stood before an enormous four-story building of deep-red brick with double balconies and elegant arches along its base. The Royal Exchange—the market for the wealthy. A bell tower rose into the sky with a carved grasshopper on the top—the mark of Sir Gresham, the merchant. A long line of dormered windows also sported grasshoppers.

Emma entered through the bell tower arches and I followed. Mute.

We passed through the arches into a wide-open courtyard filled with vendors and the mingling upper class. We walked past a statue of Sir Gresham, but I was more interested in the many statues of the English kings near the piazzas.

This was no place for a plagued. I checked my eye patch, kept my head down, and followed Emma. No need to embarrass her by getting thrown out. Few shoppers wandered about. The bell of the

Royal Exchange rang at noon and six. It was not yet noon so the vendors had not opened their shops.

Emma crossed the courtyard and headed toward a booth where a merchant set out embroidered cloths and lengths of canvas using color speech. The cloths soared from their baskets onto the table-top, resting in an attractive pattern of folds.

He wore a Blue mask, but cloths of several colors obeyed him. An Igniter. They were everywhere.

Emma reached the booth and curtsied.

"We are not yet open, madam." He set out wooden spools of yarn and thread, each stuck onto a little wooden peg for display.

"I am Emma Areben, ward of the Baron Monteagle and skilled in color speech. I wish to inquire about an apprenticeship." She handed him her letter.

He stared at it for a long time, then took it seemingly out of reflex. "I cannot take the time to train"—he looked her up and down—"such a young apprentice."

She lifted her chin. "Yes, I am young and I am a woman. But I guarantee you my skill will rival any man's." I wanted to chime in and say she was one of St. Peter's best, but the word of an eye-patched servant might hurt her cause more than help it.

The merchant removed his mask and gave Emma a sym-pathetic look. As though she was a child. As though she wasn't bursting with skill and passion and color speech.

She handed him a roll of canvas. He unfurled it and stared for a long time. My patch hindered my view, so I angled myself a bit more and caught a corner of an elaborate portrait before he rolled it up and returned it to her, breathing deeply as though winded.

Emma wanted to be a painter? It seemed so tame for her.

Once the merchant recovered, he said, "Work is unfit for your position."

Emma's gloved hands fisted. How could he respond in such a manner after seeing her skill? She took a deep breath, but I took her arm. "Emma, you don't want to apprentice for someone who doesn't value talent."

The merchant's face turned red. Emma slipped him the painting. "For you."

We walked away. Emma trembled at my side, each step stiff and each breath a hiss. We left the Royal Exchange just as the bells rang and customers left the side streets to do their shopping.

So Emma was seeking work.

Why? She had everything she needed as the ward of the Baron—money, a home, wealth, clothing, prestige. And the merchant was correct. Work *was* beneath her station.

We walked around London, without destination, for another hour. No words passed between us. We walked along the docks, watching the merchant ships travel up and down the Thames. Watching people hire small boats to take them downstream. This seemed to calm her.

"What do you think of London, Thomas?"

Her abrupt question—coming after an hour of silence— sent my mind scrambling. When I had first placed my foot upon London soil, I was struck by the stench. Dead bodies, butchered animals, refuse gutters, and Thames flow. But a month in and the stench had been overpowered by the uncertainty of life. Any moment the plague could spread; a Keeper could be caught and hung; starvation could claim someone. The wide, hollow eyes of the poor scanned the streets for stability. They found it in their conceited, oppressive king.

I gave her a safe answer. "It's not what I expected."

"Why are you here?"

I shrugged. "To find my father."

"But you found him, yes?"

I nodded, feeling the stares of dockworkers as Emma and I walked. I imagined what they saw—a well-dressed masked lady at the side of a half-blind maskless man.

"So why do you not have your color power or mask?"

"I wish I could talk about it, but I assume it's a bit like why you won't tell me about your insistence on wearing your mask." I put a little more distance between us. "You know, you really shouldn't be around me." I pointed to my eye.

As much as I wanted the payment, I didn't want it at the cost of someone's life. Emma's life.

She waved away my comment. "The plague is everywhere. I'd rather not have to abandon one of Henry's stiff escorts every other week."

"But you do it so well."

She laughed and the sound filled something inside me. I'd heard her laugh before—at St. Peter's. But the laugh never belonged to me. Not like this one.

"How long have you been seeking an apprenticeship?" The moment I asked, I wished I hadn't, because her laugh faded into a tired exhale.

"Since returning to London."

"They would be fools not to take you on."

Emma increased her pace. "Seems there are more fools in London than I thought."

The hum of voices saturated the air. We weren't near any of the markets. I craned my neck into one of the streets. "I wonder what's going on."

"Probably a street busker." Emma didn't slow, but our path took us toward the voices.

We turned up a northward street until we came across the

source of the sound. A crowd faced one direction, their backs to us. The excitement in the air carried a menacing, grim undertone.

I led Emma through the gaps of the crowd, careful to shield her from the rowdier viewers. But the moment I got my first clear view of the action, I pulled up short.

Three men stood in chains. Their masks—Blue, Yellow, and Green—were in pieces and reattached to their faces by tar. Before them, a gallows with a long ladder to the top and a single noose.

The crowd wasn't cheering for entertainment.

They were cheering for blood.

"It's not a busker." I gripped Emma's elbow, taking in the crowd, the executioner, the guards. "Let's go."

Emma didn't move. Didn't speak. But a bystander on my right elbowed me and pointed to the first masked-and-tarred man ascending the ladder. "The Keepers always go first."

A hand of dread closed about my throat.

"It's execution day." Was that a smile in his voice? "The thieves and general prisoners go next." He gestured beyond the gallows to a prison cart packed with the dirtied bodies of maskless men and boys. "I'm here to watch *that* abomination hang."

My eyes alighted on the guilty one and all I saw was a small, round black face, tiny hands, and a glare that could stop the very Thames from flowing.

I stared.

I'd never seen black skin before—not in person—though I'd heard of John Hawkins, the naval commander who captured and sold Africans to Spain. That partially caused the war between Spain and England—in which Father fought. I knew some African servants resided in England, but this was the first one I'd seen.

And he was about to hang.

"But he's—he's only a *boy*!" Emma's outrage slapped me out of my shock. The kid couldn't have been a day over ten. Were they truly going to *hang* him?

A loud *thunk* and a deafening cheer returned my attention to the gallows in time to catch the twitch of the first Keeper's body.

"We can't let this happen," Emma growled. She still faced the cage of thieves.

"It's how things are for now." The second Keeper was already to the top of the ladder when the executioners removed the noose from the first's neck. The resignation in my voice sickened me, but I clung to my knowledge of the Gunpowder Plot. It would change this. *I* would change this.

The Keeper met his fate to another chorus of cheers. My neck tensed as if it were the one breaking beneath the drop.

The third masked Keeper ascended the ladder as an executioner unlocked the prison cage and pulled out the black boy.

Emma grabbed my forearm. My skin pinched beneath her grip. "We must do something." She sounded frantic. Still focusing on the African. Did she know the lad?

I tried to tug her away. "We can't."

"Thomas!" The cheer of the crowd drowned out her scream.

I wanted out of there. We were helpless, but Emma wanted to cause a scene. If the boy was to hang for thieving, then that was punishment for his crimes. Right?

The thought felt sour.

Plagued. Keeper. Thief. By that list, I deserved to be hung too. "What can we do?" I had no sword. I had no color power.

I had no courage.

But Emma had plenty. She walked forward as the African fought his captors, and in a voice that could rival the bells of the Royal Exchange, she announced, "I would like to pay the debt on that boy and take him as a servant."

The crowd hushed so swiftly, I could hear Emma panting. Even the boy stopped fighting.

"His fate has been sealed, madam," the executioner shouted from his spot by the gallows.

"I contest that." She yanked her purse of coin from her belt. "Is there no price you will accept?"

The muttering started. She was causing a scene. My face burned for her, but at the same time I imagined myself in her spot—daring to speak out.

"He's an African. And a thief." The finality in the executioner's voice spoke volumes more than his statement. The men resumed their attempts to haul the boy up to the gallows.

Emma screamed and stalked forward.

"Someone restrain the lady, please."

I darted forward before the crowd could get to her and pulled her back with a sharp word in her ear. "Emma, they've made their decision." I kept my eyes away from the gallows.

But she planted her feet in the mud as the boy fought his captors. Though he had the ferocity of a lion, he had not the strength. Emma held her hands out to her sides and muttered color commands so fast I couldn't make out specific words.

The boy thrashed as one guard lifted him into the air and another tried to get the noose around his neck.

If only I had a blasted sword!

Emma muttered faster. Frantic. But nothing changed. Her body trembled. "Help," she finally breathed.

Her power wasn't working. There must have been other commands on the gallows. But she was so desperate, so bold in standing up for the lad despite resistance, that I did the first thing I could think of.

I ran . . .

. . . toward the boy.

I scooped a handful of mud from the ground as I went and smeared it over my face to conceal my identity.

The men got the noose around the boy's head.

I put on a burst of speed, broke from the crowd, and bowled into the two guards. The boy fell from their arms and the noose jerked around his neck as the three of us toppled down the gallows stairs.

I scrambled to my feet—coming out on top.

The African boy made a strangled croak but weighed so little that his neck didn't break. A guard pushed himself to all fours and reached for the boy's feet to give the final yank.

"No!" I kicked his arm and it cracked against the gallows post.

The boy was as agile as an acrobat. By the time I'd regained my feet, he'd pulled up his knees, swung his bound hands to his front, and was out of the noose, sprinting down an alley.

A guard fumbled for his sword.

The crowd swarmed.

I didn't even spare a glance for Emma before I took off for myself.

———✦✦———

15 June 1604

Thomas,

It was a relief to hear from you! Now that you are in London, you must visit the baker on Pudding Lane. Sugar and flour run through the veins of that family and you'll find no better pastries.

I do not understand why your father would deny you your mask. You are a grown man and it is not his right to deny you your color inheritance. A father may give his son his mask at any point in life, but usually no later than age sixteen. If Guy continues to refuse you your mask, I will visit under the authority of St. Peter's Color School and confront him.

Regarding the pursuit you speak of . . . I assume it is some sort of conspiracy plot. Be wary, Thomas. There is no easy fix for the plague. Your connection to the plague makes you vulnerable regarding finding a cure. I do not doubt your good intentions, just your discernment.

Do not follow anyone—or any rumor—blindly.

Norwood

Fourteen

Midsummer

The skin around my eye patch itched. I needed to replace the paste. I couldn't have the patch falling off in front of Henry or the Baron. But I already stood at the back entrance of the Monteagle house.

Ward, the footman, let me in. I waited in the hallway for Emma. A fortnight had passed since our escapade in the market and still my daring actions at the gallows hung over my mind like the sway of the three dead Keeper bodies.

No soldiers had pursued me. As far as I could tell, none but Emma knew my identity.

I wanted to feel the hero, but my actions shamed me. Yes, I'd helped the African boy, but not because of *my* conviction. I helped because Emma wanted him free. I hadn't spared a thought for the other imprisoned children and I'd allowed the Keepers to hang simply because that was how things were currently done.

Since that moment, I forced myself to envision the Keepers' shattered masks. The blood and tar painting their skin. I forced myself to remember the sound of the crowd.

Jeering. Cursing. Lusting for blood.

Anger pinched my throat. Those Keepers had families. They had stories. They'd spent their lives protecting the people.

Raised voices met my ears. I pulled up short outside of the sitting room. Had I been pacing?

"You don't think I should attend?" Henry asked from around the doorway.

I backpedaled, but then caught the Baron's response. "It's too soon, Henry. Of all Parliament meetings to attend, we need to be extra cautious with this one."

Parliament. At last—information! This was why I had taken this position. I refocused on my duty—my *true* duty to Keepers and Catesby and England.

"But isn't this the point in training me as the next baron?" Henry bit off the spike of his voice and his next words came out hushed. Intense. "This is my moment to leave an impression."

I kept my back flat against the wall, listening but not daring to look.

"Right now it is *my* impression that matters. And to bring my son, uninvited, will get tongues wagging and Parliament talking. Yes, you will succeed me, Henry. But right now you must support me. That is your first role."

I ran my sweating palms along my breeches. When? *When* was this meeting? I needed more details! Did the Baron have a written invitation in his study? I could sneak in and find—

"You're a terrible eavesdropper, you know." The whisper in my left ear so thoroughly spooked me, I slammed an elbow against the wall.

Henry's and the Baron's voices cut off.

I stared at Emma in horror. Blast my blind eye—she'd walked right up to me and I'd neither heard nor seen her.

Henry barreled out of the room and pulled up short before us. "What is going on?"

"I am readying myself for market." Emma handed me a small closed basket. "Carry the dinner, will you?"

I looped the basket over my arm, certain my face was either bright red or dead pale. My pounding heart seemed to reverberate down the hall, but Henry's attention remained on Emma.

"I wanted to say farewell before leaving," she said.

His suspicion melted away into something . . . tender. And possessive. "Enjoy the market."

"Can I bring anything back for you?"

"Just yourself." He reached out, as though to brush his hand against hers, but she turned and glided up the hall.

Their interaction seemed so personal. As though they shared a friendship deeper than Baron's heir and Baron's ward.

I followed her before Henry's gentle Emma-gaze could turn on me and transform to something ugly. I appreciated Emma covering for me, but not her interruption. A few more minutes and I might have had the date of Parliament.

We stepped out into the sun and started the long walk to market. Emma preferred to walk. I, on the other hand, would have appreciated a little less exercise. It always made me hungry, and my ten shillings a month didn't leave much room for pastries on Pudding Lane.

Our postures were both stiff. This was the first time we'd seen each other after the incident with the African boy. I didn't want to talk about it—or think about it.

We turned onto the path leading to the main road.

"Thank you for saving that boy, Thomas." Emma took my hand in her gloved one. I almost tugged away. The connection was too intimate, but it revealed her gratitude in a way her words could not. "You showed your true worth in that moment."

What could I say? I wasn't about to admit that I saved him for her. I wasn't even sure why I did it. "You would have done the same had your color powers obeyed."

She released my hand. The separation sent a cold breeze across my skin.

We reached the Royal Exchange as the bells rang and I learned the basket did not contain dinner. Emma pushed back the lid and withdrew a small easel on which she stretched a blank canvas.

"Please stand over there." She nodded toward the opposite side of the market. I obeyed, though a bit miffed.

Then, as people entered, Emma started to paint. And paint. And paint. Never once touching a brush and sending the colors to canvas with only color speech. From what I could tell, she was painting the cordwainer's stall—though what interest she had in painting shoes, I couldn't fathom.

I wanted to see.

Why did she make me stand opposite her? Likely because my masklessness and my eye patch would deter passersby.

The longer she painted, the more shoppers stopped to watch her. Some stood for a long while, watching and not asking questions. Finally, the cordwainer himself left his humming and his cobble work and glanced at her painting.

His humming stopped.

His smile faded.

And then he began to weep.

Emma stopped. She set down her paints and detached the canvas. When she handed it to him, he took it gingerly. He sniffed once, then muttered something to her and she shook her head, holding a palm up in refusal—of payment, likely.

The crowd hovered to ask her a few questions I couldn't catch from my post. Emma packed up her paints, gave me a nod, and then we left the Exchange.

Not a word was spoken on our walk back to Hoxton. Her painting had brought that man to tears. How could simple colors and canvas do that? What had she painted that held such power over him?

I picked at the edge of my eye patch, the sealant now dry and crusty.

"Here, let me fix that for you." Emma stepped into the shadow of a house and reached for my patch. I lurched back and her hand stilled. "I've already seen your plague. I'm not bothered. Now take off your patch."

I barely touched it and the thing came off. Whether I wanted her help or not, I needed it. My stiff, stone skin welcomed the breeze. Even though the infected skin felt nothing, it sensed the freedom of sun and wind. Someday I wouldn't need the patch.

Someday soon—after King James lay dead—I wouldn't need to fear the plague any longer.

Emma sent the now-dried sealing paste off the patch with a few color words. They slipped through her lips so easily and the grey-green crumbles obeyed almost before she finished speaking.

Once the patch sat clean in her palm, she held it up to her lips and whispered so low I couldn't catch any words. She continued like this for a full minute, but the patch didn't move. Was she having trouble controlling it?

Her hand dipped lower and lower, as though the patch equaled the weight of a brick. Her back bowed, but she kept whispering. The patch dragged her hand down. She used her free hand to hold up the other—to resist the earthward pull.

This wasn't normal. "Emma?"

"Go," she said at last to the patch and it flew from her hand, fixing itself around my eye. It sealed to my skin perfectly. No itching. No tugging. And no paste. Just color power.

"How did you . . . ?" I looked at Emma. She sagged against the wall of the house. I hurried to catch her elbow before she fell. "Emma?"

"I'm . . . fine." She got her feet, but not her strength. Her entire body trembled.

"What did you do?"

She sucked in a breath and gripped my shoulder. I held her firmly so she knew I wouldn't let her fall. "A color Compulsion."

"You mean . . . you mean this patch won't come off unless you die?" That wasn't what I wanted. That was the *last* thing I wanted. How would I get rid of the blasted leather once I was cured of the plague?

"Or unless you remove it."

I breathed again.

"I told it to obey no one but you." She braced herself with her other hand against the house wall. "Now you don't have to worry about it falling off."

No matter how badly she wanted to support herself, I could see her struggling even to keep her head up. So I willed my measly muscles to work and I lifted her into my arms. The basket handle cut into my forearm, but I took a breath and straightened.

"Oh. No, Thomas . . ."

"I didn't want the patch in exchange for your health."

She squirmed weakly. "This is normal repercussions for a Compulsion."

"I'm taking you home."

"Not carrying me, you're not!" She struggled again and I let her down—both because I wasn't sure I could physically carry her the entire way and because I certainly didn't want to if she was determined to resist me.

Her knees buckled as her shoes hit the dirt, but I kept a strong hand under her arm. She regained her footing. It was odd seeing her weakened, especially knowing how strong her mind and will were.

But she was weak because of setting a color Compulsion to my patch—a strong action that took a *lot* of training and practice. And she did it for me—to help me keep my secret.

"So what did you hear?" Emma picked her way up the road back home. At least she hadn't argued with me on that.

I kept my hand on her arm. "At the Exchange? Nothing—you were too far away for me to catch speech."

"No." A smile lined her response. "I mean, what did you hear of the Baron's conversation with Henry this morning?"

Oh. Blast. A lie leapt to the tip of my tongue, but we had agreed not to lie. And I intended to be a man of my word. "They were talking about Parliament."

"Oh, that's all?" What had she thought they were talking about? She shook her head. "That meeting can't come soon enough. Henry and the Baron have been arguing about it since the summons."

I forced a dry swallow before delivering my best neutral and mildly curious tone. "When is the meeting?"

Her face turned my way ever so slightly, as though eyeing me. I pretended not to notice.

"The seventh of July." Whether she suspected or not, she'd answered.

Dare I press my luck? "That's soon. How often do these meetings happen?"

She shrugged. "Who knows what King James will want?"

I smiled to release the tension in my chest. I'd gotten what I needed. "Of course. Forgive my curiosity. I am intrigued by the king's doings."

"Curiosity causes us to seek truth. I can't fault you for that."

Hadn't I said the same to Father once?

I'd need to be more careful in the future. As much as I wanted to hope in Emma's ignorance, she was too bright. She suspected something already, but chose not to comment on it.

On the day she *did* choose to comment or ask about my secrets . . . That's when I'd leave.

Fifteen

"Thomas Fawkes, you are the very oar to this plot's dory." Catesby clapped me on the back so hard, my lungs smarted.

We occupied the common room in his Lambeth house on the edge of the Thames. Father, Wintour, and Percy looked upon my congratulations with different expressions. Father's the same as always—masked. Wintour's round face provided a smile but with a logical contemplation.

Percy cracked his knuckles and didn't even seem to notice what a stroke of success my discovering the date was. "July is too soon for us to do anything." He fingered his Red mask. "And the mounted guards are not privy to the meetings. We'll have to wait for the official report to know what was said." His dark eyes lifted to mine. "Thomas will likely have to unearth the date of the next meeting as well. It could be as soon as a month or as distant as a year."

"He can do it." Catesby beamed. "I've no doubt. For now, let's get Guido and Thomas settled in the Whynniard house. Is everything in order?"

"They can move in upon the morrow."

It would be nice to leave the tiny rat hole of a room at the Bear. Though the Whynniard house wasn't much bigger, it just so happened to be connected to the House of Lords—our target.

Catesby, Percy, and Wintour shuffled through some papers on the table by the fire. I remained basking in my praise, for I knew that once the feeling faded it would take another several weeks of eavesdropping and conflicted thoughts of Emma before I received another extolment.

As I stepped toward the table, Father moved to my side. Beneath his mask, barely hovering above a whisper, I caught the words, "Well done, Thomas."

---

7 July 1604

"He likened himself to a *god.*" Percy threw a torn piece of paper onto the table—the Parliament report. Likely ripped from the market post boards. The new Whynniard house had barely enough room for Father and me, let alone Percy and his rage. One room, two cots, and a small stair down to the cellar that smelled of earth and roots and Thames water.

The Whynniard house sat so near the Thames, I didn't doubt the cellar had flooded with the putrid liquid more than once. What remained within the earthen walls once the water receded was most likely the feces of all London—rich or poor, it all smelled the same.

"A god, sir?" Father's tone remained low. Angry.

When Percy grew incensed, his tone spiked. But when Father grew incensed, his voice dropped until it rumbled the bones of the earth.

The use of Percy's title, *sir,* was our code to warn that others were about. Not only did the Scots—faithful followers of King

James—currently reside a few walls down, but scattered market stalls lined the street beyond our door. The area of Westminster was a mishmash of homes, politics, hawking, and business. No spoken word was guaranteed privacy.

Eavesdropping and gossip were free, and shoppers scooped up all they could to fill the shelves of their minds when they didn't have food to fill the shelves of their cupboards.

I picked up the report, written so common Londoners would know about King James's comments. But it sounded as though Percy had memorized it.

"He said kings resemble God's divine power on earth. He called his own Parliament members fools and they *still* bow to him! Those wretched Igniters!" Percy hurled his wide-brimmed hat across the room. It knocked over a candlestick.

Surely this absurd Parliament meeting would reveal to King James's members—to the Baron Monteagle—that he was a wild and paranoid man. Could they not see? Calling himself a god? Perhaps his Parliament would start questioning his reign.

This could work in our favor.

"This is no different from the meeting a few months back when he referred to Keepers as *outlaws*," Father said.

Percy paced, his sword swinging with every turn. "If the Igniters believe his foolish words, they will hunt Keepers with more vigilance. They will be relentless! Is there any hope for us?" He turned his wild eyes upon Father and me.

I stepped back; Father stepped forward. "Let it fuel your passion for our cause."

"I have to *serve* this man, Johnson." Even in his anger Percy remembered to keep up with Father's pseudonym. But he didn't seem to remember we were inside because he spat on the wood floor. I'd be the one cleaning that up later. "I have to *protect* him until our plans come to fruition. After he promised me—to my *face*—lenience for Keepers and then broke his word upon receiving the crown. On this day . . . it is too much for me."

A loud laugh and scrape of boots from the other side of the wall silenced us all. The northern-stenched Scottish commissioners.

Percy's chest still heaved and with each breath he seemed to boil nearer and nearer to an eruption. Even his shirt clung to his skin, wetted by his sweat. I retrieved his hat from the floor and thrust it into his hands. "You'd best get back to Gray's Inn, sir." Before he released his fury on the Scots and condemned us all.

He needed to sleep this off.

Percy never looked at me. He was somewhere else. But as he swept from the house, I spied his left hand slipping his Red mask from his belt.

I did not envy the men at the taverns who were unlucky enough to bet against him tonight. "Ought one of us to accompany him?" I asked Father with reluctance. "Drink might loosen his lips and he could reveal us."

"He won't return intoxicated. Percy is not one to drown his anger in ale." The way Father said the words hinted toward something more sinister than a night of grog and gambling.

"You don't think he'd . . . hurt anyone, do you?"

Father faced our single window and barely seemed to breathe, let alone move. Then, in a careful voice, "His past is not without its bloodstains."

I joined him at the window. The grime rested too thickly for us to see out into the night. Another thing for me to clean upon the morrow. "Should we do something?"

"Our fists are no match for a rabid mutt's teeth. We must leave a man's actions to his own conscience."

So we waited.

Father stood at the window as unmoving as one of the steeples above London's bells. I watched him, barely able to see the rise and fall of his breaths. He always stayed so calm, yet I knew a fire burned in his chest.

I slipped off my boots and prepared for bed when he spoke. "I was fifteen when I decided to be a Keeper." My hand stilled halfway to the bedcovers.

"Not far off of your age."

I was half a year to seventeen. The age gap seemed wider to me, but I suppose looking at it from his thirties changed Father's perspective. "I had a friend at St. Peter's—Robert Middleton. We talked often about the Igniter and Keeper war—both raised among Igniters, but unsure whether we wanted to be one or not. The White Light had spoken to both of us by this time, but neither of us responded. Not yet.

"Then the authorities discovered that Robert's aunt—Margaret—had converted her home into a secret refuge for Keepers. They took her to prison. And then, a few days later, they stoned her to death."

Not even hung, but stoned. A brutal, prolonged death at the hands of countless other people. And a woman at that. I'd never heard of a woman dying for the Keeper way.

"Margaret was killed for protecting people. That was her only crime. I saw Margaret die—with stone after stone against her small skull—and I craved her level of courage, of loyalty. So that day I became a Keeper. And I have silenced the White Light since that moment."

I tried to imagine witnessing the death of a woman like that—the aunt of a friend. I couldn't. I'd had no friends that dear to me at St. Peter's. "What happened to Robert?"

"He was caught and hung four years ago." So matter of fact.

"Why are you telling me this now?"

"Because you don't know who you are." He turned from the window, and though I couldn't see his expression, I could feel it.

Sad and strained and . . . disappointed. "These moments—these deaths—shaped my decision to become a Keeper. They stick in my mind like honey to a comb. I cannot shake them loose and they *define* me. You have none of that yet."

His response sounded like an accusation—as though I should feel guilt for not having witnessed the brutal deaths of friends. "I *am* a Keeper, Father." But the words tasted bitter as the memory of White Light's rescue from the prison cart reentered my head. "This plot is my conviction, and with each day I grow more loyal . . . in my head at least. My heart is catching up." I thought of the Keepers hung in the square. Just because I didn't show my conviction the same way Father did, didn't mean I was without conviction at all.

"I believe you, Thomas. It will come." He returned to the window, silent and still once again.

I woke to a shout. I rubbed my good eye. Blink. Rub. Blink again. Grey light. It was not yet dawn. Father no longer stood as the window sentinel. The shout had come from outside, toward the Cotton Garden at the back of the house. Too early for market or even wharfmen. It could've been a drunk, but something told me otherwise.

Across the room and past the cellar I strode, keeping myself from a run.

I burst through the door and out onto the green lawn that sloped down to the banks of the Thames in time to see Father throw a very muddy and bloody Percy into the putrid waters.

I stumbled to his side as Percy emerged with a gasp. "Fawkes, you—"

"Scrub yourself clean, Percy." Father squatted by the bank. "Before you oust us all. You've been a fool this night."

I drew up short, the dark morning barely illuminating the men. Blood caked the side of Percy's face and around his eyes . . . as though it had splashed him with his mask on.

Then I saw the mask on the bank. Covered in red splatters and strings. Most terrifying of all was the smeared shining White blood that flowed only in the veins of Igniters.

Father threw the mask to Percy. "Clean this too. Then get yourself to your duties. I'll not be back to check if your careless hide drowned. Hurry up. The shipmen will be waking. Even they won't miss the king's guard bathing in the Thames."

Percy glared at Father, gripping the raised bank with one hand and his mask with the other. The current pushed against him, but he maintained his spot. As Father stomped back up to the house, I joined him. "Is he not injured? The blood . . ."

"He's well enough."

I wanted Percy to be hurt. I wanted the blood on his face and clothes to be his. Because if not his, I dreaded knowing whom it came from. Unless . . . unless he killed the king. I drew up short, a few strides from the house.

Was King James dead?

No noise on the streets, no bells ringing. Surely there'd be chaos if the king were dead.

"Thomas, come inside."

I did as Father asked, not wanting to be seen in the same vicinity as Percy. "Should we leave here?" What if men came for Percy and he exposed us?

"Nay. Leaving would heighten suspicion. We continue with our duties as normal."

So I set to scrubbing the floor of the Whynniard house and then polishing the window.

A quarter bell later, Percy walked past me with nary a word, wearing his underclothes and carrying his mask—now washed clean. He dropped the clothes on the doorstep and disappeared up the road. While Father sent them for laundering, I set to polishing Percy's boots.

My hand swept across the leather, almost frantic. Waiting for church bells or king's men or news. Finally, as the sun rose, the market awoke with life and chatter far louder than the morning birds and bells.

I ventured among the booths, glancing at the loaves of bread but shopping for gossip. The timber-covered market stalls left no room for breath. Traders hoarded the oxygen, casting their carefully threaded words like bait to the merchants' wives.

"Good morn." I nodded to a woman weaving sticks for a basket.

"Good? Ye 'aven't 'eard, then?" The weaver's swollen ruddy face pinched together like the butt of an orange.

I ceased my browsing and swallowed hard. "Heard?" The king was dead. The plot was finished. I would get my mask.

"O' the six massacred Igniters."

I stiffened. "No."

"Their blood tore right out o' their bodies. Musta been a strong Red."

Percy.

"When? Who?" Had Percy gone after Parliament members?

"Just some wealthy folk up in Hoxton."

My coin purse slipped from my fingers and fell to the earth like the thud of a dead body after the gallows. "Hoxton?"

"Aye. I don' envy the servants up tha' way, havin' to deal with the family politics." She gave a nod, her fingers continuing with the sticks uninterrupted.

I turned from her stall, pulse pounding in my throat. Hoxton. Hoxton was large. Those six Igniters could have been anyone. Yet I couldn't stop the thundering panic.

Anyone.
Anyone.
Anyone.
One could have been Emma.

Sixteen

I pounded on the door of the Monteagle house.

Ward opened it and frowned. "It is not your day of employment." He didn't seem troubled or grief-stricken.

"I'm here to speak to Mistress Areben," I panted.

He eyed me and I knew full well the impropriety of calling on Emma at the front door outside of my employment. It sent all the wrong messages.

Ward eased the door closed. "She's occupied. You may leave your message with me."

I planted a hand on the wood to keep the door open. "So she is . . . well?"

"She was well upon rising this morning." He stepped closer. "Why? Did something happen? Was she attacked again?"

I shook my head. "I heard . . ." I *saw* a man who burst the blood out of six Igniters' bodies.

"Ward, who is calling?" Henry appeared like a gnat sensing blood. By the calm saunter I knew everyone was safe. If Emma had

134

been harmed or killed, Henry would not be at the door, looking me up and down and greeting me with, "Cyclops."

"He is asking for Mistress Areben," Ward said before leaving. The way he said it made me seem shady.

Henry's smirk darkened. "What do you want with her? It's not your day to escort her."

I was a fool. Of course Emma was fine. Percy wouldn't attack the Monteagle residence—even in a fit of rage—when I was serving them for the plot. "I had heard of an attack on Igniters in Hoxton. And I wanted to inquire after the Monteagle residents' safety." My tone came out cordial. But both he and I knew the undertones carried the utmost dislike.

"How . . . kind of you." He stepped onto the entryway and closed the door behind him. "We are all well. But now that you're here . . . You've yet to give a report of your outings with Mistress Areben."

I backed up a step to put more distance between us and ended up standing one step lower than him. This made me feel inferior— that was probably his intent. "I was unaware of my need to report."

His eyes slitted. "Now you're aware. What has she been doing?"

I allowed an eye roll to come through. "Shopping. Isn't that what women do?" I loathed the way that small statement made me feel on a similar level as Henry.

Henry didn't laugh. "What else?"

I tried to look surprised, but facial expressions weren't my strong suit since my face was part statue. "Walking. From market to market to market. She usually starts at the haberdashers on London Bridge to see what new hats have been laid out. Then along Silver Street to the wigmakers.

"By that point it's noon, so she sits in a garden or by the riverside. Once the Royal Exchange bell tower rings, she heads there." If I allowed myself to keep talking, I'd be hard-pressed to keep from lying.

Henry didn't stop eyeing me the entire time, as though examining every word for half-truths. My face felt painted with them.

"I secured your employment, Cyclops. You work for *me*. Your payment comes from *me*. So if you want to keep this role, you'll have sharp eyes and a thorough report after your excursions with Mistress Areben." His sneer could curdle cream.

"Is there something specific you would like me to watch for?"

After another pause, his scrutiny finally dissipated. "Let me know if she does anything other than shopping."

"Well, she takes walks and sits in the park—"

"Something noteworthy, Cyclops. Like talking to a master or securing an apprenticeship or mailing letters." He checked the ties on his doublet, as though collecting himself, as though adjusting his gentlemanly façade.

I turned to go.

"How is your father?"

I paused in my exit. What did he care of Father? Dangerous waters lapped at my ankles. I shouldn't reply, but to ignore the deceptively polite inquiry would scream of suspicion. "To my knowledge, he is well."

I hoped that made it seem as though I didn't see him often. In truth, I didn't. I worked in daylight; he worked at night. We shared only a few suppers a week.

"Are you not residing with him?"

"Aye, but we are both about our own business." I took a few small steps—signaling my departure, but Henry couldn't take a hint. Or he chose not to.

"I would like to meet him."

And I would like to spit on Henry's boots, but we couldn't always have what we wanted. "Perhaps someday you will." When Father stood at the side of the new Keeper monarch and doled out sentences to the Igniters of London. "Good day, Henry."

I strode away.

"Thomas!" Henry actually jogged after me. What in Thames' name? I closed my eye and took a breath before turning. Henry held out a fist. "Your month's payment."

Oh.

I reached out my hand and the coins clinked into my palm. More than last month's payment. I didn't look at them or count them in front of him. But it was too much.

Henry dropped his hand back at his side and looked up from my handful of coins. He knew it was more than I'd earned. Why? Certainly not as a gesture of goodwill. Did he want me to count them? Was he testing my honesty?

"Within the month, I will be overseeing the Baron's home on the Strand. I would be honored if you extended a supper invitation to your father." A bribe, then. He cleared his throat. "You would be welcome as well. Good day, Thomas."

This time he turned his back on me . . . and left me with a palmful of coins and questions.

The door shut and I forced myself to turn onto the main road before releasing the barrage of thoughts. I stuffed the coins into my pocket. He wanted a meeting with Father.

And it certainly wouldn't be for mere supper talk.

Henry wanted something. This was bigger than me—beyond the schoolboy feud. Did Henry know of the plot? Did he suspect me of ulterior motives with my employment?

He had always doubted my heritage, always taunted me about not truly being the son of Guy Fawkes. Even *I* had questioned my bloodline at times. After all, I'd never seen Father in person beyond my infancy. But it seemed that now that I was reunited with Father and actually *living* with him . . . Henry wanted in.

Was that why he'd hired me?

My pace grew faster until the jolt of each stomp rattled my teeth. I didn't slow. I had been a fool to run all the way to Hoxton for Emma—an Igniter and enemy. *Why* did I fear for her so?

Yes, I was her escort and we were quickly becoming more than acquaintances. But my passions resided elsewhere—with the plot. With my mask. With Keepers.

So why did I come for her? Why did I allow emotion to control me? Emotions were deceptive. They made men do foolish things like save runaway African boys from the gallows. Like bolt from Westminster to Hoxton on a whim.

Emma was my employer's ward. Nothing more.

But you have to admit she's cute.

I stopped so abruptly that I toppled sideways into a young woman shucking corn into a wooden bucket. "Watch it, slob!" She shoved me away.

"Apologies," I breathed.

White. That blasted color in my head. I thought it had left me for good. I thought I'd silenced it.

Nope. I've just been polite. If I wanted, I could hum nonsense in your ear for the rest of your life.

It could hear my thoughts, even when I wasn't directing them toward it. It was after me.

Could this day get any worse?

"Thomas!"

My head jerked up to meet her Brown-masked face. Blast it all. "Emma."

"Ward said you sought me."

"It was a mistake." I hurried on, but she caught my arm. I wrenched away, jumpy. "You should be home, Emma!"

She startled backward.

"People *died* in Hoxton last night. Igniters. Don't wander out alone right now." I pointed toward her road. "Go back."

I realized then that she held a parcel in one of her gloved hands. "I didn't know." She held out the parcel and her next request came out cool. "Are you heading to town?"

In no mood to apologize or be remotely gentlemanly, I snapped, "Where else would I be heading?"

"Well, aren't you pleasant today?" She thrust the parcel at me. "Please deliver that to the draper at the Royal Exchange."

I glowered and took the package. I deserved to be treated as a servant. I *wanted* that, right? So I bowed. "Of course, madam." The parcel was light and I suspected a painting rested inside. My foul mood evaporated. She didn't deserve my irritation. "Still no apprenticeship?"

A woman directed a gaggle of brown geese past us, up the lane. Emma took the olive branch. "None yet."

I probably should have been grateful. Once Emma secured an apprenticeship, my escort would no longer be needed. I still had information to gather from the Baron. "Why do you even need one? You are beyond most masked already. What can they teach you that you don't already know?"

"There is much I don't know, Thomas. But most of all, an apprenticeship will allow me to make my own life path. I need to be able to provide for myself." There was something she wasn't saying. I wanted to know more—to pry, to talk, to connect.

But then I remembered the events of that morning. Percy's bloodied state, his rage, the recent Parliament events. If I remained conversing with Emma, she could become involved. Endangered. And more conversation would lead to deeper friendship. No matter how much I appreciated the fact she saw beyond my plague, it wasn't enough for me to risk my life and the life of the other plotters. Or even to risk *her* life.

After the next Parliament meeting, everything would change.

King James would be dead, a Keeper would be on the throne, Parliament would be disbanded, and I would be a traitor to the crown if caught. All of London would change. No . . . all of *England*.

In that moment I realized Emma's life would change too. I could not attach myself to her beyond the professional relationship between servant and employer. But I *could* secretly hope she'd abandon the White Light nonsense and return to the Keepers.

Until then, we couldn't be friends. No matter her kindness or our kinship.

We couldn't be friends because I was going to help murder her king.

Black

1 August 1604

Norwood,

Things grow tempestuous between Keepers and Igniters here in London. How are things in York?

I've been spending more time with Emma.

T

---

30 August 1604

Norwood,

I'm sure you've heard, but Spain signed King James's peace treaty. The king held an enormous feast. The Igniters of London are celebrating—I was with an Igniter family when they found out. The Keepers are greatly despairing. A lot of us hoped Spain would invade London for the Keeper cause. Now we know what side Spain is on.

There is much I wish to talk with you about. I anxiously await your response.

T

---

10 September 1604

Norwood,

I only just heard of the execution of the Keepers in York this past July. Their names were not made public. Please tell me who they were.

Please respond to this letter, even if it be a mere sentence.

T

30 September 1604

Thomas,

St. Peter's no longer employs me. I am coming to London. And I think I would like to be part of this new undertaking of yours.

Norwood

Seventeen

19 October 1604

Today my money pouch emptied and my scabbard filled.

The smithy handed me my new sword—a rapier. As rapiers went, it was the runt of the litter—a simple handle with barely any guard, matte grey blade, and seeming to dull the longer I looked at it. But it was mine.

And even the most unimpressive sword can leave an impressive wound when in the hands of a practiced master.

I adjusted my belt. Already my right hand itched to draw the blade and wield it in a good spar. But chances were I'd be using it for more than sparring in the near future. The next meeting of Parliament was four months away—February. That was when all our fates would change.

Percy was the plotter who gathered that information. The longer he worked as one of the king's guards, the more information they served him. The deeper he got.

With a weapon at my side, I headed to Lambeth. A meeting awaited at Catesby's home.

Tonight I would meet the other plotters. And tonight I would talk to Catesby about Norwood. Norwood was to arrive at the Bear within the next couple of days. I'd made arrangements with the alewife so that Norwood had a room waiting. What would he see when he saw me again? Would he notice the change that I felt inside—the growth of confidence and purpose and identity?

I crossed London Bridge and then headed south along the Thames. It would have saved me an hour of walking had I simply rowed across the river, but best not to make my connection to Catesby too easy to spot.

His house rested on the river—a small boat mooring accessible from his door. I used the side entrance like a proper servant, tempted to leave my cloak on against the lingering chill, but I hung it up by the door.

I made my way through the hall toward the sitting room and the voices hit me. They weren't typical conversation voices. They had the subtle tones of formality, of serious discussion, of planning.

They had started the meeting without me.

I hovered by the door, just out of view, and listened in. Like a proper spy. That was why Catesby inducted me, wasn't it?

"Ever since Spain signed the peace treaty, King James has considered himself all-powerful." That voice belonged to Percy. "This very month he proclaimed himself king of Great Britain."

"Great Britain?" That thin, high voice was new to me.

"It's what he wants to call us—by combining Scotland and England. As though we are not separate. As though we would mix blood and pride and identity with those northern pigs."

Father spoke next. "I suspected the treaty was coming. When Wintour and I spoke with King Philip in April, he hardly considered our plea for him to invade England. King James is too powerful, which is the entire reason we are meeting tonight.

Instead of lamenting our disappointments, let's pour that passion into action."

"Hear, hear!"

Percy must not have heard Father's call to action, because he persisted in a low grumble, "First James commands all Keepers to either become Igniters or leave England, then he tries to outlaw our beliefs, and then the treaty. Will no one fight for us?"

"We will fight for ourselves." I finally looked to see Catesby with a fist against his opposite palm. "We can't change King James's mind—his own wife is a Keeper and even she can't sway him. All we can do is form the minds of his children. His sons must die. But Princess Elizabeth is a mere eight years—young enough to put on the throne and mold. She will be raised and advised by Keepers."

Saving Keepers and freeing England truly was up to us.

At last I strode into the room. They looked up, stunned. As though they had forgotten about me. I realized that I walked right into Catesby's house and up to the door to eavesdrop. Anyone could have done that. Anyone could have heard this conversation and caught us. I made a mental note to keep my good eye on the door during all meetings.

Someone had to.

"What do we do next?" I asked.

Catesby straightened to his full and impressive height. It made me feel like I'd encouraged him or emboldened him. I straightened too. He waved toward the fireplace. "This is Robert Keyes."

I took in the room. Catesby stood in the middle. Father and Wintour sat at a table. Percy paced by the curtained window and three new men stood by the fireplace.

The tallest of the three—Robert Keyes—stood like a portrait under scrutiny. Tall like Catesby with a giant red beard. He seemed to be the oldest of everyone and looked so jolly and cordial that I couldn't imagine him lighting a fuse to murder a country's leaders.

I liked him already.

The other two strangers could be twins in face but were opposite in body. Jack and Kit, I presumed. One stood with folded arms, wearing layer after layer of bulging muscle. A single fist to the face from him would put any man in an early grave. The other stood shoulder-to-shoulder with hardly any muscle at all. Both men had eyes only for Percy—narrowed, angry gazes.

Percy ignored them.

That wasn't good—we couldn't have unrest among our group.

I was about to introduce myself to the brothers, but Father did the honors. "Thomas, this is Jack Wright"—he gestured to the muscular beast—"the most skilled swordsman you'll ever encounter." Father then clapped the thin man on the shoulder. "And this is Kit Wright, also formidable in swordplay, but even stronger in color power."

"They are Percy's brothers-in-law," Catesby said.

At Percy's name, the brothers' narrowed eyes sent such daggers at Percy that I could almost see the footplay of the nonverbal duel taking place.

I ignored the hostility and grinned at the talk of swordplay. "Truly? Swordsmanship is one of my passions too." My hands itched to draw my new weapon and face off with Jack then and there. I wanted to grow. I wanted to earn an introduction beyond my name. Guy Fawkes, Europe's fiercest soldier. Jack Wright, the most skilled swordsman. Tom Wintour, talented linguist and lawyer.

What would mine be? Thomas Fawkes, defeater of the plague? Thomas Fawkes, the boy who saved England?

Or Thomas Fawkes, the plotter who died maskless . . .

"I knew you'd be a swordsman from the moment I saw you as an infant." Jack pushed off the wall and extended a hand. "Didn't I say that, Guy? You remember, yes?"

Father laughed. "I remember."

"You . . . knew me as an infant?" I tried to keep my jaw from hanging.

"Jack, Kit, and I went to school together," Father said. "You were wooed to sleep by the sounds of our sparring."

I liked that picture and shook Jack's hand with gusto. Kit offered his hand as well, though his grip was brief.

Father lifted his head to Catesby. I could tell he wanted to talk more about the Wright brothers—he seemed to have a friendship with them the way I did with Norwood.

My spirits lifted even higher at the thought of Norwood. After tonight's meeting, I would approach Catesby with my request to add Norwood to the plot. I had my reasoning listed out:

Norwood was a powerful Green and healer.

He had remained a loyal Keeper even through St. Peter's crossover from Keeper school to Igniter.

He kept secrets. Catesby already knew this tidbit—that Norwood had saved me and protected me from the eye of suspicious Igniters.

"Keyes has contacts for gunpowder," Catesby said. "With the recent peace treaty, retired soldiers are willing to do anything to get rid of their gunpowder stores."

I focused on the red-bearded man, waiting to hear if his voice matched his ruddy and jolly appearance. "My cousin's husband, Ambrose Rookwood, is a wealthy young Keeper up in Suffolk." Keyes's voice did indeed match his apple-cheeked grin. A man who grinned while talking about gunpowder fit our group perfectly. "He has money, gunpowder, and horses to spare."

"But we cannot tell this Rookwood about the plot." Percy stopped his pacing. "None of us knows this man. Keeper or not, he may not be willing to join such treason."

Keyes nodded like he expected this. "I have told him the

gunpowder is for the use of the English regiment in the Spanish service in Flanders. The peace treaty has opened this window for us."

Percy snorted. "Are you telling me to be thankful for that blasted piece of signed paper?"

"Of course not." Keyes's perpetual smile made every sentence out of his mouth seem covered in honey, but I could see the strength and fire behind his eyes. "But it has opened a window for us. And in a plot such as this, every window should be treated like a bugle in a battle charge."

Wintour stood from the table, like a lawyer with a prepared statement. Even standing, he looked dwarfed in a room of such tall men. "Where will we store this gunpowder if Rookwood agrees?"

Catesby opened his arms wide. "Here. Until we can move it to the Whynniard house. Because my house rests on the Thames, the unloading of barrels will not be suspicious—it is expected along the water."

Wintour cocked an eyebrow. "Will not your servant . . . What was his name?"

"Bates will not be a problem. He is loyal and does not ask questions. And I have spoken with him."

All the men went silent. We knew what "I have spoken with him" meant, for we'd all gone through the same conversation—though I did wonder if the other men had to cross swords with Catesby as I had.

So our group was up to nine: Catesby, Father, Percy, Wintour, Jack, Kit, Bates, Keyes, and me.

Catesby had the power to break each and every one of us, yet our faith remained strong with him because of his loyalty to keep our secrets. Even though I was frustrated that *he* knew Father's secrets and I didn't, I respected Catesby all the more for not revealing them.

"We need those stinking Scots to leave!" Percy burst out.

"They will eventually," Catesby said, remaining calm.

Jack didn't look appeased. "Is this a safe place, Catesby? What about the meeting room in the sewers?"

"Too wet," Father said.

A mere breath of silence followed his statement before a creak of wood tickled my ear from the hallway.

My eye darted to the door, then back to the men. They continued to talk. No one else had heard it. "Hush," I said harshly.

They immediately quieted. The crackles of the fire seemed like pistol shots in the silence. Tension tugged on my gut like the withdrawing of a dagger. I wanted to be wrong. I wanted to question what I heard. But where my left eye lacked, my left ear excelled. I rarely heard wrong.

Another creak.

Quick as lightning but silent as mist, Jack, Father, and I all drew our swords and leaped into the hallway. Empty.

Father swept down the hallway leaving behind no sound greater than the brush of cloth against skin. But Catesby strode down the hallway after him, all confident footfall and fearlessness. "I'm sure it's Bates."

As he passed me, I spotted a drop of sweat on his temple.

We heard more talking from deeper in the house. None of it sounded distressed. Jack led the way back into the sitting room, sheathing his sword. "Fool of a servant, startling us like that."

"He might have been eavesdropping." Percy's lips curled in a sneer.

"Catesby trusts him," Jack snapped, returning his hand to his sword hilt. Even though his brother, Kit, said nothing, his hand drifted to his own sword hilt too.

What was between these three? Catesby said they were related.

Perhaps that was just it.

I looked at Father, trying to read him since he hid all facial expressions. He stood tall and rigid, like a soldier on the front.

Catesby returned, breathing hard. His smile curved like an overstretched piece of string. Tight. Forced. "It was Bates." He rubbed a hand over his forehead. "He should have known to announce his presence."

Percy's face grew as red as a holly berry. "Announce his presence? We could have run him through!"

"There's no *we*," Kit muttered in Jack's ear. "Percy didn't even detect an intruder—the boy did."

"Is he going to join the meeting?" Percy asked loudly.

"No." Catesby shut the door. "He does not need all the details. He has been with me since before the Essex plot. He is a faithful Keeper and obeys without question."

Percy breathed deep like a stallion after a run. The rest of us stayed stiff.

Catesby let out a long, slow breath. "If we let fear or doubt hinder us, this scheme is over before we've started."

That was enough for me. I wanted to expel the nerves choking me. I wanted to be free, and if it took placing trust in Catesby to free myself, I would do so.

"Shall we continue?" Wintour lowered himself back in a chair. Maybe it was because he was a lawyer and thus one of the smartest in our company, but his choice to sit sucked the tension from the room.

"Keyes will secure us gunpowder," Catesby continued, as though we'd never stopped, "and once the Scots have left the Whynniard house, we can start tunneling."

"A tunnel?" I looked between the men.

"Aye, from the basement of the Whynniard house to a cavity under Parliament. We will store the gunpowder in the tunnel. We will light the gunpowder during the next Parliament meeting. God rest their souls." Catesby's face lit with a passion that stirred a fire in my own bosom.

The plan was set.

Something about digging our way beneath Parliament—beneath the very seat of King James's Igniter meeting—caused my fingers to curl around the handle of an imaginary shovel. It made me feel powerful. We were outsmarting the king.

We were taking back England.

"I will keep you informed regarding the gunpowder." Catesby turned to Percy. "Let us know when the Scots leave." Percy nodded, but his glower remained. I was thankful he was living at Gray's Inn instead of with Father and me at the Whynniard house. I didn't know if I could endure more Percy-raging or watch him leave to murder more Igniters with his Red mask.

"Any reports from the Monteagle house, Thomas?"

I startled at the sudden attention of seven men. *Don't stutter. Speak like a man.* "The Baron's son, Henry, will be moving from his Hoxton lodging to a house on the Strand. I presume the Baron will follow shortly." With Emma. "Henry has expressed interest in meeting with my father."

Jack's eyebrows popped up. "Indeed? What does the Baron's son want with a loyal Keeper soldier?" He turned to Catesby. "Could the son be a Keeper?"

I had never thought that. Henry had never shown loyalty to either side, though he *did* use multiple colors with his mask. "I am quite certain he's an Igniter, but I don't know what he wants with Father." Father said nothing to any of this.

"Henry Parker has always been drawn to the powerful masks, whether Keeper or Igniter," Catesby said. "I expect he wants to meet the famous soldier to feel important."

I stared at Catesby. He said this so nonchalantly. "Do you . . . do you know the Baron Monteagle and his family?" Did he know Emma?

"I have had conversations with their servant, Ward, in the past. Keep me updated, Thomas," Catesby said. "If Henry's inquiries increase, you might have to terminate employment. We have the new Parliament date, so there's not much more crucial information we need from the Baron. If you overhear anything of importance, you can go to Wintour. He's lodging at the Duck and Drake down the street from the Monteagle home on the Strand."

Wintour gave a wink. I liked the idea of reporting to him over food at the inn. I liked Wintour and his sharp mind.

"There will be much action in the streets tonight due to James declaring himself King of Great Britain." Father stood. "Igniters, Keepers, and Scots alike will, with their ale-addled minds, endanger many." He nodded to me. "Thomas and I will monitor tonight."

Me? I straightened. It was because of my new rapier. I'd finally be joining Father on his night excursions. It was time to show my worth . . . and my skill.

"Take caution, Guido," Catesby said. "If you are caught or attacked, we do not have the resources to free you."

"If I am caught, it will be for the cause."

He wouldn't be caught. I wouldn't let that happen. With his mask and my sword, we could subdue even the shadows.

⌐≍⌐

I stopped Catesby at the end of the meeting as the men departed at alternate times and in different directions. "Catesby, may I speak with you?"

He stopped prodding the fire and faced me. "Of course, Thomas."

Was there a tactful way to say this? "My friend from St. Peter's is coming to London. Benedict Norwood."

"Ah, the Keeper man who helped you with your plague?"

I released a breath. "Aye. He lost his employment at St. Peter's. He has expressed interest in joining the plot."

Catesby's countenance darkened in a way I'd not witnessed before. It sent ice into my chest and I immediately thought back through what part of my words might have caused this reaction.

I saw it.

"I haven't told him of the plot." Blast. This was about to get messy. "I've been writing to him and said only that I was part of something that would help England. It was because he *knows* me and my mind that he pieced together it might be something Keeper-related. It is that mindset in him that makes me think he'd be a help to us."

Catesby's darkness lessened but did not abate.

I wanted to leave the situation then and there, but I plunged on. "We could do with a Green, and he's kept the secrets of all who have ever spoken with him—particularly mine." I raised my chin. "I trust him with my life, like I trust you. I am not asking for your agreement, only for your consideration of this matter."

"I will consider it, Thomas. Let me know when he arrives in London and you and I will speak further." He returned the metal fire prod to a hook on the wall. "This plot is tenuous. We must bring on only those men who are *necessary* to its fulfillment."

"I understand." His caution was expected and I appreciated that he was even willing to discuss Norwood further. But most of all, I caught what was unspoken. He said that he must bring on only those men who were necessary to the plot's fulfillment. The men who were irreplaceable.

That spoke volumes about each man he'd chosen.

Because he'd chosen me.

Eighteen

The rapier at my side thirsted for Igniter blood.

Keepers would be captured. Keepers might even be killed. This was what Father did every night.

He saved lives.

He freed them.

And even though he did not spare the time to be the father to me that I desired, I respected him with all the loyalty of a son.

"Make certain your belt is good and tight." He checked it and tested the sharpness of my blade. Was he worried for me?

I had no space in my mind for worry. I was just anxious to finally do something at which I knew I excelled. I was going out as a warrior on a night when the Igniters were doing what they did best—hunting and imprisoning Keepers.

People like me. Like my father. Like Norwood.

If Igniters just took the time to interact with Keepers, instead of attacking without thought, they'd realize we were humans too. With passions like them. Fighting for our beliefs and our rights.

After tonight, Norwood would arrive in London and I'd tell

him of my escapade. Of my chance to fight for Keepers' freedom—for *his* freedom.

"Ready?" Father stepped away from the house.

A lump grew in my throat and I steeled my will. If a situation called for me to kill a man, I must not hesitate. "Do . . . do you think I ought to have my mask for a night like this?"

"That takes training and we don't have the time. Besides, being maskless keeps you safe from capture."

I clamped down on my irritation. "How so?"

"Because masks show one color. Igniters are identified through their blood—or through observing them controlling multiple colors. When Igniters hunt a Keeper, they slice their arm open. Igniters have strings of White Light in their blood. For Keepers—and all other people—there is one color. Red. Plain. And, in the minds of Igniters . . . guilty. But the Igniters won't attack those without a mask—you pose no profit for them. You are viewed as neutral."

That couldn't be the lone reason he continued to deny me my mask. "I don't want to be neutral. I'm a Keeper. I want to stand for my beliefs like you."

"Then do so with what you have. For now, you have safe blood and belt. And we need you alive."

I swallowed hard and wiped my palms on my breeches. "I'm ready."

"Then let's go, soldier."

The lump in my throat only grew as we stepped out the servant's entrance and onto the damp streets. October rain was kind to no man. Small drops spit on my forehead, not quite rain, but more than mist. Father set out at a swift pace, keeping to the shadows the way a squirrel navigated the branches of a willow. If I looked away for one minute, I'd lose him and his Black mask to the night.

A quarter of an hour in and I could see why Catesby recruited my father, why the Spanish army promoted him, and why Wintour took him on an embassy to King Philip.

I mimicked his footsteps, but where he was silent, I was panting. Where he was invisible, my face caught the shine of moonlight. Where he was still, my sword clanked against stone.

He finally slowed and held up a fist to stop me. We were at the Tower of London. The cruelest and most renowned place of torture and imprisonment known in England. It rose upon its hill like an unslain dragon.

"They bring Keepers here at all hours of the bell," Father said in an undertone. "Igniters will turn in a Keeper for less than a shilling and the guards will hang them to make a profit. The Keepers never defend themselves. That is true courage."

My fist pressed against my side. "How could people do such a thing?"

"Igniters believe that for each Keeper that dies, one person is cured of the plague." Father's hand touched my wrist. I looked at him, but he pointed ever so slightly toward an alley. Shadows moved. I backed against the wall and gripped the hilt of my sword. Draw only if attacked, Father said. Fists were more efficient and left less blood.

The shadows formed into two people. Two men whom I had seen once before in an alley assaulting Emma. The shorter of the two had a scar along his cheek, vaguely resembling a boot heel.

Good girl, Emma.

They approached the Tower guards, who straightened at their posts. The taller man handed over a tangle of color masks. "Their Keeper owners will be delivered at first bell by cart."

"How many?" a guard asked.

"Six." Scar Face pointed to the bundle of masks. "Count 'em."

The guard lifted them to the light. They clacked against each other, so he sifted through them. Two Brown masks, three Blue— one of which seemed very feminine—and a Green.

A Green mask with a vine pattern I'd recognize anywhere. Norwood's.

I didn't realize a gasp had slipped through my lips until a guard shouted and Father yanked me down a lane. Through shadows and dark alleys. Under awnings and past sputtering window candles. We ran until I no longer knew what street squelched underfoot. My heart pounded and my head spun.

Norwood. That was Norwood's mask. He'd been caught. He was about to be imprisoned.

Father pressed me against the wall of an empty cooper shop. "Can you not follow the simplest instructions? We need *silence*." He ran a hand through his hair. "We should still be able to intercept the delivery."

I barely caught his words. "They have Norwood." I looked up at Father, who now stood silent. "Benedict Norwood. My friend. My instructor from St. Peter's." My voice rose. "They have him!"

He must have gotten caught coming into London. Blast it all! No! We should go to Catesby. We should get Jack and Kit Wright to come fight with us.

"All the more reason to rule our emotions and outbursts tonight. We need to find the cart of Keepers. Have you seen him maskless?"

"Aye."

"Then keep an eye out for his face. Let's go. It is already past midnight."

We should go after Scar Face and his friend. "Those men attacked Mistress Areben one night," I said mostly to myself. "And she was an *Igniter*."

"The Baron Monteagle's ward?" Father asked.

"Aye."

We passed a street filled with raucous laughter. I glimpsed men slumped against houses. One lifted his tankard. "Down with the Keepers!" Ale mixed with mud.

"God save King Philip!" replied another.

"Peace and freedom at last. Now if only the Scots would go back to their stinking highlands!"

I wanted to shove all their heads into the ale barrels until their lungs filled with the liquid. Hypocrites! They claimed to crave peace and freedom; meanwhile, they attacked Keepers and imprisoned us for no reason other than different beliefs. I loathed the lot of them.

Father stopped us by the bank of the Thames beneath the shadow of a wattle-and-daub house. Laundry fluttered overhead, mimicking the tempo of my erratic pulse. "When they come, you focus on getting the prison cart open. If there are fewer than three assailants, I can keep them busy."

"I'm good with a sword."

"Swords are no match for masks."

We waited for an hour. The cool air from the Thames chilled my body but did nothing to calm my mind. Norwood. They had Norwood. Father remained a statue, as though he had no concern or care for my friend.

"What if we've missed the cart?" I finally said.

"We haven't." He pointed. All I made out were shadows. Night. Darkness. My plagued left eye forced me to turn my head to get a full view. Then I caught it. Movement. Silhouettes. Whispers. A giant box on wheels crept by. I wanted to rush it. To burst it open and incapacitate the swine who dared trade people for coin.

Father bounced on his toes. My heart leapt to my throat. I bent my stiff knees to warm my muscles. Then we advanced. I heard not a single footfall from Father's progress. I willed my movements to be as obedient.

As we drew nearer, the jeers of the captors met my ears. It sounded like more than three. In fact, as we rounded a corner, it sounded more and more like a . . . crowd.

Why would there be a crowd at two in the morning? Even the revelers ought to have been stumbling to their mats by this time.

The cart came into view again and Father slowed to a halt. It headed to a wider street.

That boarded-up cart was identical to the one in which I'd traveled to London, with a small barred window on each side.

A mob, intoxicated by King Philip's peace treaty, followed, cheering as they did at the hanging. They threw old food and dirt clods at the cart.

"Good riddance, plague bringers!"

"May the drop be quick and the swing short!"

"Deceivers! Scum! Hiding the White Light from us!" A glob of mud slammed into the side of the wagon.

"There are too many." Father's voice sounded heavy. The wagon drew closer.

"No! You do this every week. Surely you can do *some*—"

"It has never been like this. We're too late."

"No!" My shout was lost to the noise of the crowd. I wanted to scream, *"You're Guy Fawkes!"* I couldn't attack them without him. Maybe I'd overestimated Father's color power. Maybe he wasn't the Black I thought he was.

The crowd and carriage exited the alley and headed toward the Tower. I couldn't give up. "I need to know if Norwood's in there." I bolted toward the wagon, not pausing at Father's call. "Thomas!"

My actions were rash, I knew. But I also knew I'd neither sleep nor rest for the remainder of my plagued life if I didn't at least try.

I pushed through the crowd, letting the anger show on my face, so as to appear as one of them. I even let out a few shouts to release my fury, though my words of "Swine!" and "Heartless vermin!" were meant for the bodies surrounding me.

My momentum carried me through the throng and I leaped onto the wooden step, gripping the metal bars with my fists. I shoved my face against the bars. "Norwood? Norwood! Benedict Norwood!" I prayed for no answer. That would mean he wasn't there.

But then a swollen and bruised face appeared inches from mine. "Thomas?"

"No!" My cry of despair wrenched my heart. I tugged at the cage lock. "No. You shouldn't be in here! How did they take you?"

As though the crowd realized that I was not part of them, hands tugged at my clothing. Nails scraped my skin. "Get off, boy!"

I gripped harder. "No. Norwood. What can I do?"

The hands yanked me off, leaving me with a last view of Norwood's wide eyes just before a lump of horse manure splattered his face. I kept my feet and fought the masses. People released me, but not before one man pulled my sword from its scabbard.

"You're one of them, aren't you?" he shrieked, eyes red and wild. "You should be in that cart!"

Despite the sword tip at my chest, I screamed, "You should be strung up for condemning innocent men!"

He lunged, but I sidestepped him easily and planted a boot in his rear, and he flopped face-first into the mud. I retrieved my rapier and lifted it to run the drunken Igniter through, but hands grabbed me. It felt like a hundred pairs. The mob had turned the moment they realized a Keeper ran free among them.

My sword was wrenched from my hand, my boots from my feet, and a blade pressed against my throat. But then a cloud of the deepest black swept over us with an earth-shaking gust of wind. We all toppled over one another.

Screams and clangs of metal filled the night. Then, "Thomas, get out of here!"

Not Norwood's voice.

Father's.

I stumbled to my feet and searched the ground for my sword, but the street beneath my boots writhed and roiled like a sea, tossing bodies this way and that. I could make no sense of it, let alone spot my weapon.

I obeyed and ran pell-mell along the road, trusting I would eventually exit the alley. A cry of pain from somewhere to my left. Then I slammed into a wall and tumbled to the ground. A gush of warm liquid covered my face and entered my mouth.

Blood.

Had someone struck me?

I lurched back to my feet and felt around. Wood. Wheels. Metal. The prison wagon.

I fumbled for the door. My fingers brushed the lock. I yanked on it, but my hands slipped free, slick with mud. I felt on the ground for a rock, a piece of debris, anything to break the door open.

Nothing.

I pounded the lock again with my fist. I rammed my shoulder into the wood. I begged every color I'd ever studied to open the blasted thing. But the colors wouldn't obey me. Not when I didn't have a mask. I even screamed at the White Light, more in hatred than for help.

The cries of the people and the surrounding mayhem left me disoriented and lost. Father—where was he? He'd caused the black cloud. He'd caused the tempestuous ground.

Could he open the lock?

"Fath—"

An explosion of light sent me reeling back. The torch crashed against the cart. I squinted my good eye. Flames filled my vision. Fire lapped at the exterior of the prison cart. Igniters with Yellow masks spread the fire in seconds and all of Father's color powers ceased.

The screams didn't.

This time they came from inside the wagon.

"No!" I rushed to the wagon, flames now scorching the walls. Smoke billowed into the air and the fleeing mob stopped as one. People eyed the flames and then swarmed the burning wagon.

Were they going to help me?

Relief, sharp and swift, allowed me a single breath before the cry, "To the Thames!" reached me. "Don't let the fire spread to the houses!"

The wagon moved under the force of twenty pairs of hands. Those wearing masks commanded the mud and the wood of the wagon to send the cart trundling toward the Thames.

I ran after it. "Norwood! Norwood!"

With flames eating his prison, Norwood kept his face pressed against the bars. The skin on his knuckles peeled back from the heat. I couldn't get through the throng to him. Not even when the cart careened into the river.

"Norwood!"

His gaze locked with mine. The cart bobbed once, then tipped and sank beneath the Thames like a weighted body.

Nineteen

I sat on the soggy bank of the Thames for hours, staring at the spot where Norwood drowned. I didn't have enough in me to spare a care for the others in the cart—the others who were Norwoods to people in their own lives. The innocents who had just been murdered over a *disagreement*.

Already they were forgotten.

No one mourned them—they mourned only the coin they lost by not delivering those men to the Tower.

Igniters did this. Igniters who claimed to fight for freedom, who proclaimed, "White Light for all."

They murdered.

"Igniters believe that for each Keeper that dies, one person is cured of the plague," Father had said.

If it were true, then Norwood's death would have had a purpose. As it was, though . . . He died in vain. And that sickened my heart most of all.

Emma was an Igniter. She was one of them. She might not condone the actions of her fellow Igniters, but she perpetuated the problem—spreading the use of White Light and blaming Keepers for the Stone Plague. How could I have allowed myself to consort with her? To *work* for her guardian?

At the hanging in the summer, she was desperate to save the African boy, but she said nothing when the three Keepers were hung.

Father joined me on the bank for the first hour, weak from his use of Black color power and not speaking. I was glad. No words could comfort and I didn't want to talk. This was between me and Norwood.

I hadn't been there for him, yet he'd been there for me every time I'd needed him. He'd been my true father.

Guy Fawkes was a pretender.

I pushed myself to my feet. I couldn't let Norwood's story end this way. It was no longer about curing myself of the plague or convincing Father I was worthy of a mask. I would make Norwood proud.

He represented Keepers everywhere. And I would not let them down.

November passed in a blur. Keyes had secured several barrels of gunpowder from his cousin, Rookwood, so I spent most of the time helping load it into Catesby's house.

The Monteagle household was away on holiday. Good riddance. Their absence freed me to focus fully on the plot and the stewing of my fury.

Father did not invite me on any more nightly excursions. Perhaps he thought me too weak. I no longer had a sword. I hadn't even gotten to show my skill. Every time he returned to the Whynniard house, it was with a number of Keepers saved.

"Four."

"One."

"Three."

That was the extent of our interaction. He knew things had changed. I think he believed I was finally a Keeper. Finally committed to the plot. And he was right.

Now it was personal.

On some days, I found myself sitting down to write a letter to Norwood before remembering he was gone. The hollow feeling grew and grew, as though bitterness had taken a pickax to my chest. Chipping out a cold cavern.

I had no one with whom to share life.

No one to trust.

And that freed me to be emotionless.

Emma Areben sought to invade my thoughts, but I shoved her out. What did I care if she secured an apprenticeship? She was an Igniter. She was an enemy. And for now, she was gone.

❖━━✦✦━━❖

December came with a dusting of snow, which made vigilante work particularly difficult for Father. Being a Black, he could control only items completely shrouded in darkness, and winter brought out the braziers and the street dwellers to the warmth as witnesses. So he spent most of his nights observing and scouting.

He didn't have long to wait.

A week in, I entered Catesby's house in Lambeth with sodden boots and my cloak tight around my shoulders. I stepped into a house filled with conspirators—Catesby, Percy, Wintour, the brothers Kit and Jack, Father, Keyes, and—Bates? I thought Catesby said his servant wouldn't take part in the meetings.

They surrounded a cask of ale.

Percy whirled to face me, his cheeks pink from drink. He lifted his glass. "Thomas! Come join!"

I walked in, hesitant, and hung up my cloak. Then I situated myself on the left side of the room so as to keep the wall in my blind spot and the plotters in my sight.

"The Scots are gone!" Percy's proclamation was accentuated by a cheer. Only Father did not drink, his mask still secured to his face.

"Gone?" A hard joy lit in me. "So we can finally . . ." My eyes cut to Bates. He was a thin, wiry fellow and stared mostly at the ale cask.

Catesby stepped forward. "Bates is one of us, Thomas. He's officially joined the plot, taken the oath, and he's a Green."

Meaning he took the place Norwood would have filled.

I couldn't help but compare Bates to Norwood. He didn't hold a candle to my friend. Bates looked spineless. Did Catesby consult with anyone or did he just act? I didn't like that our safety and our lives now relied on another person.

But at last we would tunnel from the Whynniard house to Parliament. With Parliament meeting two months from now, we needed to set the plan into action. "When do we start?"

Catesby slapped me on the back so heartily, it knocked the breath from me. "Tomorrow, lad. Though I daresay if we gave you a shovel, you'd start this very night."

My arms longed to pour my hatred of the Igniters into manual labor. Too much time was wasted on reveling. "I would, sir."

"Have some ale. Tomorrow we fetch timber to uphold the tunnel and Jack will secure the tools."

"Are we digging all by hand?" I scanned their belts for their masks.

"Wintour and Keyes are our Browns. They will help where they can, as their energy allows."

I nodded and accepted the cup of ale, though not yet in a reveling mood. I stood by Father while the others refilled their cups. In an undertone, I asked, "When did Bates officially join?"

"Tonight. I think Catesby determined he's heard too much and might as well be inducted."

So he *had* been eavesdropping. At least he hadn't turned us in. Yet. Bates could ruin us all if he was not faithful. "May Parliament come quickly."

"Aye."

To the group, I asked, "What else of the plan? Timber tomorrow, then what?"

Catesby laughed, but Percy held my stare with narrowed eyes. "We will dig in rotations. We need to find ways to dispose of the dirt."

"How about in the Thames?" I suggested. It was forty yards or so away—that was our best option.

"Too many ships." Wintour refilled his ale. "Too many opportunities to be spotted."

"Not if we put the dirt in ale barrels." Keyes slapped a hand onto the top of the ale cask in the room. "No one would question the transport of ale. We'll drink them and then fill them with dirt, transporting them somewhere else for disposal. The countryside maybe."

Catesby toasted Keyes. "Cheers."

"What of the gunpowder?" I asked. "When will we move that to the Whynniard house?" We had barely finished hiding it in Catesby's house.

Father nudged me with his elbow. "After the tunnel is started, then you and I will row the gunpowder along the Thames and store the barrels in the tunnel."

Percy finally gave me the answer I craved. "The tunnel should be complete mid-January, a few weeks before Parliament."

He, at least, seemed to share my passion for starting on the tunnel. It unnerved me to find my desires aligning with those of the murderer in the room. But what did it matter? By the end of this plot, we'd all be murderers.

Tomorrow it would begin.

At last, I joined in the reveling.

---

19 December 1604

My muscles burned as I pulled the oars through the water. Mist hung in the air like a damp cloak, shielding Father and me from view. We'd made the trip enough times now to gauge direction without being able to see the Whynniard house. The first night of rowing, we'd misjudged so severely that we spent another hour rowing upstream.

The three barrels of gunpowder weighed the boat down so that if I didn't keep my elbows tucked, they'd dip into the icy water as I rowed. One overcorrected teeter and we'd be sunk and then frozen and then drowned in the December Thames.

Like Norwood.

But rowing one barrel across at a time would lead to too many journeys and we'd be bound to be noticed. Even these barrels were covered in straw to keep their contents from the straying eye.

Our alibi, if caught, was that we'd been delayed by drink on our way back to our master and were rowing his goods to his house before he could notice in the morning. The alibi was weak at best, but it would serve us appropriately enough to avoid suspicion a first time. If we were caught twice . . . there was no excuse. Especially if whoever did the catching decided to break open the barrels.

Large shipments of gunpowder near the Parliament of a paranoid king were bound to alert someone.

I bit down a grunt as I matched Father's oar pace. Where I'd
gained speed and strong legs from my errand runs, he maintained
strength in his arms. But now, on our fourth night of rowing, he
broke a sweat same as I did. It served as my only source of warmth
on the frigid river, but I didn't wish for summer. The stench of the
Thames beneath the heat would have made our deep breathing
near impossible.

Father lifted his oars from the water and stiffened. I imitated
him, my back to the bank. Were we preparing to dock, or had he
seen someone? I wanted to turn and look, but not at the risk of
sinking us.

Our cessation of oaring caused the boat to rotate parallel to the
bank, controlled by the current. At first, I barely saw the shoreline.
Then movement. A shadow. A person crouched over the water?

He didn't seem to have noticed us, but the shape dipped a limb
into the water. A thirsty beggar? At third morning bell?

Not even a dying beggar would dare drink Thames water.

In the silence of our held breaths, I caught a harsh whisper.
Then our boat drifted deeper into the fog and the mysterious figure faded from view. We stayed silent for several more minutes,
then Father resumed rowing. "Best to take it back tonight. No good
risking delivery with a skulking figure at the water."

We rowed back up to Catesby's house, docked, and returned
the barrels to his cellar. A wasted night. Once we informed Bates, I
freed my voice and questions. "What was that person doing?"

"Who knows what the creatures of the night do?" Evasion.
How ironic he would say that when *he* frequented the night streets.

"It sounded like color speech."

"I heard nothing." We both saw the same person, the same odd interaction with the water, yet Father seemed to hold no curiosity. I, on the other hand, wanted answers.

Igniter? Keeper? Spy? Was Father not at all worried about getting found out? Perhaps that person had been at the Thames every night, watching us, and we'd never seen him. After all, anyone could use the fog for covering as well as we did.

"We'll stay at the Bear tonight."

"No." I quickened my pace. "If we stay at the Bear, that will be outside of our norm." I looked to Father. "You walk the night as though you are made of shadow. I will follow you and we'll get to the Whynniard house unseen."

"I'm flattered by your faith in my stealth, but I think you overestimate me."

"We'll need to let the tunnelers know in the morning." I chose not to comment on his humility. "If they make any noise with that person about, it could lead to inquiries."

No argument. He led us away from the Bear. I tried to hide my surprise. He was trusting my judgment? Was I earning his respect? We crossed the shadowed London Bridge, evading a crying beggar who clutched a stone arm.

I slowed, but Father continued on with a low, "Soon, Thomas. All will be cured soon."

My breath fogged before me as we breathed deeper from the brisk pace. I anticipated my warm bed, but not the early morning. Despite our late nights of rowing, we kept up the pretenses of Percy's servants. I called Father "Johnson" when around others and he treated me like an underservant. I looked forward to the day this was all over and we had a Keeper on the throne.

Emma and the Monteagle household had returned from holiday last night. I'd have to face Emma for the first time since Norwood's death. I wasn't sure I could do it.

Father led us to the door of the Whynniard house as capably as I'd anticipated. I saw no sign of the cloaked figure. The house was dark and we left it that way as we climbed into our beds.

Morning brought in the diggers, one by one, during the bustle of dockworkers and street hawkers. First Wintour and then Keyes. Father and I descended into the basement where the wall panels sat to the side, revealing a gaping hole in the earth. The musty dirt smell filled my nostrils. A torch stuck out from a hole in the earthen wall.

Keyes came into view, walking up the tunnel with a crate of dirt. He dumped it into an empty barrel and then sneezed. A puff of dust shot from his red beard. He started when he saw us. "Bates told us you brought the powder back to Catesby's."

Father stepped into the tunnel and I followed. The tunnel sloped sharply downward, held up by thick wood framing every several feet. Wood beams rested in the dirt as makeshift steps down. A few bends in, we passed the collection of gunpowder barrels at knee height. Wintour wore his Brown mask and leaned against the wall at the end of the tunnel, a hand on his heaving chest.

He usually worked the tunnel at night because color power was much quieter than the slam of shovels and axes. But his short stature meant he was the most mobile in the tunnels too. So, unfortunately for him, he served the most shifts.

"We encountered a questionable character down the bank." Father adjusted his mask. "We returned the powder to Catesby's for the sake of caution. We'll let them sit a few days before trying again. Meanwhile, keep aware of your comings and goings. If we are watched or suspected, that will be the end of us."

Wintour tugged his mask down so it hung about his neck and wiped a sheen of sweat from his face. "Who was this person? An Igniter? A king's man?"

"It was too dark and the mist too thick, but Thomas thinks he heard color speech." So Father *was* placing stock in that. "If it was an Igniter, there's no way of knowing what he was trying to command of the White Light."

Wintour coughed into his arm. "Perhaps . . . we should stop for a few days."

Father and I nodded, though I hated the idea of delaying the plot. It was almost Christmas and Parliament would be meeting in a mere seven weeks.

Wintour and Father headed up the tunnel, leaving me to douse the torches. I stared at the end of the tunnel—smooth, cleaned dirt after Wintour's color administrations. I had not yet been instructed to pick up an ax or even carry a single crate of dirt out to the river. Gunpowder was my charge, but I envied Wintour. Even with his exhaustion and the cough that had recently arisen from breathing in so much dirt.

I wanted to dig. I wanted a mask that could move dirt in the name of a mighty and world-changing conspiracy. A mask no one could take from me. Not even an Igniter.

What had happened to Norwood's mask? He didn't live long enough for the Igniters to smash it and tar it to his face.

My frustration exploded and I slammed the dirt wall of the tunnel. My fist cracked in pain. I must have hit a rock. My knuckles smarted and grew red beneath the torchlight. I shook out my hand and my thoughts. I needed to keep my focus.

After dipping a rag in the bucket of dirty water beneath the torch, I smothered the fire. I forced down a drab breakfast of pottage, then grabbed my cloak.

Father met me at the door. "Stop by the smithy while you're out today." He passed me a slip of paper. "Your new sword should be ready."

My hand stilled on its way to grab the note. "New sword?"

His gaze rested on the paper, not meeting mine. "I looked for yours on the streets, but someone must have snatched it. I'm sorry you lost it."

I slid the note from his hand. "I am too. But you—"

He patted me on the shoulder. "See that it's sharpened before the smithy gives it to you. And make sure it fits your scabbard." He handed me my belt and scabbard.

I took it reflexively. "I—" Inhale. Try again. "Thank you, Father." I barely squeezed out the words.

He'd put in an order for a new sword. For me.

"Happy Christmas." He shut the door behind me, but I remained on the icy doorstep for a moment longer. My empty scabbard would be thankful to be filled again, particularly with the approach of Parliament. I secured the belt.

Once we blew up King James and kidnapped Princess Elizabeth, there would be much fighting. Now I was ready.

Before heading to the smithy, I walked along the Thames, casually examining the bank around the area where I thought we'd seen the cloaked figure. Too many footsteps had trampled the place for evidence and pigeons pecked at the soggy ground. Perhaps there was nothing to concern myself over.

But as I turned away—toward market—I caught a little peek of White in the grass. A stone maybe? I walked near and squatted. It was a small dagger with a handle of bone, stone, and a spot of red that looked like blood. The same type of dagger that the men in the alley had used to try to cut Emma.

For some reason, the small weapon unnerved me. I remembered what Emma said so long ago in the alley—"*You have no idea what color Compulsion they've put on it.*"

I left it where it lay. If the mysterious person came looking for it again, I didn't want him to somehow hunt me down for it.

I headed along Bridge Street to Parliament Street and then right at Charing Cross. That put me out at the Strand—the road where Monteagle's city home rested. Where Henry wanted to meet with Father. They were still residing up in Hoxton until after the holidays. I dreaded when the entire family moved to their Strand house. It was so close to the Whynniard house. It would be harder to hide. I would always be looking over my shoulder.

Their Strand house looked dark. Curtains drawn, interior dark.

Might it stay that way.

The market bustled with the thrill of Christmas four days off. Pine boughs decorated doorframes. Booths overflowed with bright fabrics, carved wooden children's masks, boxes with cloth bows, fresh bread, baubles for women's ears, necks, and fingers. I had not even considered getting Father anything.

The best gift I could give him was a dead king.

I reached the smithy, and when he handed me the rapier, I could barely take it past the surprise stiffening my muscles. While the sword was sturdy and practical, the handle was woven black and white and the name *Fawkes* engraved on the hilt. That must have doubled its cost. It wasn't needed, yet Father did it anyway.

I placed the new sword carefully in its scabbard. It fit perfectly.

The other market stalls hawked wares and reeled in the women-folk. Items twirled in the air—ribbons, cloths, handkerchiefs, baskets—obeying the color commands of their Igniter owners, trying to catch the eye of a shopper. Was it only last spring when I saw Emma and her daffodils? That had been before I knew what she was and what she supported.

The memory reminded me of how we ended up at the hanging where she cared more for the colored boy than she did for the three Keepers. She condoned their hanging without a word, and I'd dared to humiliate myself by helping her with the boy—not that I regretted it.

I had let myself enjoy her company. I didn't hate her . . . I just wished she wasn't what she was.

As though summoned by my thoughts, the Brown mask with a white flower interrupted the sea of shoppers.

There she was. Facing me. Staring. My heart thundered. I wasn't ready. I wasn't ready to see her yet.

The moment she took a step toward me, I turned away.

"Wait, Thomas!"

But I quickened my pace, then ducked behind a market stall and doubled back. I glanced over my shoulder. She faced away from me, on her tiptoes, to peer above the swollen crowd. I left the market.

What could she possibly want? I had nothing to offer her other than completing her errands and escorting her home.

But I wasn't working for her guardian today.

She had no hold over me.

I took a new route back to the Whynniard house—cutting through St. James's Park. When I entered, no one was home. With all the people shopping and meeting and walking along the streets in preparation for Christmas, it was too risky to try tunneling or moving gunpowder and dirt. The other plotters were out shopping themselves, sending gifts to their ignorant families who were unaware that, should the plot go awry, this could be their last Christmas.

I managed to post a small note to Grandmother and Grandfather, though I still felt bitter over their actions at my Color Test. Still, they raised me and I didn't want to commit treason without showing them some amount of forgiveness—as much as I could muster at least. For my own sake.

I hung up my cloak and ventured down to the basement. The planks were in place, covering the entrance of the tunnel. I could dig. No one was home. I could make progress in the tunnel and they'd have less work to do once Christmas passed. They couldn't fault me for that. I would work quietly.

I slipped upstairs to shed my shirt and boots. I tossed them by my bed, but as I headed back toward the stairs, a form passed by the window. It was barely dusk, but dark enough for the figure to hide in the shadows.

I hurried to the window and pressed my face against the glass in time to catch the wisp of a cloak as the person inched around the corner of the house . . . toward the back garden and the bank of the Thames.

Proper visitors did not go to the back. Neither did any of the conspirators. I unsheathed my new sword and ran to the garden door, keeping the fall of my bare feet as light as possible. This could be the person Father and I saw on the bank of the Thames. Someone knew about our plot.

I strode to the back door. There was no time to waste—the snooper could be in the house any moment or discovering all manner of things by peeping in windows. I threw open the garden door and leapt out, sword first.

Movement to my left.

I swung to face him and my sword flew out of my hand as though wrenched by the blade. I ducked in case he had his own weapon, but before I could regain my bearings and land a punch, a voice—a *female* voice—shouted, "Thomas!"

I stumbled back and finally took in the figure in front of me. Emma.

My adrenaline transformed to anger. She must have seen it in my face because she took a step backward. I snatched my sword from the ground, shoved it into my scabbard, and then grabbed her by the arm. "Blast you, Emma! Are you out of your *mind*?"

I pulled her away from the garden and toward the front door. My bare feet burned from the frozen earth. She squirmed, but I didn't relent. Then she yanked her arm away so hard, it threw me off balance. "Let go of me."

I rounded on her. "What are you *doing* here?" As I finally faced her, I noticed the differences in her appearance. Her clothes hung like tattered drapes instead of elegant fittings and her usually curled dark hair looked disheveled and almost black beneath her cloak hood.

"I was calling on you, you lout!" Being held at sword point hadn't shaken her ability to stand her ground. "How was I to know you'd be"—she gestured to my torso—"half-naked?"

I glanced down at my bare chest. Good thing my face was already hot from anger. It hid the embarrassment. I fumbled for something else to say. To distract. "How did you disarm me?" I hated admitting I'd been bested in swordplay by a woman, but if any woman were to do so, it would be Emma.

"I used a Grey command."

I ran a hand through my hair. "Blasted White Light."

She breathed deep through her nose as though steeling herself. For some reason I got the impression she was waiting for more of a reaction. Well, I wasn't about to succumb to White Light talk.

"You need to leave. Wait—did you *follow* me?" A gust of wind caused my muscles to tense. I folded my arms for warmth. She needed to get out of here, I needed to go back inside, and we needed to never speak again.

"Yes."

"Were you trying to sneak in?" What if Father returned and saw her? Or worse . . . Percy?

"No! I went to the back door because you are a servant. And when no one answered the front door, I thought I could inquire after you at the kitchen."

Little did she realize there *was* no kitchen. Just a one-room flat with two doors and a cellar filled with gunpowder.

Shivers made my words clipped. "What do you want with me? Why not wait until I show up to do your bidding tomorrow? Why, when you ignored me at school, do you suddenly follow and irritate the plagued maskless boy?" I wanted her to grow angry, to be insulted and stomp away.

But she placed a gloved hand on my arm. "Thomas." The kindness and caution in her voice stilled me. "I'm sorry about Norwood."

My jaw clenched so hard it discharged a headache in my temples. "How . . ." I licked my dry lips. "How could you possibly know about Norwood?"

She hung her head. "I wrote him too. I knew he was coming to London to visit you. Henry had been in contact with—with the Tower guards."

"You two talked about me?" Disgust, hot and thick, coated my throat. My friendship with Norwood invaded. By Emma. An Igniter.

Did she know he was a Keeper?

"He said I could trust you." The wind almost carried her soft words away before I could catch them. "But I'm not sure. I'm not sure he ever saw the Thomas that I'm seeing now—afraid. Selfish. Evasive." She lifted her chin. "Stone cold."

Something inside me twisted at her words.

"If I didn't know any better, Thomas Fawkes, I'd say your heart is what's infected. Much more than your eye."

"What would you know of infection?" I scoffed. "Go home, you china doll."

She only laughed—cold and emotionless like Henry would do at St. Peter's. Then she left.

Good riddance.

I could no longer feel my arms or feet, but I managed to stumble back into the Whynniard house. I stomped into the basement and tore the planks from the front of the tunnel mouth. Grabbing a pickax, I removed my sword and stalked into the darkness. Then I attacked the wall of dirt with everything I had until sweat poured down my spine.

Until my hands blistered and tore.

Until blood slithered down my forearms.

Plain. Red. Blood.

I didn't stop.

Twenty

21 December 1604

I woke to a blurry world. My good eye burned, but when I went to rub it, my hands seared. What was going on? I blinked rapidly and the raw blisters on my palms came into focus. Then I recalled digging all night.

Light shone through the small window by the door. What time was it?

I sat up, but the room spun. I blinked my good eye and felt my eye patch. It was as secured as when Emma first commanded it to adhere to my face. The dizziness increased and I groped for a bedpost. I must not have gotten as much sleep as I thought.

My stomach roiled and a knife of pain sliced into my skull. Throbbing behind my eyes.

Blast it all, I'd allowed myself to become ill. Probably from the damp nights of rowing and then my talk with Emma out in the winter air without proper attire. It was my day to serve the Monteagle house, but if this headache continued . . .

I took a deep breath and the world righted itself a bit. I clomped down the stairs to the cellar. Voices sounded from the darkness. Was Wintour already here digging? Did I sleep through his entrance?

A mumble—that was Father.

A response—Wintour.

A word: ". . . outbreak."

I entered the cellar, squinting against the torchlight. My body swayed. I should have remained in bed. But I'd made it this far.

Father and Wintour stood by the tunnel entrance. Father had a foot propped on an overturned crate. By their bent postures and severe tones, I could tell something was wrong. They must have seen that I'd dug in the tunnel and they were displeased.

I steadied myself on the wall and cleared my throat. Both their heads snapped up. Father reeled back and Wintour let out a cry, reaching a hand toward me.

I frowned, or at least tried to. My skin prickled. Stiff. Oh . . . no. My hand drifted up to my brow. Fingertips touched stone. Plague blossomed from my left eye patch up beyond my eyebrow and over most of my forehead.

"No." My plea came out as a croak. I splayed my palm. More plague along my temple and hairline. "No!"

It had spread. The dizziness, the headache, the unsettled stomach. Plague.

"Thomas . . ." Father took two steps toward me. "There's been an outbreak—"

"What do I do?" I couldn't breathe. Couldn't think.

"His patch won't cover that now." Wintour backed into the tunnel.

My gasps came faster and faster.

Was the plague in my throat? Closing up my air?

"Just . . . just hold on a couple months, Thomas," Father said. "We'll get a Keeper on the throne."

A couple *months*? It had spread overnight! I gripped Father's shoulders. "Give me my color power!"

"That won't help—"

"You have to!" My screech echoed and I cared not who heard me.

"No color power is strong enough to remove the plag—"

I shoved him away. "Do you even *want* me to live?" I stumbled up the stairs and yanked my cloak from the peg. Father stumbled out of the stairway as I pulled on my boots.

"Thomas, you shouldn't go out in your state—"

I pulled my wide-brimmed hat low on my head and swept from the house, slamming the door. Snow swirled from the sky, bringing joy to those celebrating Christmas and giving the impression of a clean, pure London.

All the snow did for me was keep a temporary record of my disjointed path away from the Whynniard house. Perhaps it was the shock of the cold, but my vision cleared a bit and the headache settled to a dull throb.

I was going to die. If the plague spread from my eye to half my forehead overnight, it might not be finished. I could be dead by supper! Father didn't seem to care.

No matter what he said, I knew the colors could cure me. They just needed to be commanded by someone powerful enough. My pace doubled. If Father wasn't going to help me and wasn't even going to enable me to help myself, then I'd have to take matters into my own hands despite my involvement in the plot.

So I set out to find the strongest color speaker I knew . . . if she'd forgive me.

My hour walk to the Monteagle house in Hoxton was nearly as chaotic as my morning. Plagued people littered the streets, some clothed for the elements and others without shoes and still in nightshirts, thrown out of their lodgings at the first sign of petrified skin.

My plague had been exposed.

I hurried across London Bridge, catching cries from behind the closed doors. How many lives were rocked by the outbreak? And how far would the outbreak spread?

Most concerning was what had caused the outbreak—Igniters? Keepers? White Light?

I passed piles of stone rat carcasses, pigeons, and even a cat—plagued overnight. Some people threw them over the edge of the bridge into the Thames. And that was why no one drank the water. One old man sat by the bank, tossing crumbs of seeds to the surviving pigeons.

Two children poked at a stone rat with sticks until their mother caught them by the ears. "Annika! Gabriel! *Do you want to turn to stone?*"

Once I turned from Old Street Road onto Hoxton, I breathed freely. What would Emma say? I'd been cruel yesterday. And she'd come to give me belated condolences. Norwood had told her she could trust me—though I wasn't sure why she'd need to or if she really *could* trust me. But if Norwood had truly written her those things, it must mean I could trust her too.

Even with her being an Igniter.

I needed help, and she was the only one I knew who would hear me out.

The Monteagle house came into view and I sagged. Part of me had wondered if I'd collapse before arriving. But what was I doing? I had come to an Igniter family for help.

My plague could be *seen*. One glimpse from the Baron and I'd be dismissed. Reported. Quarantined or perhaps imprisoned for lying to a Parliament family.

But I had to know if Emma could help me. I was dying. And I was equally as desperate as those barefooted plagued people in the streets. My head pain blinded me for a moment. I pressed my blistered palm against my forehead and the cool touch calmed the throb enough for me to think. I'd go to the back—to the kitchens—and ask for Emma there.

I passed through to the garden. Snow covered the ground like a freshly lain sheet. The evergreens glistened beneath the dawn sun, sparkling with an innocence and beauty so contrasting to the day's events.

An iron bench beckoned to me. I resisted the urge to sit and think all this through. What would Emma really be able to do? Snow crunched deep into the pebbles underfoot. Then I saw her.

I wasn't sure what I was expecting, but it had not been to see her sitting in a cushioned upright chair in the middle of the garden, wearing a fur cloak with an easel before her. I slowed and stepped off the loud gravel path. Her hood kept me from view, so I took my time approaching.

Her right hand hung suspended in the air, a palette of paint resting in her left. The different colors of paint floated in the air, like rainbow snowflakes waltzing with the wind—three shades of blue and grey and green . . .

The paint drops aligned themselves on the canvas, then spread as though pushed by a brush. But Emma did not hold a brush. She didn't even whisper instruction. Only little sentences came forth as though she and the colors were friends. "Oh, that's very nice. Yes, you two blend splendidly!"

The painting came into view and I stilled.

It was me. My face. I stood with my back to the viewer, looking over my shoulder enough to reveal my eye patch and a glare from my good eye. This painted likeness looked so . . . alone. It made me want to help him—this angry, lonely Thomas who seemed to be looking back with both longing and anger, and moving forward with reluctance.

Was that how Emma saw me?

A brown drop danced in front of her face. She giggled. "Oh, Brown, you rascal. Find your spot." It splashed against my painted hairline and then wiggled itself to form the brim of a hat, yanked low to hide the eye patch.

The painting bore a talent that demanded to be acknowledged. To remain silent would be an insult to the very core of creation. "This is exquisite," I whispered.

Emma spun so fast, her elbow knocked the canvas off the stand. I shot out my hand and caught it before it hit the snow. My thumb smeared the newly painted hat.

"You startled me." Her hands trembled as she took the painting from me and returned it to its spot. She coaxed the brown paint off my thumb and back to its spot, then covered the art piece with a small cloth.

"I . . . I paint portraits. I was . . . I was just practicing from . . . from memory."

Was she embarrassed? "I don't mind." It gave me a glimpse into her heart and, in the meantime, cracked my own. I got to see my brokenness from the outside. I hadn't realized how lost I truly was—consumed by my desire to cure myself and kill King James—until I saw myself through someone else's eyes.

"I can't help it. I *see* people. Their pain. Their burdens. And they press upon me until I release them to canvas." When Emma faced me, her hand flew to her masked mouth. "Oh, Thomas."

I wanted to cover my face the way she'd covered her canvas, but her painting already proved she saw more than I could block with a low hat brim or a hand over my face. I gave a pathetic shrug. "I didn't know where else to go."

Her gloved fingers grazed my forehead and moved my hair out of my eye. I felt like a weak fool, but she didn't treat me as such.

"Can you help me?" I didn't tell her my ideas about her using her Grey speech or White Light speech or whatever she did. She would know if she could help me or not.

"I am powerless." Her hand dropped to her side, but I snatched it with my own.

"No, you're not. You are the strongest and—and *kindest* Igniter I know. If anyone has the power to help me, it's you."

She rose from her spot on the bench, glancing toward the house. "My power comes from White Light."

My chest tightened, but I forced a swallow. "That's how you painted just now, using all the colors. With White Light, right?"

She nodded.

"Tell me more. You said White Light could stop the plague. How do you know? If that's true, why won't you command it to heal me?"

"You don't *command* the White Light." She squeezed my hand and I realized she was the only person who had ever shown me affection. "You *ask*."

I released her hand. "I can't." If I spoke to the White Light, that would go against everything Father and the others and I had been striving for. It had taken months for me to silence that annoying nag.

Only Igniters dabbled in White Light and killed innocent Keepers.

That was the one line I couldn't cross.

"It's the advice I have for you, Thomas."

I let out a long breath. I should have known better. She was too set in the Igniter way. I wanted her to be on my side, to be with me through the plot to kill King James. Because her presence filled me. When I was with her, we felt like a team. It was so different from how things were at St. Peter's.

Well, if I was going to die from the plague, I might as well show Emma the kindness I'd previously denied her. I held out my arm. "Care to take a turn around the garden?"

She didn't move. "*Can* I trust you, Thomas?" Her concern bled through her muffled voice, so I forced myself to really analyze what sort of man I was.

Trustworthy? Perhaps. Norwood thought so. Catesby and his men trusted me. "I hope so. Or at least, I strive to be worthy of your trust."

She took my arm and we headed deeper into the trees. The winter chill seemed distant with her arm in mine. We entered the orchard, though the bare branches provided little cover from the snow.

"You've been painting the masters at the Royal Exchange. Why?"

"Because I want them to see that they are more than shop owners. They are more than their trade. And of course I'd hoped they'd see my skill."

"Did you secure an apprenticeship?"

She laughed a beat under her breath. "The Baron forbids it. He has sent letters to the masters. He still allows me to paint in the home . . . as a lady does."

"That's absurd. He can't stop you from pursuing a future!"

"You might be surprised at how much he *can* stop me. And it's not about stopping me from pursuing a future. It's about directing my pursuits toward a future of his approval."

I wanted to know more, but I remembered how worn she seemed yesterday. There was no way to gauge her health. Not for the first time, I wondered if she had the plague.

I brushed snow from one of the apple tree branches, fighting my headache. "You once said you believe Keepers and their followers caused the plague." Emma remained silent. "In fact, there's a rumor that for each Keeper who dies, one plague victim is cured."

"Now *that* I don't believe."

"Other Igniters do, though. And you call yourself one of them." I tried not to sound accusing. "It's hard not to lump you in. How are you any different from those who so passionately hunt Keeper followers—like Norwood—and turn them in to the Tower for a shilling?"

Her brown gloves stretched over her clenched knuckles. "You can't judge an entire group of people by the actions of a few."

The throbbing behind my eyes increased. "They set fire to Norwood's prison cart and then pushed it into the Thames." I leaned on the trunk of a plum tree. "I was there. Your people cheered as he died."

She rounded on me. "And *your* people hid White Light from *everyone* for centuries! When it is the source of all color powers and the only color that speaks to *us.*"

"Why is White Light so important to all of you?" Were all Igniters just power hungry?

She seemed to take several calming breaths. "It changes *everything.* Our forefathers spent their whole lives seeking to bond with a single color, to control it. But White Light spends years seeking *us* out, to bond with us. None of the colors would exist without it. Wouldn't you rather connect with the source?"

Wintour's voice echoed in my head. *"Seek the source."* Would he encourage such a thing in this setting? "I'd rather be *alive*, not perishing from this blasted plague." Color power or White Light, Igniters or Keepers . . . What did it matter if I was only going to die?

"Ask White for help, Thomas. Give it a chance." She plucked at a piece of peeling bark.

I studied her face—or rather her mask. Even in the morning light and snow, I could barely make out her shadowed eyes. Before I realized it, I'd placed a hand at the side of her face—half my palm on her mask and the other in her dark curls. She stiffened.

"How can you expect me to trust your words about White Light when you won't even trust me enough to reveal your true self?" I said softly.

Her hand flew to her mask as though she was afraid I'd tear it from her face. She straightened her shoulders. "My true self has nothing to do with my face, Thomas Fawkes."

Interesting perspective. The world had associated my worth with my plague for the past two years. "Why do you hide?"

She swallowed and her voice came out thick. "For the same reason you want to."

I wanted my mask because I was ashamed of what people saw when they looked at me. I hated being defined by my plague and I was sick of being helpless. I wanted a future.

"Are you plagued?" Why did I want her to say yes? So I wouldn't feel alone?

She pushed my hand away. "Forget it, Thomas."

"You say you want to trust me. So trust me." My desire to see her face made it hard to breathe. I needed something real. "You did not shun me. Give me the opportunity to show you the same height of character."

She stopped, her head down. "I need time."

"I may not have time." Now I was begging.

"I hope you're wrong."

As she picked up her painting and went inside, I whispered, "Me too."

Then she was gone and I remained immune to the cold, staring at her back door with my good eye.

That was probably why I didn't see Henry Parker stalk up to me until he'd grabbed the collar of my shirt. "So *this* is why you wear the eye patch?"

Blast! I thought he was on the Strand! I shoved him off me. "Leave me be, Henry." I brushed my clothes straight. My secret was out.

"No, you leave *Emma* be." He matched my stride as I left. "She doesn't need to associate with Keeper caddies who can infect her with more than a plague."

I stopped to face him. We were eye-to-eye. I'd grown taller. "What are you implying?"

He got right in my face. "I'm telling you that she's spoken for. And if you overstep that, I'll make sure you're a participant in the next hanging."

Emma was spoken for? What was going on?

My brain caught up to the rest of his sentence—that I'd *hang* if I interfered. Was Henry part of the crew turning in Keepers to the Tower? "I'm finished here, Henry."

"Are you resigning?" He sneered.

I held myself tall. "I'm plagued. Do I have a choice?"

He stepped back. "I'm sure we can make an arrangement."

The way he said it made me even warier. What did he want so badly that he would risk his health and the health of his family? "Explain."

"You never took me up on my offer of supper on the Strand." When I frowned, he added, "With your father."

There it was. He wanted to meet Father for reasons I didn't

understand, but his desire was strong enough that he'd risk the plague. I didn't need employment that badly. What more information could I gather from the Baron that would even help the plot? My time here was done. "I'll take my final payment, please."

"Don't be a fool, Thomas Fawkes. You'll receive no other employment with your spreading plague. Not even your father's great name will get you work."

"I am my own man. I can make my own way."

"You are no man without your mask." He raised an eyebrow. "Why doesn't your father give you a mask? Isn't that why you came to London?"

"That is not your business."

He sneered. "Perhaps your name isn't Fawkes at all and you aren't related to the cad."

"My father is not a cad." The sword at my belt reminded me of the new side—the generous side—of Father I'd recently witnessed. "He is a good man."

Henry's sneer faded and he seemed to force civility. "Your father is a courageous color soldier and mine a coward. I suppose I envy you."

His humility was an act. I'd seen him perform in front of the headmaster at St. Peter's before, though not quite as well as he was doing now. I didn't buy it, but I mustered up my manners all the same. "And I, you, with your mask. I suppose we both must be content with what we've been given."

"I suppose." He dug in his pocket and then flipped me a coin. With a nod, he returned to the house. "Good day, Cyclops."

Bow. "Sir."

To the observer, it might seem like a mutual dismissal, but I took the long way home anyway, doubling back and routing through new paths until I no longer saw his poor attempt at following me home.

The walk back to the Whynniard house was just as weighing on my soul as the walk away from it. Plague doctors with their beaked color masks flitted from house to house, overcharging for their services and feeding off the panic.

A plague doctor and apprentice treated me when I was first diagnosed two years ago. They made no visible difference but claimed they'd slowed down the spreading. It was enough to put Grandfather and Grandmother at ease. Not me, though. I still remembered them leaning over me, the noses on their masks almost poking me in the face. I never trusted them.

As a plague doctor left one of the houses on London Bridge, I couldn't help but wonder if any of the rabid Igniters from the night of Norwood's death had woken up plagued.

I reached the Whynniard house, my stomach gnawing at my innards and my blistered hands aching from the exposure. A hay bale hung from a hook outside the door.

The sign of plague.

I knocked snow from my cloak and boots, then entered. Faint noise came from the cellar, so I headed down the stairs.

Wintour and Jack were hard at work on the tunnel. Wintour looked up when I entered the basement. His gaze rested on my face for a moment. Then, "Care to give us a hand? You did the work of three men last night."

They weren't casting me out? I gestured over my shoulder with my thumb. "The hay bale is for me, isn't it?"

Wintour actually smiled. "Aye."

"Are you not afraid of infection?"

Jack snorted. "My sister nearly died of the plague—she's still got it, but it went dormant. If I didn't catch it from her, I won't catch it from you." He dumped a crate of dirt into an empty ale cask. "Catesby knew about your plague?"

I nodded. "Aye. Upon my talk with him."

"He let you join us. I trust him."

Wintour sent a stream of dirt from the wall into a crate. "And that hay bale will keep all snoopers from venturing too close. It's our best defense! We can tunnel freely."

They saw my plague . . . as a blessing? They weren't running in fear. They weren't turning me in. They were accepting me. Like family. My heart swelled and for a moment I was speechless.

Wintour tilted his head to one of the barrels. "Care to haul this out?"

I swallowed hard, nodded, and then set to carting dirt out of the tunnel. My blistered hands burned, but it served as a distraction. As I hauled crates and scooped loose dirt, my mind turned to Emma. The plotters believed King James's death would cure the plague. But Emma believed White Light could help me.

Neither group had proof.

My best option was to try both. I believed that *Emma* believed White Light was a good thing. I'd never considered colors seeking me out. Did White Light want to control me like I wanted to control a color?

We had seven weeks until Parliament. If the elimination of King James didn't rid us of the plague, *then* perhaps I'd dabble in White Light to my heart's content without risking Father denying me my color power.

But what if I didn't make it seven weeks? As if to remind me of my predicament, my head pounded.

No one would know if I spoke to White Light, right? It had contacted me in my mind, so I ought to be able to respond nonverbally.

Did I dare? I couldn't bear the idea of waiting another seven weeks to see if I survived long enough to assist in the assassination.

My hands trembled, sending a scoop of dirt into a crate. No one understood what it was like to have the plague claiming bits of his brain with each outbreak. I wanted to be teachable. Pride had gotten me nowhere. I had to try something.

No one could know. Not even Emma.

Besides, it wasn't as if speaking to White Light would make me an Igniter.

So as I hauled another full crate of dirt to the mouth of the tunnel, I closed my good eye, took a deep breath, and thought, *This message is for White Light. You must already know I'm a Keeper, but I'm willing to speak to you about my plague. Emma says you're the source of the color power and supposedly want to bond with me. So if you're so powerful, heal my plague. Or at least give me a sign that any of Emma's words are even true. Show me what side you're on—Igniters or Keepers.*

I finished my message but then realized how foolish that was. To speak to a color—to command a color—I needed to be looking at it. But how did one look at light? Wasn't it all around us? We wouldn't have colors without it.

If I didn't hear from White or see a sign after a few days, I'd try again outside. Maybe.

Or maybe all of this was rot.

I had to believe there was some amount of truth to Emma's claim of bonding with White Light. After all, she had something—some sort of confidence or peace or increased color skill that I envied.

"Is your head hurting you?"

My eye snapped open. Father stood at the base of the cellar stairs. How long had he been there? A sick dread slammed into my gut. What had I done? "Yes, it's been hurting since morning."

He didn't say anything to that. I wasn't sure what he *would* say.

So we helped Wintour cart the dirt upstairs. Once night fell, Wintour disposed of it into the Thames using his color power and cover of darkness. He was right about the hay bale. Street wanderers gave our door a wide berth. Mutters spread fast until even the nearby market stalls relocated farther from the house.

I watched from the window—acting as lookout with the house dark. Father joined me after Jack left. "I'm sorry you have the plague."

"I'm sure you are." Father probably had visions and dreams for his son the way I did for a father. All dashed when I woke up with a stone eye.

"Your mother died of the plague, you know."

"Is that why you stopped writing?" I asked. "You thought I'd die?"

"I stopped writing because I didn't want to get attached to something fleeting." He rubbed his thumb over the hilt of his sword. "Your mother died within four weeks of contracting the plague. So I figured if you were going to face the same fate, I was better off detaching myself so that sorrow would not affect my ability to serve in the Spanish war."

I ground my teeth. Wintour sent a stream of dirt into the water.

"I see now that I was wrong."

I nodded. *Wrong* barely touched the surface. He'd been selfish, fickle, and untrustworthy . . . until recently.

Wintour returned to the cellar for another crate. One of us should help him. As I stepped away from the window, Father said, "I am pleased you can still be a part of this plot of passions. You can see, to some extent, why I acted the way I did."

"I don't see why it was so impossible for you to write a letter to your son every few months." I turned guard duty over to him. "Good night, Father." Though forgiveness had started to warm in my heart, I wasn't yet ready to show it.

"Good night, son."

I paused next to my small cot. What if I woke tomorrow with even more plague? Or what if I didn't wake at all?

A deep-earthed crash shook the Whynniard house and a billow of dirt dust exploded into the stairwell. It blinded me for a moment. Father and I raced down the stairs. We entered the cellar to fallen tunnel slats and air dust so thick we yanked our shirts up over our mouths to breathe.

A torch illuminated the mouth of the tunnel and a giant pile of dirt, timber, and stone at the first bend. "Wintour." Father lunged for the dirt pile and scrabbled through the rubble. *"Wintour!"*

Our tunnel had collapsed.

Twenty-One

24 December 1604

"This makes no sense!" Wintour strained a vein in his temple, trying to command the dirt back into place, but he fell back gasping. His Brown mask fell from his face, cracked.

We'd found him buried near the entrance of the tunnel after the cave-in three days ago. Father dug him free with his Black color power before he suffocated. A wood beam had cracked Wintour's mask and he couldn't seem to control his color. He held it in his lap like a sick child. "It was secure. I tested it every day. It shouldn't have collapsed."

"Sabotage?" Father suggested.

"Are you implying someone betrayed us?" Wintour asked.

Both of them turned to me. My pulse hammered in my ears. Ringing. It was because I talked to the White Light. I caused this. Somehow the Brown in the tunnel knew I betrayed it.

And somehow they knew.

"What do you think, Thomas?" Father asked.

"You were the last one to dig." Wintour slid a thumbnail along the crack in his mask, clearing out the packed dirt.

I shook my head. "I am one man. I barely made a dent. You tested the tunnel after I dug." I sounded guilty. They kept staring. Staring. Staring.

I'd asked for a sign. But this was punishment.

"We're not accusing you, son." Father leaned his elbows on his knees. "If we started blaming each other, where would that lead? We are asking only for your opinion."

Oh. "I . . . I am as perplexed as you."

A lie. I caused the collapse. I'd broken Keeper law. I'd betrayed everyone because I had talked to White.

＊

Catesby and Percy came that evening to inspect the damage.

"How far behind does this put us?" Catesby asked.

Percy struck the wall of dirt with a shovel. "Weeks! We might as well be starting over."

Wintour's hands hung at his sides as limply as the broken mask at his belt. "I don't understand. This shouldn't have happened."

"We'll re-tunnel," Catesby said.

"But how can we reinforce it and avoid the same catastrophe if I don't know what went wrong?" Wintour fiddled with his cracked mask. "I'm useless now."

Father rubbed dirt dust off his mask. "You still have two hands, Wintour, and a brilliant mind. We'll double the timber and have Keyes use his Brown power to pick up where you left off. At any rate, all our gunpowder is buried in there."

＊

We spent Christmas Day in the dirt. No roast goose, no spiced pudding. I stepped outside at one point to catch the London Waits passing by, playing carols. They weren't quite as skilled as York's minstrels, but their music brought a temporary balm to my heart.

By the time Percy returned from his duties at Whitehall Palace, we'd worn through every muscle in our bodies and barely dented the pile of debris. We found our first barrel of gunpowder. The earth had crushed it and mixed powder with dirt.

Father kept the torch back after that. How many more of our precious barrels were destroyed?

Percy stumbled down the stairs, dipping his shoulder against the doorframe. His Red mask had been pushed up onto the top of his head. Against his shock of white hair, it looked like blood on snow. The smell of ale filled the room—a stale but welcome alternative to the dirt we'd been breathing all day.

Father sat back on his heels. "We've barely cleared away the entrance. It's too much for Keyes. He can't lift the beams or move the dirt."

Only then did I realize how strong Wintour's color power had been.

"No matter," Percy slurred, propping himself up by the wall. "Parliament's been delayed."

Silence pressed against us. Not even the torch dared to flicker, even when Father lowered it from the mouth of the tunnel.

Shock. Despair. When Father finally seemed to find his voice, he rasped, "For how long?"

Percy shrugged. "Months. *Months.*" He yanked his mask from his head. "'S 'cause o' the plague." His gaze slipped along the wall and landed on me.

Wintour strode to him and looped an arm over his shoulder. "Let me help you back to Gray's Inn."

"B-Blasted King J-James."

Delayed. I plopped right on the pile of dirt. I wouldn't make it that long. What if there was another outbreak?

This message couldn't be ignored.

The White Light had sent its sign. It was trying to stop our plot. My breathing quickened. I didn't want to think about it. I didn't want to question my actions or involvement. I faced Father. "Do you . . . Father, is this a sign?"

He pushed himself to his feet and set the torch in its bracket. "It is, son." Was that excitement in his voice? How could he be excited over the tunnel collapse?

Unless he, too, had been thinking about White Light.

"So then what does this mean?"

He threw his arms wide. "The scheme is blessed!"

Wait, what?

"At the exact time the tunnel collapsed, Parliament was post-poned. We've been given the time we need to complete and perfect our duties."

"Time? *Time?*" I jabbed a finger toward my face. "I don't have time. My plague is spreading and you are rejoicing over the plot's delay?"

"I'm rejoicing because we have been given aid!"

"To whom do you attribute this aid?"

"The White Light."

I stared, then rose. My voice came out low. Cautious. "You . . . you speak to it?"

"No." His protestation split the pause like the snap of a horse whip. "None should ever speak to it. But it sees all. It sees us."

Was that what had happened? A sign of approval? "A Keeper would call this a sign of favor, but an Igniter might call it a warning."

"What does it matter what an Igniter might think?"

"It matters!" It mattered because I was sacrificing everything for the Keeper cause and just now realized how subjective our differences were regarding White Light. "Why are we so against bonding with White Light?"

Father rubbed his eyes through his mask holes and then addressed me as though explaining to a toddler. "White Light is the source of all color power. It is beyond our understanding. It should never be controlled."

Thus far, what he said aligned with Emma's words. Then what caused the rift between these two groups to widen so much that they wanted to *kill* each other?

Perhaps Father saw the doubt on my face. "Ages ago, White Light taught the strongest and most faithful Keepers how to speak the different color languages and then those Keepers passed that knowledge on to the public. But then a rogue Keeper named Luther resisted the Keeper way. He convinced people to speak to the White Light themselves. They started calling themselves Igniters."

This was the most Father had ever said to me in one go. Finally, I was getting answers.

"There were uprisings. Soon Keepers no longer had homes or income. Then, finally, the White Light sent a plague to punish the Igniters—to *stop* them. The plague killed Luther, but he'd already irreparably damaged the structure of the color power ways."

Did Emma know any of this? "Then why do Igniters blame the plague on Keepers?"

"Because they don't know their own history. They think Keepers killed Luther and that the plague came as punishment."

I stared at Father for a long time. "Both sides are mere opinions."

He shook his head. "What I told you is true."

He might think so. But I could no longer take a person's word on something that would affect my life. Not even Father's.

Twenty-Two

The House of Lords was not all that big—smaller than some of the cathedrals. Every time I left the Whynniard house, I looked at the House of Lords where Parliament would meet.

Where the world would end.

The building rose with a tall chimney and arched windows set into grey stones. The entire structure made a giant H shape and our Whynniard apartment rested in the right foot of that H. King James would die in the center.

I walked past it casually with Father and pictured it exploding into chunks of stone and timber, collapsing in a heap and changing history forever. The emotions that followed this internal visual were not peaceful.

The grounds bustled with its commercial enterprise. We passed a few more taverns, wine merchants, and the cookshop from which I frequently acquired dinner. I wore a new patch—wide enough to cover the plague. My hat brim did the rest.

Men with Green masks wove pine garlands in the open air with frenzied muttering, trying to sell their last wares before the holidays ended. One Brown-masked man moved his entire cart of goods from one side of the road to the Cotton Garden with color speech.

Father pointed out some crockery wares to keep up the guise of being passersby, but really we were examining the small path between the Whynniard house and Parliament to make sure the tunnel collapse wasn't visible from above. If even a single shopper had noticed something suspicious, we could be ruined.

Wintour and Keyes had been hard at work clearing it the past several days, but with little progress. Not even Father and his Black color power could move much. Wintour's mask was useless, but he dug with shovel and hand as though the entire collapse had been his fault.

Without the coin for another batch of gunpowder, we hoped the buried barrels were unspoiled.

We walked along the Thames. Ice spiked away from the shore edge. "Any sign of that figure from last week?" I asked. Was it only a week ago that we saw the skulking person by the bank?

"No. But I expect it is because of the snow. Tracks are too hard to cover up on a fresh snowfall." Father paused by the water. A few boats passed by, steering to dock on the other side. Then we made our way back, our walk at an end. No signs of tunnel collapse to the naked eye.

As we passed Parliament on the other side, I noticed a cart sitting in the street, unattended, just outside of where Parliament would meet. Two men—one Blue and one Yellow—exited from a wooden door half-set in the ground beneath the building, carrying a crate of kitchen supplies. One grunted and nearly tripped. Father and I hurried forward to help. We loaded it into the cart.

The men stretched out their strained fingers. Judging by their simple cloaks and muddied boots, we were all of equal status. "Thank ye, sirs."

"Our pleasure." Father gestured to the items in the cart. "Is this all being sold?" Now that I was closer, I caught the barrels and piles of soot-blackened kitchen materials.

"No, just cleared out a bit." One man removed his Blue mask and wiped his brow.

"Who owns the undercroft?"

The man shrugged. "The current tenant is a man named Skinner. But he doesn't live here much." He headed back inside with his partner. After a moment, Father followed, so I did too.

Descending into the undercroft felt reminiscent of the London tunnels—dark, void of warmth, pressing upon me. It was an open space with arches along every wall and thick stone pillars in two lines down the center. If my bearings were correct, we currently stood beneath Parliament. Our collapsed tunnel was supposed to end beneath my feet.

Stone floor, rock ceiling with wide wooden beams at six-foot intervals. One wall was all brick to accommodate a fireplace. The giant hallway seemed to have served as a kitchen at one time. Now the place was a mixture of muck and dust. The fireplace looked as though it hadn't been used in years.

Father removed his hat and examined the ceiling. "This is quite a space."

"Aye," said the Blue. "Seventy-seven feet long an' twenty-four feet wide. Good for storage, but not fer livin' if ye ask me. Still, some tenants use it for lodging."

Before I'd even processed his statement, Father bowed and steered me out. "Thank you, sirs." We returned to our apartment via a roundabout route so the workers wouldn't see us.

Once the door closed behind us, Father hurried to our cellar where Wintour and Jack sat eating a dinner of bread and cheese. "The undercroft beneath Parliament is being emptied," he said.

Wintour tore a chunk of bread away from the loaf and popped it into his mouth. His broken mask rested on his knee, a thick brown paste over the crack, half-dried. "Who's the tenant?"

"Some man named Skinner, but he doesn't seem to use it much. Perhaps we could make an offer to the owners that would make it ours."

Jack's eyes brightened. "Then we'd need not finish the tunnel. We could move the gunpowder straight into the undercroft." His breath quickened. "If we let that undercroft, the plot cannot fail."

"Precisely," Father said.

Wintour leapt to his feet, barely catching his mask from falling. "Jack and I will take the word to Catesby. Guy, go tell Percy at Gray's Inn. We may not have enough coin for new gunpowder, but we should have enough coin for a lease. All we need now is a convincing reason for letting the place." He swept his hat onto his head and they hurried out of the cellar.

As Father passed me, he whispered, "I believe you've had another sign."

Why didn't that comfort me the way it seemed to comfort him?

---

6 February 1605

"March twenty-fifth." Catesby paced in his sitting room.

The rest of us—except for Jack, who was late—hovered as near to the fireplace as we could. Despite Catesby's wealth of knowledge, he had barely enough coin to heat the place.

"That is when we will make the offer on the undercroft. During the Lady's Day masquerade." He scanned our group. "Percy, have you come up with an excuse to lease the place?"

Percy polished the Red mask on his belt. "I will say my wife is coming up to London to join me. And she needs lodging."

"And which wife might that be?" Jack stepped from the darkened hallway, his question colder than the frost on the lattice window. His brother, Kit, hung in the shadows behind him.

The room went silent. The fire popped. Even Catesby—our leader of golden words—stood mute.

Percy's mouth opened and closed several times. "It is the reason that matters."

Jack's fingers toyed with the hilt of his sword, but his anger seemed to run so deep that it seeped out in a pool of deadly calm. "I just want to know, should the landlord ask you the name of your wife, which name you shall give. Our sister's or the wench you wed when you abandoned Martha."

Father's head snapped to stare at Percy. "What's this?"

Percy's face reddened. He had two wives? My gut twisted. When he didn't answer, Jack persisted. "Or have you a third I've yet to learn about?"

Catesby raised a hand. "As hard as it may be, this plot goes above personal matters. Deal with this dispute in your own time, but do not let it escalate to a duel. We need you both." He was the only one who could have spoken those words without being attacked by the three steaming men.

Jack's hand slid off his hilt, but the battle had already been played out. No one would meet Percy's eyes.

Murderer. Adulterer. And we were supposedly on the same side.

"Guido will continue the guise of John Johnson—Percy's servant—and be the one to secure the lease." Catesby trundled on, despite the remaining tension. "Percy will attend the masquerade to perform his duties as the king's guard. Thomas will attend as his servant."

I started. "Me? Attend a masquerade?" I looked up to find Catesby staring intently. "But . . . I'm plagued."

"You will be wearing a cloth mask for the dance. No one will see your plague, and we need a servant who can observe nobility from the shadows."

I stood in a daze as they finalized the other plans—who would meet with the landlord, how much to offer, what to do if they refused, and so on.

But all I could think was that I was being sent to a masquerade in the king's palace. I would be in the same room as King James. I would see the man who was perpetuating this war and oppressing Keepers.

I pictured the king—dressed in layers of colored cloth, lounging behind a table of delicacies with Igniters from the gentry fawning over him. I imagined him signing decrees that exiled and executed Keepers.

If I was as inconspicuous as Catesby said I would be . . . why not simply kill the king on my own? In fact, why not turn this masquerade into an assassination?

Twenty-Three

Lady's Day
25 March 1605

I could smell the gossip.

The thrill seeped through my stiff masque attire as Percy and I approached the Palace of Whitehall. The king's residence. Though the palace was less than a mile from the Whynniard house, this was my first time getting close enough to tangle my nerves.

The palace was a city in itself. Percy and I approached through St. James's Park, which had recently opened to the public. King James had improved upon the old deer park and populated it with all manner of new decorations. Percy and I passed a man leading an elephant. At one point I saw a camel and even heard someone claim to have spotted crocodiles.

We passed aviaries and I gawked at the exotic birds, preening feathers more colorful than Emma's paint palette. Ahead, the sunset cast shadows that caused the palace buildings to seem twice as tall. Like sentinels guarding the king. Watching us.

Lines of English elm trees marked a strolling path to our right.

A few masquers walked arm in arm along it, sporting elaborate gowns and emblazoned cloth masques, near identical to the one tied to my face. Color masks remained at home this night—not for costume's sake, but by the king's decree save those with special pardon.

King James was right to be paranoid.

Ahead rose the four-towered gatehouse—Holbein Gate—the greenish-grey stone boasting its authority over the lesser structures. Red roofs sat like crowns upon the buildings' stone bodies.

Percy pointed to our left as we entered the world of nobles and kings. "Those are the Horse Guard barracks." The barracks rose above horse stables with lit windows on every floor and a tall grey bell tower.

To our right, we passed the Olde Stair Café. Then we were consumed by the crowd's madness, entering a narrow lane that forced everyone together like water from a tributary. Attendees gulped deeply from the flood of chatter.

"Did you know?" one guest tittered to another. "King James and Queen Anne employed Ben Jonson and the great architect Inigo Jones to design the masque."

"*No.* He's returned from Italy?"

"The very one."

"And Jonson only recently started performing again after killing his fellow actor in that duel."

"How thrilling!"

The excitement sent its own perfume over the masquers. Percy took his place at the gate with other guards, inspecting guests as they arrived. If he found an assassin sneaking in, would he let him pass? It would be a relief to allow someone else to do the job for us.

As enticing as it had been to dream of killing King James on my own, I knew it would not be considered a success in the grand scheme of the plot. We needed to cripple England, to shake the Igniters, to cause chaos through which Keepers could rise to leadership.

If the goal had been to kill King James, Percy would have done it by now. And if fire-hearted Percy could stay his hand, so could I.

I explored the courtyard with my eye. Endless yards of blue fabric flowed down the steps leading into the court. That cloth alone must've cost several months' wages. The blue coloring grew deeper and darker as it disappeared into the court, inviting masquers to enter a magical land.

Bubbles of all colors floated in the air, swirling around guests and then zipping off to land on someone else. I scanned the courtyard for the masked who might be controlling them but saw none.

"Alchemists, architects, Igniters, and masques . . . What an era we are in!" someone squealed.

I shifted my feet, waiting for Percy to finish his rounds of inspection.

A voice whispered in my ear, "Don't tell me you're spending the whole evening out in the *cold*. I want a dance."

I spun. A flowing silver gown slipped away into the crowd. I couldn't see her face, but the voice—and the relaxed yet elegant posture—betrayed her identity.

Emma.

Her event masque covered her entire face and neck—all black, but with a white rose over one eye. Her deep brown-black curls were gathered over one shoulder and had cloth flowers woven into them like a new garden springing from fresh-turned soil.

She glanced over her shoulder at me when she reached the bottom of the stairs. And I did the most unmanly thing that could have possibly accosted my reflexes.

I waved.

I dropped my hand—even wiped it on my doublet as though that would return some honor to me—but I still caught her giggle.

Then she took the arm of another man.

He wore deep purple and a painted cloth masque of flames. His lifted chin and cocky stature told me all I needed to know. Henry Parker. I recalled my last conversation with him. He'd said Emma was spoken for. Was he trying to claim her?

Emma walked tall. Maybe she didn't mind. Henry Parker had an honorable title and they *did* look quite regal together.

Percy and I stayed outside another half hour. Then a man with skin painted completely black, wearing a net across his bare chest and a flowing tangle of blue-and-yellow cloth about his waist, appeared at the top of the stairs.

"Let the masquerade begin." His booming voice was met with shrieks from women who had lingered outside. They scrambled up the steps, some tripping in their haste—like chickens racing after a worm.

The bubbles in the air drifted to the ground and remained there for a full minute before popping one by one, like candles going out.

Percy and I took up the rear. We entered the court as a man hollered from a balcony, "May I present—the Masque of Blackness."

I stood on the sidelines, squeezing behind a few huddled bodies. The torches dimmed throughout the court and an awed hush settled over the audience. I barely caught sight of men in the balconies above—wearing their color masks.

Then shadow consumed them.

The room hushed, but my nerves hummed. I couldn't help but get caught up in it, freeing myself from the all-consuming thoughts of the plot.

A tiny light came from the opposite end of the hall—a single lamp flame. It grew and grew, until I was sure the wall was on fire.

The blue cloths that had been on the outer steps swarmed through the doors, past my feet, and into the court, slithering like floodwater until the entire floor was covered like a giant sea.

The cloths roiled and writhed. The first lamp resumed a regular height of flame. A second lamp illuminated a small false forest on one end of the court, with a shore of creamy silk pouring into the blue sea.

In the center of the court rested an enormous concave shell. It rocked back and forth, tossed by the sea. People in elaborate costumes stood inside the shell—all blackened with paint.

Like the boy I saved.

But it didn't create the same intrigue as his natural, smooth dark skin. These painted bodies looked almost comical—or disturbing, as though they'd been dipped in tar but not feathered. The memory of the black boy snapped me out of the moment and I swept a glance over the room until I found her.

Emma stood still as a statue, tracking the giant shell as the cluster of "Negro" masquers sailed to Britannia. Blue-skinned masquers—Oceanian torchbearers—wore flowing sea green and led the shell, navigating the sea with their bare feet.

I found Emma far more interesting than the masque production. Even when the Negroes left their shell and stepped foot on Britannia's shore and their dark skin miraculously turned pale, I couldn't tear my gaze from her.

She stood ramrod straight. Henry leaned over and whispered something to her. Her hands fisted at her sides.

The crowd's applause startled me. Three men bowed in the center of the room. An announcer said, "Ben Jonson, the author of the masque; Inigo Jones, the architect; and John Dee, the renowned alchemist."

Dee bowed the lowest, his parti-colored mask shining beneath the newly lit torches like a jester's motley. I'd never seen a mask like his—with an even streak of every color crisscrossing his face. What did that mean? What was his strongest color?

"And, of course, my lovely wife . . . my Annie," King James added. One of the elaborate women stepped out of the seashell, curtsied, and joined him on the dais.

King James wore no mask, so I could see the full force of his adoration as he took his wife's hand. I could see his groomed pointed beard, the crinkles at his eyes, the movement of his neck ruff as he whispered something to the queen.

I looked away. His actions made him seem human. Even kind.

A short, stooped man spoke to the king and then the music began. A foreign phenomenon filled me—an emotion I couldn't place. The most music I'd heard was a single harpsichord that Grandmother played. But here there were lutes, trumpets, bandoras, wooden flutes, spinets . . . an orchestra of the soul.

The masquers performed a practiced dance before anyone else was free to join. I looked back to Emma's spot by the wall. Her comment about us dancing must have been in jest. I couldn't join the floor. Even with my masque covering my plague, my livery declared me a servant.

But she and Henry weren't among the dancers.

"Start mingling, Thomas," Percy said in an undertone as he passed me by. "Hover around Dee. I want to know more about him." Then he was lost in the shuffle of linen and magic. Dee? Ah, the parti-color–masked alchemist. Of course. His color power alone commanded the production—a good man to observe.

I moved to a corner of the room where a cluster of fawning admirers surrounded Dee. The traverse was easy. People didn't move for me, but neither did they stare. For once I looked like everyone else. Masqued and natural.

No one saw my plague.

No one saw my patch.

I was invisible.

Dee lifted his mask—revealing the wrinkled face of an old man. An old man who kissed the hand of every adoring lady and bowed thanks as profusely as a servant with a spring along his spine. He seemed too ancient to be responding in such a manner—like an aged grandfather flirting with other men's granddaughters.

"How long are you here for?" one woman simpered.

"I live in London, madam. Mortlake."

"How have we not seen you at court before?" asked another, shielding her flowered masque with a fan flutter. Her flirtation wasn't even subtle. And he was thrice her age! Surely none of these women actually wanted to marry the old corpse.

Then again, if he was swimming in power . . .

"I recently returned from my post as warden of Color College in Manchester." His attention flicked to me for a breath. "Excuse me, ladies, I must speak with the king."

They parted for him, but as he passed me his eyes fixed on my masque. They narrowed. What did he see? I was hidden beneath cloth and string.

Then a single word slipped from his lips, almost a whisper, as he glided past. "Plague?"

Chills deluged my skin. He couldn't know that. My face was covered. I checked my masque. How could he know? Had it spread?

He slipped into the crowd, attending to a new group of admirers.

"Did *you* know he lived in London?" a woman asked the lady next to her, her former awe turned to the harsher tone of gossip.

"He must have returned after the death of his wife and daughters."

"They *died*?" Gossip One gasped, a hand fluttering to her throat. "How?"

"Plague," said Gossip Two.

A somber hum fell over the ladies as if they were paying respects to the dead. Then Gossip Two pulled out an extra juicy piece of meat for the hounds. "Plague claimed his first two wives as well."

"*Three* wives?" Gossip One shook her head. "That man sounds cursed."

"*I* heard the king didn't even want him here tonight. Dee is old news."

"Poor man. At least *he* never got the plague."

"Not anywhere *we* can see." And then the women shuffled off in a fit of giggles.

A commotion from the garden doors drew my attention as Henry reentered the court, seemingly in a huff. He straightened his jacket and checked his hair, then put on a charming smile, so forced that his cheeks crinkled against the cloth of his masque. Where was Emma?

I tried to move through the crowd. A huddle of women stood between me and the garden. I slipped out as a distant voice called, "Ah, Henry! Can that little morsel of yours really do portraits?"

Candles lit the garden, elevated upon small pedestals as though imitating the flutter of fairies. Not many guests were out enjoying it—probably due to the chill.

A silver gown moved across the way. Emma. Alone. Even in a public location she should not be left unescorted. Anything could happen in a dark garden—particularly one this size peopled with men who referred to ladies as "morsels."

I should've kept dogging Dee, but I could not. "Are you well, Em— Mistress Areben?"

She didn't turn around, but her shoulders shook. Oh no. Was she crying? I walked up, tentative.

"I'm fine, Thomas." There were no tears in that voice. Only quivering anger.

"I see." Perhaps I should return to Dee.

She took a deep breath and then faced me. There was nothing for me to see since she still wore her event masque. "Are you out here to be some sort of knight?"

I frowned. She was the last person who needed a knight. And I was the last person who could *be* a knight. "I came to . . ." *To be with you.*

I hesitated long enough for her to turn and walk away. She headed for the hedges. I followed, though not invited. If she told me to leave, I would respect that. But I wanted her to know that I was with her. For her.

We passed a pond with seashells resting on each dormant lily instead of a flower. The garden hedges created avenues and shielded alcoves where couples could sneak away. One woman slipped into the shadows with a giggle. Her carnal lover wasn't far behind.

I adjusted the ruff at my neck. "Emma . . ." She rounded the end of a vine wall. "Wait."

A swish of cloak. I let myself run and caught her arm. Black gloves ran from fingertip to elbow. She didn't pull away, but she slowed. When she spoke again, her voice was cold. "Why are you following me?"

My hand dropped and I stopped. "To make sure you are well. I overheard a man mention your portraits to Henry—"

"You're a servant here. Don't you have duties to return to?"

That smarted. She was acting as though she wanted me to go. Maybe I should. But I'd already abandoned my post as Percy's servant. I wanted to know what had upset Emma. To defend her from whatever hold Henry had over her.

My thoughts ground to a halt with a single realization: I had put Emma over the plot.

That meant trouble. But I didn't leave. Why was I doing this? Staying? Why did I care?

"I brought some portrait paintings to show to the gentlefolk of the court." Emma pulled a roll of canvas from up her sleeve. "I got one to one person before Henry found me."

I unfurled the small roll beneath the moonlight and saw a young girl in a chair with wheels. Her brown hair swept over her shoulder, brushed but not styled. Though the thinness of her arms and neck showed her sick state, a radiant smile sent my own lips curving upward. Somehow Emma had captured beauty in the brokenness.

How did she *see* these things?

"It's astounding. They must have been impressed."

She took the portrait and returned it to her sleeve. "The gentleman was—even showed it to his wife. They have six children. I offered to paint their family, but—"

"Henry." A muscle in my jaw ticked. There was so much I wanted to say, to shout, but Emma's frustration billowed about her, and my own irritation wouldn't bring her any relief. So I breathed once. Twice. In. Out.

"You always seem to find me, Thomas. Why is that?"

"Perhaps because when I find you I always seem to find truth. Honesty. Emma, you're . . . you're *real*." Blast, that came out sounding eerie. I shouldn't open up. It would muddy the waters of Keeper versus Igniter. But my mouth wouldn't stop. "You're not afraid to speak out, to oppose wrong, to dig for truth. There's something authentic about you that I . . . I need." The eeriness continued. "I mean, that I desire." *Desire?* That made it seem like I desired *her*. "I mean—"

"I know what you mean."

I stared at Emma's black masque, her dark curls with pink silk flowers woven throughout. She could end this with a single sentence. She could avoid this dangerous conversation by dismissing me.

I hoped she would.

I prayed she wouldn't.

"What did you think of the masque performance?" However I expected her to respond, it wasn't with that.

I stepped back—finally realizing how close we stood—and shrugged. "It was fine." It was barely a memory. I'd spent the entire time watching her. "Though I don't think England's soil is magical enough to whiten human skin."

"I hated it." She trembled. I swept my cape off my shoulders and onto hers, though I suspected she wasn't actually cold. "Those Negroes in the shell were like *you*, Thomas."

I withdrew my hands. "What do you mean?" In the production they were treated as tainted because of their skin, but they turned white and "clean" once they reached land. Did she mean I was tainted by my plague?

"They acted as though the skin determines the worth of a human. As though being 'cured' or being of fair skin is the ultimate perfection." The tips of her gloved fingers reached for the left side—the plagued side—of my face. "But they're wrong. Your skin and plague don't define you."

I studied the grass. "It's easy to hear, but difficult to believe."

"Believe it."

"Do *you* believe it?" I caught her fingers. "About yourself?" About her own plague? This wasn't just for me—I knew that much from the passion behind her words.

Oh, how I wanted to see her face. "I want to know you, Emma." I stepped closer, crossing the final boundaries of propriety. "You can trust me."

I wouldn't tell anyone about her plague. I understood her

wanting to be accepted the way she was. No matter if her entire face was plagued, that wouldn't change my view of her.

I wanted to know I wasn't alone.

She leaned back, but not enough to break the touch of my hand on her masque. "Go ahead." She spoke so quietly I almost didn't catch it. Almost . . . forced.

I frowned.

"Take it off." She gestured to the masque.

My fingers itched to pull on the ties, but I dropped my arm. "No. It has to be your choice. I want you to feel free to show me your face, not pressured."

She rocked on her toes. I thought maybe she'd leave. But then she reached up and tore the masque from her face. It happened so fast I had to blink a few times to gather my bearings. Her form came into view beneath the moonlight.

There was no plague. Nothing.

Not a spot or blemish marring her dark-black skin.

Twenty-Four

Emma's chin lifted. Defiant.

A dark curl stuck to her inky skin—pressed there from her masque. A line of freckles ascended from her left upper lip and ended beneath her eye . . . like a constellation on a night sky.

I stared like an imbecile, unsure what to think. What to say. I couldn't mess this up, but all that kept repeating in my head was, *Slave skin. Slave skin. Slave skin.* I wanted the words to stop. They didn't feel like my words—they certainly weren't my heart.

Because Emma wasn't slave or servant.

She was . . . Emma. Powerful. Masked. Artist. And I imagined everything she'd been hiding and how *long* she'd been hiding. How alone she must have felt.

"I can see it in your eyes." She held my gaze, fury in hers. "You see only a lesser vessel. Slave Emma."

I shook my head. "No." Finally, my thoughts and emotions clicked into place, aligned in my mind. And I had the words—the *only* words. "I see *my* Emma."

Hesitant, I pulled her to me. Her stiffness melted away and she wrapped her arms around me.

My Emma. My Emma. My Emma.

I finally understood and felt no shame for declaring the words. We were spoken for . . . by each other. Something beyond both of us led us to each other, wove our stories into one, and on this night I realized they were too tangled to ever be separated.

That was fine with me.

"You're not disgusted?" she mumbled into my shirt.

The idea of finding her disgusting almost incited a laugh, but I swallowed it down. "No. Never. I was *surprised*, but it changes nothing." I didn't think I could have said those words a year ago, or even a few months ago. But because Emma never let my plague affect how she received and treated me, she unknowingly taught me how to think the same way.

"Henry and the Baron are the only ones who know." She stepped away. I drank in her features. Wide eyes ringed with white powder.

She gestured to the powder. "To keep my skin hidden." She tugged at a curl. "I lighten my hair as well with color power. It's been rather draining."

That was why she'd started looking so much thinner and ragged. "You're stunning." What else could I say? Her very soul was leaking out and I couldn't look away.

"In my own way, I suppose." She tucked a curl back into place.

There was no comparison. To see her skin and body was to glimpse merely a shell. As though rating a pearl by its oyster.

She lifted her masque back to her face.

"Wait . . ." I stopped her. "Why? Why must you hide?" It was illegal for anyone in England to make her a slave. What did she fear? Did she think someone might sell her to Spain?

"That's a story for another day, Thomas."

"Is it Henry?" I didn't want her to put her masque back on. What I once found beautiful now seemed only a slip of drab cloth compared to the beauty that lay underneath.

She didn't answer but held the masque against her skin. "Would you mind?"

I reached around to tie it for her, though I would have preferred to tear it away and burn it, so as to keep seeing her face, her quirks, her blinks. We had entered into something new. Something fragile, shared between only us.

I secured the knot but didn't move away. Inches separated us.

Until a hand wrenched me back by the collar. "Get off her, you *dog*."

I tripped trying to keep my feet and crashed into a hedge. It was springy and thrust me back into the light like a thousand angry hands. Henry Parker ripped my cloak from around Emma and threw it at me. I caught it as I steadied myself. Then he seemed to notice who I was. "Cyclops?"

Blast.

Henry looked between the two of us, one of his hands tight around Emma's wrist. "Is *this* why you kept him as your escort?" His knuckles whitened. I couldn't see a grimace on her face, but her eyes squinted. "Secret trysts?" His voice echoed in the garden. Others would hear. Others would come. "You could catch the *plague*!"

People would see and assume and Emma would be ruined.

I was ruined already.

"No." I pulled Henry off her. "We were—"

His fist crashed into my face and I went reeling. Screams. Onlookers. Black filled my vision, but I shook it clear, throwing my forearm up to ward off another blow that didn't come. Henry was bent over, clutching his hand to his chest.

My ears rang, but I felt very little pain.

He'd struck my plague and it broke his hand. Emma didn't run to either of us, but held herself stiff and tall. "Come, Henry. You've caused a scene."

Her ability to switch from vulnerable and masqueless to stiff and commanding left me in awe. I felt privileged that she let me in, even if just for a moment. She spun and marched back toward the palace.

"I will have your *head*, plague," Henry ground out. "Emma belongs to *me*." He followed her into the darkness.

"She doesn't *belong* to anyone!" I glared at him, though no one could see it through my masque. I fumbled with the clasp of my cloak. I needed to get away. In minutes, the entire court of King James would know about my plague and about my presence. I would be ruined and the plot put at risk.

But Emma. I had to follow.

I hurried past the gossiping onlookers, tugging my masque tight on my face, and rounded a hedge in time to catch Henry's angry voice. "You were *throwing* yourself at that plagued Keeper like some street trull."

Emma's reply was equally as vicious. "Better throwing myself at a plagued gentleman than chaining myself to a blackmailing scoundrel."

A slap of flesh on flesh hit my ears and I surged forward in time to see Emma strike Henry in return. Good girl.

Emma lifted her chin. The masque covered her face, but now I knew what to expect behind that guard. Fire. Courage. Strength. She swept past him, toward the doors.

My face burned. Pieces fell into place. Henry was using Emma somehow—threatening to reveal her skin color? She had shown herself to me, maybe even to convince me to help her.

It bent my mind imagining her needing—or asking for—help, as though a stallion needed to be taught how to buck off its captors. Couldn't she leave the Monteagle residence?

She trusted me.

I wanted to help her.

I *had* to.

I fumbled for my sword to find my belt empty. No weapons were permitted at the masquerade. Fists it was, then.

Henry rushed after Emma, but I caught his shoulder at the door. He spun so fast, I lost my grip, but he didn't strike me. He backed into the main court, knowing the crowd was a fight I couldn't win. And all he'd need to do to defeat me was raise his voice and scream, *"Plague!"*

Couples twirled in the center of the court. The orchestra filled one corner of the room. Henry barreled through gentlefolk in Emma's wake. I sidled along the walls, flattening myself against the wood to avoid being crushed by a woman's broad skirt. Once I reentered the bodies and heat and gossip, I remembered why I was at Whitehall at all.

Should I stop Henry or inform Percy? If I associated with Percy, then Henry might ask questions. I needed to distance myself from him—from the plotters—for good.

My heart failed at the thought.

Someone shoved me. Too many bodies in one place. Henry stopped beside John Dee and whispered in his ear. The waltz ended. Couples broke apart. And a multicolored mask remained in the center of the floor once all dancers left it. "May I have the court's attention!" Dee raised his hands high.

Judging by the king's frown and Queen Anne's raised eyebrows, this wasn't part of the evening's planned events. On the sidelines, I caught Henry eyeing Dee.

He'd told Dee—probably because he knew Dee could silence the room.

I quickened my pace along the wall. Where were the doors?

Dee's mask was fixed so firmly to his face, his eyes popped out of the holes like a bug's. "I have a gift for the king, but also for his people."

I slowed.

Dee scanned the crowd as the chatter turned to a hush and then curious murmurs. I was as curious as the next person . . . until his popping gaze landed on me. And stayed there. I couldn't move. This *was* about me and he knew I was plagued—he knew even before Henry divulged my secret. People turned to follow his gaze. Their frowns crinkled against their masques when they spotted me—the stunned masqued servant.

"One year ago, my beloved wife, Jane, and my three daughters were claimed by the Stone Plague."

King James made a small gesture with one hand and Percy appeared at his side.

"It convicted me . . . and *freed* me . . . to pour myself into the art of alchemy and color speech."

The king whispered something into Percy's ear. Percy nodded and then headed toward Dee, his hand sliding to the hilt of his sword. *Yes! Hurry, Percy. Stop his mouth!*

Dee's words quickened as all the while he stared at me. "And after a year of sacrifice, I return to London with a gift. This boy"—he swept a giant arm over his head, leveling a finger at me—"is dying of plague."

The gasps squeezed me until I couldn't breathe. Percy stumbled to a halt.

"Our king is hesitant to entrust his people to me, but here I stand before you—with you as my witnesses—that there *is* a cure, and I have it." The murmurs increased to a full-on clamor until Dee held out a hand. "Come here, boy!"

As though drawn by an invisible rope, I took one step after another toward Dee. What else could I do? The hall had turned mute. King James leaned forward from his seat on the dais, eyes narrowed.

I wanted to run.

I wanted to be cured.

I wanted to attack Henry.

He stood with Emma on the edge of the court. Watching. Emma had a hand to her mouth. Onlookers stepped away as I passed them. An aisle formed. When Percy looked to the king, King James held up a palm. To wait. To see what happened to me?

I reached Dee and stopped, the soft brush of my boots against the polished dance floor seeming like a scream of noise amidst such silence.

Dee breathed hard while looking at me. His breath smelled of weak wine. "Remove your masque, boy."

I glanced at Percy. What could I do? He gave no acknowledgment or direction, so I tore the masque away. Perhaps then Dee would see I *wasn't* a boy.

Dee grabbed my face with his gnarled fingers. I tried to pull back, but he hooked a finger in my stone eye socket and his thumb in the soft skin beneath my chin.

The touch felt invasive and triggered revulsion. But his strong fingers didn't relent, no matter how hard I pulled away. If anything, they tightened, digging their cracked nails into the soft skin beneath my jaw.

"I am neither Keeper nor Igniter." His voice slipped forth like a chant. Dark. Thick. Filling the room. "Knowledge, science, and the arts of alchemy are my masters. They have allowed me to be a warrior for you. A warrior against this plague. Behold!"

The lanterns flickered. Dee entered into a fierce muttering. I couldn't understand his words. They sounded like German.

Panic flooded me. My good eye left Dee's crazed popping eyes and searched until it found Emma. The whites of her eyes conveyed the same apprehension I felt. She stepped forward, but Henry yanked her back and hissed something in her ear.

My skin prickled and the room spun. The pressure of Dee's thumb and forefinger grew stronger and stronger, digging between my bones. Colors exploded in my mind like knives thrust through my skull.

A hundred voices—dark and chanting like Dee's words—hummed and rippled and surged. Could no one else hear them? They grew louder. Dee's fingers tighter. My fear stronger.

I let out a bellow and wrenched away. Too many colors. Too many sounds. I collided with the ground and cracked an elbow against the polished stone.

My cheeks burned. I felt—rather than saw—everyone's scrutiny upon me. I tried to push to my feet, but the dizziness was only just abating. Nothing felt different. Stiffness pulled at my left eye as it always had. It hadn't worked.

I rested on all fours, breathing heavily. Gasping.

It echoed in the dead room.

Then a woman screamed. I caught a face staring at me from the floor. From *in* the floor. I reeled away, but even as I crab-crawled backward, my mind registered the face. Combed-back dark hair, pale skin, and astonished wide blue eyes.

Two of them.

Mine.

Twenty-Five

I lifted a trembling hand to my face, barely registering the cacophony of voices. But before my fingers touched my skin, I knew I was cured. Because I could see the left side of the room without turning my head.

I closed my right eye—my good eye.

Still I saw. I saw King James on his feet, eyes round as oranges. I saw Percy, jaw slack. I saw Dee . . . shaking and sweating and then slumping to the ground. The king's men rushed to help him. Good thing, too, because the onlookers swarmed Dee next, shouting all manner of pleas.

"My baby has the plague, please come heal her!"

"Teach us how to do this!"

"What color did you command?"

"You don't speak to White Light at all?"

The loudest voice of all came from across the room. "Lies!" Emma pointed an accusing finger. "I don't know what colors you spoke to, but only White Light can cure. This isn't right."

Henry yanked her from the room as Dee was brought before

King James. I wasn't even sure Dee *heard* Emma. I kept touching my new eye—blinking for the first time in two years. It still felt stiff and grainy, like the plague rested *beneath* my skin now. But what did it matter?

I. Could. See.

"What the girl says is true," the king said. "White Light is the greatest and purest of the color powers."

"Then why has it not saved the plagued?" Even with Dee's bowed head and tone of humility, the question came out as a challenge.

This Dee fellow could be a great addition to the plot.

"We will talk of this privately." With a single look from the king, the guards took a compliant Dee away. Yet Dee had made his point.

I was cured.

I was new, and all of London had seen it. Even Emma. So why was she so vehement against Dee? Did she know something about him, or was she simply offended on behalf of White Light?

Dee was almost out of the room when a firm hand gripped my shoulder. I startled and looked up. Percy steered me out of the room into an antechamber off one side of the king's dais.

He lowered his mouth to my ear. "Say anything about the plot and I'll stab you in the back."

"What?"

His fingers dug into my muscles. Then he threw me into a chair and stood guard. The room was empty except us two. Before I could utter a word, King James himself strode in. My confusion and nerves doubled.

Here was the king. *Just* the king—in a room with two plotters who planned to murder him. King James wore clothing stuffed with padding to guard against knife attacks. His bent legs sent him into the room at a waddle. Three more men entered the room and stood behind him. Percy took his place at King James's side.

I stared at the king, trying to see what Percy saw. Trying to hate like Percy hated. Trying to remember all the things that King James had allowed to happen.

"Were ye truly plagued, young man?" the king asked in a thick Scottish brogue.

He didn't call me boy. "Yes, Your Majesty." I trained my eyes on the ground. It spread out so wide now that I had my full sight. A broad expanse of world revealed with each blink.

"When did ye contract the plague?"

I willed myself to act obedient and submissive. *Answer questions, do not offer information.* "Two springs ago. It started with my eye and spread to my forehead just this last outbreak."

"Where did ye contract i'? What be your name? And who be your master?" The questions came fast. Thick.

Don't look at Percy. Don't look. "I . . . I contracted it in York, sire." Percy stared me down from behind the king. "My name is Thomas and . . . and . . ." I couldn't tell him I worked for Percy and I didn't dare give him Father's pseudonym. "I am a caddy—an errand boy—for the Baron Monteagle." Or at least I was. "They are an Igniter family, sire."

"You were nae plant?"

I frowned and felt a surge of exhilaration to have both eyebrows obey. "A plant, Your Majesty?"

"A fake," Percy interrupted. "One of Dee's helpers."

"N-No. Of course not."

King James turned his eyes to Percy. "Do ye sense any lying?"

Percy appraised me a final time. "None, my liege."

"Very well. Send the man home."

Man. Not *boy.* The king believed me.

I was out of the chair and in the road before I could process the turn of events. Percy said nothing more to me, so I did the one thing that made sense. I headed back to the Whynniard house, taking in the winter stars with full sight for the first time in two years.

What would Father say when he saw me? Would he be proud? Would he give me my mask and color power?

I was cured. My entire goal for becoming a masked had been met. No more fear of death. The life or assassination of King James didn't change my fate.

For the first time, I was free.

And that freedom begged me to ask myself a certain frightening and dangerous question: Now that I was cured . . . did I still have reason to be part of the Gunpowder Plot?

Brown

Twenty-Six

"Thomas!" Father's entrance into the Whynniard house took me by such surprise, I drew my sword.

He stood in the doorway, one hand still on the knob. Frozen.

I sheathed my rapier. "I'm impressed you recognized me." I still hadn't gotten used to how broad the world seemed now that I took it in with two eyes—even our pathetic apartment seemed larger.

Father stood aghast for another moment, then slammed the door behind him and swept off his hat. "So King James is dead, then?"

"Um . . . no."

Confusion devoured the delight in his voice. "But how are you cured?" Then something like apprehension sent him backing toward the door. "What did you do, Thomas?"

The way he asked it sent a shard of guilt into my chest. What did he think I'd done? Given myself over to White Light? "I didn't do anything," I growled. "An alchemist in the king's court—John Dee—healed me."

"Igniter?"

"No." I told him everything. I told him about Henry finding me in the garden—though I left out any mention of Emma. I told how he'd revealed my plague to Dee and then Dee healed me in front of everyone. "He said he's neither Keeper nor Igniter. He has nothing to do with White Light—he just overpowers the different colors and bends them to his will."

Father paced the length of the entry. "Does Catesby know?"

"Not yet, but Percy will undoubtedly fill him in before the night is out."

Back and forth. Back and forth. "I don't trust it."

"I've always known a strong enough color command could cure me." I had been right all this time. Norwood hadn't believed me, Father hadn't believed me, even Emma hadn't believed me—yet here it was. I never stopped believing.

"But others have tried—never to any avail."

"They weren't strong enough," I said.

"*I* tried with your mother."

"Then you aren't strong enough!" Why didn't he get it? Dee did it. I was living proof. Father could protest and deny and scratch his honorable head all he liked, but both of my eyes now saw and blinked and held his gaze.

His chest heaved. His pacing stopped. "I suppose you're right."

"I'm sorry, Father." I hadn't meant to deflate him. "But . . . aren't you pleased that I'm no longer plagued?"

"Of course. I just . . . I want to understand so we can spread that to the rest of England."

I clamped my mouth shut. I had thought only of myself. My plague. My healing. My future.

Father thought of England. Of others.

There were so many ways I wanted to be different from Guy Fawkes. But in this . . . in this I wished I were more like him.

"If Igniters were able to see that the plague is not the Keepers' fault, maybe they'll stop capturing and killing us," he said.

I unbuckled my sword belt and hung it up. *"For every Keeper that dies, the Igniters believe someone is cured of the plague."* "You're right, Father. We should talk to Catesby. Perhaps he will know more about Dee." I tried to think broader—beyond the now. "What does this mean for the plot?"

"Nothing has changed."

"Not even with King James? You think his death and the death of Parliament will still cure the plague?"

"I do. And even if it doesn't, it will release Keepers from oppression and execution. We were successful in our offer on the undercroft of Parliament." He discarded his hat. "You will still have to keep your face hidden, Thomas. Those at the masquerade who saw you will recognize you on the street. You will draw attention to us."

"Why don't you give me my mask, then?" The words hung in the air like the plague hay bale outside the door. Bound with tension and silent messages.

Say yes.

"I will discuss it with Catesby."

At least it wasn't a no.

---

28 March 1605

"Are you *certain* you can see?" Catesby bent at the waist, putting his face right up close to mine and staring at the skin around my eye socket.

"Yes, sir." I tapped my cheekbone. "To my mind, it still feels stiff and tough, as though it is made of stone, but my sight is returned to me. I suppose those are the aftereffects of being plagued."

It had been three days since the masquerade and we'd secured the lease for the undercroft. But the gunpowder remained buried in the Whynniard tunnel.

Catesby shook his head and stepped back to the table in his meeting room at Lambeth. "I don't understand. You say John Dee was a guest of King James? Wouldn't that mean he's an Igniter?"

Percy stepped up at this. "He was not a guest of King James. Dee entered the court as part of Ben Jonson's troupe of masquerade conductors. Prior to the masquerade, John Dee had been refused from court. To my knowledge, he and King James have always disliked one another."

"Indeed?" Catesby rubbed his chin, smoothing out his trimmed beard. I looked between him and Father. When would Father bring up my mask?

We discussed plans of tunnel digging and funds and whether or not we should abandon the trapped gunpowder and risk ordering a new batch.

Catesby accepted my healing without much ado. His ease of acceptance sent a message of normalcy to the other plotters. It abated their fear, their overexcitement, their rash conclusions.

We went our separate ways after the meeting, each bolstered with the success of the plot and the continuous good news. Father stayed behind.

I thought back to Christmas when the plague had an outbreak and the tunnel collapsed and then Parliament was delayed. At that time it had seemed like such a sign from White Light—a sign that we should abandon the plot.

But what about these new signs? The undercroft? My healing?

I found myself not back at the Whynniard house but instead at the Bear, where I paid for an ale and a piece of parchment.

I needed to write Emma. I had so many questions—about her

safety, about Dee, about Henry, about White Light. I especially wanted to tell her how privileged I felt when she trusted me enough to show her face.

But that mustn't go in a letter.

If Henry was tightening his hold on Emma, I didn't want him intercepting the letter. What might he do if he knew she'd trusted me with something so private?

So I wrote with familiarity but avoided the topic I most wanted to address. If she replied, I'd know it was safe to say more.

Emma,

My plague is gone. I can't explain what happened at the Whitehall masquerade, but I'm curious—why did you believe Dee was lying? My sight has returned and I truly believe I might be cured.

Are you safe? You can come to me at any time. For anything. I want to talk. I am willing to listen. Even about White Light.

Thomas
The Bear at Bridgefoot

When I had posted the letter and returned to the Whynniard house, Father was already there. The question about my mask didn't even make it past my lips.

"Catesby says you are to have your mask." He sounded resigned. That wasn't the attitude I'd hoped for.

"Do you even want to make me one? Do you even wish color power upon me?" It sounded petty even to me.

"Of course, especially because you have shown yourself a loyal Keeper through and through since Norwood's death."

I tried not to squirm. How was it that when I *felt* loyal to the Keepers upon first joining the plot, he called me undecided, yet now that I was truly confused about White Light's role in this plot, he called me loyal?

"This isn't what I wanted it to look like," he said.

"I don't understand."

"When Maria caught the plague and died so quickly after your birth, I left you with your grandparents. I had planned to make you the strongest, most intricate mask. The more powerful I grew at color power, the better mask I could create."

I knew fathers made masks for their sons, and mothers for their daughters, but I didn't realize their color power affected the mask they made.

"So I joined the Spanish army—they are a Keeper country, and at the time they were at war with the Dutch. I could fight for Keepers without fighting against England. There I was free. And there I trained. During my travels I gathered the best materials—carving tools used by Keeper royalty, wood that had been preserved in a Keeper monastery and blessed every day for a century. But then I received word of your plague."

"And you never thought of me again." The thought didn't sting this time. I could see his life more clearly. Why would he leave his career for a dying son?

"Not until the day you lay in the mud at my feet." An expelled sigh left his body bent and withered-looking. "I'm sorry, Thomas. I gave up on hope, and you suffered for my cowardice."

"I forgive you." And this time, I meant it. We'd entered a new place of openness—a state of being that I'd always imagined a father and son to have. It felt stalwart—like nothing could crumble it.

"I've left what exists of your mask in Spain. It will take travel and time for me to retrieve it and complete it, but Catesby has given me permission and an errand to complete during the trip."

"When will you leave?"

"Next month." His answers to my questions came so swiftly and clearly, I didn't want to stop.

"Father . . . why don't you ever take off your mask?"

"Because no one has a right to see beneath it. I've built myself into what I am. I'm proud of that. The last time I took it off was for your mother."

"Will you ever take it off for me?"

A long pause. The scrape of feet on a rough wood floor. A clearing of the throat. "No."

It took two weeks for me to receive a return letter at the Bear, but when I opened it, a silver crown fell out.

18 April 1605
To Thomas Fawkes,

You've been rehired per the request of the Baron Monteagle. Included in this letter is advance payment. If you are willing, please report to the Monteagle house on the Strand on the first Monday of every month beginning in June. If you are not willing, please return the crown.

Respectfully,
Henry Parker

I laughed so loud, several patrons looked up from their dinners. I pocketed the letter—and the crown—and left. Henry thought I'd come running back to employment at his summons?

I imagined him having to write that letter. I imagined him fuming at the Baron's command. It was no mystery why the Baron wanted me rehired—or why Henry accentuated that it wasn't *his* desire. I had been a miracle at the masquerade. I then told King James I'd been working for the Baron Monteagle, and the king wanted to make sure it was true. Knowing the priorities of the Baron, he paid me a crown so he could say that the miracle boy worked for his family.

Status was everything to him—or at least worth a crown.

The fact that Henry replied to my letter—and not Emma—told me she probably never read it. Should I take them up on this offer to keep an eye on Emma? Or should I reject it because we were fast approaching Parliament?

I'd talk it out with Catesby at the meeting tonight—the last meeting we were to have before Father left for Spain to make my mask. I headed toward Lambeth. My fingers fiddled with the crown in my pocket. The weight of the coin felt like a promised future.

Perhaps I didn't need to talk to Catesby.

After all, I was cured and the plot was progressing. Once it succeeded, I'd no longer be with the group, right? We'd go our separate ways in freedom. I needed to have coin and a plan. I hadn't thought beyond curing my plague.

And if the plot failed, well, I'd likely hang.

I left the crown in my pocket. For now, I'd take it. In a few days I'd show up at the Monteagle house on the Strand and see what happened.

I turned onto Church Street. The spring showers had created quagmires in the streets—trapping carts in the mud. Gravel had been scattered over Church Street, but it didn't help much.

I picked my way across the dry patches of ground just as a large rock fell from the sky.

I sprang backward, swallowing a shout, the *thump* of the rock still resonating in my chest. I'd drawn my sword, ready.

What in Thames' name? Had someone sent it after me with color power? An Igniter?

Henry?

I glanced up, but there was no cathedral steeple to throw it off of. I adjusted my footing, ready for an attack, but one final glance at the rock stilled my reflexes. It held a familiar shape. A stocky branch of stone off one side, ending in a small point.

It wasn't a rock.

It was a *pigeon*.

I nudged it with my toe and it rolled over, exposing a feathery underside with a half-stone wing. The pigeon had died from the plague *in the sky*. That meant the plague had spread through the beast so swiftly it had gone from flapping to falling within seconds.

Was there another outbreak?

I sheathed my sword and bolted for Catesby's home. I made it through the door, up the stairs, and into the parlor before I'd taken three even breaths. I burst into the crowded room, but the first person my eyes alighted on was not Catesby. It wasn't even a plotter.

There by the fire, with a parti-colored mask on his belt, stood John Dee the alchemist.

"Thomas, at last!" Catesby shut the door behind me. "Meet our newest member."

Twenty-Seven

What was *he* doing here?

Maybe he can cure the pigeon.

I snorted at White Light's jest before I realized it had spoken to me. For the first time in *months*. Since before the masquerade and the tunnel collapse and my employment by the Baron.

Here it was and its first words were about a *pigeon*?

I wasn't sure what emotion was showing on my face—shock at Dee's appearance? Fear at White Light's voice? Humor over the pigeon statement?

"How's your eye?" Dee asked.

My hand drifted upward, tapping the skin almost of its own accord. "Still cured."

"Good."

I thought about what this meant. John Dee. Newest member. Catesby told him about us?

The trust I'd had in Catesby when he'd added members in the past—Keyes, Bates, the Wright brothers—cracked with this new addition. Maybe because Dee seemed so eager to grab attention.

Father seemed to feel the same way. "You just turned every eye upon you at the Lady's Day masquerade," he said to Dee. "That puts the rest of us at risk. Why are you here when you're not even a Keeper?"

"I'm not an Igniter, if that's what you're implying."

"It's not." Father's response came out flat. Thin.

Dee cleared his throat, but it didn't strike me as a nervous clearing. More like preparation for a speech. I still hadn't gotten past my surprise to offer him a proper thank-you for changing—and saving—my life.

I could have done that, you know. You just never asked.

Dee's stare bore into me. Did *he* know White Light was speaking to me? I wanted to shout, "It's not my fault. I don't know why it keeps picking me." But I *was* the one who spoke to it before Christmas—before the tunnel collapse.

So maybe it was my fault.

Dee sat in a chair with his back to the fire, blocking the heat. The chill hit the room immediately. "I allowed Catesby to question me, as is, apparently, the standard with this plot. But I feel it only fair to allow the rest of you to do the same."

The flaming backdrop turned Dee into an imposing figure. He gestured to the other seats. "Please, sit."

We sat. I wanted to know his story. I wanted to understand.

"Why do you want to take part in this plot?" Father asked.

Dee leaned back in the chair. "I was once the top advisor of Queen Elizabeth."

His statement struck me like stone knuckles to the gut. "Queen Elizabeth was the Igniter monarch who started this war!"

Dee nodded serenely, like he'd expected this response. Maybe even hoped for it. "I didn't care what side she was on, and she didn't care what side *I* was on. In her mind, I was a neutral party—able to give advice without bias. And for me, she provided the finances and support for my research, travels, and pursuit of knowledge. We had a deep friendship." The first semblance of vulnerability bled into his voice. "King James has no interest in allowing me back into court, hearing my advice, or funding my research. He has no respect for what Queen Elizabeth valued."

"So this is about your pride." Wintour loosed the statement as fearless as the lawyer he was.

Dee shrugged. "Perhaps. We are all passionate about something—you about Keeper persecution and I about knowledge and color arts. I spent half my lifetime creating a library of research, guidance, and tomes on color power. The queen herself visited my home and library at Mortlake weekly. But when I returned to London this past December, my house was destroyed and the library was ransacked."

The intake of several hissing breaths punctuated his statement. Any masked would have loved to have access to such research on color power and White Light and even swordplay. Quality books and research were difficult to come by, even for St. Peter's Color School. To lose such valuables would have been devastating.

"Queen Elizabeth helped fund my collection and I, in return, helped guide her sea captains and generals and other masked leaders. But King James said its destruction was not the crown's problem. He placed no value in my lifetime of work serving the crown. So you see, gentlemen, why I want a hand in removing him from the throne and raising up little Princess Elizabeth."

"For money?" Wintour asked. I liked how he continued to prod into Dee's motivations.

"For *status*." Dee adjusted his chair to the left of the fireplace and warmth flowed back into the rest of the room. "For purpose. Surely you can understand that. I went from being invaluable to the crown and a *world*-changer through my research to an outcast from the court with a ruined library."

Wintour nodded but then asked, "Why doesn't King James trust you?"

"Because I'm against White Light. You're Keepers. My aversion to White Light should please you."

"Keepers aren't against White Light," Father corrected. "Just against responding to its calls, because it addles the mind and makes you power-hungry. Proven by Igniters."

Emma wasn't power-hungry. I didn't appreciate the generalizations and paranoia that Keepers seemed to hold about White Light and Igniters.

Silence reigned until the crackles of the fire took the throne.

Finally, Catesby looked around. "Satisfied?"

I stared at Dee—he stared back. Waiting. So I gave in. "How did you cure me?"

"I used a color Compulsion. It sent me to my bed for two weeks after the masquerade."

So it *had* come down to strength. "But how are you so strong?" And how could I become the same?

"The same way I'm so old. Time. You must never relent in your study of color. There is more to learn than you will ever understand." Dee stood from the table. "Are we done here, Catesby? I have things to attend to."

Percy addressed Catesby as well, though jutted his chin toward Dee. "I just want to know why we need him."

Catesby opened the door—a signal that we were finished. But not before he said, "Because he can open the tunnel back up for us. He can unearth our gunpowder."

30 May 1605

"When I return, I'll have your mask." Father slung his cape over one arm and donned his broad-brimmed black hat. With his mask beneath, he looked a force to be reckoned with.

"When will you be back?" Even two months after the masquerade, the full movement of my face and scope of my vision felt unnatural. Sometimes I imagined my skin was stiffening again. Maybe the paranoia would never fully abate.

"Travel is never predictable. That's how adventure shows up." Father had decided my duty to the plot was more important, so I was staying behind. But that was exactly why I wanted to go. I wasn't sure what my role was anymore. I knew my external duty—serve the Baron, blow up the king, discover the new Parliament date.

But the closer and closer we got to setting the plot in order, the less I liked the idea of murdering so many people. How did that make Keepers any different from the Igniters? The Igniters murdered hundreds of us over the course of years. We would return the favor in a single night.

It seemed more a way to start another war than to stop one.

Father stepped outside and mounted the dapple-grey horse provided to him by Catesby. "Likely a month or two."

I nodded. At least he gave me an estimate.

"The Keepers need you while I'm gone, Thomas. You are a strong enough swordsman to defend them." With a squeeze of his heels, Father was off. Trot, trot, trotting through the wet morning mist left over from May's rain showers.

I watched him go. My tension and nerves left with him, as though stowed in his saddle packs. He was safe from Henry Parker's inquiries and he'd return with my mask. I just needed to bide my time.

———— ✦ ————

I returned to the Whynniard house and prepared for my first day returning to Monteagle's service. I was ready to see Emma again.

Emma.

Her name rested in my mind, so simple—the opposite of her. Like a mask hiding the strength and complexity of her character. I'd waited dutifully until my day of service—not writing her any letters, not inquiring after her.

Not risking my chance to see her and confirm her well-being.

The time I spent waiting for this day had gnawed at my innards as though I'd swallowed the Stone Plague.

It had been a whole year since I discovered Emma dispatching the ruffians by the Tower of London. We were quite different people back then. I was now seventeen and about to receive my mask.

And she . . . Perhaps she wasn't so different. But she made herself known to me. Vulnerable. And that made *me* different.

I didn't just want to see her. I wanted to know more about her desires to become a portraitist. I wanted to make that happen.

I wanted to be the opposite of Henry and the Baron and encourage her to use her talents as cobblestones to pave the way to her independence. I wanted her to rattle the earth and be the start of a new masquerade that told the story of a young black girl who had color power beyond the men and peers of her city and wasn't afraid to use it.

The Strand was one of the widest roads in London and my breaths always came easier because I wasn't shoving through bodies or dodging puddles of refuse. It felt cleaner than the other streets too. People dumped their waste out their back windows rather than the front.

That's how you knew the wealthy lived here.

I arrived at the Monteagle house on the Strand through a back alley, circling around so that they wouldn't see me arriving from the direction of the Whynniard house. I knocked on the back door and Ward the footman answered. He didn't greet me or say anything other than, "This way."

This house was much smaller than the Monteagle home in Hoxton, but also more luxurious. Oil lamps in every glass window—though unlit because it was still early afternoon. Embroidered curtains hung delicately tied away from the glass, and each piece of furniture was stained a deep, rich burgundy.

I entered a sitting room. The Baron stood at my entrance, alone in the room. "Ah, good, you have accepted our offer."

I gave a bow. "Thank you for your generosity." Though I knew the Baron's offer existed only to increase his reputation as a benefactor. He showed a height of character in taking me back on despite the fact I'd endangered his entire family with my plague.

"You will accompany me to Whitehall today. I have business to attend to."

"Of course, sir." Whitehall? Was he visiting the king?

I followed him toward the front door. I wanted to ask about Emma. I wanted to ask about Henry.

But it wasn't my place. And no matter how many glances I sent to the hallways or shadows, I saw no one but Ward.

We rode to Whitehall. I used one of the stable horses, thankful I had learned how to ride at St. Peter's. It didn't take long and I wondered why we'd ridden at all when it was so close, but then I remembered that the Baron's heartbeat survived on appearances.

With the clip of each horse's hoof, people of the street looked up. They saw, first, the Baron and then me. Some returned to their business without a second glance, but others—the more wealthy who had been at the masquerade—watched me with widening eyes and lowering jaws. ·

They recognized me as the plagued boy who'd been healed.

And now I understood why the Baron took me with him.

I kept my horse a half-length behind the Baron's. We took the road past the House of Lords. I averted my eyes, which may have looked more suspicious than if I had glanced at it.

"Parliament meets here." The Baron pointed.

It took me a moment to realize he was talking to me. I thought it would go against his high status to speak to me in such a familiar manner in public.

"It is an honor to serve King James as one of his members."

I was sure it was. But supposedly it had also been the Baron's "honor" to serve the Keepers before he was imprisoned by Queen Elizabeth. The Baron was too much of a follower to commit to any side. As long as the monarch was pleased with him, he would remain whatever that monarch wanted. "How often does Parliament meet?"

"It varies—especially with the plague outbreaks. The next meeting is slotted for November fifth, but who knows if that will hold." Just like that he had handed me the information I needed. I pocketed the date—the final missing piece from the plot.

We arrived at Whitehall and the Baron entered for whatever business he had. I stood with the horses by the steps to the main hall. This is where I'd seen Emma in her silver gown. The last time I was here, I'd seen her face.

I could still bring it up to my memory—under the moonlight and dark as the most alluring shadow. Was she still at the Hoxton house?

The Baron didn't return for another three hours. I remained standing as an obedient and patient manservant, though the wandering of my mind could entertain me for only so long.

When he finally exited, he looked pleased.

He mounted and waited for me to join him astride my borrowed horse before he asked, "Have you ever met the Earl of Salisbury?"

I thought of the short, stooped man speaking to King James at the masquerade. "Isn't he a noble?"

"The king raised the little man to the peerage last year. The king calls him 'my little beagle.'" The Baron laughed, then threw a glance over his shoulder back toward Whitehall as though the Earl might be following us.

I didn't laugh, though I probably should have indulged the Baron.

I knew how irritating disparaging titles could be—like *Cyclops*. Though I'd take Cyclops over "little beagle" any day.

"Anyway, good man. Good conversation." The Baron cleared his throat. "My brother-in-law, Francis Tresham, comes to town in a fortnight. He will likely require your services."

I bowed in understanding. "Of course, sir."

The Baron adjusted his reins and didn't speak again until we'd returned to the Strand. By this time, it was evening. I saw to the horses and my stomach rumbled as they munched on a mound of hay.

I entered the home to ensure my duties were no longer needed and nearly collided with Emma around a corner.

She reeled backward and I instinctively put out a hand to catch hers so she wouldn't fall. "Thomas!" She yanked her hand from mine, spun on her heel, and walked away.

I hadn't even had time to process her presence.

"Ah yes, the Cyclops is back." Henry didn't even grant me a greeting as he turned to pour the Baron some brandy. The Baron snickered as he had when talking about the Earl's nickname.

But I remained staring after Emma. She practically *fled* from me. Apparently her thoughts during our separation had taken a different turn than mine. Perhaps she was ashamed for having shown me her face. Or maybe she was angry about—even afraid of—my cure?

I couldn't stop the plummet of my stomach or the frustration of not understanding. If I was to be a bauble on the Baron's belt, that wasn't worth two crowns per month.

"I think he scared away my poor betrothed." Henry handed the Baron the balloon glass.

My mouth went dry. Betrothed?

Henry turned slowly with a wolf smile. "Hadn't you heard?"

"Congratulations," I said without emotion. So that was why Emma had reacted the way she did. I faced the Baron. "Will you be needing anything else, sir?"

The Baron, more focused on his brandy than the conversation, didn't spare a glance. "No. Thank you."

I bowed and left, my cheeks burning. As I reached the back door, Emma showed up to hand me my hat from the rack. I took it but couldn't choke out a thank-you.

She opened the door. "Good day, Mister Fawkes." Her voice came out soft and subdued—a new side of Emma that I suspected came from binding herself to Henry Parker.

I wanted to yank her from the house and remind her who she was. She wasn't some baron-in-training's plaything. She wasn't some wealthy wife who would have to hide her own skin color at the command of her husband.

She was fire and life.

She was awe and starlight.

But because I didn't want to embarrass her and I didn't want to bring down Henry's wrath upon her, I poured all those words, all those thoughts, all those emotions into the most sincere bow

I could execute. I held her gaze and willed her to see that I still admired her . . . and that I still knew her core.

If this was the last time I would see her, I didn't want her to see any animosity or judgment.

"Good day, my lady."

Twenty-Eight

It probably wasn't my best idea to expel my frustration with my rapier blade, but what were swords for?

I wended my way through the dark alleys, hand on my hilt. Itching to use it in a battle once and for all—and to redeem my pathetic attempts during Norwood's capture eight months ago. Without color power, I'd have to be more creative in my attempts to free the Keeper prisoners.

I passed along the back side of the Strand, ducking under the lit windows and sliding through the shadows. I'd walked this path so many times, I knew the proper route of shadows to reach the Tower undetected.

Two revelers stumbled out of the Duck and Drake, masks swinging on their belts just as drunkenly as their owners. That was where I'd first seen Father and not known it. I'd thought he was reveling, but he'd actually been swearing himself into the Gunpowder Plot.

As the two men swayed down an alley, three dark shadows slunk behind them. I pulled up short. The three followers carried swords and rope. They wore their masks—all of which were Blue. They struck me as Igniters out for blood.

Or worse . . . for masks.

I couldn't let those drunks get jumped and turned into the Tower. They made it to the docks before the three Blues revealed themselves by sending a rope around one drunk's ankle using color speech. Igniter scum. The Keepers didn't even scream, the ale too thick in their minds to allow them to register fear.

I stepped behind the Igniters and drew my sword. "Leave them be." I attacked before they could turn, adrenaline sending my sword slices and parries through the air at a speed beyond my regular skill. One Igniter caught a foot over a plank and stumbled backward into the Thames. Two to go.

One drunk guffawed at the blunder . . . until a sword pierced through his left lung. He screamed and dropped to one knee. When the Igniter withdrew his sword, the wounded drunk flopped sideways, half his body over the edge of the dock, pouring his red blood into the river. Keeper.

"How dare you." I faced off with the remaining two, bending my wrist and holding the blade a few inches lower so as to lure them closer by giving the impression of a shorter blade and shorter reach of my arm.

One took the bait. I deflected his strike easily with my guard. A quick jab into his shoulder broke his stance and sent him reeling back. That bought me some time. It wouldn't be long before they used their color pow—

A slap of water hit my face.

The shock of cold and stench broke my footing. I swept the water from my face with my free arm in time to see the two Igniters advancing—both wearing their masks and swords aloft. I deflected their united attack, but another splash struck my face.

And another.

Another.

There was nothing for it. I reeled backward—away from where I knew the swords to be. If I couldn't see, I couldn't fight. But I didn't have much of a choice as scoops of water pummeled me. I barely sucked in a fresh breath between attacks and focused on keeping my fist around my sword.

A sting at my thigh. I yelled. The jab was weak, but that meant they were close enough to send their points into my heart. I tried to outrun the water, but the attack doubled. The other Igniter must have emerged from the Thames because a dock barrel upended and rolled along the boardwalk toward my shins. I attempted a leap over it, but it caught my leading foot and I fell hard on my back.

The barrel changed directions and came for my head. I scrambled for my feet, but the constant drenching of Thames water made it hard enough to breathe, let alone regain my balance. I couldn't find it in me to flee. Not with a sword in my hand. Not if it meant abandoning these reckless drunk Keepers to the noose.

But were they worth dying for?

I hauled myself to my feet with the help of a line of crates, blinking the water out of my eyes.

Then another figure strode onto the dock, behind the two Igniters. A cloak billowed about his body and a hood covered his face. He didn't still his footfalls. The Igniters spun.

This new figure had no sword, but his fists held two small daggers. Daggers of stone.

Fear devoured my bravery. This was the man—this *had* to be the man who had been on the bank of the Thames. The abandoned dagger on the shore matched.

The way he entered the battle left no room for doubt . . . We were all dead men.

The two remaining Igniters focused their attacks on the new man. I turned to get the remaining drunk Keeper out of there. The stabbed Keeper had bled out into the Thames. His skin was so pale and drained that, even if he were still breathing, I could offer no help.

I dragged the remaining Keeper up the stairs away from the boardwalk. "Where do you live?" I demanded.

He kept looking over his shoulder at the mystery man. Too drunk to be concerned for his comrade. If fate favored him, he might wake up and never remember the flopping bloodless body of his drinking companion.

"Where do you live, man?"

Still no answer. The sounds of fighting were distant enough that I spared a glance over my shoulder.

The cloaked man darted in with his daggers and cut each Igniter. One. Two. They barely stumbled. They barely checked their swords. His little daggers would do nothing against them except stick them like annoying bee stings. Should I help?

Blast it all.

I shoved the Keeper into the Duck and Drake. The innkeeper had his nightcap on and was carrying a candle to lock the inn door. I flicked him a twopence. "Put this man up and don't let him leave until he's sober."

I didn't stay to see if the innkeeper caught the coin.

I didn't stay to see if the Keeper kept his feet when I released his arm.

Sword still drawn, I returned to the dock. The third Igniter had crawled from the Thames and retrieved his own sword. It was now three on one. They all bled red blood with white strings from their sword arms.

Should I really take this mysterious man's side? One of *his* daggers had been used to try to cut Emma when I first met her in London.

But leaving a man to fight three-on-one made me as much a coward as he would be a hero. So I ran down the boardwalk, sword at the ready.

The sopping-wet Igniter met my advance. I dispatched his sword in a single defensive twirl, but my strike stilled at a scream.

The other two Igniters had dropped their swords and clawed at their throats. Was the man attacking them with something using his color power? They recoiled from him.

A sliver of color peeked through the mystery man's hood—Yellow. Or was it Brown? I peered closer.

He shouted something. The brim of my hat yanked down over my face and stuck there. Something hard struck my side. I toppled and threw out my arms to catch myself, but the post of the board-walk caught me in the temple.

⁙

I woke to pain in my ribs and scattered light in my eyes. Someone kicked me again in the side and I groaned, waving a hand. A third kick came, harder.

Now I was angry.

"Get up, beggar. This is my dock and you're deterring custom-ers. As if the plague wasn't enough trouble for one morning. You're lucky I haven't confiscated your sword."

My sword. I blinked my eyes open. My lashes met the press of black cloth. Beams of light slipped through the weave of my hat. I yanked the brim up and made out a man in brown fisher garb with a coil of rope over his shoulder. A few other men wandered the docks.

I could see out of only one eye. My hand flew up to the left side of my face. Not stone. Just tender and so swollen my lid couldn't open.

"Looks like you lost." The fisherman chuckled and headed up the boardwalk. "Learn to pick your fights, boy."

I stumbled to my feet, my sword still in hand. I barely looked as I sheathed it, trying mainly to keep my balance. My memories slogged through my fatigue and headache, trying to catch up.

Then I saw three forms lying on a tarp. I inched closer until I saw the webbed grey plague ringing their throats, petrifying their air supply. Their masks were smashed practically to powder and sprinkled over their chests like bread crumbs.

These were the three Igniters from last night.

All dead.

All plagued.

And I'd glimpsed the mask of the man who'd done it. The flash of Yellow repeated in my head—but it was so shadowed. It might have been Brown. Or even Red.

Blast it all!

All I knew was this was the same figure who'd lurked at the bank of the Thames. The man with the odd daggers. He'd sent my hat brim over my eyes—as if he was afraid of my knowing his identity.

Did I know any Yellows?

What was he doing every night with those daggers? And why did he leave me on the dock to wake so confused?

The Thames churned, muddy like poor man's stew. Its spinning current promised chill and death. I watched the brown water, smelled the fish slime from the docks, and heard gulls overhead, circling for the discarded fish guts. The noise of the dockworkers beat like a drum against my skull, shoving my questions to the wayside. I was in no shape to riddle out these new questions. I barely made it back to my bed in the Whynniard house before my knees gave out.

Still, I forced myself to pull off my boots and lay them by the door. Then I removed my hat.

A folded slip of paper fell to the ground, sticking to the grime on my boot. Where did that come from? I unstuck it and opened it.

Tomorrow. In our alley. The handwriting swept across the page with long handles and sharp peaks—fierce and elegant.

Our alley?

A relieved laugh escaped me.

Emma. She had slipped it into my hat on my way out of the Monteagle house on the Strand. And "our alley" was the alley in which we first came together in London.

She wanted to meet. It wasn't the end of us. I should have known she wouldn't dismiss me like that—after everything.

I headed to the alley shortly before the morning's ninth bell. I wanted to wait for Emma, not the other way around. I didn't know what time she'd arrive, so I planned to be there all day if need be.

Caddies ran to and fro, delivering messages for their masters. I passed London Bridge and a string of nicer homes. An African girl hung out laundry on a rope stretched from one window to the neighbor's. I stared at her as I jogged past. For the past two months, every time I passed a person with skin darker than mine, I imagined what they could be. I imagined what talents hid inside of them that they couldn't show to others because Europe didn't understand them yet.

What would they be like if they were all allowed to don masks, like Emma did? Or better yet, what could they be if people didn't halt or judge or command based on skin?

My entire thinking had been flipped. It was disorienting. Overwhelming in a way that demanded change and action. What talents rested inside this girl hanging laundry? Was she an actress? Did she have a mind for science? Was she a powerful color-speaker like Emma?

The church bells chimed nine.

I ran on, careened to the right, and skidded to a halt in the alley where I first saw Emma in London. It was empty save the patches of shadows. Now, more than ever, I wanted to see her and talk.

I kept my eyes trained on the main road. Every gown that passed caught my eye. Every woman with summer gloves on or a lace ruffle at the throat. She could be Emma . . . expertly hiding her skin color.

But she'd shown herself to me. She'd trusted me and let me in. I knew what hid behind her mask and beneath her gloves, and I felt incredibly privileged.

Perhaps she wouldn't come. Maybe she'd changed her mind, or Henry found out about her message. That thought grew a lump in my throat. He'd called her his betrothed.

An hour passed. I paced the alley.

A couple walked past with a black servant girl in a stained brown dress and apron trailing behind, balancing a basket on her hip. I shook my head and paced the other direction. My mind still jumped to the word *servant* when I saw someone with dark skin.

My culture had affected my thinking without my consent. How many other things had it shaped without my knowing it? It made me want to examine things—to seek the heart of matters. Of skin color, of Keepers, of Igniters, of White Light, of all my assumptions.

How many of us acted and spoke out and fought for beliefs that we held because our environment told us to? As much as I wanted to blame my England, I knew the blame sat with me. I hadn't trained myself to discern. To examine. To seek the *source*.

That was about to change.

"Have you already forgotten what I look like?"

I spun and found myself face-to-face with the girl with the basket. Then I saw the curls. The constellation of freckles. The wide eyes. "Emma."

She stood there. No emotion. No comment. But her fingers picked at the reeds of the basket. Was she . . . nervous?

I found my voice. "Not forgotten. I've thought of you every single day since the masquerade. I just . . . wasn't expecting you to show up in—"

"Servant clothes?"

"—disguise."

"Oh." Then she grinned. And my heart turned so violently in my chest it ached with a confusing bittersweetness. I wanted the world to see Emma's smile, but she'd had to hide it. For years.

"You're so beautiful." The words slipped out before I could catch them. But I didn't want to stop them. I never wanted to stop telling her.

"And you're so . . . bruised." She wrinkled her face. "What happened?"

"Ah yes." I tapped the portion of my face battered from the dock post. "I guess you still have to stare at the unsightly Thomas."

"Your plague was never unsightly." She adjusted the basket on her hip.

"Shall I take that for you?" I reached for it, but she pulled it out of reach.

"No. It's already odd enough for people to see you talking to

265

me in public. But should you carry my basket for me, word might spread through the web of servants. The less conspicuous we are, the better."

"But . . . you're free right now. You're . . ." I gestured to her. "You're not having to hide yourself. Can't you walk and do as you please?"

"I'm sure I could, but all of London would be watching."

"I just . . . don't understand." I knew black skin was uncommon— my own reaction to it was proof enough of that. Curiosity was natural. But why would it hinder her?

"You were at the masquerade, Thomas. You saw the performance." She brushed her fingers along my bare arm. "You are pure-skinned."

Absurd. That she would call *me* pure-skinned—a man who had been plagued for two full years. But that was how the Masque of Blackness presented the people of England. "It shouldn't have anything to do with skin! Plagued or African or masked. There's too much fear and prejudice in England right now." I ground my teeth. "Because of King James and the war between Keepers and Igniters. If people would just—"

"You've had one moment of clarity and now you think you have all the answers." She gave a grim smile. "Take a breath, Thomas. There has always been fear. There will always be fear. It's up to us to stand tall, even when the fear demands we bow to it."

"I'm fighting for freedom, Emma." I couldn't tell her any more than that, but I wanted her to know I was doing something. Once we got a Keeper on the throne, we could stop the war. The plague. The deaths. We could make a new England. We had Dee on our side now.

Igniters controlled us. Well . . . *most* Igniters. Not Emma. Never Emma.

Once the Igniters—except Emma—were exiled, England would have order. Freedom. Keepers accepted others.

"Be careful, Thomas." The way she said this sent my skin tingling. "Be careful that you're fighting for the right cause."

I snorted. "What, for the Igniters?"

"No. Don't fight for the Igniters. Don't fight for the Keepers."

I pressed both hands against one of the house walls, taking a deep breath. "Shouldn't I fight for what I believe in?"

"It's not as simple as that. Fighting for what you believe in is too subjective."

I raised my head to meet her eyes.

"We need to fight for *truth*. Your beliefs can be misguided."

"So can yours," I ground out, defensive, though I wasn't sure why. Hadn't I been thinking the same thing before she entered the alley?

"Exactly. Both Igniters and Keepers and people in between fight for their own agendas . . . instead of being willing to discuss and seek what's *right*."

I tried not to sneer. "Do you really think there's some ultimate truth out there?"

She laughed. "Of course there is! It is the foundation of morals and justice. A foundation of truth represents what life was intended to be."

"And how do *you* know what was intended to be?"

Somehow I sensed the answer before she gave it. "I go back to the beginning."

"The White Light?" I rolled my eyes. Both of them. "You're so deceived by Igniter talk you can't see it."

She pointed a stiff finger to my face. "Have you ever responded to it?"

"Yes! And it gave confusing signs."

"So ask for more. Keep seeking. Don't you see?"

"I *want* to see!" My shout echoed down the alley and I sucked in a breath. Even though my eyes were finally clear, I still felt so blind. Our reunion wasn't going at all how I'd hoped. "Emma . . . White Light wasn't the one who got rid of my plague. John Dee did."

Her eyes narrowed. "He abuses the color powers. Colors are meant to be coaxed, spoken to in their own language. Treated with respect—and then they obey. Dee's ways *force* colors to obey. To control them without White Light's authority is to break them and twist them to do things they shouldn't."

I agreed that he was knowledge-hungry, but how was that any different from Igniters? "Whatever he is or does, his way worked. How many more people could he cure if King James gave him authority to?"

"I'm sure King James has his reasons."

I wanted her to be right, but did she know how the king called himself a god? Did she know how he exiled every Keeper? Did she know that there was a plague outbreak the day he rode into London to settle on the throne? "King James promised the Keepers freedom, but the moment he sat on the throne, he doubled the restrictions!"

"That's because the moment he stepped foot in England, Keepers tried to murder him! I'm sure that made him think twice."

Blood pumped in my ears. I wanted to vent these thoughts, but I didn't want our meeting to be an argument. I wanted to hold her passions and views, but I needed to know they were right. I needed to do what both she and I had already expressed—get to the core of things. Go to the beginning.

But on my own.

I couldn't let her shape my decision just because I cared about her. And I couldn't let Father shape my decisions just because I wanted to please him.

I swallowed once. Twice. The words stuck thick and bulgy in my throat. I forced them down and sought a new avenue of conversation. "Was it hard to get away?"

She shook her head and her dark, earthy curls swept into her face. "It will be harder to return. Henry will be angry."

I wanted to go somewhere and really *be* with Emma. Not hiding in some dark alley, cold and suspicious-looking, at risk of having a bucket of waste upended on our heads. So I held out an arm. "May I treat you to a pastry?"

Her somber face broke into a grin. "Only if it's the baker on Pudding Lane."

I raised an eyebrow. "The best."

She looped her arm in mine. I let her keep the basket. One of the cloths gave a poor attempt at concealing a lump. "Why aren't you wearing your mask?"

"There's so much paranoia in the streets about the plague and the war between Igniters and Keepers, best not to add black skin with a mask to the mix. There is no law against my having a mask, but neither is there a law in favor of it. It's those grey lines that send innocents to the noose."

We walked slowly down the cobblestone street, turning onto another wide lane made of dirt. Two men stood on either end of an enormous log held up by crossed mounts, each one gripping the end of a saw. Back and forth. Back and forth.

We smelled the bakery before we actually saw the wooden sign displaying a painted stalk of wheat. Fresh bread, scones, and warm pasties filled with hash. Every few sniffs would mix with the stench of raw meat and fish from the surrounding stalls. I alternated salivating and gagging.

Emma hung back while I stepped up to the baker's window. A young girl with a long blond braid slung over her shoulder flipped a bowl of dough upside down onto a huge flat wooden spatula. Then she shoved it into the burning oven.

The heat of the oven radiated through the serving window. It would be a nice workplace in winter, but I didn't envy the girl now that summer was heating up. I ordered two scones.

She handed them to me and I used one of the cloths from Emma's basket to keep in the heat. Fresh. Perfect.

We wended our way down Pudding Lane. Scattered straw helped lessen the amount of muck on the street—one of the busiest lanes for the poor of London.

I led Emma around a pushcart and through a group of women shopping for vegetables. A shipyard worker nearly ran us over with a basket of fish on his shoulder. We finally made it to Grace Church Street and then London Bridge, and then I knew where I'd take her.

We left London Bridge and turned right onto the Bankside, then to Maiden Lane. Emma's intake of breath told me when she saw it.

The Globe Theater.

Built a few years ago by the Lord Chamberlain's Men, the daub was still white in the weathered grey wooden framing, rising three stories from the earth. The green roof consisted more of moss growth than thatch. The promise it held of story and performance from Sir William Shakespeare was enough to lift it to a height of awe.

From its brick base up to the thatched roof, the round theater represented acceptance for all. Built with cheap materials, it was accessible to both rich and poor. Currently, the wooden doors were closed, but I caught movement through the small square windows in the second story.

The actors were there. Perhaps even Shakespeare.

Emma and I found a place on the stretch of field beyond the Globe and sat with our scones. Already my stomach grumbled for dinner, but I nibbled the pastry to hold me over. "Have you ever attended one of his plays?"

She shook her head. "Henry won't let me. Not even when we were invited to Whitehall for Shakespeare's performance of a play called *Othello*."

I lowered my scone. "What hold does Henry have over you?"

Emma stared at her scone, then shoved half of it in her mouth. I would have laughed at her bulging cheeks, but instead I took a bite of my own scone so she wouldn't feel like the only one chewing.

When she finally swallowed, she seemed to have gathered strength. Who knew the power contained in a scone? "It's a long story, Thomas."

"I'm willing to listen."

Her hands plopped into her lap. I couldn't stop staring at her— the way her dark eyelashes kissed her cheeks with each blink, or how her line of freckles seemed like a tearstain, or how her mouth formed words carefully, gently, when she finally spoke. "My father was a navigator under John Hawkins."

I'd heard of John Hawkins. He'd transformed Queen Elizabeth's navy and died a wealthy man from enslaving Africans and selling them to Spain.

"During one of their trips, he met my mother. He was barely seventeen at the time, but he used most of his navy payment to purchase her and free her from her Spanish owner. Once they returned to England, he offered to set her up with money and a small lodging. Instead, she married him. Father left the navy, refusing to participate any longer in the trade, and then joined the gentry."

I could see the strength of her father's convictions in Emma.

But the downward tilt of her eyes told me the story didn't end happily.

"He kept his marriage to Mama as much of a secret as he could—for her safety. Many knew he'd married foreign, but didn't realize he'd married black. Those who did know couldn't understand why he wed her. They said he should marry well and marry white and hire my mother as a servant and concubine." She darted a glance up at me. My distaste must have shown on my face because she laughed. "You'd be surprised at how common that is, Thomas. But thankfully my father was a man of honor."

Her use of *was* instead of *is* didn't escape me.

"Mama was a musician," she went on. "I loved watching her play the lute, tabor, viol-de-gamboys . . . Eventually I painted her. She was my first portrait. I can't paint only people because I don't simply *see* people. I see their stories. Their emotions. *That* is what I paint."

I recalled the painting of me—and how seeing it stirred a deep sense of being *known* in me. Then I thought of the cobbler weeping over the portrait in the Royal Exchange. It didn't seem so odd now.

"Mama always felt sorrow that she wouldn't be able to make me a mask, since she had no mask of her own. After I started painting, she sought out every bit of information she could find—writing letters to masters, seeking out books, questioning my father. Then she carved me a mask. She begged and begged the White Light to put color power into the mask. And the white rose showed up." Emma removed her mask from the basket and handed it to me.

It was heavier than I'd expected. "It's exquisite." My fingers ran over the white rose, smooth and sleek. Would my mask be this heavy? This smooth?

"White Light instructed me in the colors. Mama was so proud. But when she contracted a fever, doctors refused to attend her because they feared her black skin. They didn't know what it meant or what it might do to their color powers. Father was furious and wrote to every doctor." Her lip quirked up to one side. "One finally came—though he was more an herbalist than a color doctor."

"Norwood." I could tell by the way she looked at me that she expected me to piece it together. "But he's an apothecary."

"Yet he came."

Even as a Keeper, he went to her family's aid. All that time at St. Peter's, he'd known about Emma's heritage and secret.

"He couldn't save her, but I never forgot his heart. Then, two years later, a Keeper shot my father in the back during a hunting expedition."

My breath stalled. "Shot? But . . . why?"

"Because Father supported King James."

Her father was killed for being an Igniter. So often I had viewed Igniters as being the killers, but now I saw it went both ways. Emma had more reason to hate Keepers than I had to hate Igniters. Yet she didn't hate me—she didn't seem to hate *anyone*.

"The Baron Monteagle—who had frequently sought my father's advice on certain matters—agreed to take me in. He knew about my color power. It would build his reputation and show him as charitable. But he said I was never to remove my mask except to eat in private. He sent Henry to fetch me and take me to St. Peter's Color School with him."

"The Baron is a coward."

"Don't judge him too harshly. Look at what happened to my parents. People thought less of my father once he married my mother. We were shunned from public events—no matter how appropriate they were for our station. Those sorts of things would distress the Baron to no end."

I liked the Baron less and less. I could see from whom Henry got his charm.

"Thomas, you have to understand that black skin is seen as being from the devil. The gentry don't believe an African will ever hear from White Light. They believe we are so evil we cannot have color power."

I gestured to her mask. "But you are proof otherwise!"

"I am an exception. My mask came from Mama's pleading. I don't know how people will react—"

"You will tame their prejudice."

"I can't." Her voice sounded so small.

"Why no—"

"Because I'm afraid!"

The wind caught away her exclamation, leaving an echo in my chest—an echo of my own struggles. Fear of revealing myself and reaping the reactions. I understood more than she knew.

I stopped pressing her and instead returned to her story. "So you and Henry went to St. Peter's."

"I wore my mask all hours of every day. I didn't know how long the Baron would keep me as his ward, and since I couldn't provide for myself, I trained in color power with hopes of securing an apprenticeship."

"Why doesn't Henry want you to have an apprenticeship?"

"Because I am a lady. Noble families don't work. For me to take on an apprenticeship would shame the Monteagle name."

"It's for *pride*?"

"That and because Henry's color power is a lie." She sounded sad, like she pitied him. "The Baron has high expectations for Henry, but Henry can't command the colors. They don't obey him."

That didn't make sense. "I saw him at St. Peter's. He was the best in our class."

She took her mask from me, returning it to the basket. "That was me. I hid behind doors during his tests. I was the one command-ing the colors and earning his grades and prestige." She grimaced.

"But why would you do that? Why would you lie like that and lessen yourself?" Did she care for Henry?

"Because we needed each other. I needed his secrecy so that I could have a position and future at St. Peter's. He needed me so that he could earn his father's approval and inheritance."

"You can leave him now, though, right? You have color power. You have talent. You have everything you need!"

Her fist clenched around a clump of grass and the small blades tore from their roots. "I'm an African *woman*, Thomas. An African. I can't just leave. The way to move on is if I secure a reputation as a portraitist . . . or if I marry. Society demands—"

"Forget society! Just . . . run away." It sounded rash coming from my mouth, but I could think of nothing else.

"And become some street dell? No. Henry has eliminated my chances of an apprenticeship through threats and letters. He wants me at his side forever. If I continue to pursue an apprenticeship, he and the Baron will take my mask from me."

"They have no right!" I was shouting now and caught myself before my words drifted too far to the ears of passersby.

"Where would I go?" Emma continued. "What would I do? Hang laundry for some lord's family? Henry and the Baron hold my skin color over me like a whip to a horse's rear. One step out of line and I'll be penniless. No master will take me in London and I'd have no means of traveling. No matter my skill, I wouldn't last one night on the streets."

Vagabonds, ruffians, fraters, Igniters hunting Keepers, whore-houses . . . What woman could combat all of that alone and penniless? Chill bumps dotted my arms. "Can't you expose Henry's secret?"

She breathed deep through her nostrils and released the captive grass. Several pieces stuck to her palm and she picked them off one by one. "It's not worth exposing my own. Besides, I will not do to him what I fear he will do to me."

"Not even if he exposed you?"

She looked up. "Not even then."

I wanted to say so many things. I wanted to tell her that *I* would help her. But the Gunpowder Plot still owned my allegiance. "There's no one else you can go live with?"

She brushed the grass from her skirt. "Norwood was coming down here to see what he could do. That was my last option. And now"—her voice almost disappeared under a gust of wind—"now Henry wishes to marry."

So it was true. I had hoped, until this moment, that his comment was a lie. "Why does he want this?"

"I'm the only one who truly knows him. And until you, he was the only one who knew *me*. It is not such a wild idea. I think he's afraid. He doesn't know who he is without me. What woman will have him if he can't even master color power? He's already been trying to train under strong Igniters—even seeking out Keepers with no success."

I couldn't imagine Emma bowing to the whim of that snake for the rest of her life. Caged. Tamed. It would ruin her. Not for the first time, I was glad I'd broken Henry's hand at the masquerade.

"He has no right to cage you." The coldness of my words would have frozen the very beams of sunlight lighting Emma's cheeks.

She looked up—not surprised, but hopeful.

"I'll help you get away. You can go to a different town where they don't know Henry. Where you can paint portraits and make a living with or without a man."

"And live under a false name? Hiding who I am so Henry doesn't find me? That is not freedom." She tried a smile. It wavered.

"Well, you can't marry Henry."

"The Baron has the final say. His son marrying his ward would paint him as an even greater benefactor."

I shouldn't respond. I shouldn't. "What if the Baron dies?" He was a Parliament member—he was a victim of the plot. His death might free Emma. My stomach turned sick at the thought.

She paused a long time, possibly offended by the question. I prayed she didn't read into it, but how could she not? "Henry would become my guardian. He could marry me the very next day if he so wished."

That couldn't be the answer. "Why does he have that power? You're just a ward! You shouldn't *have* to marry!"

"I *want* to marry someday, Thomas. Life as a spinster is much more difficult than life as a wife—but I don't want to marry for ease. I want to marry the right man."

A weird twist tightened in my stomach. I hadn't really thought of marrying anyone. Not even Emma, though I admired her. I hadn't put in much thought beyond finding a cure.

Emma lifted her eyes and I saw the hesitancy in them—like she was waiting to see if I accepted her openness. Or if I'd be open in return. I wanted to tell her about the plot—tell her that I could be dead in a few months. Tell her I *wanted* to help her, but I couldn't until I had my mask.

"Ask me, Thomas," she whispered.

The words hung on the tip of my tongue. *Come away with me.* Even if the impropriety would shock the Baron into a heart attack. Even if it was only to get her away from Henry, we could do it.

But Henry would hunt us. The very crown might come after us if Henry revealed Emma's heritage and my political standing. And if the plotters were caught and revealed names, my treason would condemn Emma. And fleeing would do nothing to save Keepers or plagued.

This was getting too entangled.

"I can't." Those words sliced through my lips like a knife being yanked out of my throat.

She straightened, as though combating the temptation to slump in defeat. "I understand."

But she couldn't. She had no idea why. I wanted her to know my secrets like I now knew hers.

"So what have you been up to since the masque?" Her voice was thin iron—hard, cold, but a façade of cordiality.

I wasn't ready to switch to me. I hadn't thought up what to say. But then, why not the truth? Or at least part of it. "I've been trying to rescue Keepers who are being sold to the Tower for hanging."

Her eyebrows shot up. "You have?"

"Well, I'm trying to." My endeavors seemed a bit lackluster when I really thought about what I'd done—dragged one drunken Keeper back to an inn filled with ale. For all I knew, he had died the next night. "Father had been doing it, but he's away for a few months so I'm trying to fill the shoes of a very powerful Black."

"It's not fair that he expects you to do this without color power."

A sudden urge to defend him rose up in me. "He'll be returning with a mask."

"He's made you wait long enough. But you and your father need to be cautious. Henry goes out at night too. He may not be skilled with a mask, but his blade would put any man's swordsmanship to the test."

"I've sparred with him before." He *was* skilled, but not enough to best me. Henry had trained while also pouring his focus into color power. "What does he do when he goes out?"

She shook her head. "I don't know, but I think he's training under someone."

I remembered him whispering in John Dee's ear at the masquerade. "Who?"

"He won't tell me."

Because he knew Emma wouldn't approve. He knew Emma hated Dee. I'd bet my rapier Henry was meeting with Dee. I'd never introduced him to Father, so he'd had to pursue someone else famous and skilled to train him.

But why would Dee take Henry on as an apprentice if Henry had no color power? Dee was intent on deepening knowledge and making connections that got him closer to the crown. Then again, once we blew up Parliament, Henry would be the new Baron.

"Will you go out again tonight?" she asked. "To help the Keepers?"

"I think so."

A pause. "I will go too. With you."

"Why would you do that? You're an Igniter."

"Just because I'm an Igniter doesn't mean I want people to be murdered or imprisoned for coin."

As if I didn't already respect her beyond what I believed humanly possible. "You would do that?"

"Your comment about the Keepers at that hanging got to me, Thomas. In a good way. In a changing way. You were right—I'd spared no thought for them. I don't want to be like that. And once my thinking changed, the colors obeyed me even better and I painted your portrait."

"Funny how we both taught each other the same lesson." I helped her up from the grass and we made our way back toward London Bridge. "Are you certain you want to help me?"

She popped an eyebrow. "Are you sure you want to try to stop me? You have only a sword and I have only a mask. Together, we are a force to be reckoned with." She sounded like she wanted this. This danger and adventure. I couldn't deny her that.

"What about Henry? If he finds out—"

"Remember, he's gone at night too." A sly grin painted her face. "I'll meet you here at midnight."

"In that case . . . bring your mask."

Twenty-Nine

The prison carriage stopped at the side gate of the Tower of London, led by two Igniter captors.

It hadn't been hard to find the Tower in the dark. As we'd wended our way from the Strand in the shadows, my sword did not clank against stones or bushes. We'd kept to the edges of the lanes but did not venture onto any grass—its soft whooshing would betray our presence more than the fall of leather on packed dirt. Emma followed me softly, though her skirts swished more than I would have liked.

We'd arrived in the alley without a whiff of detection. It was hard to quell my saunter. I'd done it as well as Father could have. He would be proud. And even if he wasn't, *I* was proud of how far I'd come.

I was no longer the boy hiding behind ale barrels at the Duck and Drake planning to steal a man's coin purse.

The creak of metal hinges refocused my thoughts. Two guards came forward from the Tower to meet the cart. The Igniters held up a bundle of masks. The guards took the masks, then handed over coin to pay for the captured Keepers.

I looked at Emma with a silent, *"Are you ready?"*

Her wide eyes met mine and I caught the sound of her excited quickening breath. I felt like I was finally giving *her* something—a moment of action, of power, an opportunity to show herself . . . even if it was just to me.

She nodded and we made our move.

Emma went for the cart. I went for the men—two guards and two Igniters.

I sent the point of my sword where it would best serve us— through the mask straps of the two guards. Before they could respond, I'd sliced the masks off the Igniters too. Then the swords flew. At last, something I could defend against.

I lunged for the guard on my right and released my skill. My sword tip drew blood. So did his. Scratches, slices, twirling. He lunged and I spun to my left. Steel caught my sleeve, but not flesh. It didn't take the others long to surround me.

With a snap, I slashed my blade into my opponent's side. Shallow, but enough to cause him pause. I leaped out from the midst of them and darted a glance to the cage. Emma sent a quick color command to one of the Igniter's boots, securing him to the ground. He cried out and lost balance.

"Keep your focus!" I called. I appreciated the help, but she needed to save her color energy for if things went awry.

Emma gave a sharp nod, then slammed a rock against the door lock. Voices cried from behind the bars and wood. Calling for freedom.

An Igniter spun toward the noise, then lunged for his mask in the dirt. I stabbed my sword toward his hand. When he recoiled, I kicked the mask out of the way. I was tempted to stomp on it and shatter it . . . but that was one thing I couldn't bring myself to do. It broke the standards of honor.

Arms cinched around my body from behind. I yelled as a guard yanked my sword from my hand. I stomped on his bare foot and my heel cracked through bone. He screamed and released me, stumbling backward until he tripped over the boots he'd abandoned after Emma's color command.

Well done, Emma!

She hadn't gotten the prison cart door open yet. There must be a color command on the lock. The Igniter on the ground retrieved his mask and turned toward her.

"Emma!" I yelled in warning.

She looked up, sent a spray of dirt at his face, then ran. The men didn't pursue. Ha. The fools thought she was fleeing.

I went after my sword—dropped by Broken Foot—but the other Igniter used his color power to send my cape up over my face. I batted it away, but four arms trapped me. The cloth slid away at the same time that one of the guards yanked up my sleeve and sliced his blade across my forearm. I flinched as a burst of blood flowed forth. Deep red beneath the moonlight.

"I don't see any White in 'im." The guard wiped his blade on my sleeve.

"Does he have a mask?" one of the Igniters said.

The guard felt around my belt. "No. But I can kill him right here and still get coin from our captain."

I tensed.

Broken Foot dragged himself forward with a drawn dagger. He wouldn't even give me the honor of death by sword? I tried to throw off the other guard restraining me, but I might as well have been wrestling an oak.

He yanked my head back, exposing my throat. I got in one last swallow.

Then the prison cart lurched so violently, every Keeper prisoner cried out. Broken Foot spun. The cart bucked again. It creaked and then rose.

Into.

The.

Air.

I stared slack-jawed. Higher and higher it went. The occupants screamed. Bony fingers gripped the metal bars. Then the wheels began to spin, as though a giant hand cranked them. Faster and faster.

How . . . ?

The guards stared with arms drooping. The Igniter captors reeled back.

Then I saw her on a rooftop, arms outstretched and entire body trembling. Emma was lifting the cart. Alone. It had taken six Browns to push the thing into the Thames when Norwood drowned. Yet there she stood, showing her power to the world.

The White Light in her veins pulsed so strongly it shone through her clothing like morning sunbeams. The Igniter beside me dropped to his knees. I barely found my footing enough to make a break for it, toward the alleys. There was nothing I could do by gaping.

The wheels broke from the wagon. One after the other, they spiraled toward the guards and Igniters—one for each man.

Crack.

The first guard fell like an abandoned rag doll. The second wheel hit the next guard before he'd even checked on his fellow. The two Igniter captors tried to run, but Emma sent them sprawling. Once they woke, their headaches would rival any they'd had after a full night of reveling.

I paused, balanced on one foot. All seemed done, but then with a gasp from Emma, the prison cart crashed to the street and split apart. Keeper prisoners shoved cracked timber off themselves and stumbled out of the wreckage. One retrieved their bundle of masks.

Another stood in awe, staring up at where Emma had stood. "Why . . . why would an Igniter save us?" one asked.

"Come on!" The first ran into the dark. The other followed while two young boys darted away, snatching up the Igniters' masks as they went.

A window lit above. We'd woken nearby residents.

I searched the rooftop for Emma. Where was she? Then I thought of what she'd done. Having used that level of color power, she could be incapacitated . . .

"Emma!" I bolted to the back of the alley and found her access point to the roof—barrels pushed up against the herringbone brick walls. I scrambled up, hauling myself to the roof by a support beam. I crawled to where she'd stood, but she wasn't there. More lights came on as I knocked wooden shingles loose.

She must have fallen.

I slid down the shingles, ignoring the slivers that bit my thighs, and dropped to the ground with a grunt.

The Tower had awoken.

The town had awoken.

"Emma!" I shouted.

"Will you *stop* shouting my name for all the street to hear?" she hissed from behind me.

I spun. She leaned against the brick wall, mask hanging around her neck, breathing hard but looking exhilarated. The glow from the White Light in her veins dimmed with each pulse.

This girl . . .

"Time to go." I took her gloved hand and we sprinted into the darkness.

Not quite the smooth rescue that Father would have orchestrated, but we'd done the job. We were still breathing heavily several minutes after we stopped. "You were brilliant," I said.

"I've never done something of that magnitude before." She wiped her curls from her forehead.

"How did you manage it?"

"It was more like a feeling. I barely had to think and the colors obeyed. Everything felt so—right."

I tried to imagine what other people might say—what the king would say—if they saw what Emma had done. They would fear her. And fear turned people wild.

Still, I was proud of her. And I found myself drawn to that glow in her skin.

The guard had cut open my arm and plain red blood had run out. A confused disappointment formed in my throat. Why didn't I feel like a Keeper? Why didn't I feel the conviction that Father and Catesby and Percy seemed to hold on to? What was I?

Not masked, barely Keeper, and certainly not Igniter despite the few times I'd talked to the White Light. Seeing the glow in Emma's skin and the joy on her face, recalling what she'd done to that cart . . . made me want to talk to it again.

It made me want to understand.

Thirty

13 July 1605

"My collapse will likely last a week. Maybe two." Dee stood before the caved-in tunnel in his bedclothes.

"Thomas will care for you," Catesby said from beside the cot we'd carried into the cellar.

Dee nodded. "I know he will."

I didn't like being assigned the nursemaid to Dee, especially when I was so confused about my commitment to this plot.

Catesby, Wintour, Jack, and Percy crowded into the cellar with me. Dee couldn't fix the tunnel, but he could lift the dirt long enough for us to retrieve the gunpowder. Or so he said.

"Are you ready, men?" Dee asked in a somber voice.

We all nodded as though steeling our nerves for a death duel. Catesby, Jack, and Percy all wore their masks. Wintour's was still cracked beyond repair but remained on his belt all the same.

Dee took a breath that filled his chest like a swollen cow carcass. Then he tied his multicolored mask to his face. He didn't even use color power to knot the ties—not wasting a single ounce of the energy that would be sent to the tunnel.

He faced the mouth of the tunnel as a soldier of the sea might face a leviathan. The rest of us held our breath. Dee's inhales and exhales filled our ears. He seemed to be steeling himself for the job. That or gathering energy from the audience. He *was* a performer, after all.

He lifted his hands. German spilled from Dee's mouth. A great rumble shook the cellar. I squinted, though no dust reached my eyes. Dee had control over even that.

The great timbers that had lodged themselves in the wall of the tunnel cracked and then rotated. Dee swept an arm to the side and the beams lurched upward, forming a square arch in the tunnel. Rocks and dirt showered the floor of the tunnel.

I looked from the upright beams to Dee's quaking body. Was he weakened? Was he almost depleted? Catesby seemed to be thinking along the same lines because he moved the cot closer behind Dee, to catch him upon collapse.

But then Dee opened his mouth wide like a gaping fish and released a bellow that would have shaken the tunnel by volume alone. Wintour grimaced and I imagined the passersby above hearing Dee's roar.

Perhaps they would blame it on the plague bale that still hung in front of the Whynniard house door.

His roar sent a blast up the tunnel, shoving debris and dirt mess back into place in the walls—leaving behind a smooth, cleared pathway into the earth.

Wintour, Keyes, Percy, and Jack darted into the tunnel and rolled out the barrels one by one. I pulled them out of the opening. Dee grew pale. He trembled and dust fell in the tunnel.

"Hurry!" I shouted.

The men ran up again. A third time. Sending barrels rolling toward the opening—one after the other. I hauled them out, shoulders burning.

A timber beam crashed to the floor. "Get out of there!" Catesby hollered.

They obeyed and barely stumbled through the opening when the dirt crashed down with a rumble and Dee's body melted onto the cot. All of us panted. We'd rescued thirty-six barrels of gunpowder.

For the first time since losing his mask to this plot, Wintour cracked a smile. He might have even let out a whoop had the public streets above not been so near.

Percy pushed past me and the two of them aligned the barrels as easily as a boy might roll a hoop along a country path.

And so the plot continued.

———✦✦———

27 July 1605

King James was said to return from his hunting trip tomorrow. Apparently killing wildlife was more important to the king of England than the fact his people were still killing each other.

While the king was away hunting, certain men spent their evenings moving the last of the gunpowder barrels from the Whynniard house across Cotton Garden and into the undercroft of his own Parliament.

I was one of those men. Still plague-free and using both working eyes to take in the thirty-six barrels of gunpowder stacked atop each other against the back wall. The sight of them sent my heart racing. The last steps of the plot were in order.

And for some reason, I continued to help. And help. And help. Because I was too unsure to make up my mind.

"Dee says the plague persists because such a wild Igniter king sits on the throne." Percy brushed the dirt off his hands. "He warned that when the king returns to London, there will probably be an outbreak."

Dee had been talking like that ever since he woke in the Whynniard house. He had returned to his home this afternoon and I was pleased to be rid of him. I'd barely been able to take a free breath on account of his needing care or food or cleaning or reading material or sending me out to scatter seeds for the brainless pigeons and ducks. His neediness had made slipping away to meet with Emma almost impossible these past two weeks.

We stacked logs of firewood for another hour to cover the gunpowder. With it all near the fireplace, it looked like a regular stockpile. The perfect cover-up. One portion remained thin enough to access the gunpowder—both to check it and to light it. When the time came.

Who would be the one assigned to lighting the match?

Once finished, I took the cart back to Catesby's. I did so armed, just in case. Emma and I had spent night after night rescuing Keepers—every time she could slip away. It was harder for her lately because Henry had been staying home—further convincing me that he was training under Dee.

She would often try to explain to the Igniters that their choice to capture or kill Keepers was wrong. They never listened. Lust for dominance and money did that to some people, but I admired Emma for trying.

On the way home from Lambeth, I passed by Emma's house on the Strand. The lights were still on. As Parliament grew closer, I hadn't decided yet if I would tell Emma of my involvement—or ask her advice.

The more time we spent together—me seeing her understand the White Light inside her—the more we began to meld.

As one team.

As one mind.

Did that mean I was becoming an Igniter?

Every now and then I slipped my sword blade along my finger to make sure no White ran in my blood. Sometimes I was relieved.

Other times . . .

Father would arrive home soon with my mask. I was ready for it, but not for the reasons he might've thought. I wanted to see what would happen when I bonded. What would the colors do? What would White Light say? And how would I respond? I knew in my heart that I would try speaking the language of multiple colors. Why *shouldn't* I? I trusted Emma's approach to color power more than anyone's.

I walked the river, not yet ready to return to the Whynniard house. I kept my eyes open for the cloaked figure. After speaking with Emma, I couldn't stop picturing the man as Henry Parker. But Henry had no color power, so it couldn't be.

It was foolish to seek the cloaked man again. He'd already proven he could best me, but he hadn't killed me. A desire for understanding—for truth—gnawed at my gut. A new feeling. It meant sometimes thinking along the lines of what Father had instructed but then also sometimes venturing away from those lines to find the answers for myself, as Emma advised.

My train of thought felt rebellious, but also . . . organic. Cleansing. Like that was what men were supposed to do. Be seek-ers of the answers and the truth. To be above the influence and opinions of the outspoken.

Father said he'd done that, yet he refused to talk about White Light when I asked. His pursuit of truth meant nothing if he wasn't willing to share it.

My scouring of the banks and alleys revealed nothing. I saw a few shadows here and there, but nothing more than a few revelers, plagued beggars, and entwined couples. I gave coin to the beggars, along with whispered promises that a cure was coming, then returned home and slept fitfully, a blinding voice whispering in my mind . . . in my dreams.

And me responding.

* * *

The king returned. People talked. Some cheered. Percy kicked things.

The sooner this plot ended, the sooner I could make my *own* way in life. If our plot succeeded.

A crowd hovered on the banks of the Thames with the king back in Whitehall. Searchers of gossip. They liked to see which nobles came and went from the palace. I joined in as a scout.

As ladies left Whitehall and passed me by, I pretended to stroll as though enjoying the view, but gossipers always had a higher pitch than the average converser. All the better to gather information.

"Isn't that the boy who was cured of the plague on Lady's Day?"

Blast. I continued to walk, knowing by the increase in their voices that they'd turned to glance at my back—not pausing in their chittering. "Do you really think Dee did that? Do you think he can heal the plagued?"

"You saw it, didn't you?" the first woman asked.

"No, I was out in the garden with— Well, I was out in the garden." Her friend gasped, but the second woman plowed on. "Anyway, I heard Dee sent the king a warning against an upcoming plague outbreak."

Dee did *what*?

The first woman waved her hand as though shooing a bee. "How can anyone know if an outbreak is coming?"

I strained for the other woman's response, but by then they were too far away. Dee sent the king a warning. I wondered if Catesby knew that he was consorting with the king. Trying to earn his favor.

And what better way to earn the king's favor than to reveal a plot of regicide?

No. Catesby trusted Dee. Dee had completed his role—he'd retrieved the gunpowder and set the plot back on course. But could he really predict an outbreak?

I tapped my skin. Still healed, but still stiff on the inside.

Night fell and I ended up at the Thames. The waters lost a bit of their stench once the sun set, allowing the cool breeze to flow over the banks. It was the one peace I really found. Perhaps it was the idea of the water constantly moving, traveling, going. It was never stuck.

Never like me.

It made me feel free. In a couple of months I *would* be free— either through death or through the success of the plot and reception of my mask.

I passed two beggars asleep in a doorway—one snoring and the other whimpering. It wasn't cold out, but perhaps his thin frame was chilled. As I passed them by, he wiped something from his arm. Liquid. Blood?

I slowed, but a cry from ahead claimed my attention. A young lady stood arm in arm with a tall man on the threshold of one of the nicer houses. But before the door closed, I caught her concerned exclamation: "I'm *bleeding*, Joseph. Right here on my wrist."

"Well, what did you do this time?" a male voice replied as the door closed. Moments later, light shone through the oiled linen over their window as a candle was lit.

A shadow passed between two trees far up the bank. My blood curdled with premonition. Pigeons clucked and pecked at the ground by the Thames, making it difficult to hear the shadow's footsteps.

I quickened my pace. With the moon blocked by tight alley roofs, it was a strain to see much, but then the stars illuminated the flash of a knife as the figure passed a group of gentlemen. One let out a surprised exclamation. His fellows laughed.

What was happening?

I brushed past them, giving the body of a stone rat a wide berth. A pool of blood spread on the ground beside it. The trail of sliced flesh and Stone Plague sent me into a run. I softened the slam of my boots and checked my breathing, wrapping myself in the cloak of silence perfected through Father's training.

Then I saw him. Hooded. Swift. Silent.

A dark mass gliding up the street with purposeful speed. The man passed by a sleeping beggar, but not before I saw the jab of a blade, heard the surprised grunt, caught a splash of blood.

This man was cutting people. Beggars, ladies, gentlemen, rats.

Was this Henry Parker?

I waited for him to round a corner, then knelt by the still-sleeping beggar. The cut was shallow. So what was the mysterious figure's purpose?

I continued my chase, but when I turned the corner, the alley lay dark and empty. I drew up short. Either the man had broken into a run or he'd . . .

I looked over my shoulder in time to see the figure raise his stone-bladed dagger. There was no reflex quick enough to dodge in time, but he didn't throw it. He caught himself.

As though he knew me.

He backed out of the alley, but I lurched after him. "Wait." The moonlight caught a piece of his mask. A line of Yellow, a splash of Green, a streak of Red crisscrossing—

His dagger flew.

I ducked and rolled. The blade stuck in my shoulder. I yelled and drew my sword as I found my feet, my shoulder stinging. With a mutter, the dagger tore from my shoulder and returned to his hand. I gritted my teeth, but when I looked up, he was gone.

Dee.

I pursued, but no shadow or alley or window light had anything to show. Already my mind questioned what I saw. I cupped a hand over my wound.

The color power this man used on the docks matched Dee's skill. When he thought I'd seen his mask, he sent my hat brim over my eyes. Tonight, when I saw him under the moonlight, he stuck me and fled.

I needed to find him. What was he *doing*?

I hurried away from the alley, away from the bleeding beggars. I forced myself to pass by the Duck and Drake where Wintour lodged, because if Dee was watching me, he would surely silence me for good if he thought I was going for help. I unsheathed my rapier, but he could command it out of my hands. It was more for the sense of safety and defense.

Against every instinct, I returned to the Whynniard house.

I locked the door behind me and closed the shutters. My hands trembled as I lit the candles. My hands never trembled—it would weaken my swordplay. Perhaps it was from blood loss.

I stripped off my clothes to examine the gash on my shoulder—on my sword arm. Annoying.

The blood ran down the back of my shoulder. It burned. I

craned my head but couldn't quite glimpse the whole cut. Then . . .
I caught a color. A flash woven in with the red and flesh tones. My
breath caught. Was that . . . Was there color power in my blood?
Did I see . . . White?

I ran to the cellar, taking the steps two at a time, dripping blood
behind me. I grabbed one of the torch mirrors we'd used when tunneling and stumbled back up the stairs into the light. I angled the
mirror behind my shoulder, straining to get a view.

Too much blood.

I rested the mirror on the windowsill and crouched down so I
could see my shoulder and attend to it at the same time. Using a
rag, I smeared away some of the blood, examined it on the cloth.
Nothing. I looked in the mirror again.

There.

White?

I touched it and brought my fingers in front of my face. Red.

I got as close to the mirror as I could without smearing blood
on it, the trembling making its way through my entire body. The
light color grew. Mingled with more blood. Wait . . . It wasn't
white. My knees buckled. The grey color lining my cut like the
raised stitching of a buttonhole was the Stone Plague.

It was back.

How could it be back? My mind answered the question even
before it finished asking it. Dee. His strange dagger had somehow
infected me. He was infecting the gentry, the common folk, the
beggars.

My breath clogged my throat, fighting to get out.

Dee, who fed pigeons that then fell from the sky like giant
hailstones.

Dee, who was the only man able to cure me of my plague.

Dee, who warned of an outbreak.

He didn't just know about the plague. He *controlled* the plague. And he'd infected me.

The longer I stared at my new wound, the less control I maintained over my panic. Blood pulsed and pulsed. The bits of stone stared at me like eyes through a red face. I tried to block it with my free hand. Blood bubbled out of the wound. The stone scratched the pad of my finger. Dread poured into my gut. I couldn't be plagued again. I couldn't let this happen.

I couldn't let Dee get away with this. His cure was a lie.

Even now, he was either watching my door or continuing to cut unsuspecting people so they would walk around unknowingly spreading the plague to their friends and families. Tomorrow people would think there'd been an outbreak. They'd blame it on the king's return.

The stone pushed against the palm of my hand.

I removed my hand and looked again. It was still there, like a dead island in a sea of blood. Was it wider than before?

I snatched the mirror from the sill and held it right above the plague, angling toward the candle flame. As I watched the reflection, a portion of plague cracked and then crawled over another centimeter of my skin.

It was . . . spreading.

I whipped a knife from the food board and set the blade against the skin of my shoulder. I hesitated for a moment but then remembered how my plague defined me. How it crippled me. How it made me weak in Father's eyes and unworthy in the eyes of others.

I stuffed my hanging shirtsleeve into my mouth. Deep breath through the nose.

Then I sliced through my flesh, peeling off the portion of stone in one swift motion. The shirtsleeve muffled my scream but did nothing to stop the violent trembling that racked my body. The dagger fell from my hand.

I couldn't stand. The wound screamed with me until I ran out of air. Once I took a breath, logic returned and I tore the shirt from my mouth, using it to stop the blood.

A sickening ache spread through my chest. When I looked in the mirror next, my face was pale. Blood cascaded down my arm, dripping onto the floor and running down my pants.

I smeared away the mess and grimaced as the cloth rubbed the raw of my wound. But I had to know if I got it all. I couldn't rest or heal until I knew I'd cut the Stone Plague away. I leaned close to the mirror, angling my shoulder close to the glass.

Red. Blood. Liquid. Flesh.

Grey.

"No." I dropped the cloth and shoved my bare fingers into the wound, numb to the pain in my desperation to feel what I thought I saw. Then a rough scratch. The stone was still there. Too deep to cut out.

It had sent down its roots.

As I stared in the mirror, the stone made its appearance. A cracked line from the wound ran along my collarbone. Chills sprang from crown to toes. I stared at the string of stone. A tiny thread of plague wriggled like a worm beneath my skin, then wended its way from my collar up to the soft flesh of my neck.

It . . . was alive.

The worm broke into ten smaller threads and spread like a tree stretching its branches. Up the left side of my neck. Scaling up my jawline and clawing its way to my eye. My bloodied hand fell away from my shoulder.

I was a dead man.

"Wintour," I whispered. "I must get to Wintour." To warn him—to tell him about Dee.

I fumbled for the latch, not caring if Dee was outside.

The door swung open just as the skin on my face stiffened. I could feel the plague's fingernails picking their way across my flesh. To my eye.

I blinked once before the left side of the street went dark as plague overtook my eye. Only it didn't stop there. The branches spread. Blended.

I crashed into the doorframe.

The branches connected into a spiderweb.

I stumbled over the threshold.

From webbing to a sea, the plague flowed from my left eye up to my forehead. The headache came like a hammer to my skull and I clapped a bloody hand to my temple, not realizing I still had the mirror in it. The glass smashed against my skull and shattered.

As I careened into the night, I held a shard in front of my face. I couldn't tear my gaze away, even when the plague rolled across my forehead to my remaining eye.

I was watching myself die.

And the one thought that broke through the cloud of despair was that I didn't want to die alone.

I lifted my eyes. The last thing I saw before the plague took my other eye was the bale of straw still on its hook in front of the Whynniard house.

My vision darkened. The headache sent me reeling backward. I collided with the ground and gasped for breath in the darkness. Was the plague seeping into my lungs?

The bale creaked over my head. A knife pierced my brain.

I couldn't see.

Couldn't think.

Couldn't breathe.

I sucked in a final wisp and tried to shout. For Wintour. For Percy. For Jack.

The plague poured down my throat and barely a whisper emerged, carrying the name of the only one I truly wanted beside me. "Fa . . . ther."

Thirty-One

I'm the only one who can save you, Thomas.

Not . . . you.

Why won't you let me?

I . . . can't.

You're being stubborn, you know.

Father. Keepers. The plot.

And Emma?

Emma . . .

She and I are one. Is that distasteful to you?

No. She's . . . I want to be like her.

But she is like me.

You are . . . dangerous.

Yes. Yes, I am.

. . .

But I'm worth it.

I am . . . afraid.

I am here.

Very well . . . Do as you will.

———✦———

A hand in mine. Warm breath on my face. Darkness. Silence. But not death. Not yet.

White

Thirty-Two

15 August 1605

"How long . . . been like this?"

Words slipped into my consciousness, jumbled. My sluggish brain tried to piece them together.

". . . plague outbreak . . . King James's return . . . three weeks . . ."

Confused. Overwhelmed. I wanted to return to the darkness.

"Three weeks?"

My mind latched onto this voice—the fishing line that hooked my curiosity . . . my desire to find the light.

"The seizures stopped . . . days ago." This tone carried familiar notes too. "I'm sorry, Guido. He . . . useless to . . . plot."

"I will not abandon him."

"He is not dead . . . but neither is he alive."

The words came smoother now. Where was I? *Who* was I? Why the darkness?

Movement. Cloth on cloth, leather on wood, *click, click, click.* A creak. A latch. Silence.

The line to the trusted voice broke. No more words to hear.

Nothing to draw me out of my prison. I descended once more into the darkness.

⊶ ⇄ ⊷

16 August 1605

"Thomas."

A spark of light. I groped for it, wanting to be freed of the dark sludge. *Help me.*

"Thomas."

I pulled myself from the sludge, the darkness dripping from me as the fishing line slowly reeled me up. Out. Toward the light. *Again.* The line slowed, slowed, stopped. Darkness lapped at my ankles, trying to sink its fingers back into me and return me to my mental coffin. *Don't leave me!*

"Thomas?" This time the voice carried despair. But the line tugged me upward again. Away from the sludge. My lungs filled. My mind awoke.

I knew that voice. Deep. Rich. Craved.

Father? No response.

"He's gone, Guido. Nothing more than a breathing body." That voice halted my upward motion. Was it talking about me? "We have limited resources as it is. You need to let him go. We can't have you catching the plague too."

Click. Click. Click. A creak. A closing door.

No. Don't leave!

The fishing line grew slick as the darkness tried to loosen my grip. Somehow I knew that if I descended into that dark pool again, I'd never resurface.

Something shook me. My entire consciousness lurched from

the movement. "Surely you can hear *something*. The plague isn't in your ears."

The line reeled me up so fast I barely managed to keep hold. Then I was out. I was free and I was awake.

"F . . . Father?" I wasn't sure if the full word actually came out. Transferring the word from my mind to my lips left me gasping. My mouth barely moved.

I was awake. And with my waking came a flood of memory. Plague. Plot. Death. Dee.

I tried another word, but a grunt came out.

"Thomas!" A movement on my mattress. I sagged to one side.

I tried to lift my eyelids. They didn't obey. Where was the light? Why couldn't I open my eyes? I lifted my left hand. Just barely. It flopped onto my stomach, but then another hand was in mine. A strong and callused one.

"Catesby!" Father's shout pierced my mind like the clang of London's bells. Perhaps Father noticed the tension in my limbs because he lowered his voice again. "Thomas, are you truly awake?"

"I . . ." I couldn't say more—one, because it took so much effort to form a single sound, and two, because I didn't know if I was. I couldn't see. But with every word he spoke, my mind woke more.

Noise burst into the room. Voices. Catesby and Wintour and Percy and Father. And suddenly I was being moved and jostled. Too many voices. Water down my throat. A call for a healer.

Not Dee, I thought. *Not Dee.*

<hr/>

It took two full days before I was able to speak normally again. I never once returned to the slimy darkness that had consumed me for—according to Father—three weeks.

They got me sitting up again.

They got me breathing right again.

They got me eating solid food.

But no one could get me to see again. According to Wintour, he'd found me two days after my collapse—two days after a massive plague outbreak. He'd found me seizing on the ground. I'd remained in and out of seizures for weeks—neither speaking nor responding to any prompting or call.

My sight was gone—the majority of my face fully stone. Eyes. Forehead. Cheeks. The left side of my neck and shoulder. But not my throat. Not my airway or mouth or nostrils.

I'd watched the plague slither into my mouth.

White had saved me.

I was changed. I could feel it, but not identify it. Whoever I was when I collapsed, I was no longer. There was an unrest in me because now I knew Dee caused the plague. The death of King James would cure no one.

I had a new enemy.

"Not even Dee could heal you," Wintour said, and my spine stiffened. Of course Dee couldn't cure me. He had no desire to. He wanted me dead because now I knew his secret.

I needed to tell Catesby, but I couldn't purge his words from my mind. *"He is not dead . . . but neither is he alive."* He saw me as a waste of resources. Would he respect any of my words if I tried to rid the plotters of another member?

"When did I finally respond?" I asked.

"Not until Guy returned." Wintour grabbed my hand and placed a bowl in it. I reached with my other for the spoon. At least they were letting me feed myself now. But it brought little solace. I found myself longing to be plagued like the old days. In one eye. Ashamed, but still functional.

Now I couldn't even feed myself without help. Perhaps, with practice, that would change. But . . .

The darkness was lonely.

* * *

"You've some letters." Father's voice came out hesitant. "I fetched them from the Bear."

I had letters? "From whom?" As the words passed my lips, I knew.

"I've not opened them. But the seal is Monteagle."

Emma.

I held out a hand and thick parchment brushed against my palms. Several letters, then. What must Emma have been thinking? I'd disappeared. She had likely visited our rendezvous spot and waited for hours. I hated the idea of her waiting alone.

"I delivered a letter to the Monteagle house, informing them you were taken ill."

What did Emma's letters say?

I would never know unless I asked someone else to read them for me. And that, I couldn't do, no matter how severe my curiosity. If she wrote anything of White Light, I would be questioned. Doubted. She would endanger herself.

And endanger me.

I hadn't forgotten my last conversation with White Light. It felt like a dream or another life—a lullaby in a plagued mind. But it had happened. My soul knew it more than my mind.

I'd spoken to the White Light. I'd accepted it. I didn't know what that entailed, but none of the plotters could know until I figured it out.

"Is there something between you and Monteagle's ward?"

I'd almost forgotten Father was there. "Nothing more than my duties and conversation." And secrets and deep trust.

"She's an Igniter, Thomas. You cannot involve yourself with her. Perhaps your plague is a sign of—"

"It's a sign of nothing!" I fisted the letters. "I'm plagued because—"

A knock on the door.

Father's weight left the bed. Sick dread entered my gut. "Don't answer it," I said, but the creak of the wood on metal drowned out my plea.

I strained my ears, angling my left one from habit. Street chatter gusted through the entry with the breeze. The wind smelled of earth and bodies and Thames. Despite its threads of stench, I welcomed it far more than the dirty walls of this apartment.

The door closed again. "Who was that, Father?"

"Who do you think?" John Dee responded.

I recoiled against the wall. "Get away!"

"So you know. I'd suspected you caught enough of a glimpse of my mask, so let me remind you of what you've seen me do. I silenced those three Igniters on the dock within seconds. I lifted the entire tunnel to free the gunpowder and it barely took a toll on me—"

"You were bedridden for two weeks."

"When other men would have been put out for a month. Or *dead*. My point is . . . You know my power. And you wouldn't want that power to go against any of your plotter friends now, would you? I could tear their Keeper blood right out of their bodies like your friend Percy is so skilled at doing. With a single command I could crack their skulls open like eggshells. I can spill your names to the king."

"That would thwart your own plans to raise Princess Elizabeth."

"Do you think I can't recover? I've lived through plots even

Catesby couldn't have dreamed up. Every threat I make has been thought out, planned out. All of which can be avoided by your silence. After all, you don't want *Emma* endangered . . ."

I swallowed hard, my Adam's apple scraping against pieces of Stone Plague. He'd won. And he knew it.

He left.

The desire to say something to Father or Catesby sat like hot water in my mouth that I wanted to spew, but Dee was right. I'd seen his power.

I needed to think this through.

My head pounded. I leaned against the pillow as the door creaked again. The change in footfalls revealed Father's entrance. I said nothing, for now.

I thumbed Emma's letters, unsure where to direct my thoughts. Three. Three letters. There was so much I wished to know—their dates, their contents, their purposes. Was she in trouble with Henry?

The more I let my mind question, the more it spiraled into paranoia. Would Dee cut her next?

The unknown contents tormented me. The blindness ate at me. I finally slid the letters under my mattress as though they never existed.

I wished Father had never told me about them.

---

20 September 1605

It took several days for my strength to return enough so I could venture into the cellar at the sound of foot scuffles. I was sick of spending so much time in my bed, waiting for something to happen—the plague to finish the job, White Light to say something, Dee to murder me, the plot to end.

The footsteps belonged to Father. I never thought I'd be able to differentiate between something so common as footsteps, but now that my eyes were gone, my ears seemed to step in to fill the gap.

I held my arms out to guide me down the stairs. But soon I found it was easier to go off of memory than to try to guide myself physically. I stopped on the first step and envisioned the apartment. Down the stairs, through the door if it was closed, don't trip over the line of crates.

I made my way down the stairs at a regular pace, grasping for some semblance of normal. I misjudged the bottom step and stumbled. My knee hit something and then there was a clatter. Blast it all.

"Thomas? What are you—"

"I cannot remain in that bed one moment longer." Surely Father understood.

Silence.

"I just . . . I'm tired of the view." My lips quirked up; the humor freed a level of tension that had been building in my chest. *I* could jest about my situation.

"The . . . view?" I caught the smile in his voice. Good. "Well then, I've a fire for us. Shall we warm upstairs?"

I headed back to the main room. Father didn't take my elbow or try to guide me.

My hip caught the doorframe. Bruise. I realigned and walked around it, settling onto what I knew was the bench beside the hearth. A crackle. Pop. Warmth. "Are we alone?"

"Aye." Father's voice came from in front of me, beside the hearth. Higher up, as though standing. I pictured his regular posture—one elbow high on the mantel, the other hand resting at his side or on his sword hilt if he wore it.

"How is the plot?" No one had given me any updates. Catesby had made it clear I had nothing to offer. To be cut out of it when we were so close left me shamed. But it affirmed that the plot truly was their main focus, beyond even care for each other.

"We hit a few snags but recovered. November fifth can't come soon enough."

Barely a month away. "What sort of snags?" Did they find out about Dee?

Father's boots scuffed the ground. "The gunpowder . . . When I returned and checked it, some was decayed."

I straightened. "Decayed?"

"Gunpowder is not meant to be stored that long. With all the delays from the tunnel collapse and prolonging of Parliament, it was only a matter of time. Catesby is looking into getting more."

All that powder. All that coin. Wasted. Was it Dee?

That was me.

I dared not move or speak. White Light's voice seemed so loud in my mind, I was sure Father had heard it.

There was no more guesswork.

White Light was against this plot.

And if it could collapse a tunnel and decay gunpowder, what else could it do?

"Will we be rowing it across the Thames again?" I forced myself to ask. Could Father detect the war inside me? If White Light was against the plot and I continued helping with it, what might it do to me?

Don't blame me. You'd be doing it to yourself.

It had been easy to surrender myself to it when I was dying. What did surrender mean now that I was well? White Light had saved my life, yes. But it had left me blind from plague.

"Thomas . . . you can't possibly expect to help row. You could put the plot at risk." The warning in Father's voice told me plenty. The plotters had discussed this among themselves.

"What was Catesby's conclusion? Now that I'm not a lifeless slug upon my bed, has he come up with an idea other than simply letting me die?"

"He concerns himself only with the plot." Father sighed. "He has brought in a new conspirator."

"Who?"

"Ambrose Rookwood."

I knew that name. "The man who provided us with gunpowder?"

"Aye."

"He is trustworthy?"

"Rookwood's wife is cousin to Keyes. He is a horse breeder. We think he suspected something already and we need the steeds. With the recently decayed gunpowder, we need his resources."

I angled my face to the fire, letting the warmth touch the bits of skin that remained exposed. For a moment I imagined how Father must view me—a face like a statue. Expressionless. Disgusting. But then, how different was it really from his own? He never removed his mask.

And now . . . I'd never know what he truly looked like.

He was supposed to have returned with my mask, but now that I had a face of stone, I didn't have the heart to ask for it.

"What can I do, Thomas?" A movement. Then silence. As though he almost came to me.

"I don't know, Father." I stretched out my legs in front of the bench. "When the stone started to spread, I thought . . . I thought it was the end. I was certain I would die."

"How did it happen? I've never heard of the plague spreading in such a manner."

I fiddled with my belt as though I'd find my sword there. I

wanted to tell him. I wanted to say Dee's name out loud. But to put all the plotters at risk like that . . . I cared about them too much.

So I told the truth without a name. "The mysterious man from the banks of the Thames. He was wounding people on the street, so silently and swiftly no one even knew it was him. I followed him, but he took me by surprise. Cut my shoulder and the plague arose from the wound."

"From his sword?"

"A dagger."

"Then someone has learned the secrets of the Stone Plague." Father's footsteps marked his way across the room. "How is this possible?"

"Don't you see? The Stone Plague isn't some curse. It's a color Compulsion. Killing King James won't change that."

A rustle of clothing—the lifting of his hat from the peg. "We will talk more of this tonight."

I stood up. "Where are you going?" Was it nightfall already?

"Catesby's. There's a meeting. I'll bring home supper."

Noon, then. "I'll join you." I headed toward the door but knocked my outstretched hand against the window. I redirected, heading for where my boots ought to be.

"No, Thomas. You're not recovered enough and Catesby's forbidden it for now."

"Why?" Did Catesby know about the White Light?

"The walk to Lambeth is long and you're hardly recuperated. Besides, we can't hide your plague. You would draw attention. I'm sorry."

By the time I opened my mouth for a response, the door had closed. Again, I was left alone. I hated the idea of sitting in the Whynniard house. I'd been in there for weeks. *Weeks.* I couldn't stay.

If Dee was threatening the other plotters—threatening my *father*—then I needed to go, despite my illness.

I fumbled for my boots. On my first attempt I put them on the wrong feet and I growled at the empty room. Once I got them right and hooked my sword belt on, I grabbed my hat and pulled it as low as it would go. I didn't need to worry about it blocking my vision, for I had none.

I tried one cloak after another until I finally found the worn familiarity of my own. Then I burst outside. I was hoping to run after Father, but now that I was out in the street, the onslaught of disorientation hit me. Voices, smells, sounds. Swirling. Digging their way into my midnight mind.

The world was . . . louder. Broader.

And I didn't feel a part of it. Life maintained its too-fast dance and, like at the masquerade, I felt pressed against the wall. Suffocating beneath the weight of my difference.

"Father?" I knew he wasn't around to hear, but the earth wouldn't release its hold on me—as though the very ground had spoken color speech to the roots of fear and they entangled my boots.

I took several deep breaths, then headed to the left, as that would take me to London Bridge and thence to Lambeth. But I'd turned too soon and strode through a gutter with a splash.

I lurched out of it and rammed into a body. "Get off!" someone shouted. The voices grew louder—hawkers and buskers and shoppers. I stretched my hands in front of me, every centimeter of skin burning from shame.

All eyes on me.

All sounds in me.

All fear controlling me.

"Father?" I didn't even hear my own voice. I rushed forward—if only I could catch up. Shout loud enough for him to hear—to know that I would not be caged. I was strong. Persistent. Like him.

I struck the side of a house and my elbow cracked on brick. What was that house doing there? I was heading straight up the road. I thought.

I turned again, took two steps, and met another building. "Father!" Blast it all. I broke into a cautious run, arms outstretched and hat brim pulled low. "Father! John Johnson! Father!"

A goose honked in response, followed by a strike from someone's cane. "Plague! Plague! This boy has the plague!"

Another strike from the cane. I threw my hands up to protect my little bit of exposed face and turned away from the strikes until the angry cry faded, until the noise faded.

Until the world faded.

I could go forward no more. But neither could I go back. Because I was lost.

Thirty-Three

Father found me.

All day and evening I had waited, crouched in an alley with a double cloak of humility over my shoulders. Even when my gut twisted from hunger, I stayed.

He asked no questions. I offered no answers. We entered the Whynniard house and he handed me a cold pasty. I took it to my cot by the window—not that it mattered. My view remained the same no matter where I sat or ate.

Dark.

Blind.

Alone.

——✦——

The next morning—at least I assumed it was morning due to the scent of eggs and sausages brought from the Duck and Drake—I fetched a sheet of parchment and sat at the letter desk beneath the window.

If I couldn't read Emma's letters, I'd write her one of my own.

But how could I explain all that had transpired over the past month of silence between us? If so much had happened on my end, how much had *she* dealt with?

I fumbled for a quill and inkwell. I traced the corners of the paper with my fingers to make sure I set the nib on parchment and not on the wood of the table. No matter my words, this letter would look terrible. Best to get straight to the point.

Dear Emma,

 The Stone Plague has blinded me. I have only just received your letters and cannot read them.

My nib paused, but I didn't lift for fear of losing my place. What else was there to say? The letter wouldn't hold half my heart and I didn't want to risk Henry reading the contents.

I couldn't continue rescuing Keepers with Emma. I couldn't continue employment with the Baron. I couldn't do anything to save Emma from Henry.

So I scribbled out a final sentence.

 It is best if you forget me.

      T

I folded it and managed a messy wax seal that resulted in more hot wax on my fingers than on the parchment. I pressed a thumb into the soft wax instead of a seal.

Then came the hard part.

I ventured outside again—the sun banishing my need for a cloak. I went until I heard voices. Sea brine and sweat reached my nose. I was near the Thames. My boots clunked onto the board-walk and I stopped. "I am in need of a caddy!"

A few voices stopped their chatter. No one approached me. Finally, I lifted the sealed letter and raised my voice. "Where is a caddy?"

"Here, sir." The timid voice came from beside my left elbow.

Relief. I handed the boy the letter and a few pence. "Deliver this to the Monteagle house on the Strand. To Emma Areben, the Baron's ward." I punctuated this request with another pence.

"Yessir. That'll be another twopence, sir."

"Why the increase?"

"You're plagued, sir. Riskin' my life, I am."

I liked this kid. I gave him another twopence. A patter of foot-steps signaled his departure.

The caddy carried away not only my letter, but also any obliga-tion or guilt I felt over looking out for Emma. I couldn't risk putting her on Dee's list of prey if he was making life threats against my companions.

I headed back to the Whynniard house, but this time I allowed my ears to guide me more than my hands. Not much improvement, but it at least gave me a sense of self-sufficiency.

How ought I to move forward? Should I expose Dee and risk everyone's life?

But what if I let it play out? What if I kept my silence and allowed Dee to complete the plot? Then Catesby and the others would see that King James played no part in the plague. But . . . three hundred men would still die.

I knew in my bones White was against the plot.

Could I even do anything?

I saved you for a reason.

I stopped in my tracks. The voice of White Light shook me no less than the first time I heard it. But this time instead of the voice sending the chill of fear into my veins, I warmed from the inside out.

Why didn't *it* do anything? Why didn't it obliterate the plague on its own?

What, do you expect me to do everything?

I resumed my slow walk back to the Whynniard house. And I made the choice to engage. *I don't even have a mask. What do you expect me to do, oh vague one?*

Hope in me.

How dare it speak of hope? I was *blind*.

White Light claimed to have saved me, but it had left me helpless. What cruel trickery was that? *What power do* you *have?*

I caught the echo of a low chuckle in my mind. It iced my skin. *Watch closely, oh doubter.*

And then . . .

I saw.

A pinprick of light interrupted the blackness that consumed me. My tired, unused pupils couldn't focus. The light blurred but grew like an approaching lantern. And as it drew near, I caught a shape. Not just a ball of light, but a figure. Like a human.

His hands spun in circles, as though painting the darkness. And colors came. Brown. Yellow. Blue. Grey. Green. Red.

Speak my language, Thomas.

I stared at the silhouette. *What is your language?*

Pick one.

Was I about to receive my color power? Was the White Light doing what Father was supposed to have done?

Pick one.

"Grey." The moment the word passed my lips, a flash of visuals popped into my sight. Cobblestones on the ground, the rocks of a cottage to my left—I recognized that cottage. Rain clouds above, a rat slurping at the gutter, the swish of a grey skirt passing me by.

Then the scene faded. Back to blackness, leaving the White Light figure in my vision.

I just saw grey. Grey items all around me. I licked my lips. Tasted stone dust. This time my voice croaked. "Grey."

Again, the flash. The visuals. I caught the cloak of a man walking across my path. The abandoned pail in the dirt, the coal-like water sloshing in the gutters. The scene lasted a ten count at most.

Again. The White Light sounded amused. I was playing into its hands, but the hunger for sight compelled me to obey.

"Brown." A flash of dirt road winding away from the cobbled path, mud on my boots, breeches hanging from wooden clothespins in the air, the trunks and branches of three trees to my right, the wood beams of a wattle-and-daub house beyond the trees.

It faded, but my clarity grew.

White had given me sight . . . through colors. How . . . ? *How?*

No answer. I hadn't moved an inch. And I remained that way for another hour. "Red." A tunic, a sunburned scalp, a cardinal. "Blue." The Thames, the sky, a patch of flowers, a woman's head covering. "Green." Grass, leaves, the jerkin of a dockworker.

I spoke the name of every color and every time I received a flash of scene. A flash of sight. Bizarre. Unheard of. The White Light was mocking the Stone Plague by using the colors. It wasn't a cure, but it was what I needed to rejoin the plotters.

They wouldn't understand the change, but Emma would.

And now . . . now I could read her letters.

Thirty-Four

"How is that possible?" Father stopped in the street and the waves of shoppers in the market flowed past him like an unbroken river.

"*Black*," I whispered and caught a flash of his mask facing me and his wide-brimmed hat illuminated by the autumn sun. I shouldn't have said anything, but I had to. I had to let him know that I could see bits and pieces so that he would convince Catesby to let me rejoin the group.

But I shouldn't have lied.

And I definitely should not continue lying. "I think the plague is receding a little. But I can see as though through a narrow tunnel."

"Are you sure? I've never heard of the plague receding."

He sounded uneasy. I didn't blame him. Up until me, the plague had been predictable. Someone got infected, and either they died within a few weeks or the plague went dormant on their skin forever.

I was an anomaly.

I was unpredictable—in more ways than my plague experience. I was the only one who knew how the plague spread, and *who* spread it. "So do you think Catesby will take me back?" I ended the question with a whispered, *"Black,"* to see his reaction.

Father looked me up and down. "I will demand it myself."

<hr />

30 July 1605

Thomas,

You weren't at our meeting place last night. I know there was a plague outbreak last week. Are you well?

Emma

6 August 1605

Thomas,

Henry's been going out every night—I know he's training with someone. He used his mask for the first time. I think he has color power now. And it's growing.

Emma

23 August 1605

Thomas,

I haven't heard from you, so I'm not even sure if my letters are making it out, but Henry has confined me to the house.

The Baron gave his consent for us to marry.

Emma

I had told her to forget me. I had deserted her because I was embarrassed and helpless in my blindness. What a fickle man I was, that I would abandon Emma after we finally established a friendship and a trust that transcended our differences, fears, and secrets.

She had joined me in my weakness, in my struggle for truth, in my secrets, and never once abandoned me.

I pulled on my cloak, tugged down my hat, and strode out the door, whispering, *"Brown,"* to reveal the path before me.

Where are you going, Thomas? Somehow I sensed that White Light asked it less out of curiosity and more out of an invitation for me to include it.

I'm going to Emma. No more secrets.

And I would do right by her.

Thirty-Five

22 September 1605

"I don't know what to say." Emma and I stood on the edge of the Thames around a small bonfire contained in a metal basket elevated on a pole in the ground. She wore servant clothing with her mask tucked beneath the apron about her waist.

I hadn't gotten through everything. I'd told her only of the plot.

"You were going to let the Baron die." Her breath quickened, but her voice lowered. "You were going to *kill* him and leave me to Henry's whims."

The fire crackled loudly enough to cover our voices, but it wouldn't be long until night fell and others joined us against the oncoming fall chill. We should have met somewhere more private.

I shouldn't have told her.

I needed to tell her more.

"Yellow," I whispered to continue staring at the flames so as not to be consumed by the blindness. I couldn't bear to stare at darkness while listening to her voice. I felt separated. Distant. "I'm not going to let the Baron die."

"You can't promise that." Lower. Deeper. Darker. For the first time I wondered if Emma could actually reach a place of anger that could not be overcome by acceptance and forgiveness.

She might actually turn me away.

She might turn me *in*.

A chill clenched my heart that no bonfire could warm. "I want to help you, Emma."

"You can't. And I don't need your help." Something changed in her tone—a cold hardness that I had suspected was coming. "You've been committed to these plotters the entire time that I've been vulnerable with you. I shared my secrets and you *increased* yours."

"*Yellow*," I whispered again. Flames nearly blinded me. "Emma, I'm telling you now. You were bolder than I was. You were willing to trust me and it just took me longer to know how to do the same."

"It took too long." She backed away. Her voice grew distant.

I reached after her. "Please listen. Extend your grace one moment longer. Don't leave me."

She sighed. "I'm not that fickle." What she didn't say was that *I* was that fickle. "Is there more to this plot I should know about?" The tiredness in her voice made me want to keep it to myself—not to burden her any further.

"No. But there's more to *me*." I drew my rapier, trying to still my trembling. Then I sliced the blade across my palm.

I didn't need to speak a color name to see the thread of White flowing from my hand. It commanded a presence of its own that transcended my blindness. Like a snake of light across my stage of black.

Emma gasped and her two hands wrenched my bleeding one to her. "Thomas!" Her voice spiked into a squeal so fast I almost forgot her anger from moments ago. "When? *When?*"

My throat burned. I swallowed several times before I could share the most intimate part of my story. I had bonded with White Light and felt like I'd finally . . . *arrived*. Arrived at my full potential as a person. She was the only one who could understand.

So I told her.

I told her of White reaching out to me the day of the Color Test, and then on the road to London, and then in the prison cart. I told her how it led me to her and how it annoyed me to no end with its sassiness, yet beneath it all was a depth I'd seen in only one other person.

Her.

I told her about Dee. The daggers. The plague.

"White saved me. It's the reason I can see. When I speak color names, it shows me all the items of that color surrounding me. So when I say, 'Brown'"—a flash of skin and freckles and earthen hair—"I see you." Those final three words came out as a whisper.

She still held my hand, her demeanor resuming the Emma I knew. "Thomas . . . White is letting you see and letting you survive because you are meant to *stop* this plot. Only *you* can do this." She exclaimed this with a longing, as though I had a clear purpose that she envied.

But I had no idea how to go about stopping the plot. I was the least important and least respected member. I was no one. "I'm only trying to fix the things I allowed to happen."

"They would have happened with or without you. But you're on the inside. *This* is why White Light got you to London."

———— ❧ ————

My visit with Emma was the final straw.

Something on your mind?

There seemed to be genuine concern in White's voice. It knew my internal anguish. *What do I do?*

If I gave you advice, would you take it?

How should I know? It depends on the advice!

I was just curious. You don't have to be so snappish.

I'm in a foul mood.

It probably won't help if I say you brought it upon yourself.

So much for *that* conversation. And Emma *liked* having this voice in her head?

Emma's not snappish.

Would you stop? Just give me your advice.

Well, I never said I'd give you advice. I was just curious if you would take it.

Blast it all—

It's nothing I haven't already told you.

And what would that be?

That this plot is not of me.

Tell Catesby that. He's doing all of this for you.

A lot of people do things "for" me, but without my guidance. I have never asked for murder. I have never asked for force or blind rage. I've only ever asked for people to respond to my voice. To color-bond with me and let me show them what I can do.

And that was enough.

Catesby planned this attack to free Keepers and return balance to our interaction with White Light. But even White Light was against it. For once, I desired to follow White Light's instructions—no matter how sassy or sarcastic—beyond the temptations of someone else's.

———※———

Thirteen days until Parliament

Coward.

Traitor.

Liar.

Igniter.

These would be my new names . . . once I abandoned the plot.

White Light didn't want to be caged anymore by the Keepers. I could understand that. I didn't want to be plagued or maskless or cowardly anymore.

When I looked at Father, I wanted to please him. But when I looked at Emma, I wanted to *be* her. There was a life and fullness and *rightness* about her color skills that came from White Light.

This war between Keepers and Igniters was complete chaos.

But it wasn't my role to *stop* the chaos. My role was to enter the chaos and bring restoration in the midst of it.

And blowing up three hundred Parliament members and the king of England wasn't restoration. It was death with no phoenix to rise out of it. Catesby thought this scourge of England would free us to be *us*. But what if the action of pursuing freedom actually changed us into something we didn't recognize?

Did murder ever free anyone?

This plot was a revolution built on corpses. It wasn't how things were supposed to be.

With a thick dose of conviction but no plan, I headed to Bread Street for one of the final plotters' meetings. I had no idea how to tell Father, how to confront Dee, how to inform Catesby that I was no longer in support of this plot . . .

That I had now become their greatest threat.

Thirty-Six

"Gentlemen, the plot is upon us." Catesby's voice echoed like the stroke of midnight.

Five of us sat at a table in the Mitre tavern under the guise of a supper party. I muttered through the colors—Grey, Yellow, Red, Blue, Green—until I found the one that showed me the most of the scene. Brown.

Table, chairs, floor, hair, and some bits of clothing. On either side of me sat Father and Wintour. I knew their forms and postures well enough. Across from me were Catesby and a figure I'd never seen before. A stranger?

"This is my cousin, Francis Tresham—recruited a couple weeks ago." Catesby's arm gestured to the new form on his left. "His recent inheritance will pay for our escapes after the explosion."

Another plotter added with Parliament only two weeks away? "Gentlemen," Tresham said.

I knew Tresham's name but didn't say anything. He was the Baron's brother-in-law. Surely Catesby knew this. As we sat in discussion, I contemplated Catesby's irrationalism. How had I not seen it before?

He conducted himself as a powerful and wise leader, but no one else recruited new men. Only *Catesby* knew our stories and we blindly trusted him. Here he was—mere days before the plot—adding another man.

I allowed my view of the scene to settle into darkness so my ears would focus more on Catesby's words than the distraction of Tresham's presence.

"Guido, you will light the fuse." As though the entire tavern had heard the finality of Catesby's declaration, the building went silent—one of those spine-chilling moments when everyone takes a breath at the same time.

My hair rose, but before a panicked thought could form, the ruckus picked up again. The creak of Father's chair told me he leaned forward. "It would be my honor."

"You have experience with setting explosives. And your dwelling near Parliament is the perfect situation."

"And what after that?" Wintour asked. "How shall Guy escape?"

A sip of mead. A swallow. A clunk of tankard on wood. "Once the fuse is lit, you need to flee beyond the explosion," Catesby said. "You and Thomas will take a boat along the Thames to a ship hired by Tresham. It will take you to Flanders, where you will be Guido Fawkes once again. You will report the news to the Keepers there."

Father's sharp inhale was the closest thing to joy I'd heard from him. I whispered, *"Black,"* to see his mask, as if it would hold an expression. Though the mask remained as mysterious as always with its painted half smile, his energized posture gave the impression that he would leap from his chair to do Catesby's bidding.

"Thomas, you shall be with the skiff and have it ready to row Guido to your escape ship." The scene faded, but not before I saw

Catesby's black hat swing to face me. "You can pretend to sleep in it that night—with your plague evident for any passersby to see so they will think you are a street dweller."

I swallowed hard, thankful—for the first time—that my face could show no expression through the plague. It was a good plan, but I wouldn't be enacting it. Hopefully, before Parliament in two weeks, I could convince Father to abandon the plot.

If Father refused, I would go to Catesby. And likely hang.

"Will this plot condemn us all?" Tresham asked in a low voice. "How do you know this action is the right course?"

A fellow doubter? I was glad it was he who asked, not me.

"It must be done." That was all Catesby said, and it seemed to be enough. The way he said it implied there was no alternative and we were England's last hope.

And everyone accepted it. Did they have no thoughts of their own?

Supper progressed as a few other details were laid. Catesby would join a contact of his—Everard Digby—for a hunting party in the north. That disguised party would gather Princess Elizabeth from her dwelling in the Midlands.

"Dee will meet us back at Whitehall once the king and Parliament are dead," Catesby said.

"You do realize my brother-in-law, the Baron Monteagle, will be in Parliament that day." Tresham's statement struck the table like a battering ram.

I wanted to hear Catesby's response. I had told Emma the Baron would not die in this plot. Tresham just might help me ensure his safety. A niggling hope rested in the back of my mind—that one of Catesby's new additions would prove unfaithful and stop the plot. That they would do the dirty work for me.

"None of us desire innocent deaths," Catesby said gravely.

"Admirable sentiments, but to what end?" Tresham said.

I whispered, *"Brown,"* to check the room for any eavesdroppers. My vision showed tables, tankards, and mud on boots and cloak hems. None were near us.

"I've thought long on this, Francis." Catesby folded his weathered hands on the table. "The plot is beyond our personal cares. We must pray that White Light will guide the innocents away from Parliament that day."

"Aye," Father said.

Again Catesby delivered words like a doctor delivered an antidote to sick veins. The table calmed, but no one seemed completely settled.

That was the nature of the plot.

Unsettling.

There was no clear way out that would leave anyone—least of all me—guiltless or at peace. Catesby asked us to sacrifice not only our lives for Keeper freedom but our own consciences and morals.

During the long route back to the Whynniard house, Father and I walked in silence. I focused mainly on whispering, *"Black,"* so as not to stumble on the less familiar path. Father kept the pace slow enough that I could pick my way with some amount of ease.

He seemed energized—not a good time for me to confess my new stance on the plot. But as we walked, I wondered if I even *should* share about my bond with White Light. He and Catesby just might kill me and move forward with the plot.

After all, Father had said a passionate, "Aye," when Catesby said the plot was beyond our personal cares. Would Father remain loyal to Catesby, or would he be loyal to me?

I wasn't willing to find out.

My thoughts searched for alternatives. Tresham feared for the Baron. I feared for Emma. Was there some way that I could expose the plot without exposing those involved? Could I possibly save everyone's lives and remain anonymous?

We arrived at the Whynniard house, but Father went right back out again to share Catesby's plans with Wintour at the Duck and Drake.

I was alone.

And I knew what I needed to do.

With color whispers, I made my way to the desk and withdrew a slip of parchment. I dipped my quill into the ink, set the nib to paper, and scratched out:

To my lord, the Baron Monteagle . . .

Thirty-Seven

Ten days until Parliament

I'm sorry, Father.

I'm sorry, Catesby.

I'm sorry, Wintour and Percy and Jack and Norwood and Keyes and Bates and Kit.

I'm not sorry, Dee.

The streets were oddly silent even though it was not yet seven in the evening. I stuck to the shadows as though I were on a mission to rescue Keepers, but this mission was far deadlier and more worthwhile.

If all went as hoped, both Keeper and Igniter lives would be saved. I'd chosen my words as carefully as a king chooses his guards, leaving the message anonymous but informative enough to do the job.

. . . I advise you, if you value your life, to devise some excuse to be absent from this next Parliament . . .

The Baron supped from the plate of self-preservation. He would read that as a warning, just as I intended.

. . . there shall be a terrible blow . . .

This would give him an idea of an attack. An assassination.

. . . the danger is past as soon as you have burnt the letter . . .

It would bring home the importance of the warning—and hopefully keep anyone from recognizing my handwriting. Even if he didn't burn the letter, I'd only ever written to Emma, Norwood, and Father.

. . . make good use of it.

The Baron had committed himself to King James. I trusted he would report the warning to the king. Then word would reach Catesby that the king suspected an attack and all would settle.

When this started, Catesby said the Gunpowder Plot was his last attempt. If it failed—if the flame was snuffed—it would all be over. Permanently, I prayed.

"Black, Black, Black," I muttered to keep an eye on the road and alleys around me, though the shadows were hard to make out through the darkness of my own blindness. I switched to *"Brown, Brown, Brown,"* and caught a bit more of the road under the sparse candlelight flickering through windows.

I arrived at the Monteagle house on the Strand, but the windows were dark and shuttered. Blast. They must be supping in Hoxton for the night. I hadn't intended to be out so long. I continued along the lane, remembering the many times I'd walked this route to report as Emma's escort.

Now, with any luck, I would be her savior.

I would leave the letter at the door or through a window. But when I reached London's Gate, a cloaked figure conversed with the gate guard. I couldn't risk being seen by anyone, so I ducked into the shadows and listened.

"Finishing up some evening duties," the man said. I knew that voice.

"It's good to see you again, Ward," the guard said.

I threw my hood over my face and yanked my hat down over my eyes. I couldn't have run across a more perfect interruption.

You're welcome.

I swallowed a laugh and waited for Ward to pass through the gate. After giving him a minute's head start, I followed through. Then I broke into a jog, muttering color names with each step so as to keep myself from tripping. It didn't fully eradicate the mishaps, but eventually I saw his brown cloak ahead. I put on a burst, tugging my cloak up.

"Sir," I called in as low a voice as I could muster. "Are you servant to the Baron Monteagle?"

Ward turned just as my view faded. "Aye, who asks?"

"Brown," I whispered for a final burst of sight, then to Ward, "There is a message for him. Take it with haste." I shoved the letter into his hand and then departed before he could question me further. He called after me, but I turned a corner and then navigated the shadows until I knew he'd not find me.

My heart pounded so fiercely, I forced several deep breaths to keep myself from growing ill. I'd done it. There was no going back. I'd betrayed everyone.

I'd betrayed Father.

But I was saving Emma. I was saving all of the members of Parliament. And in the end, I was saving Father and Catesby and the others.

So why did my greatest moment of bravery make me feel more like a coward than ever before?

I started the slow walk back to the Whynniard house. All madness would break free over the next several days. I wasn't ready. But perhaps bravery meant entering into a storm you already knew would destroy you.

I didn't sleep all night. I tried not to toss or turn, though I doubted Father would have questioned the cause of my insomnia. The plot was a mere week away—and there were plenty of reasons to have an active mind.

Yet I couldn't help wondering.

Should I have gone to him first? Ought I to have reached out to a plotter first?

If they'd suspected my doubt, they might have taken fierce action to stop me.

Morning dawned bright, according to Father, though none of it broke through my plagued eyes. I didn't want to rise, even after the long night of unease. I didn't want to face the day. I didn't want to think of what color I'd need to whisper in order to see.

I went about the day on edge, waiting for a summons or a knock on the door from the king's men. I should tell Father. I should say something and confess so he wouldn't be taken by surprise.

But every time the words formed on my lips, I sucked them back.

I was allowed to keep my secrets—for today at least. I'd let the betrayal play out. But as the day passed, I steeled myself for the repercussions.

Father would disown me.

Jack would possibly challenge me to a duel.

Percy would kill me with or without a duel.

Catesby would hang me from the nearest sycamore.

"We are to convene at Catesby's for supper to finalize plans before he leaves for the hunting party." Father handed me my cloak.

The last thing I wanted to do was spend the evening with the men who might kill me. But to refuse would be even more condemning. I took my cloak.

We crossed London Bridge. I trailed behind Father, whispering, *"Black,"* so as to keep his cape in sight. We arrived at Catesby's Lambeth home to a humble but hot supper of vegetable pottage with bread and ale. Wintour, Tresham, and Bates were the other plotters present. Dee never came to any of the meetings—he received reports from Bates so as not to be seen consorting with Catesby.

I was glad I wouldn't have to juggle his threats and my betrayal with him in the room.

No one said anything out of the ordinary as we sat to supper, which meant no one knew about the letter yet. They didn't suspect me. They were continuing on with the plot like normal. Maybe the Baron never even received the letter. Maybe Ward had recognized me and never delivered it.

I sat next to Tresham and we dug into the pottage. Barely had we taken a single bite when a knock sounded on the door.

The word *"Brown"* slipped from my mouth like a curse word so I could have a flash of the room. I caught enough of Catesby's facial expression to register his surprise.

Every piece of cutlery and word of discussion stilled. Then, with a stiff calm, Catesby said, "Bates, see to the door."

I wanted to hide. Whoever stood outside would walk in to see Catesby supping with his cousin, a plagued boy, and a masked vigilante. There would be questions. If it was the king's guard, we were caught already.

I wasn't ready.

I should have told Father.

Blasted White Light. I wasn't strong enough for this.

Bates reentered the room, his boots the only set of footsteps I caught. "It is Ward, the Baron Monteagle's servant." His tone sounded grave. "He looks anxious and says he has important news for us."

Ward. Ward had recognized me. Ward had read the letter. Was Ward . . . a Keeper?

"Let him in." Catesby's chair scraped as he stood.

I gripped the table, unsure whether to leave, to watch, or simply to shout out my guilt then and there.

A shorter stride preceded the entrance of a seventh body into the dining room. "Catesby, the Baron has had a letter warning him about a plot."

Sometimes silence can deafen an ear greater than pistol fire. That was the case as Ward's breathless statement crashed into the room.

I waited for his gaze to land on me, his finger to lift, Catesby's sword to run me through. I allowed my blindness to consume me so I wouldn't have to see it happen—wouldn't have to see the looks of betrayal and disgust.

"Tell us everything," Catesby said.

"Yesterday, around seven, a hooded man ran after me. He was of tall, lean stature, and after confirming I served the Baron, he shoved the letter into my hand. I could not read it as it was sealed, but the writing was of such a scrawl that the Baron called for my aid in deciphering it."

Had he not recognized me? I whispered a few color names—enough to show me the silhouette of the scene. Everyone faced Ward. No one focused on me and Ward was intent on Catesby.

I hadn't been found out. It was both a relief and a cause for despair.

"The letter warned the Baron not to attend Parliament because of forthcoming punishment. It urged him to retire to the country. It said something about a terrible blow."

My limited view revealed Catesby running a hand down his face before I returned to darkness.

"The letter ended with a command for the Baron to burn the letter."

"And did he?" Catesby asked, though I could tell by his tone that he didn't expect the Baron to have done so, just as I never thought he would.

"No. That night he took it to Whitehall."

My body grew numb from the frantic pumping of my emotion-filled blood. He'd done it. He'd delivered it to the palace.

"Has the king read it yet?" Catesby croaked.

"Not to my knowledge. King James returns from hunting in a few days. The letter is with the king's man Salisbury."

Wintour spoke urgently. "Catesby, what should—"

"Thank you, Ward." Catesby's voice moved across the room. After a moment, footsteps subsided and a door closed. Ward was gone. Then I remembered: he wasn't part of the plot. Catesby would be foolish to admit anything or show any proper concern in front of him. But Ward *was* a loyal Keeper. He didn't know the details, but he was clearly in support of whatever he suspected Catesby to be doing.

The *shing* of metal from scabbard broke our stunned silence, and I muttered, *"Grey,"* to see where the sound had come from. A silver blade hung in the air from my left, from where Wintour stood.

It pointed toward me just as Catesby returned.

"It was you," Wintour growled.

I leaned back in my chair, but not in hopes of escaping. I didn't even draw my own rapier.

"Traitor!" Catesby screamed from the doorway, displaying a snap in control that cleaved my heart.

I needed to explain. They needed to know the White Light was against this plot. "I—"

"No!" Tresham shouted from my side.

Was he . . . defending me?

"It wasn't me!" A clatter of wood on wood.

"*Brown,*" I whispered in time to see Tresham's figure tumble out of his seat and back against the wall. Wintour and Catesby advanced.

They thought it was *Tresham*?

Catesby drew his own sword. "You were concerned for your brother-in-law, the Baron. You tried to warn him. *Admit it!*"

"No. It wasn't me!" Tears lined Tresham's voice.

"Confess, or we shall hang you this moment."

Hang? That would be the plotters' fate should any of us get caught by the king or his men. Traitors to the crown. They were treating Tresham like a traitor to our beloved England.

Whispered color names showed me enough. Wintour with a coil of rope, Catesby holding Tresham at sword point, Tresham on his knees with his hands clasped in front of him.

I needed to speak up before Catesby and Wintour followed through.

"Do you not think Ward would have recognized me as Monteagle's kin?" Tresham pleaded. "Or at least my voice? He said the letter bearer was tall. I am the shortest among us save Wintour!"

He took a breath. Would it be his last? Wintour already had a noose made from the rope in his hand.

"Why would I write it in a letter?" Tresham's voice grew more and more shrill.

I needed to confess. It was devouring me more than the plague had ever devoured my skin.

"I sup with Monteagle weekly," Tresham went on. "I could

have warned him in person a hundred times over if I wanted and avoided any sort of evidence."

At last the noose was lowered, the swords sheathed, and the tempers abated. Catesby and Wintour backed away from Tresham's pathetic form. I'd just seen the two men who had always remained the calmest during this plot snap.

"There is a traitor in our midst." Catesby breathed deep through his nose. "We must exercise all caution. Let's hope the letter was vague enough to cause the king no worry."

No. It needed to convince the plotters that our game was up. It took me three swallows before I could force out any words. "Does this not put everyone at risk? Should we—should we consider abandoning the plot?"

"Not yet, Thomas. We will see how this plays out. We need to keep our ears to the ground for any news."

I prayed there would be news. I prayed the king would see the warning in the letter and take enough action to dissuade my friends from going through with this treason and murder.

"Guido, you must watch the gunpowder this week for any sign of inspection. It will be of great risk to you."

"I will do it gladly and without fear," Father replied.

No! This letter was supposed to instill fear, not bolster their mettle.

"None of us are to mention the letter to anyone—least of all to Monteagle."

Father shifted in his chair. "What of the other plotters? Keyes, Rookwood, Percy?"

"Keep it all silent for now," Catesby commanded. "It may not be a threat to the plot in the end."

I prayed he was wrong. If the letter didn't work, I'd have to think of something else. And I wasn't sure I had the stomach for more betrayal.

The next day passed with no inquiries.

And then the next.

Father checked the undercroft every evening. And every evening I prayed he'd find something.

Every evening he came back with a relieved report of safety.

I grew tenser and tenser with each passing sunset. We were at the end of October. The king would be back in London tomorrow. Then, in five days, thirteen passionate men—no longer including myself—would bury him in fire, gunpowder, and treason.

Ought I go to the king myself? Would he even believe a blind plagued boy like me? I might still be hung for taking part in the plotting. But maybe he'd offer forgiveness if I also revealed Dee's hand in the spread of the plague.

White Light was being annoyingly silent and I didn't want to put Emma at risk by visiting the Monteagle home, so I waited. And waited. And soon found myself in the undercroft of Parliament with Father, inspecting the barrels of gunpowder.

The room remained dark, save for a single candle. Father stood in the center of the room, mask tight against his face, sending two barrels into the air, rearranging them, and settling them down again. As long as I whispered, "*Brown*" repeatedly, I could see most of what he was doing.

Even through my fuzzy, shadowed view, I was left in awe of his color power.

With mere words and commands, he stacked bundles of firewood around the barrels, making sure the gunpowder was all close together so that when he lit the fuse there would be a crushing explosion.

The entire plot rode on Father lighting the match.

Keyes and Rookwood arrived in London the next day. We didn't meet with them, nor did we mention anything of the letter.

But it was also a day on which I hoped to meet with Emma in our alley. I'd sent a caddy that morning with a verbal message: "Would Mistress Areben like a scone from Pudding Lane?" I hoped she recognized it as coming from me. I didn't dare write a letter with my blind, messy handwriting again.

The need for her insight sent me running to the alley to wait all day. I wasn't strong enough to carry such a colossal weight of secrets. I needed help with the burden.

My emotions sloshed against my conviction like the waves of the Thames. I had done the right thing, sending that letter. But it felt like I was sacrificing my father and friends for the Baron—a spineless monarch-pleaser. Still, I couldn't—in my right mind—send him to his death at Parliament.

And that was what set me apart from the other plotters. Even Father.

I was in my right mind, and the rest of them were blinded by their passions.

Or was it, perhaps, the other way around?

I whispered the colors that had now become a custom when walking the streets of London. Yellow for the light, Brown for the ground, Red for the flushed faces and rich clothing, and Grey for the weapons.

The snaps of scene revealed the alley that had become a part of my story, sunlight on the rooftops despite the chill of autumn and a clump of stone-dead rats in the gutter. Dee's doing.

I sensed her before I whispered, *"Brown,"* and saw her lovely mask. What I really wanted to see was her skin and face. Brown showed it to me with all its intricacies.

"Emma." The relief that sent her name from my lips released the suffocating amount of tension coiled in my shoulders.

"Did you hear of the letter?" she asked in an undertone, glancing around. She was still dressed as the Baron's ward, so it must not have been easy to get away.

"Yes."

"You sent it, didn't you? I knew your scrawl—it was your blind writing. Different from your hand before your plague."

Well, that made this easier. "Aye. Do you think the Baron will attend Parliament?"

"He's already said he will not go, but he's hoping for action from the king." She headed out of the alley. "I will be missed soon. The Baron returned to his house on the Strand to be within better range of the king if he calls."

I walked with her, making sure I ducked my head so as not to impugn her character by revealing my plague. "He took it to the king?"

"King James returns this night. I do not know what action he'll take, but the king has survived many a plot. Even though people call him paranoid, I find him shrewd. He will know what to do with the letter."

"I pray for his wisdom." It was my first nod to the White Light, though I couldn't completely find ease in its voice. After all, it was only a *voice*. I knew it had power—my small glimpses of sight were evidence of that. But it was hard to think that a voice and a dangerous color could alter so many aspects of our world.

We arrived at the back door of the Strand house. I alternated *"Brown"* and *"Yellow"* whispers so as to see Emma. She pressed her back against the door. I stepped closer to keep us beneath the shadows of the roof overhang. Her breath brushed my cheek.

So many twists. So many plots in the hearts of so many men. Dee and the plague. Catesby and the king. Henry and Emma. "Be careful, Emma." My moment of vision faded, but instead of speaking the name of another color, I leaned closer to where I knew she was and said quietly, "When this ends, I will come for you."

Those words were spoken with deeper conviction and determination than any vow I'd given to the Gunpowder Plot.

"I'll be ready." She opened the door behind her and slipped away. "Be safe."

I felt cold without her presence and imagined her inches away from me for another few seconds. Then I returned to the main street.

Safe? What a concept. Oh no, a traitor could never be safe, no matter how much he longed for it. And no matter who offered it.

I had sealed my fate with the first drop of ink.

Thirty-Eight

One day until Parliament

I had failed.

"Northumberland says there is nothing out of the ordinary," Percy reported.

The king had dismissed my letter.

He wasn't as shrewd as Emma had thought.

It was the night of the plot and the last of our party stood around Catesby and his horse—Father, me, Percy, Wintour, and Keyes. Jack and Bates would be joining Catesby on their own steeds.

The king was going to die upon the morning if I didn't think of something.

Tonight I would have to challenge Father. I would have to stop him from lighting the fuse. How could King James, the most paranoid monarch in Europe, continue on with Parliament after my letter?

"Did you say anything of Parliament?" Jack hauled himself into the saddle of his horse.

"Nay," Percy said without remorse. Northumberland—the man

who had lent Percy money, gotten him his position as one of the king's fifty horsemen, and secured a lodging for him in London— was going to attend Parliament in the morning.

And Percy was going to let him die.

"I am willing to abide the uttermost trials for this action." Percy and Catesby shook hands.

"You are brave men." Catesby settled the reins in his hands. "The best." With a squeeze from Catesby, the horse carried him away from London. Bates and Jack followed.

They would join Digby's "hunting party" in the north, which was conveniently camped eight miles from young Princess Elizabeth. They would abduct her at the same time Father lit the fuse for Parliament.

Or at least at the same time Father was *supposed* to light the fuse.

"Grey, Grey, Grey, Grey," I whispered until Catesby faded from view past a bend in the road.

I might never see him again.

He could be caught or killed because of my betrayal, but I had to believe that he, Bates, and Jack would be safer outside of London. They might be able to escape with their lives once I halted the plot.

Was this right? Could I betray them? After all, they were fighting for what they believed in. For what I used to believe in. But didn't most bold acts arise from someone's belief?

Belief needs to be founded in more than just personal convictions.

But I am choosing to believe in you.

I am not subjective. I am foundational.

I knew this answer because Emma gave it to me months ago. Only this time, I *felt* the answer.

"Wintour will be at his lodging in the Duck and Drake, and I at Gray's Inn when the explosion happens." Percy was our new commander. "Fawkes will guard the undercroft all night and light the fuse. Thomas will man the rowboat. I will have four horses ready for departure after the explosion for Kit, Keyes, Wintour, and me. We will join Catesby up north for the abduction of Princess Elizabeth."

So much planning. Over a year of it. Could I truly destroy all their hopes? Possibly their freedom?

Rustling sounds came from Keyes. I whispered through the colors until I saw a pocket watch float from his form to Father's. "To properly time the explosion. Catesby has one too."

"Fight bravely. Speak your color languages clearly." Percy's motivational words were nothing compared to Catesby's. His came out forceful and sour. Bitter. "Until tomorrow."

"Until tomorrow," the others muttered. I didn't join in.

Then we went our separate ways.

I walked with Father back toward Parliament. He checked for passersby and then entered the undercroft. I followed him down the stairs. The sound of boots on stone echoed strong against my ears. My sword weighed down my belt, reluctant to be drawn against my own father.

Was this the moment? Should I challenge? Should I strike without warning? Did I even have a chance of defeating him with my blindness?

"Come here, Thomas." I followed the sound of Father's steps toward the stocks of gunpowder.

I heard the scrape of something sliding against the floor and then a box was set into my hands. I whispered, *Brown,* and the scene came into view. It was, indeed, a box of wood. My hands trembled and I couldn't bring myself to undo the latch.

The scene faded, but I felt the pressure of Father's hands as he lifted the latch for me. I whispered the box back into view and then ran through the other colors until another item entered my vision.

Smooth, raw wood humming with the desire to bond.

My mask.

Thirty-Nine

The mask sat there, a pale, spotted wood with a painted black mouth.

Everything that had brought me to London sat before me in a box—a gift that I had finally earned. Or so Father thought.

"Can you see it?" He grabbed a torch from the wall and lit it.

"I can see it." My solemn tone stilled his hands.

The one thing enabling me to see the mask was the one voice I swore to Father that I would never speak to.

"Do you— Are you pleased?"

I set the box on top of one of the barrels, hating myself. "I can't accept it."

I wanted the mask. I wanted my color power. I wanted to bond with colors like all those before me. I could take it and run. But my conscience would burn me from the inside until I was nothing but a shadow of ash.

"You've earned it, son." Father lifted the mask from the box and held it out to me. "You've proven yourself over and over again—through your patience, your persistence, your trustworthiness."

I wished he'd stop talking.

I whispered through the colors, staring at the perfect mask as self-torture. "I can't use it."

"Because of your plague?" He stepped closer. "I'm sure it will still bond."

I shook my head. "It's not that."

The mask drooped.

"I . . ." For a moment I was glad of my blindness. Glad of Father's incessant mask-wearing so I wouldn't have to see his reaction. "I wrote the letter."

I didn't know what I'd expected—a question, perhaps. Or maybe even disbelief. But Father's sharp silence pinched my throat like the noose I was bound to wear by morning.

"I wrote the letter to Monteagle. I can't be part of the plot. I have to—I have to stop it. I can't let you go through with it."

This wasn't how it was supposed to happen. I was supposed to wait until the lighting of the match, but I couldn't hold the betrayal in any longer.

I owed this to Father.

More silence. Was he even hearing me? *"Black,"* I muttered so I could see his mask.

It stared at me, an expressionless skeleton lit by the deadly flicker of the torch. "What did you just say?"

"Black," I said louder, and it brought him even more into focus. "I have to speak the color names to see. The White Light has been doing that. I've—I've been talking to the White Light. It showed me that—that it wanted to bond with me. Without it, I'm completely blind."

The scene faded and I forced out the final words. "I'm an Igniter."

My voice clogged and I couldn't go on. I imagined that Father was looking at me the way Catesby had looked at Tresham. With disgust. Ashamed. To him, I looked and sounded like a spineless coward.

But I'd never forced myself to be so courageous in my entire life.

"You betrayed us." Cold. Hollow. Detached.

I lifted my chin. "I had to. Otherwise I'd be betraying myself . . . and White Light."

"Have you no honor to stand for your beliefs?"

"Standing for my beliefs isn't always the same as standing for truth." There was no going back now. As the words spilled forth, I realized finally how much I believed them. How much they'd become a part of me. "Catesby claimed to be doing this for Keepers and for White Light, but the White Light is *against* it. There have been signs over and over again—the tunnel collapse, the outbreak, the Parliament delays, the decaying of powder, more outbreaks, another delay . . . Can you not see?"

"Those are the fates trying to hinder us! All good pursuits require stamina to conquer setbacks. Stamina you clearly don't have."

My hands fisted. "You're wrong."

"What would you have us do? Let the Igniters reign?"

"I would have you not build a life of freedom on a foundation of corpses!"

"I thought you wanted to be healed!" Father sucked in a breath. I didn't realize his voice could grow so loud.

"I have been." I touched my stone cheek. "But the healing has been internal. I cannot stand by and watch Catesby and the others murder three hundred Parliament members and a king—however corrupt, paranoid, or ignorant he is."

Father took several deep breaths through his nose. "You won't."

Wood splintered from behind me and something grabbed my ankle. I stumbled away and drew my sword. "Black!" I shouted, but

Father no longer stood near me. He hovered in the back corner of the room, muttering color speech.

A force yanked my feet from beneath me. I threw out my hands to catch myself and landed in . . . sand? No. I sniffed. Gunpowder.

"Black," I repeated and took in the scene. The barrels and bundles of wood had separated to create a path back toward the wall. Loose gunpowder pushed and carried my body toward the small space. A tendril of powder slid between my palm and sword hilt until it pushed my fingers apart from the metal.

"Father!" A barrel knocked me back as I struggled to get away. Ropes slithered from around the firewood bundles to tie my ankles and wrists. A dark strip of cloth covered in gunpowder dust tied around my mouth just as my vision faded.

The scrape of wood on stone and the pressure of round bodies around me told me the barrels had returned to their places, trapping me amidst the barrels and beneath stacks of wood. They pressed me down into the ground. I could still breathe, but each inhale brought in dust and gunpowder. I coughed. Choked.

My breaths came faster as my mind caught up to my predicament.

I was trapped. Surrounded by thirty-six barrels of gunpowder that would be lit by my father's own hand.

Forty

My tomb of gunpowder and barrels barely left room for shallow breathing. I'd tried to shift the wood bundles from above, but they only pressed down harder as though with a mind of their own.

Father wasn't going to hang me. He was going to give me up to the plot. He was treating me like an Igniter attending Parliament.

I focused on inhaling and exhaling and tried not to think of the tightness of the barrels closing in around me—of the tomb of stone tumbling down upon me. Of suffocation and darkness.

An hour passed and no amount of struggling loosened the walls of my cage. My saliva mixed with the gunpowder and turned into a paste on my tongue. I tried not to swallow, but time and overthinking sent the sludge down my throat. I gagged, picturing the black goop seeping into my lungs.

I should have taken my mask. I should have known he'd stop me like this and now I was powerless.

Whoosh! White Light to the rescue!

Sigh. *I'm not in the mood for banter.* Was it blind?

Who says it's banter?

What exactly can you do, then? The conversation did help keep my mind off the fact I was slowly suffocating.

I can provide company . . . and good conversation, of course.

I let out a long breath that rebounded right onto my face. *I tried. I really tried.*

Yes, you did. The bantering tone disappeared. *But your father did not.*

A weight that had nothing to do with the wood burying me lifted. Father's unwillingness to hear me out was not my fault. *Have you ever spoken to him?*

I speak to everyone. But it's up to them to speak back.

I can't imagine why anyone wouldn't want your winning personality in their head all the time.

I caught White Light's chuckle. I wasn't alone. Every time we spoke I was reminded why I was rebelling against the plot. The White Light had been a helper to me. Annoying sometimes, yes, but always accessible.

A creak of hinges. A patter of footfalls. An exclamation—not Father's voice. "That's quite a load of firewood!"

I stilled.

"Aye." Father laughed, but I caught the tension in his voice.

"Is this your place?" a low, thick voice asked. The Baron! He was here? He'd left his cushions to come to Parliament on a search. I didn't recognize the voice of the first man, but hope surged in me. They were taking action.

Perhaps they would examine the pile of firewood and find me. But then . . . then Father would be imprisoned. Maybe even locked in the Tower of London.

I wanted the plot stopped. I didn't want my friends—or Father—caught.

"I'm naught but a servant." Father sounded far off. Leaving the undercroft, perhaps?

The voices turned too distant for me to catch. They were leaving. That was it? They saw an enormous pile of firewood and barrels and they *left*? Why did the Baron come and not Henry? Not that I wanted Henry to be the hero, but he, at least, would have had the sense to scrutinize the situation.

No sounds returned.

Not for hours.

I shoved at the wood on top of me. It scraped against my exposed skin, burrowing splinters deep. I bucked against the bonds but knocked my head against the back wall. No matter how much I screamed through the rag, the sound barely reached my own ears, let alone someone passing on the street.

A hundred scenarios entered my mind.

Perhaps they caught Father.

Maybe Father had changed his mind and was now telling the other plotters to abandon the plan. But if that were so, wouldn't he free me?

Or maybe Father was telling them of my betrayal and they were coming after me.

Or nothing had happened and Father left for a final meal, planning to return again in the early hours to light the fuse upon the meeting of Parliament. Murdering me in the process.

I need to get out of here.

I was no match for Father and his mask.

I needed to get to the king.

The cloth around my mouth had grown so soggy from saliva, I could move it around a bit more. Finally, I managed a mumble. "Brown." It was enough to show the barrels and wood around me. But I saw no tool to help me escape. "Black." Shadows wavered from the distant torchlight. Not much different from my blindness. I tried all the other colors, demanding help from them.

Black, Grey, Brown, Red, Yellow, Blue, Green. Nothing, nothing, nothing, nothing.

They weren't enough. No single color would obey me or blend. I didn't know how to be an Igniter. I didn't know how to be a Keeper. I had no mask.

Let me be your mask.

My heart stilled. I wasn't sure what that meant, but with a deep, powder-filled breath, I said one final name. "White."

Fire burst inside my core, and for a wild moment, I thought the gunpowder had been ignited. It pressed against my chest from the inside, like some growing ball of flame trying to push its way out. My ribs were going to snap. My breath died. What was this madness?

A deep-throated yell scratched my throat.

Blind pain.

Pressure built behind my eyes. Was I having another seizure? My cheek split open with a crack. I screamed. Heat swept down the right side of my face. Blood? Bile? I couldn't even lift my hand to check.

Stone on stone and cracking sounds joined the fiery agony. My face was splitting apart, my eyes bursting from my head, my throat soldering shut. This was it. This was death.

Light blinded me—so bright, I felt it in the center of my skull. I slapped my hands over my eyes, trying to shield myself from the needles piercing every bit of me.

Then, in a breath, the pain evaporated.

I lay panting, palms pressed to my eyes. Only then did I realize they were no longer bound. The skin around my wrists burned and hissed from each bump against wood. Raw. I kept my hands over my eyes until my mind could cool.

White . . . what did you do?

The danger was real.

My palms rubbed against stone cheekbones, but something was off. I removed one hand and something slipped from my face. Something thick, solid, and stone. It landed on my leg and I blinked away the dust.

Wait. I blinked again, rubbed my eyes, and took in the barrels inches from my nose. I could see them plain as daylight. Every grain of wood, every crack, every seam.

My sight had been returned. I touched my face with the tips of my fingers. Skin. Supple, soft, healed skin. It didn't feel like when Dee healed me—no stiffness or fear resting in the pores. No threat of the plague returning. No, from both the inside and outside, my skin felt cleansed.

Then I looked down into my lap at the weight that had fallen from my face.

Fragments of bleached stone bound by fire and light, forming an oval. I flipped the curved piece of art over and saw two eye holes, a nose space, and a firm-set expression.

It was a mask.

A mask made from the plague that White Light had purged from my body. But it wasn't like any of the masks I'd ever seen before.

This one was White.

I yanked the gag from my mouth, and when I tried to straighten, the wood above me adjusted with my force. It was no longer under Father's command. I picked up the mask in my lap—*my* mask. There were no ribbons on the side to tie it to my face.

I almost didn't want to touch it to my skin—what if it stayed there and I was plagued again? Having my sight back, my skin back, was enough reward for me. I could be content.

But my task wasn't over yet.

Now I'd been equipped to do what I must.

I pressed the mask against my face. It fit perfectly. Comfortably. And when I let go, it stayed there—held on by some other force. The mouth and nose area allowed me to breathe easily. Nothing impeded my vision. Every color voice welcomed me with a hum. Waiting to join in action. I felt them around me rather than saw them.

I must say, you look stunning. Very manly and intimidating and all that.

I grinned.

Okay, but really—how do you like it?

The mask felt both separate from me and yet a part of me—a tool. The White Light, however, had become part of my identity. "It's perfect."

When I lowered my hands from the mask, I realized my veins were glowing, which was why I could see the barrels and wood around me. I looked at the barrels on each side. "Move."

The word had barely passed my lips before they obeyed. And I knew it wasn't because of me. It was because of the White Light in my veins, on my mask.

I untied my ankles, brushed the gunpowder off me, and stood, barely able to see over the piles of wood into the undercroft. The torch Father left behind had almost gone out. The main source of light came from beneath my skin. But with each breath, it diminished. I remembered when Emma looked this way after moving the prison cart.

I retrieved my rapier.

The door creaked open and I ducked behind a barrel.

In walked Father, but he no longer wore his servant clothing. Tall black boots clung to his calves, with sharp spurs at the heels.

He wore his cloak and wide-brimmed black hat. Sword at his side, mask tight against his face.

John Johnson was gone.

Tonight Father was the warrior, Guy Fawkes.

And I would have to fight him.

Forty-One

"What have you done?"

I hovered my hand over my sword as a response to Father's question. "Father, please listen—"

"You are truly lost." His voice broke. "I wonder if there was ever really a chance of saving you."

"I'm *not lost*! I have wrestled with this for the past year and made the decision to bond with White Light out of my own clear mind. You never even gave White Light a chance."

"It's too dangerous."

"Since when have *you* feared danger?"

He slid his rapier from its scabbard. "I don't want to have to do this."

I left my sword undrawn for a moment longer. "You don't have to. I am trying to save lives, Father. I am still against the oppression of Keepers. I'm not a power-hungry Igniter. I just know that this act of murder will not result in restoration."

I caught the droop of his arm. The sag of his shoulders. As though he actually considered my words for a moment. But then a deep resolve seemed to fill his chest and he took his stance. *"En garde."*

I barely slipped my sword from its sheath before he attacked. My throat burned, but not as hot as my muscles were about to. I deflected his cut, allowing the years of training and practice to flow back into my limbs.

The irony of fighting the man who gifted me my sword was not lost on me.

His movements were swift and sharp—honed by years of battle. He had always boasted Jack's talent with a sword, but already I knew Father was beyond my skill.

I thrust with my anguish.

I parried with my despair.

I cut with my resignation.

Father and I would never be father and son. Not the way I'd hoped for so many years. Not the way it was supposed to be. It was as though we were born to have a draw. Neither one of us willing to kill the other. And neither one willing to back down.

How would this end?

The bells chimed one in the morning. We had a mere six hours before Parliament and the most I'd done was tire myself.

Father had the stamina of a soldier in battle. He never relented. Never took a breath. And when my rapier tip glanced off his guard and pierced his shoulder, he spoke his first color command.

My boots tore from my feet and flew across the room as I tumbled onto my back. I tucked into a roll and came up on my feet again, my cloak tangled around my head. I threw up my sword with one hand as the other hand yanked the fabric away.

My sword met metal.

I willed up some sort of color command, but I didn't know how to use it. *All right, White, how do I do this thing?* I parried Father's attacks while I looked for something to send flying his way. I didn't want to risk the torch lighting the gunpowder, so I asked a bundle of wood to lurch toward his head. He deflected it with barely a word.

"You can't stop me." Father popped forward, and with a twirl of his blade and a command from behind his mask, my sword went spinning from my hand.

I stood stunned, his blade against my chest.

Then the fight went out of me. I took my mask from my face and dropped my arms to my sides. If he was going to run me through, I would at least allow him to see my face—something he never granted me.

He'd won.

Why did White Light do *nothing*? When I'd first stood from Father's bonds in the sea of gunpowder, I thought it would be no contest. I had White Light in my veins, I had a mask unlike any other and I was fighting for the right cause.

"Your White Light didn't help you."

Then I understood. "That's because its battles are not physical. It's spending too much time fighting for your loyalty. For your heart."

"You sound like a woman."

I swept into a bow, the sword point pricking my sternum. "Why, thank you." I liked being compared to Emma, even though Father intended it as a petty insult. "I see now that this plot is more important to you than any lives—mine, innocents', even your own."

"I won't kill you, Thomas."

"You buried me beneath the gunpowder!"

"I wouldn't have left you there—"

"Catesby would have. He *wanted* to let me die."

Father shook his head. "I didn't let him."

"But you *trust* him."

"Why shouldn't I?"

How could Father not see? "Because he's not of stable mind! Don't you question all the new men he's added to the plot these last few months? He doesn't care who dies or who lives. He collects our stories and uses them as blackmail."

"You don't know him."

It was my last chance to talk Father down from this treason and murder. "He added John Dee to the plot. And Dee is the one spreading the plague."

Not just spreading, Thomas.

So my suspicions were correct. "He *controls* the plague, Father. And Catesby knows this."

Father stared. "That can't be true."

"It was Dee who cut me that night. How else would he 'cure' me at the masquerade? It's a color Compulsion that he reverses. He was on the bank during our rowing. He has sent color Compulsions to the grains he feeds the pigeons. And those pigeons spread the plague to the rats, who spread it to the water, which spreads it to us."

"No. Catesby can't have known."

That was his response? I just told him Dee. Created. The. Plague. And Father was defending Catesby. "Don't you hear yourself? You're more concerned about Catesby's innocence than the plague of all England! You really think Catesby would have added Dee to the plot without interrogating him about his control over the plague? Catesby knew, and he allowed you and the other plotters to continue with this scheme under the lie that it would heal England of the plague and save the Keepers."

"No—"

There came a pounding at the door. Both Father and I jumped, and I instinctively stepped to his side, retrieving my sword. The action surprised me, but what stunned me even more was Father sweeping me behind him as though he was protecting me.

The pounding came again, solidifying the suspicion that it was not one of our own. It was an enemy of the plot, and even though I welcomed their entrance, I didn't want Father to be caught.

I grabbed his arm from behind. "You need to leave. Get out of here, Father. They'll kill you."

He paused for a moment and then shoved me behind the barrels. "Stay out of sight."

"No! I—"

"You have to warn the others if this goes poorly. Especially if what you say about Dee is true. You've done enough to condemn them already. Save their lives if you can."

He sent my lost boots into my chest with a quick command, then stepped away as the door burst open. I crouched behind the piles of wood. Four men entered—the first of whom was a knight I'd seen before at the masquerade. Then the Baron. Then Henry.

And finally . . . John Dee.

The sight of his multicolored mask and belt of strange stone daggers boiled my blood. His traitorous nature was confirmed.

An odd group for an attack. Judging by their unceremonious topple into the undercroft, swords still sheathed and torches lit, I gathered they hadn't expected resistance.

This was a search party.

A search party that had found an armed warrior with a Black mask, two wheellock pistols, and a sword in hand.

Henry gave a shout and drew his sword before the others registered the threat. "Who are you?" Henry didn't recognize Father. All this time he tried to get me to introduce him to Guy Fawkes, he never actually knew what Guy Fawkes looked like. Father had done well to keep his fame linked to his name but not his mask.

"I might ask the same thing," Father responded with a tone of utmost surprise.

The knight stepped forward, wearing a mask of Brown. "I am Sir Knevett. What is your business at this hour of the bell?" Knevett looked him up and down. "And with such weaponry?"

I could already tell that he would challenge Father. "I am merely a servant," Father said.

Dee remained silent—because to expose Father would allow Father to expose him.

Dee had never been loyal to the plot. He'd been loyal to whatever would further his status at court. And exposing a plot of regicide would surely endear him to King James.

"Whom do you serve?" Knevett demanded.

Father hesitated.

"This is the same man who was here earlier." The Baron pointed a finger. "But now dressed for battle!"

"Bind him," Knevett said.

"Nay!" Father sheathed his sword and held out his hands. Even I believed him to be a nervous servant. "I am but a footman—John Johnson—startled by your intrusion. What do you want?"

His act didn't deter them. Both the Baron and Dee carried coils of rope. Dee sent them swirling toward Father. Father shouted a command and the ropes twitched but didn't stop. I had exhausted him.

Why didn't he expose Dee?

"You cannot undo my commands," Dee said smugly.

Father's voice turned to steel. "Your death will undo any Compulsion you've ever set, Dee. You know that, don't you?"

"All masked know that." With a jerk of Dee's chin, the ropes rose into the air.

"Dee, you know this man?" the Baron inquired.

"Is that why you've been training an apprentice?" Father asked. "To further your practice of sending the plague into the blood of weak and helpless people?"

So he believed me.

Dee's eyebrows shot up so high, they popped over the top of his mask. "I don't—"

"You ought to be sent to the Tower for what you've done to our people!" Father screamed—all nervous servant act gone.

"I think I *do* recognize this man," Dee said in a dangerous voice. "He's Thomas Percy's servant."

Father and I tensed. Percy's name had been given. He was now implicated.

"You know nothing of me." Father's tone was deadly. "Least of all whom I serve." Then he turned to the knight. "This man, Dee, is the cause of the plague, Knevett! It is him you should be arresting—" A coil cinched around his neck, cutting off his air.

"Didn't I see you with another man recently?" Dee continued. "Robert Catesby, was it?"

Dee was giving away the names of each plotter. Soon they would all be exposed. And they would all be hunted.

"I said bind him!" Knevett shouted.

Dee resumed his command of the ropes and they coiled around Father. Father writhed away from them, brandishing his rapier. Henry fiddled with the bundles of wood and I ducked farther behind the piles. It didn't take him long. "There's gunpowder." He threw a bundle of sticks to the side and exposed some of the barrels. "Barrels and barrels of gunpowder!"

"I'm taking you to the Tower," Knevett said.

The ropes tugged Father forward and he stumbled to keep his feet. He slashed his rapier at the ropes with his free hand. "This alchemist cut my son. Sent the plague into him and blinded him—because my boy saw what he was doing and tried to stop him."

The rope around his throat cinched again, and this time didn't loosen.

For once, being called a "boy" didn't anger me. It was the first time Father had claimed me as his own. I choked back a cry.

"Ah yes, you *do* have a son, don't you?" Dee tapped the chin of his mask as though thinking.

Father stilled.

"What was his name again?"

Father shook his head violently. They were going to give my name. And then I'd be a dead man, no matter that I sent the letter or tried to stop the plot.

"It started with a *T*, didn't it?"

Finally, Father dropped his sword and they contained him. Worst of all, once his back was turned to me and they hauled him to the undercroft door, Dee ripped Father's mask from his face.

"No," I cried, but my voice was lost in the slam of the door. I didn't see his face. They had torn his pride and honor from him. And he let them.

Because of me.

I hadn't defended him. I hadn't joined the fight. But that was because Father gave himself up for me—to keep my name anonymous. So I tightened my sword belt.

I had a new target.

Forty-Two

"I will look for this Thomas Percy." Dee handed Sir Knevett Father's mask. They headed along the Thames toward the Tower. I followed close enough to hear but not be caught. Not yet.

I kept my White mask on my face—neither Henry nor Dee would recognize me with it on.

"I'll have a warrant for his arrest soon." Knevett tossed his cape over Father's head to increase Father's disorientation. "Report your findings, Dee. And thank you for volunteering your help. Your color skill has been invaluable this night."

With Father so disarmed and unmasked, he would be no match for Knevett or the Baron. Or anyone, for that matter. I hated seeing him so subdued.

Dee bowed, shook hands with Henry, and then left. I bounced on the balls of my feet, ready to follow, but one step into my pursuit I caught a glint from Henry's fist. He curled his fingers around one of Dee's plague-inducing daggers.

Henry seemed uncomfortable, adjusting and readjusting the

Fawkes

dagger. But determination won out and he strode after Knevett, the Baron, and Father.

He was about to silence Father.

Of course. He was Dee's apprentice. And if Father was going to the Tower, he would be interrogated. Though I knew he wouldn't give away any of our names, he would most certainly expose Dee as much as he could.

But if Father was infected with the plague, the Igniters would think that he caught the plague as retribution for betraying his country. They would see it as a sign.

No one realized the plague wasn't a sign of anything. It was a deadly color Compulsion started by an old alchemist.

All these years of blaming. Of wars. Of killing. Caused by Dee's creation.

Dee was neither Keeper nor Igniter, yet seemingly was against so much. What exactly did he fight *for*?

The same thing most men fight for.

Enlighten me.

Themselves.

Suddenly the night felt too old. Too short. I had no time. I needed to stop Henry. I needed to stop Dee. I needed to find Wintour to tell him the plot was up. I needed to warn the others who were also under Catesby's spell.

One step at a time. You're not alone.

Right. I hurried after the entourage headed for the Tower. Henry was creeping closer and closer to Father's bound silhouette. One slice in Father's calf. One cut to his throat. One prick of that stone blade and the plague would send its roots into Father's body.

I couldn't see the dagger, but I focused on the colors. Grey stone. Carved bone. And before sending the command, I thought of White's voice around me. In me.

373

"Come to me."

The dagger flew from Henry's fist to my shadowed hiding place so fast I lurched backward to avoid getting struck in the face. I didn't think it would obey so willingly.

Perhaps the plague was tired of being controlled. It was ready to be defeated.

Henry spun in my direction. But before he could come after the dagger, I sent it into the gutter. With any luck, the color Compulsion would be null soon.

Father had been delivered to the guards of the Tower. The gates closed. Henry had lost his chance.

As much as I would have liked to remain and fight him, I needed to stop Dee from catching Percy. I needed to stop Dee from doing anything.

And I needed help.

⋯⟫⟪⋯

Emma came to her window at the Strand house within seconds of my knock. Clothed, masked, intimidating. She had been waiting for the Baron and Henry to return.

She recoiled when she saw me and moved to pull the window closed again, but I caught the edge with one hand and lowered my mask with the other. The moment her eyes met mine, she gasped.

I expected questions. A "How?" or "What happened?" But she stared, then brushed her gloved fingers along my jawline. "You're whole."

I savored the moment and then grabbed her hand. "Emma, I need you." Father would be ashamed to hear me sounding so dependent on a woman, but I felt only relief. Because Emma and I were fluid—two streams who became a river when out on the streets together. She brought a calm and understanding that no one else could.

She asked no questions, just left the window for a minute and arrived at the back door with her cloak. She took my hand. "What is going on?"

I tugged her toward the street but then pulled up short. What was I *doing*? Emma could be killed. I faced her. "Dee is the plague. He has been spreading it his entire life. It's all one giant color Compulsion."

"How is that possible?"

"He helped with the plot for a time, but my letter caused him to switch back to the Igniter side. He's helped send my father to the Tower and now he's after Percy. I need to stop him before he exposes and kills all the plotters. And I can't do it alone." My chest heaved as I expelled this unspoken request.

Emma didn't move or say anything for a long time. I tried not to grow impatient. I needed to go—but I couldn't expect her to risk her life on impulse. It needed to be her decision. But then I realized something else might be stopping her.

"I know these friends of mine are Keepers. Assassins. They don't deserve rescue or warning, but . . ."

"Everyone deserves a chance to make right." She lifted her chin and straightened her mask. "Besides, more than that, Dee must be stopped if he is truly the perpetuator of the plague. I will help you, Thomas." Excitement bled into her voice with that last statement.

"You could die. *We* could die. I ask you because you're the strongest mask I know."

"You are not the only voice asking me to help save lives."

She likes me more than you.

I grinned, bolstered. *But I'm better looking.*

Only because of that mask I made you.

We broke into a fast stride. "Where is Henry?" Emma steered me toward the stable.

"Last I saw at the Tower—but he might be back any moment. He was trying to cut my father with one of those daggers—" I skidded to a stop. "Those daggers. They're the same ones that were used by the thugs who tried to cut your arm." I rounded on Emma. "They weren't trying to check your Igniter status. They were trying to *plague* you. If they'd succeeded in cutting you . . ."

Her eyes widened behind the mask.

Had my blood not already been aflame, this would have set it to boiling. Dee had gone after Emma. *My* Emma. Probably to infect an Igniter family to get to King James.

I wondered if Henry knew this about his mentor.

⊷ ⚏ ⊶

Soldiers filled the night streets, holding lanterns aloft and knocking on doors. We pressed against a wall and watched, not wanting to raise suspicion.

"Awake! Get up!" They turned the lords out of their houses. "There is a warrant for the arrest of Thomas Percy. Find him!" I caught some of the descriptions and commands. "Tall man . . . stooping shoulders . . . broad beard . . . white hair . . . Keep him alive."

"Wait here." I left Emma and darted to the Duck and Drake a few buildings down. Most of the patrons were awake from the hubbub in the street. I passed the whisperers, the fire, the inn man, and took the back steps two at a time until I was pounding on Wintour's door.

It opened within seconds, and though his sword wasn't drawn, he wore his cracked mask and looked ready for a fight. "Who's—Thomas?"

I saw first the frown of confusion—my plague was, after all, completely gone. I kept my mask on my belt beneath my cloak.

"Father was caught." My voice pinched at the words. I wanted to say more but feet pounded up the steps behind me. Both Wintour and I spun. Kit—Jack's brother—barreled down the hall.

"The matter is discovered," he panted. "I overheard Lord Worcester summoning the Baron Monteagle and going to fetch Northumberland. People are looking for Percy." His message delivered, his face fell and he dropped to a knee.

Wintour helped him back to his feet, showing a strength of sorrow in his composure. "Then you must hasten to Percy's lodging and bid him begone."

Kit gave a fierce nod and stumbled back to the stairs.

"What of you?" I took Wintour's arm. "You must flee." Did he catch the fact I didn't say *we*?

"I will stay and see the uttermost."

I wanted him to leave. He had always been kind to me, and if somehow Father gave up the plotters' names, then Wintour would—No. Father would not betray anyone.

"Dee has betrayed us," I said.

"But Catesby trusted him."

"He is the cause of the plague. It is a color Compulsion that has caused war and abused England."

This revelation broke through Wintour's composure and he fell against the doorframe. It took a moment for him to recover. "He knows Catesby's location. He knows—he knows the plans. We are undone." Then, as though remembering I was there, Wintour grasped my shoulder. I thought to help stabilize himself. "You must warn him, Thomas."

A repeat of Father's command. I must obey. It was my last duty to Catesby, even though I doubted more than ever that he would listen. Perhaps the others might—Keyes, Bates, Jack . . .

I squeezed Wintour's arm, sending what reassurance I could. It felt rotten. Like I was still acting the role of a plotter, yet all these things had happened because of me. Because of my letter.

When I exited the inn, Henry had Emma's arm in his grip. I lurched into a shadow and slipped my mask onto my face so that if he *did* see me, he wouldn't recognize me.

"What are you doing out here?" Henry demanded, dragging her back to the Monteagle house. I followed, inching along the walls.

"I was left *alone* in our house with soldiers shouting on the streets. I came out to help."

"There are *murderers* on the loose, Emma!" He darted a glance around. "Go back inside and bolt the door."

He turned to leave, but Emma grabbed his sleeve. "Wait! Henry, where are you going?" I caught true concern in her voice, reminding me of their odd bond—one of shared troubles, but also of Henry's blackmail.

"I'm going to battle, Emma."

"What? With whom? *For* whom? Against whom?"

"With John Dee, the alchemist—"

"Your master," she supplied.

"Ah. You know about that." He sounded pleased. Proud. "Yes, he's been training me. He helped expose an assassination plot. He knows where the plotters are hiding out and he's leading an army there for the king."

"The king trusts him?" I could hear the disgust in her voice.

"Maybe not, but Dee is a mighty warrior and infiltrated the traitors' group."

My fist tightened against my sword hilt. Dee had deceived all of us. And Catesby had trusted him like a fool. *Keep talking, Emma.*

"Why must you accompany him? You are no soldier of the mask."

"I am a soldier of the sword and flint. And Dee has a specialized armory that will stop these Keepers once and for all. The king does not need to know. All he will see after this battle is how Dee was able to direct the plague into the hearts of the rebels."

"The plague?"

Henry took Emma's hands in his. "Round shot, daggers, musket balls . . . Dee has bonded the Stone Plague to each. It's taken him years. Once the king sees how these work, there will be no more wars. England will be the greatest country in the world. England will control the plague."

"Henry, listen to yourself—"

A shout and the fire of a musket broke the night air, followed by screams. Henry shoved Emma toward the house. "Get inside. Stay safe."

"But—"

"I'll survive this. I'm with Dee." He swept her into an embrace. I stiffened. Henry saw her into the house, checked the lock, and then ran in the direction of Whitehall.

Dee was arming the king's men with plague firearms. He must have sent color Compulsions to each and every musket ball, bonding it with the plague. I couldn't even begin to fathom the skill or study that would have taken.

Perhaps it was the reason Dee joined the plot in the first place—to use Father, Catesby, and the rest of us as bait for his plan to unleash his final project.

The plotters had to be warned. I owed them this much. But what of Emma? I looked toward the Monteagle house. Henry was right. She'd be safe there.

In fact, I shouldn't tempt her.

Tell her I'm sorry.

I'm not a petty messenger. Tell her yourself. Abandonment is not love.

379

Spare me the lecture. I broke into a jog. *I'm protecting her.*

And you honestly think she'll stay behind? Do you even know her?

It's easier this way. I exited the Strand and turned right on Charing Cross.

Now you're making excuses. You'd be surprised how often I see people do this. It rarely ends well.

Is that your way of giving advice?

Is that your way of acknowledging it or ignoring it?

I pulled up short at St. James's Park, breathing hard. Footsteps crunched behind me. I spun.

"It is *so* much easier to ride in men's clothing." Emma rode up on a chestnut mare, wearing dirty servant breeches and an enormous hat pulled low over her masked face. I wouldn't have known it was her had she not spoken.

"Emma. Go back—"

She slid from the horse's back. "White advised me to retrieve my horse, so I obeyed." She didn't even sound perturbed that I'd left without her.

I tried not to let the exhaustion into my voice. "I'm going to warn the others. It's two days' ride north."

"But what of Dee?"

"He could be on his way to Catesby and the men as we speak." I mounted with effort. "Do what you can here." I looked down at her. "I don't know what will happen." Was I riding to my death?

"I'll see for myself, thank you very much."

She grabbed the edges of the saddle to hoist herself up, but I pressed a hand to her shoulder. "No."

She grabbed my arm. "Thomas Fawkes, I am coming with you!"

I was going to be sick. "You are an Igniter. In the heat of this plot, they *will* kill you."

She held the mare's bridle so tight, her gloves squeaked beneath the strain of her clenched knuckles. "Not a single day has been promised to me. Do not deny me this moment."

"I need you safe. If I fail, who will finish this?"

She lifted her mask so I could see her face—her beautiful, fiercely confident face. "Safety is an illusion, Thomas Fawkes." Her statement made me think of White Light and how it told me it wasn't safe either. "And if you fail, then I will fail at your side."

A muscle pulsed in her clenched jaw. Then she linked her hands behind my neck and pulled my lips to hers. The kiss flooded me with that rare sense of full acceptance. As though all of me was enough for her—even with my brokenness.

The mare sidestepped just as we separated. She held my stare with wide eyes of her own. My chest heaved.

And then I reached down and lifted her into the saddle, though she didn't need much help.

As though sensing that any words spoken after such a moment would be inadequate, the mare hopped away in a trot. Alone, I had felt ill-equipped to face whatever was ahead. But with Emma in my arms, the battle did not seem so bleak.

She returned her mask to her face. I pulled my own down and we headed away from the Thames. Whether to death, to capture, or to life, we would still ride.

Together.

I grinned. "I had no idea how stubborn you are."

"Oh, don't fool yourself. You've known all along." She directed the mare toward the gate. "And you like it."

One point for me.

Forty-Three

Emma and I made it out of London just as the ports closed and a watch was set on all gates. There'd be no returning without being questioned.

I ran a mental map of England through my head. We'd studied it many times during Catesby's meetings. "Let's head to Huddington Court—Wintour's brother's house."

That was the last we spoke, for few words could be shared at a canter. The mare couldn't keep up the pace, so we slowed and rode through the night. It was cold, dark, and my pulse never slowed the entire ride. At one point Emma started to slip, but I caught her.

She woke and shook her head with an apology.

"Sleep," I said. "For I cannot. I won't let you fall." She assented and leaned back into me. I took the reins and relished the moment of togetherness. What would happen to us after this? If we survived, then what?

By the time we arrived at the wattle-and-daub Huddington Court home on the second day, the mare was frothing and had a limp to her right foreleg. My fingers were numb from the chill November wind and the overcast sky removed any possible heat of sun.

We crossed the stone bridge at a walk and I took in the three-story home with a chimney like a brick steeple. Dormers poked out of the long thatched roofs. Smoke rose from the chimney. Someone was there. "Stay with the mare," I told Emma and approached the front door. I tucked my mask into my belt. It would be no good to announce myself as an Igniter upon first greeting.

I knocked and waited. And waited. And waited. I knocked again. Finally, a short young woman opened the door. "May I help you?"

Now what? I couldn't very well ask about Catesby. What side was she on? She looked nervous. I didn't see a mask.

"I am a friend of Robert and Thomas Wintour. Are they—are they here?"

She shook her head. "I'm sorry."

"Do you know where they've gone?"

She shut the door so that only her face was visible with narrowed eyes. "There are a lot of strange folk about. I don't know who you are."

I bowed. "Forgive me. I'm Thomas Fawkes. Son of Guy Fawkes." She would at least know that name and be able to determine if I was trustworthy or not.

The door opened another centimeter. "Guy Fawkes, you say?"

I nodded.

"You'd best come in then."

I forced myself not to look back toward where Emma was hiding with the horse and entered.

"Robert is my husband. You may call me Gertrude. He left here with Catesby and the others this very morning."

Well, she trusted me. "Where to? I must find them, for I have an urgent message to deliver."

"They already know the plot is foiled."

"There is more than that."

"They've gone to raid Alnwick Castle. They're going to make a stand at Holbeche House." At this, she thrust a lace handkerchief to her nose and muffled a sob.

She didn't think they were going to come back.

"Gertrude. Tell me everything."

Her story wasn't long, but it was enough to give me my next destination. She allowed Emma to come in, but both Emma and I hid our masks. Gertrude fed us and we slept—warm for once, but not at peace. At daybreak, we were back on the mare. Gertrude had said she'd offer a horse if she had one, but Catesby and the men had taken all the stable to hasten their journey.

She said they'd gathered at least fifty men to fight.

How many men did Dee have?

<hr />

The skies sent down gale after gale of icy rain, soaking us through the bone. My mind was as numb as my half-frozen body. The steeples popping up over the hilly horizon looked blurry—was that the rain or my own fog?

The going was slow. With each town we passed through, we were met with stares colder than the weather. As though they'd encountered unpleasant strangers and had no desire to deal with more.

Sorry about the rain.

This is your *doing?*

I'm doing everything I can to change Catesby's mind.

The mare plodded along. I looked to the skies. *Maybe add some hail.*

Emma and I bypassed Alnwick Castle—they were likely gone from there by now and it was out of our way. With any luck, we'd arrive at Holbeche House a half day after Catesby. We would warn him—tell the men of Dee's betrayal. Of the oncoming army.

When our ride crested a hill in Staffordshire the next morning, the expanse of England lay before us—covered in late-autumn green and valleys filled with thick fog. I thought I saw movement far off in the fog. Horses maybe? A rider?

"Should we ride for them?" Emma whispered.

I nodded. If it was Catesby and his men, this worked even more in our favor. But if it was Dee and his plague army, we would at least know their destination. I spurred on the mare and we approached from the back right. I donned my mask, remembering, again, that I now had color power.

My mind was so used to existing as a maskless that I didn't even jump to the idea of color commands.

The group was a posse of men. Townsmen, by the look of it. Each wore a sword on his belt and carried a matchlock musket. Each sported a mask of one color or another. I scanned for the multicolor mask near the front. Nothing.

"Join us, men!"

I spun to see a man astride a horse, waving to us. Emma tugged her hat lower over her face. The cloak helped hide her small frame.

"What is your name and errand?" I called back.

"I am Sheriff of Staffordshire. We seek Robert Catesby and his gang of traitors to the crown. They raided Alnwick Castle and have taken shelter at Holbeche House. The king's men are meeting us within the hour and then we attack."

Within the hour.

One hour.

The sheriff turned his steed and barked orders at a man sending matchlock rifles from a flatbed wagon to a line of men, using color speech.

Emma and I dismounted and my knees nearly buckled from the long riding. I didn't dare ride away after the sheriff drew such attention to us.

"I need to get to Holbeche House before the posse attacks," I whispered to Emma, leading the mare up the line of soldiers.

"At best, we have three hours." Her rusty whisper mingled with the clank of metal and creaking of leather boots. "One for Dee's army to arrive, one for their preparation, and then one for them to walk to Holbeche."

"You're not coming." On this, I wouldn't budge.

"I did *not* come all this way to—"

I hauled her toward a copse of trees. "You *can't* come. You are an Igniter—"

"So are you!"

"—and they will kill you, Emma. Instantly. Without question—no matter your sex or good intentions. And if you're there, they won't listen to me."

She clamped her lips shut.

"If they are making a stand, they care not for their lives, nor whose lives they destroy in the process."

"Then why warn them at all? If you already know they won't listen, then why are you going there?"

I lowered my voice further. "I know *Catesby* won't listen. He is the leader. But there are other men there—followers who have been gathered by Catesby in the heat of Keeper passion." I thought of Rookwood and Bates, whom I barely knew. Jack and Kit—Father's childhood friends. Wintour, *my* friend. "If I can save even one life from this oncoming slaughter, it is my duty. I should have stopped Catesby earlier—"

"You did what you could. Today you are an honorable man."

She called me honorable, and from the outside I might seem that way. But inside, I didn't want to go to Holbeche House. I didn't want to warn anyone and I didn't want to fight anyone. I would much rather disappear to a small English village and purge my memory of this whole ordeal.

I supposed it wasn't shameful to have those desires. As long as they didn't rule me. "Keep the mare."

"No, you must take her." Emma shoved the reins into my hands. "I already draw too much attention being a small African woman."

"Keep your mask on."

"I will, Thomas. But I'm still a woman and I still look like one. I don't need a horse to draw the men's eyes to me."

Voices in the camp rose to shouts and greetings—so loud I was certain they were yelling at us for a moment. But then I saw an army of men crest the hill, leading horse-drawn cart after cart of weapons and bags of musket ball. Crates of small daggers.

At the front of this army rode Dee in his multicolored mask and, at his side, Henry Parker.

I backpedaled into the trees so fast, the mare broke into a trot to keep up. Once the oaks blocked us from Dee and Henry's view, I hoisted Emma into the saddle. "On second thought, maybe you should come with me."

Forty-Four

Holbeche House looked brand-new. As though constructed and polished only to be destroyed in battle. No stains or rot or growing ivy.

It had two stories with dormered windows in an attic. Dutch gables decorated side wings on each end of the house. Emma and I hung in the tree line. I dismounted and left her with the mare. This time, at least she didn't argue.

"Please come back to me, Thomas."

I pulled off my mask and tucked it into my belt—the White face turned against my thigh. I didn't like hiding it—or hiding what the White Light had done for me—but an Igniter mask was deadlier than a war flag. "I'll try."

"If you don't, then I'm coming after you."

"Don't you dare." I gave her my full attention. "There's no reason to, Emma." I placed my hands on her shoulders. "What happens in that house is meant to happen."

"What if you don't get out in time? What if Dee and his army attack while you're in there? You'll be seen as a traitor. You'll be massacred!"

"I am not going in alone."

Her eyes darted to my mask. It took her several breaths to calm and seemingly remind herself of all the things she'd once told me about White Light. "All right. I'll be here."

I squeezed her hand and then left, not wanting to prolong my departure any more. Otherwise I might not depart at all.

I could creep across the field or try to approach the house in a roundabout way. But that might heighten their suspicion of me. So instead, I strode across the field with my hands held away from my sides. Unarmed.

But not unafraid.

The skies drizzled. I strode foot over foot as though through a fire, my skin burning from a confusing mixture of shame and conviction. Shame for letting things get so far. Conviction over why I did the things I did.

I was saving lives.

That was really what this all came down to. It started with the African boy at the hanging. And then with the Keepers at the Tower. And then with the three hundred Parliament members and the king.

White Light had been training me this entire time, and I hadn't seen it until now.

This was my *contra tempo*.

This was my *coup de main*.

And I strode onto the battlefield as though it were the field of a duel. Emma was my second. No audience.

I passed through a wall into the courtyard with no incident. The gate was still open. Once closed, this house would be well fortified. I approached the entrance door and still no one stopped me. Perhaps Catesby and the men weren't even at Holbeche House.

Maybe they'd fled. They'd seen sense and weren't actually making a stand.

"It's Thomas!" someone shouted from inside. "Thomas Fawkes has come!"

My heart sank. That was Jack's voice.

They thought I was coming as an ally. To fight with them. Not for the first time, I wondered if Emma would be left in that tree line indefinitely. Waiting for my corpse to come out.

I entered the house and shut the door firmly behind me. The interior was cold and dark yet smelled of acrid smoke. I blinked several times so my eyes would adjust.

Hands clasped my shoulders and I looked into the face of Jack Wright. "Wintour said you were cured." He wore a grin, with undertones of resignation and ferocity. No true joy.

"Father was taken." It seemed the only thing to say to the man who grew up with Father. Who sparred with him and was partly the cause of Father's commitment to the Keeper way.

A grimace overtook the grin. "We will avenge him."

It had already been days. *Days* that Father was in the Tower. They could have tortured him to death by now. A hollow suction in the pit of my stomach fed on what little hope remained. "I couldn't help him. He told me to warn you."

"Then you'd best come in to Catesby." Jack didn't take my coat, acknowledging that the chill in the house was not my imagination. "We had an accident. The gunpowder got wet, and when spread by the fire to dry, a spark took to it."

That explained the smell.

The pulse in my throat tapped double time to my footsteps as I made my way into the main room. I wanted to scream that soldiers were coming—that they must leave—but this needed to be handled delicately.

In a wide room with a scorched hearth and burnt rug, I saw him. Catesby stood at the window, frenziedly polishing his mottled Grey mask. A spray of soot covered his face, blackened with the touch of fire. Blood slipped from gashes in his skin.

He turned from the window. Slowly. And the first thing his eyes landed on was my mask at my belt. It had spun right way out—revealing the White. "Thomas."

I didn't move. Didn't dare drop my hand to the mask in case the other plotters in the room noticed. But Catesby knew.

And he'd not listen to me now.

"The"—I swallowed—"the soldiers are coming."

The room stilled in the preparations. Men—most of whom I didn't recognize—faced me. Catesby didn't seem to care what I was about to say or that I was about to affect the men's morale. His indifference stung, driving the blade of betrayal deeper. He'd only ever truly loved the plot—as though it was a woman to whom he was bound.

I believed he cared about the plotters too—Wintour, Percy, Father, Jack—but his care for them did not run as deeply as his commitment to the plot. It had blinded him. It had overtaken his mind.

I couldn't save him. But I could possibly save the others.

I looked around the room at the men—Bates, Keyes, Rookwood, Percy, Catesby, Jack, Kit—and I didn't want them to die. "The Sheriff of Staffordshire has a posse of two hundred men. They are barely two hours behind me." At their intake of breath, I delivered the final blow. "Dee is at the head."

"Dee?" Bates asked. "The alchemist who controls all colors?"

I nodded. "The very one." I watched their courage slip from their shoulders like the fall of a cloak.

"Ah, but reinforcements are coming!" a man crowed, coming up beside me. He wore gaudy and bright clothing. Even in the darkened house, he stood out like a bloom among thistles and looked a handful of years older than I was. I'd heard of Everard Digby's flashy clothing. But he acted as though he wasn't about to engage in warfare.

I took in what he'd said and looked out the window. "Where from?"

"From the towns we've passed—people too shy to step forward under the scrutiny of their folk. But now they follow. They've been following. They've been behind us this whole time."

"I have seen no one else."

His hope seemed to fade and he rushed to the window as though to prove reinforcements were behind him. Jack stepped up to the window and laid a hand on his shoulder. "It seems that those weren't reinforcements we heard, Digby. Those were soldiers. The king's men."

That was the last straw. Men fought for the door. Not everybody left, but those who did took horses and abandoned their weapons. Relief burgeoned inside me. Those men—the ones Catesby might consider cowards—were now safe. Alive and safe.

Catesby didn't try to stop them. But once the clamor for the door ended, once the men had sprinted across the courtyard and fled on horseback to all corners of England, he returned his attention to the room.

And he counted. "Of our plotters we have Jack, Kit, Rookwood, and Percy left." He didn't include me.

"Catesby, should this not be abandoned?" I asked. Whatever pride I had left was not worth the cost of cowardice.

He clapped my shoulder, as he always did before a final statement. "We mean to die here, Thomas. I begrudge you nothing if you go."

"You begrudge me nothing?" I couldn't leave without him

knowing—without confessing. Bile and saliva and sorrow mounted in my throat. "Catesby, I wrote that letter. To the Baron. It was me!"

I wanted to apologize, but how could I ask forgiveness for trying to save lives, to stop a war, to find truth?

His gaze transformed into disgust. He shoved me away.

"I had to! With the lives of three hundred people in my palm, how could you ask me to murder them all? That is not my right. That is not my role—no matter how passionate I am for a cause."

"You've sent us all to our graves. You chose them over us."

"You *don't have to die here*! You are *choosing* death!"

Jack wouldn't meet my eyes. "Better death than the Tower," he muttered.

"You don't need to go to the Tower." Were they so determined to perish as martyrs? "Flee this house of darkness. Go with your lives and freedom!"

If Catesby's eyes narrowed any farther, they would close altogether. "Cowardice is not our way. We will not follow your example."

I stood my ground, reminding myself that I was not a coward. Reminding myself that White Light had asked for my action. It had freed me, healed me, and used me for this purpose.

The door burst open and Tom Wintour tumbled in, sweat plastering his hair to his round face and tears dried on his cheeks. He lurched into the main room, gaze clamped onto the hearth. A frown. His eyes lifted. Searched the room. And when they found Catesby, all traces of worry and despair were shattered by a leap of his eyebrows and such joyful surprise it seemed as though he'd completely forgotten we were about to meet our ends. Wintour rushed to him. "They—they said you had died. From gunpowder in the hearth."

"I am about to die, dear Wintour. That is our fate here." Catesby dismissed me with a turn of his shoulder. I was nothing to him but vermin beneath his boot.

"And I will take such part as you do." They embraced and something in me broke.

It was time for me to leave. I'd done my part. I'd said my piece. And if I didn't get out now, I'd—

Jack jumped away from the window. "They are here." He faced Catesby like a soldier reporting to his commander. "They are closing in on the wall. Gather your arms, men!"

Forty-Five

I didn't fear death, but neither did I crave it.

Not like the handful of men—of friends—before me, strapping their masks to their faces. Loading their wheellock barrels. Dispensing of their scabbards, knowing they'd have no reason to sheathe a sword again after this moment.

They had something worth dying for.

Ah, but you have something they don't.

And what's that?

Something worth living for.

White was right. I wanted to live—to spend a life discovering what White Light and I could do together. I wanted to go after Father and see if I could somehow get him pardoned. I wanted to be with Emma.

She knew me—all of me—and still loved me. Kissed me. Fought with me and joined me. We were designed for each other.

Took you long enough.

Ha-ha.

It only took her a couple of months to reach the same conclusion.

Yes, well, she's always been ahead of me in school.

No witty quip to that.

So does this mean I'll survive today's battle?

Just because you were designed for each other doesn't mean you'll be together.

Ouch. *So . . . I'm going to die?*

Focus.

Catesby strapped on his mask.

I backed away from the window. If I was found in this house, I would be accused of treason. So I would fight. But not with Catesby. And not against him.

I would fight Dee.

"Do we know how many?" Wintour eased up to the window and stole a glance.

Jack shook his head.

"Don't do this, men," I said. "There are two hundred soldiers out there. With Dee's army, maybe more. There is no reason to die here!"

Wintour acted as though I hadn't spoken. "We need to know." He looked to Catesby, who gave a nod and cocked his pistol. "I will find out." He left the house.

"Wintour, stop!" I hadn't seen a single soldier yet, but my heart still thundered for him. As the plea left my mind, a *crack* rent the air and a musket ball struck him.

Wintour fell, his sword tumbling from his hand. "No!" I cried.

Catesby and I hurried to the window. The wall surrounding Holbeche House tore itself from the ground like a giant snake rearing its head. A line of soldiers—all wearing Grey masks—stood arm in arm, commanding the wall.

After a moment of bated breath, the hovering stone flew over to the right and crashed back to the ground.

So much for the fortification.

The Staffordshire posse advanced. An army to take on a smattering of traitorous rebels.

Wintour lay on the grass between the posse and the house. Catesby brandished his sword. "To arms! To arms!"

Kit and Jack ran outside, masks on. Jack sprinted to the well and it exploded with a gush of water, flooding the line of oncoming soldiers. The first line fell, tumbling over each other in the wave of water.

Kit used his Green power to send the grassy lawn roiling and churning. Impossible to stand on.

Then a mask rose from the fray, lifting and balancing on the arm of an oak tree, as though cradled in the hand of a giant.

A multicolored mask.

Dee fisted two pistols, held them straight in front of him, and . . .

Pop. Jack fell. *Pop.* Kit folded.

From that distance, Dee must have used color power to direct the bullets. The Wright brothers writhed on the ground for a moment. The roiling green earth stilled. The water from the well settled. I stared at their fallen bodies. Blood flowed from their chests . . . and then came the Stone Plague. It rolled from the wounds toward their faces and throats.

I yelled, but the plague consumed them. Dee's weapons left no wounded.

Two of his witnesses were dead.

Wintour crawled toward the house. He was alive! With a glance over his shoulder, he got to his feet, clutching his sword arm. He picked up his weapon as he ran and made it into the house just as another one of Dee's bullets blasted into the wood frame.

Blood pulsed from Wintour's wound, dripping on the floor as he fell into the room. Catesby helped him up. "Stand by me, Mr. Tom, and we will die together."

"I've a cracked mask and have lost the use of my right arm," Wintour grunted. "I fear that will cause me to be taken."

In the minds of the plotters, to be taken was a fate far worse than death.

A fate that my father had drawn.

And so they stood side by side for their last stand. Percy joined them. To see them in a line, facing their deaths, drew me in, like all heroic feats seemed to do. I wanted to be part of something great. I wanted to stand alongside them.

But they no longer stood for something I could fight for.

Movement from the door caught my eye and I spun, finally drawing my sword.

It wasn't a man. It was the Stone Plague from Dee's bullet that had struck the wood in pursuit of Wintour. It crawled from the hole and scrabbled at the wood like an animal seeking flesh. The beam of the door crackled like a log in the fire as the stone overtook it.

I stared. How . . . ? How could the plague spread across something inanimate? My gaze slid from the beam to the dead bodies of the Wright brothers, only to see more plague flowing like the well water from their corpses to the lawn. Across the grass toward the lines of soldiers. The soldiers backed away, breaking any semblance of formation.

I could see the whites of Dee's eyes even from his spot on the oak branch.

He'd gone too far. And now his new weaponry was spreading plague through the earth. To the king's men.

A soldier screamed as the plague snagged his boot. He ran away, but with every other footprint, plague was left behind. Spreading from new puddles of death.

Mayhem struck.

Soon the plague would crawl down their throats and suffocate them. Stop their hearts, petrify their lungs.

I darted from the room as the glass from the window shattered. I spun in time to see both Percy and Catesby fall—a single bullet blowing through Percy's chest and into Catesby's neck.

Wintour let out an anguished cry and dropped to Catesby's side. So be it. I turned away from the scene and ran. I tensed for a shot to find me—to pierce my back or my head. For a sword to meet me around a corner.

I stuck my mask to my face. Hopefully the White would prove me to be an ally. Heat burst into my veins from the mask. The color voices surrounded me—calling for help, wishing to be commanded. Wanting to obey.

I knew the moment Dee spotted me from his branch because the oak lowered him to the ground, depositing its master onto the chessboard as the queen.

To stop this spreading plague, I'd have to stop Dee. I was the pawn making a dash for the other side.

Dee spun upon my approach and threw so fast I barely registered the small knife that stuck in the forehead of my mask.

As though repulsed, the mask writhed and pushed the blade out. It tumbled to the ground, the tip melted halfway to the hilt.

"That's a neat trick," Dee growled.

"White Light has all sorts of tricks up its sleeves."

"What are you doing, boy? I'm on your side."

"Forgive me if I don't believe you when you throw daggers to *infect* me." Dee was good at playing both sides, but there was only one side to which he was truly loyal—his own. "I fight for White Light." I advanced with my sword point first. "You spread the plague."

He heaved a sigh. "No one ever thinks grand enough. I *created* it, boy. I was barely older than you—that should give an idea of what you're up against."

Created it. "*You* murdered Luther?" He had started the war. "And your wives?"

I watched his hands with hawk eyes in case he tried to throw something again. But the attack came from behind. Something wrapped around my neck. A noose. I reached to tear it away and felt leaves. Vines. They were tight, but I was stronger. I tore them away. They responded with a burst of new arms, coiled together to create an unbreakable noose.

"They couldn't give me children to whom to pass on my legacy." Dee stood over me. The vines yanked me to the ground. I released my sword to fight with both hands. *No, no, no!* I couldn't break them. I was choking.

My vision darkened, blood pounding behind my eyes.

Hello! I'm RIGHT. HERE.

"Then do something!" I hollered with my last breath.

Why do you even have a mask?

If the White Light had been a physical person within reach, I would have throttled him. But then I understood. I'd succumbed to my own power in my moment of panic. I calmed and thought a command to Green. *Release me. You have no power over me.*

Dee was controlling the Green vines with his own color speech. It was more powerful than I'd ever seen. But I commanded Green with White Light's authority.

The vines recoiled as if struck and heat poured into my face from the inside of my mask. I scrambled back to my feet to see Dee send another dagger into the chest of a young soldier no taller than me who had been trying to yank the vines away.

The soldier fell, grabbing at the dagger.

I stepped between Dee and the boy and sent my focus into my

mask. I felt the flutter of grass beneath our feet, in my skin. I heard it humming and my veins throbbed. *You will obey me now.*

The Green will bowed. And then, with a snap, the grass sent Dee onto his back, like the flick of a rug. I advanced, sword drawn. Dee's mask hung askew—his round eyes startled. He saw. He knew. White Light would win.

A bullet whizzed by my ear and I lurched back. A body interrupted my advance, sword aloft. "At last. No more school sparring, Cyclops. This duel will reap blood."

"Henry, you idiot!" I deflected his blade as easily as when we sparred as schoolmates. "I'm on your side."

"Well, I'm not on yours." He lunged and I sidestepped, keeping one eye on Dee. He went for a thrust, a slight inhale giving him away. I jabbed with my sword—too far away to strike him, but close enough to affright him into a sloppy defense.

Dee had gained his feet.

Henry's breath released in white clouds and he licked his dry lips. When he went for another strike, I executed a swift *contra tempo*—gaining control and stepping forward with a quick jab to the soft crook of his shoulder.

The blade sank.

He hissed.

Blood splashed.

It happened so fast, I wasn't sure how deep I'd jabbed. For a moment, I feared I'd sliced clean through him.

I took two steps back, lowing my rapier as a bright-red stain spread along his shirt. But he didn't lower his sword—not even when he grimaced so fiercely his eyes shut.

He raised his sword again, but then his eyes left our duel for a moment, so alarmed I almost looked over my shoulder. But I'd fall for no feint. Henry's gaze snapped back to me, then back to a spot behind me, and he abandoned our battle, running around me and back toward the house.

I let the fool go and pursued Dee.

But then Henry screamed from behind me. "Dee!" The panic in his voice sent its own shard of concern into me. I shouldn't look. I should stay focused on my target, but then, "Dee, Dee! Help!"

I looked over my shoulder. Henry knelt over the downed soldier boy. Stone Plague spread from the blade in the soldier's chest like a drop of ink in a bowl of milk—up the boy's light clothing, toward his scarf-covered throat, and disappeared beneath his smooth Brown mask.

A Brown mask with a white rose over the eye.

The world slowed as I caught the stray dark curl that had escaped the cap, the bulky gloves over the dainty hands, the feminine touch to the frightened gasp.

Emma.

"No!" Ice slid through my body.

Henry screamed Dee's name louder and louder, tearing at the plague, wrenching the dagger from Emma's chest, pulling her mask away and revealing her beautiful dark skin. Wide eyes. Tears of fear. "It's getting her! Dee, stop it!"

I. Just. Stared.

Emma . . . *my Emma* . . . was dying of plague.

Dee sprinted across the courtyard, across the plagued ground away from us. He reached the stone outer wall. The giant squares of rock lifted into a crude arch to let him through. Once he crossed to the other side, they slammed back into place with a tremor that jolted me out of my stunned state.

Emma's hands clutched at her throat, the plague weaving and slithering into her skin. Henry screamed enough for the both of us. There was only one thing to do—one way to stop that plague.

I bolted after Dee.

No, Thomas.

Emma was dying. I couldn't look back. I couldn't bear to see the stone slipping down her throat. Suffocating her. Why was the plague even affecting her? She was bonded with the White Light just as I was—even *more* than I was!

I reached the portion of stone Dee had passed through and slammed against it. "Open up, Grey." The stones shuddered. "Open. *Open!*" I pounded the stone with my fist. *White. White! Move the stones!*

No response.

"Do something!" I bellowed.

My concern is not in that direction.

I scrabbled against the stone, trying to scale it by sheer willpower.

Dee is not the answer.

I looked back to Emma and Henry. He held her in his arms and sobbed into her neck. She wasn't moving. All I saw was stone. And I understood.

I sprinted back to them and pulled her from his arms. Tears smeared behind my own mask. I couldn't think straight. "Emma. *Emma! I'm here.*"

She didn't look like herself—all pale cracked stone and wide-open, unseeing eyes. My mask grew hot before I even sent a command to the plague. *"Remove yourself from her."*

I sensed the plague shake its head, still under Dee's color Compulsion. My inner eye dove into the plague's heart. *Where do I go?*

To the left.

I navigated the cracks and the infection.

Here?

Deeper.

403

I saw the plague's grip over Emma's heart. Its knuckles pinching her veins and stilling her blood.

There.

I ground my teeth against the screaming. "*You. Will. Release. Her.*"

The plague shrank away. Resisting. But its defiance held no power, because against Dee's will and even its own will, the stone receded from Emma's nose. "*Faster!*"

It slunk back like a sulking child, pooling around the blade.

Her limp body slumped on the lumpy ground. "Emma." I shook her. "Emma!"

"Get *off* her!" Henry shoved me and I almost lost my grip.

But my mind was spinning. Analyzing. Examining her body with the color power.

Lungs. Heart. Breath. Death.

My mind's eye returned to her heart. It pulsed weakly like a fish too long out of water. She was alive, but barely. The heat from my mask sent sweat sliding down my temples. And I sought the Red of her blood. The Red of her tissue.

I placed one hand over her bleeding chest and one hand over mine—feeling for my own heartbeat.

Every time it struck my palm, I sent a command to hers. "*Pulse.*"

Tha-thump. My heart.

. . . *th . . . u . . . m . . . p.* Hers.

"*Pulse. Pulse.*"

. . . *tha . . . thump.* Her heart picked up, like a stallion in a race. *Tha-thump. Tha-thump.* Faster. Faster. *Thathumpthathumpthathump.*

I reeled back with a gasp, releasing Red from the commands.

Emma sucked in a sudden breath through her nose. Then another. Her eyes fluttered open. And I fought the urge to weep. She was alive. *You did it.*

We did it.

She saw me and time seemed to stop. For one synchronized heartbeat, I was all she saw. She was alive. She was safe . . . for now. Despite the dagger wound. She was so beautiful that my chest felt like *it* was the one with the dagger in it.

Her attention slid to Henry. She lifted her hand and rested it against his trembling, sniveling face. "It's well. I'm all right."

He nodded and wiped a sleeve across his face.

She returned her sweet gaze to me. "D-Dee . . ."

I bowed my head. "He got away."

Emma's eyebrows crashed together. "Where is he?"

"He escaped through the wall." I waved to the stones. "There. A few minutes ago." A hundred years ago, it felt.

Emma struggled to her feet with a cry, then clutched her chest. Blood bubbled from the wound. "Emma!" Henry gasped.

"I'm well," she choked. "The layers . . ." No matter how many layers of clothing she wore, there was still blood streaming out of her chest.

"Blast it all, Emma." I barely registered the madness around me. I barely gave a thought to the plague or the bodies or the plotters.

But then Emma swayed and stumbled toward the wall. "Hurry, Thomas."

I returned to the moment. To the war. And then I saw Holbeche House—consumed by the plague. It crawled along the lawn toward us. And while I no longer feared for either of us, I saw it latch onto Henry's boots. He stabbed at it with his rapier, but the blade clanged uselessly.

"Go, Emma!" he shouted. "Hurry! Stop him!"

The stone crawled up his calves. Past his knees.

Emma and I rushed to the wall. Did she think she could move the stones like Dee had? No. She couldn't. Because her mask lay in the plagued grass behind us.

"We should go around!" I hollered. "Where is the horse?"

Emma reached for a stone that had been left loose by Dee and stuck out a few inches. Was she trying to climb over? I hoisted her up until she balanced on the stone with her tiptoes. The top of the wall reached her chest and she clutched at it with one arm. With the other hand, she pulled her musket over her shoulder and leveled it on the top of the wall.

She was going to *shoot* him? Could she even *see* him?

I hauled myself up on the stone lip, using my body to steady Emma, but also for a view. Far afield Dee ran away from the battle with the irregular gait of an old man unaccustomed to physical exertion.

He was too far. Barely a speck.

I remembered how he'd taken down Jack and Kit. How he'd shot Wintour.

Emma cocked the trigger.

I thought of my mother, taken by the plague. Norwood.

She pressed her eye to the sight. Trembled.

I pictured the plagued woman in the graveyard.

I closed my eyes and sent my consciousness down into the barrel of the musket, past the flint and the pan, until I found the ball. Until I saw the grey metal, molded and smoothed.

I felt Grey's obedience. I felt its response to the White on my mask. Its bow to its sovereign.

So when Emma breathed out slowly and squeezed the trigger, a command slipped through my lips with the barest whisper.

A color command to the bullet.

"Fly true."

Forty-Six

The aftermath of battle was as bloody and revolting as the flop of Dee's dead body mid-run.

The Stone Plague cracked and crumbled off the walls of Holbeche House into dust. Henry shook himself free and spat the dust from his mouth. Some downed soldiers rose with coughing fits.

Most did not rise at all.

Emma had lost a lot of blood, so I lowered her to the now-safe ground. "I'm fine. I'm fine." But I could tell she was weak.

Henry ran straight over and tended her. I'd never seen him act so gently toward anything or anyone.

He looked around and then moved to place Emma's mask back on her face. I stopped him. "No. Let her be."

He slapped my hand away. "*You* are why she's out here. You are why she's injured and almost died!"

Never mind that I'd helped Emma save *his* life. "She came of her own will. You can't cage her."

"Leave us!" he shrieked with wild eyes, fumbling for his rapier.

Emma stilled his hand. "What?" His angry demeanor crumbled. "What do you need? Water? A healer?"

"I need you to let me go."

"You're *not* going to die."

"No. But I *am* going with Thomas." She closed her wound with her own mask, then sat up and winced.

He acted as though he hadn't heard. "I'm taking you back to Hoxton!"

"When he comes for me, I'm going." Emma lifted her eyes to mine. "I'll be ready."

⚡

Soldiers plundered the battlefield, stripping the boots and silk stockings off of Jack's body, rummaging through Catesby's pockets, trampling lifeless fingers and yanking off rings.

The soldiers who had survived Dee's plague touched their skin, their faces, their chests—pale with open mouths. They knew. They knew the plague had claimed them and somehow left. Several of them wandered in awe, trying to understand.

The plague was no longer. Not on the blades, not on the soldiers, not on the musket balls—all were free. It had been snuffed with the extinguishing of Dee's life. Such havoc caused by a single man.

One soldier had seen Emma and me send the bullet into the back of Dee's skull. That was all that was needed. He told anyone who would listen that an African girl and a boy with a White mask had killed the plague master with a single shot.

Any fears I had of being captured and killed fled as soldier after soldier wrung my hand, peered at my unusual mask, and ran out to inspect Dee's body. Many were too wary to approach Emma, but several offered her bows and helped settle her into a wagon with a healer.

Rookwood and Wintour were the last two plotters living, and they were manhandled before being sent straight back to London. I didn't even get to see them—to try to help them. Everything happened so fast. And everything stirred up conflicting emotions.

Relief and despair.

Freedom and guilt.

Success and failure.

The soldiers gathered all the masks of the plotters. I insisted they bury Catesby, Percy, and the Wright brothers. They obeyed reluctantly, but it brought me some measure of peace.

The leader of the company, a man named Walsh, took the stabled horses as spoils of battle, but I managed to claim Emma's mare. I rode her back alone. Back to London. Back to investigate the fate of my father.

It had been four days.

---

8 November 1605

"Tell me everything." King James turned my White mask over in his hands. I could read nothing on his face and barely think beyond the cold stone beneath my knees and the soldiers on either side of me.

Hero I might be called, but King James knew I had been at the Holbeche House. He knew my last name matched that of the famous soldier in the Tower dungeons.

So I told him what I could.

I focused on my personal journey—my pursuit of White Light. Or, rather, its pursuit of me. I tried my best not to compromise my friends, even though they'd been captured and many killed.

Within the first minutes of my return to London, I'd inquired at the Tower gate after John Johnson. They said his true name was Guido Fawkes and that he'd surrendered the names of the plotters.

They must have pressed him hard. It was with the greatest strain that I kept from weeping in front of the king. I left out bits about Father, not to be vague but because I couldn't push the words past the thickness in my throat. "I was to row us to an escaping ship, but instead I challenged him."

"Ye incriminate yourself, young Fawkes."

I nodded. "So be it." If Father could stand being taken to the Tower, then so could I. Perhaps I would see him. Perhaps I could—what? Encourage him? He likely wished I was dead.

King James turned my mask over and over. "But ye have also freed England of the plague." He didn't seem too concerned about arresting me. Perhaps my mask spoke of my change of heart—and maybe White Light had whispered some banter in his ear. I supposed the healing of an entire country was enough to excuse me from being the son of one of the plotters.

"It was a joint effort, sire," I corrected. "Emma Areben, ward to the Baron Monteagle, fired the shot."

"She and I have already spoken. She be a bold one, tha'. Would nae leave my court until I agreed to make clear the mask rights for those of color." He chuckled. "So wha' reward would ye ask of me?"

A reward was the last thing I wanted. I felt more like I deserved a cell in the Tower. "Ridding England of the plague is reward enough for me."

"Ye killed Dee before he could train an apprentice in the ways of the Stone Plague. He been tormenting our continent since Luther's death. You freed nae only England but all of Europe."

Huzzah.

"I offer this reward only once."

I bit my tongue to hold back the refusal. *Think, Thomas. Don't be a fool and throw away such an opportunity.* If I were going to make a request, I would not hold back. I would be bold.

I wanted something that would better the world. I thought of all the times Percy complained that King James had broken his promise. What would he ask of the king? What would Catesby ask of the king?

"Stop the executions of the Keepers."

King James leaned back in is throne. "And wha' would happen then? They would form a group and pack my Parliament full of gunpowder. To ask this be to ask for my death."

I saw his point. "But why must they be hunted and hanged as they have been?"

"They have other options. They can become Igniters, or they can leave England. Those who stay and are imprisoned are those who have chosen to defy me."

Didn't he realize that they disobeyed because they wanted him to stop persecuting them? How could they focus on discovering White Light when King James kept them too busy trying to guard their own survival?

I took several deep breaths. My fate already balanced on a wire, and if he would not grant me that request, then I would look to other needs.

Silence hung over the hall. I flicked a look up. King James looked amused. "If Your Majesty is willing"—I could not remain silent while kneeling before him—"I ask for the freedom of Guido Fawkes."

Forty-Seven

"Tha' be impossible." There was no softness in King James's face. He handed my mask back to a guard, who delivered it to me.

I took it and tied it to my belt. Its return was a show of faith from the king—he was someone who understood the White Light.

"Your father be a traitor to the crown—guilty of high treason—and will die a traitor's death."

My stomach dropped like a convict on the gallows. A traitor's death. Hung until near dead, then disemboweled while still alive. And then cut into pieces and burned.

All in front of a cheering crowd.

I knew the sentence must be passed, but I had hoped for mercy.

I swallowed my dread. "I seem to want the impossible."

"It be those who dream of the impossible who end up defying the very word."

I gathered what remained of my willpower. "Then let me amend my request to this: allow me to visit my father. As a mercy to a father and son." King James had children. Surely he understood the importance of such a relationship.

But maybe it was different for monarchs.

"Ye may visit him on the eve of his execution. Will ye claim this as your reward?"

"Thank you, Your Majesty." I rose and he dismissed me with a nod.

As I backed from the room, something felt off. Incomplete. Like I'd missed an opportunity. What had I left unsaid? Unasked?

King James rose from his throne, but then I stopped. "Your Majesty."

I did not look at his face, certain I'd encounter a thick impatience. "Would you allow Mistress Areben to paint the queen's portrait? And if you or the queen finds the portrait favorable, might you provide Mistress Areben with a letter of recommendation?"

"I gave ye one request, Thomas Fawkes."

"And I have taken advantage of it." So why didn't I feel regret? "I apologize only for taking up your time. Each of these requests weighs too heavily on my heart for me to neglect mentioning either one."

"I will see to i'."

For that reason alone, I was glad I did not help kill King James.

⁕

The night streets of London were not as dark as they once were. I strode through a London different from that of eighteen months ago. Hay bales no longer hung on hooks in front of houses. Bonfires lit every corner in their metal cages with night folk around them swapping stories.

But in every group I passed, no one talked about the eradication of the plague. They talked only of Guy Fawkes. Guy Fawkes. Guy Fawkes and the traitors. His name was now famous for a new reason.

I stopped at a bonfire to warm my hands and catch the conversation. A child stood opposite the fire from me, playing with a straw man on a stick. She held it over the flames until it caught fire. She squealed. "The Guy is burning!"

The men at the fire laughed. "How's he like *them* flames?"

I recoiled and hurried down the streets. More and more I saw the straw men. Burned on a stick. Hung from a noose and then burned. Torn to pieces between two children, like a wishbone.

These miniature straw Guy Fawkeses were made from the plague hay bales. "'E's caught and we be cured," someone said.

The people thought Father's capture cured the plague. They thought the plotters' demise had set them free. No matter the gossip from the soldiers or the story that was told to King James, everyone liked a stretched tale more than the straight one. Just as they claimed that Keepers had started the plague, now they claimed the capture of Keeper traitors stopped it.

Their ignorance disgusted me. An insult to White Light and how it stopped the plot and destroyed the plague by speaking to me and to Emma. It had been patient with us. Taught us—taught me how to follow and how to use color speech.

Yet it received no credit.

"Burn! Burn! Burn!" Some older children threw straw man after straw man into the fire. "Guy Fawkes, Guy Fawkes, 'twas his intent," they chanted, "to blow up the king and Parliament!"

"But he was catch'd," a boy joined in. "With a dark lantern and a burning match!"

I could watch no longer.

Father had held so long to his pride. To his mask. To his legacy. And now his name represented something sinister. His name caused people to rejoice in death.

Why, oh why, hadn't he listened? Why hadn't he looked for truth himself instead of building his life and passions on the fear of it?

I slept at an inn on Cheapside—not the Bear and not the Duck and Drake. Too many memories there.

———※———

Two days later, I had a message from the king . . . for Emma.

He wanted her to come paint the queen's portrait and he'd called me to caddy the letter to her—another small favor.

Today was the day. I strode to the Strand. If Emma had already visited with the king three days before, she was well enough.

I'd been thinking long and hard on how to approach Henry. Just because the plague had ended and the plot was unearthed— just because Dee was dead and King James was defining the mask laws for those of color—didn't mean Emma was free.

Henry had worked with Dee. He had trained under Dee. He had *helped* Dee with the Stone Plague weapons and led those soldiers to a battle that ended up with half of them dead. Yet he was pardoned simply because he was the son of a Parliament member, and an Igniter, and involved in the capture of Father.

He loved Emma with a dangerous ferocity . . . and was determined to smother her into his pet.

I was going to free her once and for all.

———※———

I knocked on the door to the Monteagle household as a gentleman might—as a messenger who came from the king might. I was as poor and scrappy and stubborn as I'd always been . . . but my honor had matured. It had straightened my spine, lifted my chin, and strengthened my voice.

Ward opened the door, saw me, and shook his head. "'Twas a bad choice to come here, Mister Fawkes."

"I have a message from the king," I said with a voice as firm as the steel in my scabbard. "For Mistress Areben."

Ward's brow popped up as though he'd been struck in the face by a splash of water. "Do come in, sir." As he walked down the familiar hall, I caught his mutter, "Though king's caddy or not, this won't be pleasant."

As I was led into the empty sitting room to wait, I heard them through the ceiling.

"How can you be *angry* about this? I will be free to wear my mask on my belt like everyone else. Like *you*!" It seemed Emma had made a full recovery—at least her lungs had.

"I won't let you go out like that if King James *does* pass a law. You have been too reckless."

"I don't need your permission!" she shouted.

"You are my *betrothed*!" A slam followed by fast stomps. They stopped, I caught Ward's low mutter, and then the footsteps came my way.

I steeled myself.

Henry blasted into the sitting room, a bandage around the shoulder I wounded. When he saw me, revulsion crawled onto his face like a resident insect. "You think that because you have color power you can enter my home and visit my future wife?"

"I've entered your home upon the king's orders." I lifted the sealed parchment. "With a message for Emma."

Henry held out his hand and I almost laughed. As. If.

"I will deliver it to her directly—"

"I am the lord of this hou—"

"—or not at all." I let the words drop like a gauntlet thrown between us.

We stood in stalemate. Fire in his gaze. Ice in mine.

"She is not yet well enough for visitors."

"I am *perfectly* well enough!" came Emma's shout from the floor above.

I barely swallowed the grin. I'd missed her. I cocked my head to one side. "I demand, by order of the king, that you take me to her."

Henry strode out of the room. I followed and we tromped up a narrow staircase to a closed door. Henry opened it and we swept in to a second-level sitting room where Emma reclined on a long couch by the window.

She stood upon our entrance, but kept a hand on the back of the couch for support.

I handed Emma the roll of parchment. She took it without removing her gaze from my face. It was our first time seeing each other since the skirmish at Holbeche House.

It seemed as though we were meeting for the first time. And yet as though we knew each other's very core.

"Very well. You've delivered your letter." Henry stepped between us. "I will see you to the door."

"Are you ready?" I said to Emma.

Henry shoved me into the hallway. He saw me all the way to the entry, and that was when I spun on him. "You have no hold over Emma."

Henry laughed in my face, so loud that spittle sprayed my skin. But nothing is quite so smothering as a silent room where no one joins in. "I'm her betrothed."

"By force alone." I settled my weight. "You teamed with Dee

417

and almost *killed* her." The outburst hung between us like the echo of a rifle shot.

"Dee was out of control."

"Why would Dee take you as an apprentice anyway? You are a baron's son—an apprenticeship is below your station."

"I wasn't his apprentice. I saw what he could do with the Stone Plague, and in exchange for my silence, he trained me in color speech the way St. Peter's never could. You have no right to Emma's hand."

"And you think you *do*?" Henry would do whatever it took—team with whoever would take him—to achieve his desires. It was time for that to end.

"I'm afraid there's been a misunderstanding here." Both Henry and I flinched at Emma's voice. She stood at the edge of the entry, her curls floating about her face like black fire. She wore her peasant dress with her mask at her belt. She had a travel bag in her hand.

Both Henry and I reached to steady her, but she hovered just out of reach. "You see, my hand is not for the taking." She met Henry's scowl. "It's for the giving."

She stepped forward and slid her bare hand into my outstretched one. "I'm leaving, Henry." Her other hand clenched the message from the king—the invitation to paint a portrait—against the handle of the bag.

Henry wouldn't look at her. "You can't. People don't understand you like I do. They fear you."

"I have to hope that will change someday." Her fingers tightened around mine. Warm. Solid. Confident.

I let her fight her own duel.

She deserved that honor.

Her voice softened. "We had our time. And I think fondly of

the days of our friendship. But I belong to no one—not the Baron and certainly not you."

He glowered at me. "You would have her run away with you and *work* as a common maid?"

"No. I would have her live the life and use the talents for which she has been designed. To squander her skills and her delights would be to deny her life purpose. It would be cruelest of all to purge her of her very soul."

Emma took the first step off the threshold. "Good-bye, Henry."

Henry stood there like a wilted cornstalk.

I didn't wait around.

Emma and I walked away together. Neither of us looked back.

Forty-Eight

30 January 1606

The Tower smelled of blood.

I entered through black spiked gates that creaked on their hinges as though rarely opened. As though reminding me that prisoners never got out . . . until hung.

The executions were slated for tomorrow. I'd spent the time since Holbeche House imagining all manners of reunions—none of them happy ones. The last I'd seen of Father, he was being dragged into the Tower while I hid in the street shadows.

Did he even know what had happened to the other plotters?

Did he know what I'd done?

"This way." The warden led me to the Tower. The sun was setting. Half the pale stones were lit and the lower half darkened. I felt as though I was watching the hope drain from the very rocks.

We entered the icy stairs of the Tower. Torchlight bounced off the walls, but even its flicker seemed cold—snuffed by the frozen stones. Did Father have a cloak? A blanket? Anything to keep him warm?

Wintour was somewhere within these walls, but I was not allowed to see him. I had a feeling he wouldn't want to see me either—he wouldn't understand why I was free and he was condemned.

We passed the cells of other prisoners—could hear their groans, but not see their faces. Though the floors and routes bore only stains and no refuse, the Tower stank beyond anything the Thames could achieve. It wasn't just human waste I smelled. It was sorrow. Hopelessness.

"Here." The warden stopped at a door of metal bars. He pounded on them. "Visitor. Come into the light." He didn't wait to see if Father obeyed. Just left me, but still kept me in sight. No one escaped the Tower, and he wasn't about to allow a young man to threaten that reputation, even if he had permission from the king himself.

I peered through the cell bars into the shadows. I saw no movement, no color. No light. "Father?"

Nothing. No sound.

"Father, it's me, Thomas." Maybe he was sleeping. Or unconscious. Perhaps he was even dead—how often did the guards check their prisoners?

A clink of chains. "Why are you here?"

It was his voice, and yet not. Instead of the solid tenor I'd come to know, it was a scratchy wisp of a thing. My nerves cringed at the pain in it.

"I . . ." There were no right words. "Father, I'm sorry."

"Leave me."

I gripped the bars, though I didn't know if he was looking at me. "I would rather perish with you than leave you in loathing of me." *Please come. Please come into the light so I can see you.*

"I don't fault you. You were too young." Too young to be part of the plot. Too young to be trustworthy. Too young to receive my mask.

"It is not the immaturity of my age that swayed me, Father.

There was a different voice speaking reason into my ear—a voice I grew to trust." I wanted him to say it. I wanted to know that he knew.

"White Light."

"The voice you were trying to protect. You were faithful to your beliefs, but it was your beliefs that were set awry." Could he see the anguish on my face? Could he see how desperately I wanted him to understand?

A low, humorous laugh. "Do you think," he said, "that after torture beyond what you've ever dared to imagine, I would sway now?"

My vision blurred as I peered into the gloom. "Will you not speak to me face-to-face? Will you not come forward?"

Another clink of chains. Then I saw a small corner of black wood. His mask? But something was off. It was only a piece. Then another one came visible as he moved into the limited light. They'd smashed his mask into four pieces and reattached it to his face with nails and tar. The chunks of mask nailed to his skull and cheekbones glowed like a sickly skeleton.

I stared at his broken mask—hiding a face that I would never see revealed. Now representing his shame. For a fierce moment, I wished I could take his place. But the best I could do was try to make him understand. This was my chance. Be bold now or be guilty forever. "I don't ask you to sway. I ask you to listen. If White calls out to you, will you listen?"

Father slunk back into the half shadows, low to the ground as though living on all fours.

"I wish I could have seen your face."

"A mask is a man's honor. A man's pride." His usually bold and strong statement sounded halfhearted.

I lifted my White mask from my belt. "If that's true, why don't you respect mine?"

"You meddled with White Light to get it. It is not of honest means." He lifted a hand to pick at the dead skin around his mask shards.

"I never asked for it!" My voice echoed off the stones. "I never asked for White to speak to me or to create a mask. Of its own accord, it led me, warned me, cured me, and helped me defeat John Dee. It used me to eradicate the plague. It saved . . . it saved me." My voice clogged. "Why are those things so wrong to you? I might have had the stone eye, but you are the blind one."

He remained silent at my insult. My next statement was quiet. Resigned. "I sought the source—like Wintour is always encouraging us to do. And . . . it answered me. White Light is the source of color power and it showed me truth."

"You succumbed to its will!"

"No, I sought to understand its will and I found that I agree with it. How can you claim to fight for White's name if you won't even speak to it?"

The mask pieces on his face clattered together as he cringed. He turned his face away and I barely heard his response. "You know the answer. It's too dangerous."

"More dangerous than trying to blow up the king?" I leaned closer. "Father, fear has never held you back from anything. Why are you afraid of this?"

"Skilled and knowledgeable Keepers have protected us for generations." He sounded like he was trying to convince himself.

"So you are going to trust the voice of a man above the voice of the first color that *designed* color power and made it bond with our masks?"

A broken sigh. Father seemed to be resigning himself to the fact we'd never agree. Perhaps I should do the same. "What are you trying to accomplish, Thomas?"

"I want you to know that my decision was worth it." That was what it came down to. "You need to set aside your fear. Bonding with White Light was worth every single heartache and regret that I will live with until I die. And I couldn't let you perish without knowing that."

"Thank you, Thomas."

I didn't move. The guard—sensing the end to our conversation—came to escort me out. I gripped the bars. "Please, Father—please tell me you'll try."

He shook his head slowly, as though in pain.

"Time to go," the guard muttered.

"Please!" I pleaded through the bars. "Do this one thing. If not for you, then for *me!*"

He lowered his head onto his knees, his greasy hair falling like a curtain between us. The guard tugged at my arm. But then I heard it—the barest broken whisper. *"For you."*

Forty-Nine

Dawn approached to the countdown of my heartbeat.

Emma and I stood at the gallows, dressed in thick cloaks. Beside us, a wagon was loaded with what few belongings we shared between us—mainly canvases and her bottles of paint. After the hanging, we were leaving London. Together.

She, with a glowing portraitist recommendation from the queen herself. I, with a mask on my belt and a small pouch of what remained of my reward money. And both of us free. Almost more than the queen's recommendation letter, Emma clutched another proclamation to her chest that she'd torn from the doorfront of the church.

A new edict that all English people—whether they be of colored skin or white—should train with a mask.

Granted, no master or masked was willing to train those of color. Yet. But the first step had been taken.

A crowd had gathered—the largest one I'd ever seen at a hanging. They called for blood. Many carried straw men strung up on sticks that they waved over their heads. I couldn't understand the thirst.

I was born too soft to have such bloodlust. But a man can be both soft and strong, maintaining hope for the world. Emma had shown me hope.

She held my hand in hers while we watched the proceedings—her mask around her waist, revealing her stunning black skin and hair in all their glory. We got stares, but she held her chin high. Some people even stumbled away from her, giving a wide berth. I didn't know why they feared her.

Perhaps it was the same type of fear Father battled—fear of the unknown.

I didn't want to watch the hanging, but I had to see this plot through. I owed it to my comrades. To Father.

Rookwood went first. The platform rose above the crowd and a line of guards kept the people at bay—some still threw rocks. A ladder led to the top of the hanging post. Rookwood crawled up, adorned with a broken mask and bruised body. As his boots landed on each peg, a flash of his talents and qualities entered my mind. Even in the little time I knew him, I'd learned he was one of England's most skilled horsemen and a stalwart soldier. Talents wasted because of his commitment to murder.

I admired him for his bravery—for his concern for Keepers and willingness to do what was needed to stop the persecution.

He reached the top of the ladder. A man slipped the noose around his neck. Then Rookwood leaped from the ladder and met his death with the crack of a neck. The crowd booed. They wanted him to survive the fall so he would suffer the disemboweling.

I was thankful he was dead.

Did anyone in the crowd have the courage these men did?

Wintour climbed the gallows next. Still short, but almost all his pudginess gone. I wouldn't have recognized him without his mask shards stuck to his face with pins and tar. He looked over the crowd as he ascended the ladder. Who was he looking for? Me?

His face stopped, turned in my direction. I couldn't tell if it was because he saw me or someone else, but I gave a nod. He nodded back and my heart broke. Thus, Wintour ascended—a stubborn but kindhearted man who had negotiated with kings and fought loyally, who had never once feared the noose.

His drop left me ill.

Father was the last.

Two soldiers had to drag him to the gallows. He looked unconscious, and his entire form changed from the mighty vigilante I once followed through shadows. His legs shook, knobby and barely strong enough to support him. What had they done to him?

They deposited him on the ladder and left him the honor of climbing it himself. The mask pieces on his face were smeared with fresh blood.

The crowd started chanting, "Fawkes! Fawkes! Fawkes!" Not in an admiring way. His name—*our* name—had left the greatest mark on London's people because Father was the first one captured. They were chanting for his death.

He forced one foot over the other, headed toward the gallows. He made it halfway up the ladder before he stilled, looping an arm through the rungs to catch his breath. The crowd screeched for his death. They mocked his weakness.

Everything within me cried, *I can't watch this!* But I would not leave. I would not leave him this time.

"Father!" I screamed above the crowd.

No one stopped, but Father stilled and then scanned. Emma's hand tightened in mine. I waved my free hand, choking. I wanted him to see me. I wanted to *be* with him when he died. I wanted him to have some sort of hope—some tiny measure of comfort in his death. The knowledge that I loved him, however little he might value that.

Then he saw me. He gripped the ladder rung so tightly, his knuckles turned white.

He must hate me.

But then he reached up with his free hand and wrenched the pieces of mask from his face, one after the other. He threw them to the ground and the crowd lunged for them. I didn't know what they planned to do with them and I didn't care. Because for the first time . . .

I saw my father's face.

And it was kind.

Broken, twisted, bleeding, and bruised, but filled with a fierce strength that buoyed my courage beyond what it had ever been. In the clench of his jaw, the lift of his head, and the crinkle of his eyes . . . I saw pride.

In me.

The guard behind him struck him with a stick and Father continued his ascent, keeping his eyes on me. Near the top, he stopped, looping an arm through the rung to stabilize himself.

"Do you see?" he cried.

The crowd hushed, hungry to devour the convict's last words. What they didn't catch in his question was the wild joy. And that was when I saw the flash . . . the glimmer of White mingling with the blood that slipped from the nail holes.

White Light.

The hangman had had enough. He reached down and yanked Father upward, breaking Father's balance. His foot slipped; his hand groped for a hold and met nothing.

Father knocked against the side of the ladder and then fell, headlong, to the cobblestoned ground. I didn't see him land and the crowd's exclamation drowned out the sound. But I shoved through bodies, dragging Emma behind me.

Then I saw him, lying in a twisted form, but with a relaxed body. Free of pain. White and Red pooling around his head.

The executioner checked him. The masses held a collective breath. "Dead," he proclaimed.

Some groaned. Others cheered.

I. Breathed.

Take care of him.

I never stopped.

Emma said not a word until I finally turned away. "It is done."

I nodded. "Let's go."

We didn't stay to see them drawn and quartered—that was the excessive step that appeased the crowds and proclaimed them traitors. Their heads—with their cracked masks—would be stuck on spikes above London Bridge or maybe even the Parliament building.

But Emma and I were leaving the city of death—the city where my life changed and we both found truth. It was bittersweet, but the newness of the future sustained our hearts.

I couldn't stop thinking of how Father abandoned his pride and threw his mask pieces to the ground. When he pointed to his face and screamed, *"Do you see?"* It was as if he were saying, *"Do you see what you did?"* And it was something for which he was thanking me. Something of which he was proud. A new mask for him to wear—of blood and light.

I would never know what exactly happened to him the last night he spent in his cell, and I knew White Light wouldn't tell me if I asked. But what mattered was that it had happened.

Father had seen what I'd seen. He'd seen the wall that the Keepers had built between themselves and White Light. He'd seen the misunderstanding that Igniters had about using its power.

He'd seen truth.

We climbed into the wagon. I grabbed the reins and flicked the mare's flanks. We rolled through the empty streets, passing shops and market stalls that had once been places of secret meetings and a hesitant relationship between Emma and me.

I had entered London in a prison cart, set on revenge and riddled with plague.

I left a free man—free of prison, revenge, and my plague. But what a cost I'd had to pay. I'd handed over my pride, my cowardice, and my relationships. In return, I found life.

"How are you doing?" Emma asked once we'd broken free from the city and rolled through the countryside.

I would be annoyed if that question came from anyone else. "I'm sorrowful . . . but no longer burdened."

She rested her head on my shoulder. I put my arm around her. A small flare of warmth came from where my mask rested at my belt.

Before I received my mask, I didn't know who I was—my skill, my purpose, my identity. I thought I was supposed to know. But instead, I learned how to search—how to track down the origins of skill, purpose, and identity. How to get to the source.

It's really not that hard, you know. I'm right here.

My lips curved. It was almost a smile.

I still didn't know exactly who I was going to become.

—I pulled my White mask free and set it against my face, warmth flying through my veins—

But it was time to find out.

Author's Note

What's True and What's Not

My dear reader, you made it. To be honest, I wasn't sure *I'd* make it to the end of this story. This book is historical fiction (with a fantasy twist), but so much of it is built off a true story. I wanted it to be as historically accurate as possible outside of my creation of Thomas and color power. I think you'll be surprised to find out what aspects are true. And to think . . . I used to find history boring.

The Gunpowder Plot was real—one of countless failed attempts to assassinate King James. All the plotters were real men—Catesby, Wintour, Percy, Jack, Kit, Bates, Keyes, Rookwood, Fawkes—and their involvement, roles, descriptions, and deaths are as accurate as the history books allow. The plotters not really touched on in this story were Tresham, Digby, and Tom Wintour's brother, Robert.

Yes, Catesby was the ringleader and Percy was an undercover mounted guard. And yes, those two were killed by a single bullet that passed through them both.

Guy Fawkes is the most infamous because he was caught in the belly of Parliament with the gunpowder. Yes, he really did die by falling off the gallows ladder. For his sake, I'm glad.

I wanted to tell their stories. Because every story, every stance, every passion, and every war has two sides. Sometimes three. Sometimes more. And Thomas's story is one of exploring, of seeking, of examining and digging for truth. His and Emma's story is one of *listening*. Much healing can be found through the commitment to listen and the willingness to talk the hard talks and dig for truth.

So, speaking of truth . . .

What's True

The Masque of Blackness was a real masquerade put on by Ben Jonson—and yes, it showed black-skinned travelers turning white when they set foot on land in England. While slavery was not legal in England, there was clearly an opinion about people of color that affected their acceptance into society.

Although slavery was illegal in England, Queen Elizabeth did allow John Hawkins to start and profit off the slave trade. But by the 1600s, a black community began to form in England—sometimes called the first. They were ordinary working class, often employed as servants, musicians, dancers, and entertainers. But at this time in England, very few inhabitants of London had seen black people before; some were fascinated and some were uneasy. Most were paranoid and labeled blacks as terrible creatures. Through Thomas's story, I wanted to capture what it might be like for a light-skinned person to encounter a dark-skinned person with fresh eyes—free of a lengthy history of racism. While Thomas was still impacted by his environment and the *knowledge* of the slave trade, he was able to see Emma for who she was and to see her skin color as something startlingly unique and beautiful.

A movie—and true story—that deeply moved me and inspired me for Emma's character was the movie *Belle*. Go watch it.

What's Stretched

Thomas Fawkes. He may or may not have existed—go do your own digging and see what you find. There's a mysterious record of his birth, but nothing more. So I snagged that loophole and made it my own. While there is a single record of his existence, I *did* fiddle with a few dates to make sure that he was the correct age for the story. I'm an author. I can do that. ;-)

John Dee was a real man—an alchemist known for having the greatest library in England. But—to my knowledge—he wasn't involved in the plot in any way. But he was perfectly set up to serve as one of my villains.

The plague existed and terrorized people (though obviously it wasn't turning people to stone). However, it wasn't officially eradicated from England until 1666, during the Great Fire of London (which was started by Emma's favorite bakery on Pudding Lane. Oopsie.).

Emma Areben was not the Baron Monteagle's ward. To my knowledge, the Baron never even had a ward. Emma comes straight from my imagination, but represents real women and people of diverse backgrounds and skin color caught up in this culture of newness, caution, and change.

DISCUSSION QUESTIONS

1. Thomas felt incomplete because of his plague. Have you ever had an injury or an illness that made you feel that way?

2. Thomas was caught between two sides—the Keepers who wanted to be free of oppression and the Igniters who wanted to be free to use color speech as they pleased. In the end, Thomas realized he had to find the truth for himself. What ways can you search for truth or seek the source of matters relevant to you today?

3. When Thomas started figuring out his own stance on the war, he felt like he *had* to stay in the plot so as not to let everyone down. Do you ever find yourself being swayed by pressure from others?

4. Some people—like Catesby—are very passionate about their cause. They are easy to follow and cheer for. What are some pros and cons of a persuasive personality?

5. Emma treated Thomas as a regular man—acknowledging his difference and accepting him as he was. Her treatment of him taught him to respond the same way to her when she

revealed herself to him. Is there someone in your life who is different or has a difference? How can you show them love as they are?

6. Have you ever felt like you needed to hide your true self? Why?

7. Sometimes we fear things we can't control—like White Light. What do you think is a healthy approach to these fears?

Acknowledgments

Books are not meant to be written alone, just like life shouldn't be lived alone. So many people walked me (okay, cheered and carried and dragged me) through the wild journey of writing *Fawkes*. Picture me blubbering and stuffing my face with chocolate as I try to make it through this list of thank yous:

First and always foremost is my everything. Yahweh. You are Father; you are savior; you are helper. I used to picture you as always serious, but the journey of writing this book revealed to me a delightful playfulness in our relationship. Thank you for answering every single one of my panicked prayers over my writing.

Mister Ninja—my greatest encouragement and greatest love after our true Leader. No romance I write comes close to the one we're living. Mom, Dad, Liza, Shawn, Binsk, and Melanie—I don't think you realize how much your love and support makes me cry. *You* are my favorite story. The Brandes clan—for all the games, ice cream, laughter, and wildness that keeps me sane between all the deadlines.

Karen Ball and Steve Laube—my cheerleaders who first saw

"me" in this story. Who kept me writing for the right reasons. And who are my champions.

To my sisters: Mary Weber—you handed me this story nugget and then helped keep me from going completely crazy with my writing mood swings. Thank you for such endless soul care. Sara Ella—your pep talks and Skype calls and motivational texts and dear, dear friendship made this book possible. Ashley Townsend (aka: Marianne Dashwood)—my first ever fangirl. You squeal the loudest and totally get me. You are cherished more than you'll ever know. <3 Eleanor

To my fantastic publishing team: Becky Monds—you suffered through the terrible first draft and yet saw the heart. Thank you for reading the story and not the words. Jamie Chavez and Jodi Hughes—for tolerating all my preferences and helping me get this story where it needed to be. Amanda Bostic—for being our fearless leader. Kristen—for blowing my mind with this cover. I'm still drooling. Paul, Allison, and the rest of the TN crew—for your tireless energy and all you do for us authors. <3

To Erik and Donna Thoennes—for allowing me into your home and for hearing the heart of my story. Those conversations were a turning point for me, where I no longer feared writing Fawkes poorly but instead committed only to writing it faithfully. And to the Thoennes kids—I still hope to write a book-turned-movie that you will all star in someday. ;-)

Allen Arnold—for listening to my fears, for praying over me and my book, and for seeing the heart of this story. Katie Grace—for being my Owl Ninja and my go-to person for all the things and all the word wars. Katie Danforth—for cheering me through literally every stage of writing this book. My beta readers Ashley Townsend and Rosalie Valentine—that extra little duel between Thomas and Henry was for you. Jill Williamson, Lindsay Franklin,

S. D. Grimm, Emilie Hendryx, Clint Hall, Kara Swanson, and all the other dear authors who are my cherished community.

To my Ninjas—for loving me, encouraging me no matter my busyness, and for always sending Oreos. (I've left a little something for you in Chapter 8.) To the Mitchtams—you guys helped me knock out the ending in three days. Camp NaNo for the wiiiiin! To my Realmie Roomies: Katie Grace, Tricia Mingerink, and Ashley Townsend—for understanding that if I didn't write to candlelight I would die.

Thank you to the Wildly Unbalanced Writers, OYANers, Enclave Authors, my Biola family, CCH, and the Speculati for being my people. Thank you Mister Guard at the Tower of London who told me all the secrets about Guy Fawkes and sent me on a merry chase to find Ambrose Rookwood's signature carved in the wall.

To research authors Antonia Fraser, Ian Mortimer, John Paul Davis, and David and Ben Crystal—for writing history books and dictionaries that allowed me to truly breathe life into Thomas's world.

And of course, to my readers: Despite the umbrella term, I truly adore each and every one of you. Every note, every comment, every message is such a balm to my heart. Thank you for reading Thomas's story and being my friend no matter if you like my books or not—*you* are what's important to me. <3

Shalom.

About the Author

Photo by Emilie Hendryx from E. A. Creative Photography

Nadine Brandes once spent four days as a sea cook in the name of book research. She is the author of the award-winning Out of Time series and her inner fangirl perks up at the mention of soul-talk, Quidditch, bookstagram, and Oreos. When she's not busy writing novels about bold living, she's adventuring through Middle Earth or taste-testing a new chai. She and her Auror husband live in a Tiny House on wheels. Current mission: paint the world in shalom.

⊸———≑⊸———⊸

Website: NadineBrandes.com
Instagram: NadineBrandes
Facebook: NadineBrandesAuthor
Twitter: @NadineBrandes